CITY OF BRIDGES

THE SEVEN PORTALS SERIES

ANDRE JONES

ALIEN
PRESS

✺ Created with Vellum

AUTHOR'S NOTE

It is a sad but true story, that this particular book is two decades in the making!

City of Bridges came about when I was 'fed up' with 'silly rules' obstructing keen roleplaying in games like Dungeons and Dragons, Middle Earth Role Playing (MERPs) etc .. so I decided to design my own roleplaying system.

After several months of 'brainstorming', I devised a gaming system and a fantasy world, with its own races (species), religions and ancient history. - I even got a group of friends over to game-test it!
I then joined the Navy, and my gaming aspirations drowned …
but I could always write … and so on those long shifts cruising the world's oceans (it's pretty boring after the first month!) I got out a trusty old laptop and started word by word, chapter by chapter…

What you see today is a far cry of the original story line … let's just say the discarded prologue (now modified) for Book 1 is now Chapter 2 in Book 3.

Regardless of how it came about, I do hope you enjoy the read, and can immerse yourself in this wondrous fantasy world.

Please consider leaving a Review

Help other readers find this epic fantasy series by leaving a review on Amazon, Goodreads, BookBub, or any other website. Even simple ones like 'I loved it' really help with a book – and an author's – success.

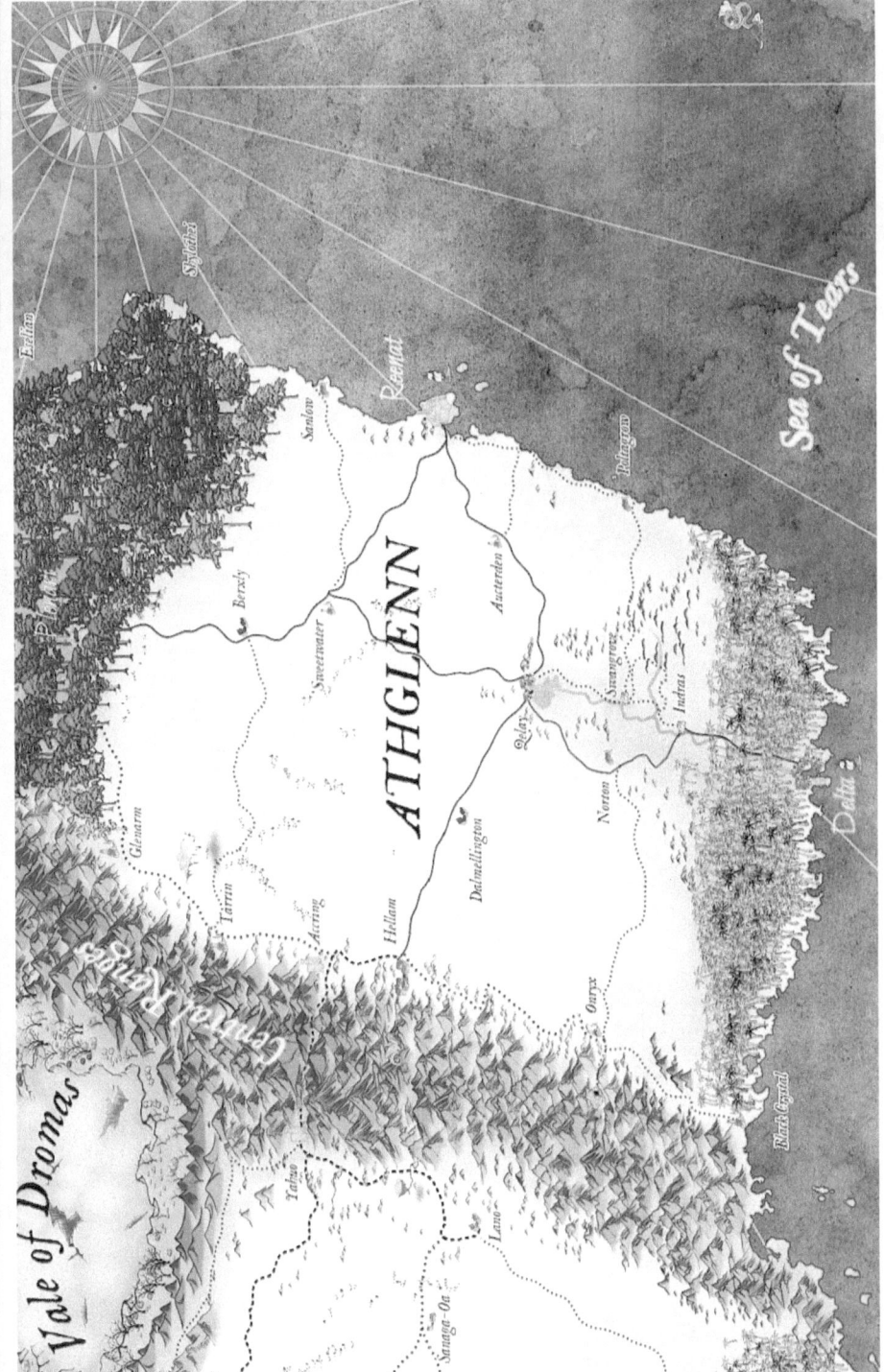

1

THE MESSENGER

LEONIE WAITED SILENTLY, BLENDING INTO THE SHADOWS, AIDED BY her fine layer of glossy black fur and dark clothing. Her view encompassed the centuries-old palace, its walls rough quarried stone, the windows on the upper levels blocked up.

From her vantage point on the rooftop of a large warehouse in Portside, she looked north-east across the harbour over the sprawling island city of Delta. The wealthy and elite lived on this side, with the poor, the unclean, the crossbreeds and half-breeds shunned to the low-lying eastern sector where the swamp was most prominent. All other citizens lived in-between; their location dependent on their social standing.

It took a little time to get over here; bridges linked the many islands making up the bulk of the city. If you knew your way around like she did, you could avoid the guarded checkpoints.

She did not visit Portside often. It was too open, too clean and the streets too well-lit and patrolled. It was regarded as far too dangerous for most, unlike the shadowy backstreets of Dock-side; her familiar grounds to the east. *But the pickings are much better over here*, she reminded herself. Any unauthorised cross-breeds found in the area were subject to severe penalty; branding was the initial punishment, fingers and toes went next.

The Grand Plaza, jutting into the harbour, was where the bulk of trading took place, and therefore deemed neutral territory, open to everyone. When strolling through the Plaza, Leonie often heard travellers comment on how picturesque the port was, some comparing it to the ancient and glorious city of Reenat, the capital of Athglenn.

Delta might look beautiful, but beneath the façade lay a cesspool of greed, intolerance and corruption. Religious sects constantly vied for dominance. Opportunists were there for whatever information they could sell. And half-bloods were less than nothing. As a crossbreed and thief raised in the slums, she knew the seedier side. Any tainted lineage was despised by the full-blooded, bringing disdain and ridicule mostly, or violence if they could get away with it.

The Eternal Gardens stood near the base of the palace outer wall closest to the water. They had been created as a remembrance for those who perished in the blaze which destroyed the city's most elegant structure, the Temple of Eternix.

Leonie shivered. Cold despair washed over her at the disturbing memory of children and women losing their lives in the smoke and flames; her mother one of them. Leaning against a chimney, she took a moment to calm herself and restore her poise. It was dangerous enough travelling the roofs at night. She didn't need any mental distractions.

A large obelisk stood at the end of the street. As Leonie watched, the crystal at its peak began to glow with a magical aura, as did other monuments scattered around the city.

Unexpected movement distracted Leonie's contemplation of the obelisk. Two shadowy human figures made their way along the tiled rooftops of the buildings to her left, heading towards the waterfront. Her uncanny balance enabled her to use the sloping rooftops with ease, but humans usually stuck to the gloom and shadows of the alleys below.

Over the years Jade, her mentor and boss, repeatedly warned her; curiosity was her biggest weakness. Leonie agreed. Who these two figures were and what they were up to consumed her.

No other thief in the city matched her skills, but this pair showed remarkable speed and agility. *I need answers.*

Swiftly paralleling their course, she kept one lane between them, her bare paws making little noise on the slate tiles. *What are they doing?* The figures furtively moved with a clear purpose. *Who or what would call for such scrutiny from these two?*

Her attention snapped back to the Palace. Five armoured riders were exiting through the main gates.

"Interesting," she muttered, curious what could make guards leave the palace so early in the morning and in such a hurry. She rhythmically balled then flexed the fingers of her paws, claws extending and retracting reflexively as she gazed across the streets below. The guards were making their way down the road, turning at the junction, heading towards the docks.

Dropping lithely onto a balcony, Leonie gathered herself before the drop to street level. Once on the ground, she crossed the lane, silently melding with the shadows along the wall of the same building as the would-be burglars, using the eaves as cover.

A few strides in front of her, a door opened, casting a shaft of light across the cobblestones. Too close to evade, she passed the door in a flash, hoping she would be unnoticed in her dark, close-fitting attire. A noisome odour assailed her as she passed, her nose wrinkling in recognition.

Dogs!

No sooner had the thought formed when two small terriers darted out, setting up a constant yapping. The noise they made belied their pathetically small stature. These dogs were no physical threat but could alert others to Leonie's presence. Picking up speed, she sprinted down an alley, heading for the smelliest pile of refuse she could find hoping they'd lose her scent or at least their interest in her. Sure enough, within moments, the racket faded as the dogs found something more appealing. Now she could concentrate on determining the exact whereabouts of the strangers. She was concerned the dogs may have alerted them.

Pausing at the alley's exit, she scanned the area carefully. The street ended at the wharf where a newly arrived ship had docked. Coming from the direction of the gangplank, a man swaggered down the centre of the street. He carried a heavy satchel over one shoulder, oblivious to the attention from the rooftop pair.

His dark clothing and small cape were of good quality, but the twin gryphon plumes jutting from his hat marked him a guild courier. Anyone who interfered with their passage would be liable for severe punishment, which no doubt resulted in his cock-sure attitude. He was still about twenty paces away but moving closer, walking down the centre of the road.

Leonie hugged the shadows. Judging from the occasional creaking above, the devious pair must be close. The man's lack of awareness appalled her. *Some people are so deaf.*

"Psst. You're in danger." Gaining the courier's attention, she pointed up.

The man tensed and looked around, his gaze locking onto her location. Stepping away, his hand rested on the pommel of his blade.

"Move to cover. Quickly!" she hissed.

At the same time, a dark shape slid down a rope four paces to Leonie's left. Except for the narrow slit around the eyes, a dark grey close-fitting suit covered the figure from head to foot.

In one fluid motion, the courier leapt back drawing his rapier. A faint hiss sounded, simultaneously. Something tiny struck the road near where he'd been standing.

Darts? Leonie's hackles raised. *Assassins!*

Silently, the assassin on the ground pulled a blowpipe from a slim arm pocket. Leonie crept up close behind him. He'd finished loading and was raising the pipe to his lips when a sudden yapping nearby caused him to hesitate.

The assassin turned towards the sound, noticing Leonie's presence. He raised an arm to fend off her claw-swipe, face showing his surprise. The impact of her strike knocked the blowpipe from his grasp and lacerated his right wrist. Recovering, he manoeuvred to give himself room, drew a blade with his left hand and flicked it at her with barely a glance.

Leonie saw its dull glow the moment he drew it. *Power!* She jumped straight up, twisting nimbly. The dagger embedded in her left calf. Hissing in pain, she spun in mid-air, kicked off the wall, and flung herself at him. Clawed rage descended.

Fear etched the assassin's face; his eyes widened and mouth opened in shock. He uttered a cry in a foreign language. Swift on his feet, he dove to the side, tripping on the uneven flagstones. The yapping dogs were quick to move in with the excitement.

The courier stepped in and thrust his rapier between the writhing frenzy of dogs. The assassin groaned as the blade deeply penetrated the light armour and ribs.

Leonie landed gingerly beside the dead man. She gritted her teeth as she swiftly pulled the assassin's dagger from her calf. "Too bad you missed those mutts."

Before he could reply, the courier stiffened and fell to the cobbles at her feet.

Ignoring the blood running down her leg, Leonie dragged him under an awning. From his reaction to the dart, it was a fast-acting poison.

The courier convulsed. He tried to say something, but his lungs were almost paralysed. He feebly attempted to pass his satchel to her. A message entered her head.

Take to Qelay. Styx. Hrolta— The thought hit her mind as his body spasmed one final time. He gave a last gasp. Leonie froze at the sight of his bleeding eyes and frothy mouth. His hand tightened on her arm one last time before he died.

The dogs grew silent; one of them distracted by something behind her. With the dagger still in her paw, she reacted purely on reflex, spinning and hurling the dagger from the hip at the approaching shadow. Snagging the satchel with a claw, she leapt away without a backward glance. She landed a few paces further than the average human could. The injured leg failed her, turning her exit into an untidy sprawl. Rolling awkwardly, she came up hard against a wall. She was about to get up to bolt away but realised there was no follow-up attack. Three dark life-less figures lay in the street.

The dogs sensed something unusual in the night; maybe the smell of death affected them. They started howling a short distance away. Yapping was one thing, but this din would draw a curious crowd. Picking up a stone, she hurled it at them, scoring a glancing blow. One dog yelped and ran off; its companion followed, taking their noise with them.

Slinging the satchel over her shoulders, she limped closer to the bodies.

The first assassin lay in a pool of his own blood; the courier *and* the second assassin had blood and froth covering their faces. The dagger which she'd thrown was the same dagger that hit her. Her instinctive throw did not hit a vital area, but he was just as dead. Stunned by the realisation, she tried to quell a rising panic. She'd been poisoned too! *Why aren't I dead now? How much time have I got?*

Finding nothing more than another glowing dagger, two blowpipes, and a small wallet of darts, she stowed what she could in the satchel. Perhaps these items could reveal informa-tion; maybe the type of poison used, or the particular clan of assassins involved.

Slashing a length from the courier's cape, Leonie bandaged her leg wound to staunch the bleeding. Tempting as it was to examine the bag's contents, the clatter of approaching hooves gave her notice to be on her way.

"Time to go," she muttered, plucking the plumes from the courier's hat as an afterthought. Whatever house the courier represented, they'd want to know what happened. Sliding the courier's rapier through her belt, she melted into the shadows as the palace guards trotted into sight.

After almost stumbling into a patrol of guardsmen a few blocks later, she slowed down. The bag's contents bounced, the weight bruising her shoulder and back as she moved awkwardly. *What's so important to assassinate a courier?* she wondered repeatedly. Curiosity burned within her to check out the satchel's contents, but not as much as the fire in her leg. *Jart'lekk assassins don't come cheap.*

Leonie pushed on before she became another victim. She recalled the horrible deaths of the others; their contorted faces of froth and blood.

Tightening the straps so the heavy satchel wouldn't bounce, she returned to Dockside, fighting the strong urge to curl up in a corner and sleep. Returning proved difficult. Her left leg refused to cooperate; her whole side began to numb. It wasn't until she felt the coarse planks of Dockside beneath her paws, she realised she was well within the Taker's guild territory. Staggering, Leonie leaned heavily against a rough wooden wall. She noticed the spotter sitting in the shadows. *Asleep,* her mind vaguely registered. *He's earned a rude awakening.* When she moved, her leg buckled, turning her step into a full collapse.

———

Opening her eyes, Leonie groaned. Jagged agony knifed through her head. She turned away from the sunlight streaming in through the window. After a short pause allowing her nausea to subside, she slowly cracked her eyes open again.

She found herself in a vaguely familiar room. Her fuzzy mind refused to work. Motes of dust swirled gently, rising and falling as they passed through the fingers of light clawing their way to the back of her eyes.

Averting her eyes from the harsh light, she saw a jug and cup on a table by the bed. Her fingers fumbled, spilling half the contents over her and the sheets. It was all she could do to raise the cup to her lips and drain it before slumping into the pillows. Darkness engulfed her again, dragging her back into unconsciousness. With a rattle, the dropped cup hit the floor and rolled away.

• • •

She heard a door open and close. Soft footsteps approached. Her eyes fluttered open.

"Morning," Jade greeted her.

Leonie's attempted reply was a mere grunt.

"Cat got your tongue?" Jade placed the satchel at the end of the bed. "I'm glad you returned to the land of the living." She poured water, then helped Leonie sit up. "Your continued existence with us wasn't cheap. Luckily you had the foresight to bring samples. It's capable of killing a man in thirty seconds."

"I counted twenty," Leonie croaked.

"Ah, we can speak. Good. The herb lore to counteract the poisons of the Jart'lekk isn't well-known. Your resilience to the poison is astounding." Jade placed the jug and glass on the table. "The apothecary didn't think you'd make it. I'll have to pay him extra. I don't like assassins wandering my streets, or trying to kill you." Jade pulled up a chair beside the bed and lifted the flap of the bag. "I can only assume curiosity got the better of you, and you got a tad too close. Again." She crossed her long legs and sat back, fingering the plumes in her hands. "Enlighten me. What happened?"

With frequent pauses to drink and catch her strength, Leonie related all she could. By the end, it had exhausted her.

Jade stood up with a nod. "You need more rest. I'll get the boys out to dig up what they can. If the Jart'lekk know who you are, you're not safe. They hate loose ends, and with the death of two of them, they will seek vengeance." She was through the door before Leonie could reply.

Leonie lay back, frustrated at the weakness that assailed her. *Why assassins? What was so important?* She succumbed to a sleep filled with disturbing images of running down dark alleys, footsteps all around, yet with no one in sight.

2

A NEW FOE

A BOY ESCORTED EVLIN TO THE CRYSTAL INN'S TOP FLOOR, ushering her through a door into a large room where he left her with a quick bow.

The luxury amazed her. Opulent carpets covered areas of marble tile floor, paintings and tapestries adorned the walls. Expensive, plush furniture caught her eye as well. In her short life, Evlin rarely allowed herself moments to consider a better world. In her world, daydreaming was a hazardous preoccupation; loss of concentration could mean death or injury.

As a thin slip of a girl with bland, blonde hair and forgettable appearance, the only attention she usually received was the back of a hand or worse. What Evlin lacked in physical prowess she more than made up with pure rage and cruelty.

Years ago, in another small village, a would-be mark had bested her. Recognising her potential, he decided to spare her, training her to focus her rage towards enhancing her skills. The training had transformed her life. All the things making her an unwanted member of society made her an ideal candidate to join the Jart'lekk. Now all she wanted was to do her job and please her master.

Evlin suppressed a shiver at the sight of him, in awe of his abilities. Wearing the close-fitting standard dark grey suit of the Jart'lekk, he was her master, as he was to any taking the Blood Oath.

On entering, she bowed. Beside him stood a pudgy man dressed in blue baggy leggings and tunic of silk. He looked too unfit to be a guild member. If her intelligence was correct, he was Daras, from the Savant's Guild; the supplier of information and payment for this contract. Holding a creamy pastry in each hand, he gobbled one, then the other.

"You summoned me, master?" she addressed the head of the Jart'lekk.

"I did." His dark eyes were never still, always searching. "You've done well. I have received favourable reports from many chapters. Today I require the use of your *Seeker* talent." He offered Evlin a selection of desserts from the table.

She recognised none of them, choosing a small tart and taking a modest nibble from the edge of the offering. "I serve in whatever way I can, master."

"You've heard about this morning's occurrence?"

"I visited the area as soon as I heard."

He nodded, expecting no less. "And your findings?"

"The blood evidence shows, at least one of the Enemy left injured. Surviving the poison is a mystery, but from that contact, her essence was imprinted onto this dagger found in our man." She pulled it out of her sheath.

Forged in sacred ritual within the Opsyss temple, the weapon's design was typically used by all guild members. A small reservoir built into the scabbard meant drawing the blade caused a drop of poison to coat the sharp edge.

"Care to explain?" Her master raised his trimmed eyebrows.

"During moments of battle or great stress, the aura every-body has intensifies, leaving an identifiable life sign to those with the *Seeker* talent. This dagger tasted her blood, making the imprinted signature even stronger."

"You say *her*. How many were there, and how can you assume it was a female poisoned?" Daras asked.

Evlin turned to the fat sage. He was eyeing yet another pastry. "My *Seeker* sense conveys this signature as female. No one is capable of surviving our poison. As no body has been located, *she* must have been removed, indicating at least two people. I am unaware if they were part of it, or merely passing by."

"How can a couple people best your top assassins?" Daras asked. "How did they get close enough? Why am I paying such huge sums of gold if anyone – even a female – can do the job?"

"I'm a female." Evlin looked the sage in the eye. "You think I am not good enough?" Out of the corner of her eye, she noticed her master smirking at Daras's discomfort.

The sage stepped back uneasily since Evlin still held the dagger. "Not at all, but an untrained woman? How? Has one of the Jart'lekk gone rogue?"

"The Jart'lekk has no rogues, and this is not an average woman. She is very different."

"How so? What makes this one so special?" her master asked.

Evlin smiled. "Master, she's only part human. Her aura indicates she has a mixture of traits."

"A half-caste? Are you sure?" Daras asked in surprise.

"From her blood, I am positive."

"I cannot fathom anyone in the area helping crossbreed scum," Daras said.

"How would you go about eliminating this problem?" Her master considered a pastry on the plate in front of him, ignoring Daras.

Sheathing the dagger, she replied, "Exterminate every half-caste in Delta."

"That's one method." He delicately licked a crumb off his lip. "But creating anger at us within the city is not our goal."

"Anger over half-castes being exterminated?"

"No, at wholesale slaughter. Though they may despise half-breeds, crossbreeds – call them what you will – the people will become fearful of us——"

"They should be fearful." Evlin quickly looked down, chagrined at herself for interrupting her master.

"Not to the extent the populace would make demands of the authorities; they may call in the guards. I prefer our organisation to keep a lower profile."

"The *Codex* now has the attention of several temples, the Brotherhood of the Flame, and the Watchers in particular." Daras said. "Both are focused on little else right now."

"Let me worry about temple interference," the master replied to Daras.

"I will locate her." Evlin nodded.

"You have her bounty, but the book comes first."

"But master, she has killed two—"

"I'm not one for repeating myself, Evlin." His eyes drilled into her soul.

Evlin dropped to her knees. "Forgive me, master. The book is primary, as you command. My blood is your blood." She gave Daras a withering look in return for his smirk.

———

Three days of boredom was all Leonie could stand. Hissing, arguing, and clawed threats reverberated through the Taker's Guild House. To save his skin, the apothecary declared her recovered and able to go outside. After a fresh change of clothes, she quickly headed for the door.

Out of habit, Leonie kept to the shadows when approaching the waterfront. At the sound of a soft footfall on the planks around the nearest corner, her hackles rose and ears twitched. The thought of being attacked by assassins crossed her mind. Maybe this wasn't such a good idea? She was positive no one survived the recent encounter. No witness to point an accusing claw.

Damn these narrow alleys. Damn the refuse, too. She braced for an attack.

A gust of wind stirred the dust. Her keen nose picked up the familiar scent of an illios mixed with the garbage. Leonie relaxed, retracting her claws.

"Hi, Feiron," she said, recognising her friend as he strolled around the corner.

"Damn. What gave me away? You haven't ssuddenly developed pssychic abilitiez, have you?"

She grimaced at the tone of his sibilant voice; it didn't take long for the lisping and slurring to irritate. The forked tongue of a vorien made it challenging to capture the nuances of the common language. He sounded authentic, but it was an unpleasant experience.

"No." Leonie grinned. "It was your smell." She paused at the lane's exit, letting her eyes adjust to the bright daylight. "Luckily you shapechangers have a distinct aroma."

"Thanks. It's sso nice to be appreciated." He caught up with her. Pulling two fruits from his pouch he offered her one.

Leonie declined with a shudder. "The last time I ate one of those, the fur on my tail fell out." She admired the way his scales glistened. The darker tips on the dorsal fins were perfectly formed for a mature male.

Over the Bridgeway, the pair dodged merchants and carts going about their daily business and made their way on to a pier jutting out into the canal. To the left, the harbour opened to the Great Southern Sea. To the right stretched the waterfront and the bulk of the city beyond hugging the coastal hills. In front lay the myriad islands haphazardly connected by bridges of every size, shape and colour. Diamond Island was the largest and where the Grand Plaza was situated. The headland opposite them, which made up the western arm of the harbour, was crowned by the Palace.

As they walked along the pier, she turned to him, appraising him in full light. "Looks like you've got that new shape down to a fine detail." She nimbly stepped over a loose board. "Too bad you can't change your scent. Not that I find it objectionable, but it's not what a vorien smells like."

"Perhaps I could mask my natural scent by strapping a few

fish around my waist." Feiron bit into his fruit, through the rind. The juice dribbling down his chin was absorbed through his scales.

"If you think it'd help." She grinned at the idea of him moving around the town with the stench of dead fish in his wake. Stopping by the railing at the end of the pier, she used the opportunity to rest. "How do you do that? Bite, I mean."

"We can harden our skin in small areas and shape it to an edge firm enough to slice into soft tissue, like fruit."

They found themselves beside a small shrine dedicated to Onin-le, a minor water deity. Both spat in it as was customary, sharing their body-water. Feiron then fanned his fins in an intricate display, as expected of one of the aquatic races.

"Why bite though? Doesn't your race usually absorb food through the skin?"

"Yes, but it's good practise. Having food dissolve on one's face isn't a good way to maintain my disguise."

"Good point. What brings you down here to this part of town? And why disguised as a merman? Don't you illios go to pieces in water?"

"What you say is true. Prolonged immersion in water, especially seawater, would have a debilitating effect on my endoplasm."

"Okay, okay." She held her paws up to fend off a lecture. "You dissolve, right?"

"In a word, yes. My reason for being here is standing beside me."

"Me! Why?" Her tail twitched.

"My mentor and your boss are colluding with each other. They suggested we team up for a trip."

Leonie watched with interest as he changed back into his natural form. A translucent, grey blob now replaced the shape of the almost humanoid fish. "That's hard on the eyes. A warning would have been nice?"

He took another bite of his fruit. "I'm aware you don't enjoy being out of town, but your boss insisted. I think she's worried for you."

Leonie shrugged, relieved his speech was back to normal.

They watched as a small fleet of fishing vessels sailed out through The Teeth, a series of sharp rocky outcrops rising from the mouth of the harbour.

"So, looks like we're both heading to Qelay. What's your task?"

Feiron hesitated. "Your task has priority. On the return, I need to visit the Central Ranges. I've already arranged for transport and supplies. Other than your charming company and natural skills, you need not supply anything more."

"I understand what I have to do, what's the nature of your trip?" she asked, idly watching a school of redfins darting around the pylons of the small pier.

"Oh, nothing really. A small matter of collecting a few eggshells," he replied vaguely.

"Eggshells? Why go to the mountains? We'll be away over a week or more in that trek. There are dozens of farms much closer." Leonie turned to Feiron, eyeing him dubiously. When in his natural state, she never knew what part of his body she was addressing.

"Because that's where volcanoes are," he said, trying to sound casual. "They have the ideal conditions for wyverns to nest."

"Wyverns? Volcanoes?" Her tail lashed back and forth. "By the whiskers of Slistorf. Is your mentor crazy?"

"Possibly, but think of how much fun we'll have."

"Fun? How can this be fun?" She was about to protest further but stopped and sighed. Less than an hour ago, she had been complaining about wanting to go out.

The wind changed direction, bringing with it the foul odour from the nearby tannery and the exposed mudflats of the ebbing tide. Turning, they retraced their steps, a well-chosen moment, as Leonie did not think she could stomach the stench much longer.

Feiron oozed behind as they moved off the pier, crossed Bridgeway and wended their way towards the Web; aptly named with its many crisscrossed alleys and lanes. It was filled with nooks and crannies containing nasty surprises for the unwary.

"Why wyvern eggs?" she asked.

"These shells have rare properties. You may remember, my mentor is an alchemist. She wants; I fetch. But, after this trip, I'll have finished my obligations and will be free to do as I wish."

"No one's that free."

"I'm sure the shells alone will suffice." He paused. "But then, imagine the look on her face if we brought an entire egg, one that hatched in her lab—"

"Imagine the trouble we'll be in for bringing a live wyvern into the city. Imagine what I'll do to you if you think about it again!"

"At the least, we can see a volcano up close and maybe even a real wyvern. I know it's a lot to ask, but there's no one else I know or trust well enough to depend on in a crisis."

"Stop." She pivoted on the spot, causing him to ooze around one of her legs. "If we're going to help each other, don't mention crisis. Remove it from your vocabulary. I don't want to meet a wyvern – up close or within rock throwing distance. I want to retire old and with all my limbs still attached."

"This is so exciting." He hugged her with his enthusiasm. The embrace felt like being swaddled in warm jelly.

"That's your way of showing your gratitude, is it?" She automatically adjusted her stance to maintain her balance. "Where can I contact you?"

He reformed beside her. "My cart and supplies are in the warehouse on the second-last block along the North Mall; the one with the grey doors."

"Alright. I better go find Jade."

"I haven't told you what you'll get for the assistance," Feiron called out as she turned away.

"Let's see how successful we are. I don't need much."

"Do I hear correctly? Do my ears deceive? A thief knocking back a profit?"

"That, my friend, will cost you dearly." She shook a clawed finger at him. "And in case you haven't noticed, you've no *ears* to deceive. You're a talking blob. All we know of wyverns is from rumourmongers on street corners, or bard tales we hear in taverns. There's no guarantee of hoarded treasure, so don't make promises you can't keep." Her lithe form disappeared in the shadows almost instantly.

3

AN UNEXPECTED TRIP

SLINKING ALONG THE SHADOWY LANES, LEONIE WORKED HER WAY deeper into the Web, trying to fathom what this venture would entail. She had been out in the surrounding jungle previously, but not far. Her skills-set best suited an urban environment. *It ruined my fur for a week!* She shuddered at the memory.

In her current condition, perhaps a ride in the country might do her some good. Leonie hated being weak and inactive, but not fool enough to think she was ready to return to work.

When she rounded the corner, she came face to face with a pair of guards. After a moment of shock, Leonie dived to the side as a guard reached out.

"It's one of them rrell half-breeds." The two guards turned to give pursuit.

Leonie landed, rolled then bounded along the narrow alley. She cursed herself for being so careless. Running in broad daylight would only bring more attention.

In her weakened condition, she could still handle the both of them, but her boss frowned at dead guards in the Web. Relying on instincts, a surge of adrenalin, and perhaps a touch of luck, she decided on her next course of action.

Within a few strides, she sprang onto a barrel then up

the wall. Her claws dug into the woodwork. With barely time to bunch her muscles, she leapt and twisted to the opposite surface. Two more jumps, zigzagging between the close-in buildings; she grasped the overhang and flipped onto the roof. Crossbow bolts peppered the wall, following her trail.

Sucking in huge gasps, she lay flat on her back on the shingles. Even that minimal exertion made her feel as useless as a kitten. The sounds from below indicated the guards hadn't given up. *Next time won't be so easy.* Leonie dragged herself to her feet, taking stock of her location. She bounded across the rooftops, jumping the small gaps in her stride, and continued on her way to Jade's.

To satisfy herself all was clear, she discreetly circled the block twice. Pausing at a blank section of wall between two discarded barrels, she found a knothole, bent down and blew a long raspberry followed by a short one. Within a few seconds, she heard the wall creak.

"Who comes up with these ridiculous passwords, Ro?" she asked the looming figure within as he removed the panel.

The mute shrugged his massive shoulders, sliding the wall back into place after she stepped through. He signed his greeting and led the way up the narrow stairs.

Without waiting for a response to his knock, Rohan entered the room at the top of the staircase. Inside, Netoha waited with a spear at the ready. On seeing them both, she relaxed, greeting them with a warm smile. Netoha laid down her weapon and poured a glass of water, handing it to Leonie with a wink.

Behind the scroll-littered desk, the slim figure looked up briefly. "Ah, glad you survived your walk." Jade waved to a chair; a sheaf of papers clutched in her hand.

Arm in arm with Ro, Netoha pulled the door closed behind them.

"They make a nice couple," Leonie said.

Jade did not respond, immersed in the papers on the desk, her green eyes scanning every document.

With a sigh, Leonie turned to a large, faded tapestry across the room depicting the continent of Shak'aran. She examined the terrain between Delta and the lands to the north, tracing the Urmaq River to Qelay to get an idea of what she'd be up against.

"Have any trouble?" Finally, Jade stood up. "I hear patrols are searching for rrells."

"Nothing I couldn't handle. They were easy enough to evade."

"No body count? Good. We've plenty enough troubles."

"How'd they know where to look?"

"You *do* have a history. I reckon the wounds on the assassin's arm clued them into a rrell – or half-rrell," she corrected, "being involved. Claw marks tend to be exclusive to your kind. There are few half-rrells with your particular traits. I reckon it's time for you to get out of town. Let things quiet down." Jade picked up her glass of wine and joined her by the tapestry. "Coincidently, I've arranged for you to tag along with a friend of yours on his expedition."

"So, I gather, but I dare say hardly a coincidence."

"You know me too well. You've not travelled much, but there's a whole wide world to experience." Jade spread her arms out, almost spilling her wine. "The fresh air will do you good. Plus, Feiron has some unique abilities that may come in handy." She pulled a familiar satchel from behind her desk. "I was doing some snooping around the Savant Guildhall since the attack." The table shook when the tome thudded down among the scrolls. "They're calling this the *Seer's Codex*."

Leonie reached for it, surprised at the weight. "That's all? I thought there'd be more." She turned the pages, browsing through the script. Most of the writing was a different language.

"Other than what you tossed in? No. This belt has two scabbards, but one dagger."

"I left the other one in the assassin."

Jade nodded. "The Jart'lekk will want to find the killer. They will be relentless. Other players are getting involved. Besides the Palace, a few priests are asking questions. You've stumbled onto something big."

Thumbing through the heavy pages, Leonie considered the implications of Jade's comment. The Jart'lekk weren't a trifling matter, despite her recent successes. If it involved the temples, there was no telling where this would lead.

"Clearly, this book has to be taken to Qelay, to a hroltahg named Styx," Jade said.

"If it's so important, why can't this Styx come here? Why was the courier solo? Armed escorts would be a good idea."

"Sources inform me the book was discovered recently. It was supposed to be a secret. Anything more than a courier on a routine errand may have been considered out of place. An armed escort would have drawn attention. As to the rollo situation, our illustrious Lord Zander despises hroltahgs, hence their ban from the city."

"Doesn't he despise everyone?" Leonie mumbled. "I've read my share of books; this one's unusual. Why is it so heavy? I don't recognise any of this writing."

"Agreed. I've not been able to make much of the esoteric details and predictions. Information from the sages is scarce. Ironically, when it comes to sharing knowledge, their lips are tighter than a vorien's arsehole. In the wrong hands, this book could be extremely dangerous; it must be delivered to the hroltahgs sooner than later. Simply knowing of this *Codex* is risky. I trust you without question. You're already aware of the dangers involved and proved you can handle it."

"Any idea who the Jart'lekk work for?" From what Leonie heard, you couldn't reason with these people. Once they had a task to do, they would not stop until they succeeded or died in the attempt. "Surely the temples aren't hiring assassins. Don't they do their own dirty work?"

"I've got snoops around the harbour, but you'll be long gone before we know anything. With assassins lurking the streets, the safest place is anywhere but Delta." She looked steadily into

Leonie's violet eyes. "I'm relying on you to deliver this book to Qelay and get back in one piece."

Jade sat down, back to business. "Styx will probably be at White Cliffs – a rollo hangout in Qelay. I'm sure he's expecting someone. With their telepathic abilities, they will know of you long before you even see him."

"What do hroltahgs look like? I've never seen one."

"Rollos are an unusual lot. Short, solid and round. Nick-named because of the way they move. They'd be formidable opponents if they weren't pacifists."

"Why does Zander hate them so much, if they're no threat? Why the ban?"

"It's said he hates their psionic talents the most. You can't keep any secrets from them, and Zander is a man of many secrets. He wants to remain so."

"I can see how that'd be annoying." Leonie replaced the book into the satchel. "One other thing bothering me is, why me? Surely those bookworm sages have their own channels to deliver messages."

"True, but not all the sages trust each other; there's always infighting. They've got their different philosophies and can't seem to agree on anything. Most have some alignment with one temple or another. I suspect some of them work indirectly for Lord Zander, which might explain those guards, and his aware-ness of the courier's arrival.

"Because Zander wants this text so much," Jade continued, "I want it out of Delta more. Trouble with assassins and fractious temples is bad enough. We don't need more grief with the Royal Guards. If sages can't depend on each other – believing hroltahgs are best to deal with it – then I for one won't argue. Neither will you." She reached into a drawer and pulled out a pouch. "For any expenses incurred. Maintain a low profile and be quick. So, no stealing." She tossed the pouch.

Casually snatching it out of the air, Leonie pocketed the pouch. *To be throwing around money, she must be worried.* Leonie hid her surprise.

"Take it easy out there and enjoy the wide-open spaces."

"The fact Zander may want it is reason enough for me to smuggle it out, but your money's always good to have." With the satchel slung casually over her shoulder, Leonie closed the door on Jade's curses.

4

QUESTIONS TO BE ANSWERED

BACK ON THE STREET, LEONIE REMAINED VIGILANT AS SHE HEADED to her humble home. Hidden within the attic of a little-used warehouse, it provided easy access to the roof. Being strategically located on the corner provided a good view of the streets below.

Once inside, she swapped the satchel for a backpack, tossing in a change of clothing along with the *Seer's Codex*. She grabbed an old travelling cloak from a peg on the wall and donned it before heading off. Avoiding as many people as possible, she made her way to North Mall and the warehouse Feiron mentioned.

One of its two main doors stood ajar when she arrived. Peering into the dim interior, she counted four stalls along each side wall. A bald man stood harnessing a small cart to a di'anth, towards the rear of the building. Quietly, she slipped inside and approached from the shadows, using a stack of wine barrels as cover. There was no vorien in sight.

The di'anth's odour was pungent, and sometimes she wished her sense of smell wasn't so acute. The seven-foot-long reptoid's legs were muscular and slightly bowed, ending in large webbed feet. Its thick tail swished on the straw-riddled floor. Within moments her keen nose picked out the familiar illios scent emanating from the direction of the old man.

"Need a hand?" She stepped up behind him. If she had startled him by her sudden appearance, he did not show it, much to her disappointment.

"Almost done, thanks." Feiron now used a soft, high-pitched voice, but nowhere near as irritating as the vorien lisp. "I gather things went okay with your boss?"

Leonie considered what to say. She'd known him over a year. In that time, she could not recall him ever losing his cool. It was only fair to let him know the risks involved.

"You could say that." She moved closer, lowering her voice. "I have a package to deliver." She held paws up to fend off questions. "I should also tell you others might be searching for it."

"Oh, well." Finished with the harness, he straightened up. "Maybe this trip won't be as boring as I had expected... unless we meet wyverns."

"We'll most probably be in danger," she insisted. "We may have assassins after us if they find out we have this. I want you to know—"

A young stable-hand entered through a side door. Leonie glanced at him warily. Everyone was a potential informant in this city.

"This is Argus." Feiron filled the silence, pointing to the beast.

"Are we ready to go?" Leonie asked as she gave the animal a rub on its thick neck. "The sooner we're out of here the better."

"Argus can't answer you," her companion quipped. "Yes, we're packed." Walking around the cart, he conducted a final check.

Leonie nodded, climbing onto the seat. She politely waved to the kid as he wheeled a barrow towards the door. Feiron joined her a moment later. "Who are we now?" she asked.

"Oh, sorry. Like my new disguise? I am now Hectr, a merchant of some success who keeps on the move. This way, I can come and go as I please."

"A smuggler you mean. Good." Discreetly, she removed the *Codex* from her backpack. "Can you hide this somewhere secure?" she asked Feiron quietly. "There might be searches."

"Sure." The illios took the book and, with a manoeuvre hard on the eyes, encompassed it within his body mass. The book seemed to slide into him.

"Ugh." Leonie stared in equal amounts of fascination and disgust.

"How do I look?"

"Looks like you're getting fat." Pulling her hood up, she covered her distinctive ears.

He chuckled and flicked the reins. Argus lurched off towards the open door and the cobbled street beyond, his webbed feet slapping the ground with each stride. As they turned onto the street, Leonie spotted an armoured squad on horseback in the distance, heading in their direction. They didn't appear to be in a rush, so no alarm. Yet.

"I'd like to get to the gates before they do," she tactfully pointed out. "Without being too obvious, I suggest more speed, otherwise this might be a short venture."

With the loosening of the reins, Argus leant forward. Judicious handling by Feiron kept the di'anth's speed in check. Their actions didn't merit undue attention, and the approaching guards didn't hail them.

Nearer the gates, the road widened into a small square. In the centre of the square, an obelisk stuck out from a well-tended garden circle. Leonie dared a quick glance to see if it was glowing. It was. She made sure she was well-covered with her hood and cloak.

The cart trundled along the road and soon reached the main gate. The usual four guards were on duty, looking tired after a long, boring watch. Three men stepped up to the cart, leaving one by the gate with his spear at the ready.

"Leavin' our fair city, are we?" the senior guardsman asked while the others made a close inspection of the cart's contents.

"Greetings to you too, constable. I'm Hectr Cerrin. We're off to Indras to drop off supplies, thence on to Sorbaa to exchange more goods." Feiron handed over documents from a small chest under the seat. "The reason for our departure is that Shi-Ela, Goddess of Luck, isn't with me. I lost most of my money on a game of Dare, and lack the funds for another night—"

"Don't need a speech," the guard said brusquely. "Been here long?"

"Unfortunately, no. In and out," Hectr replied. "Too busy to sightsee; and now too poor to indulge in the many cultural wonders."

Leonie noted the guard examined the papers carefully. He turned his attention to the search when they uncovered the back of the cart.

Feiron also noted the extra scrutiny. "Someone steal the crown jewels?"

"Smart-arse," the corporal muttered. He turned to Leonie. "And who might you be?" He spat onto the road.

"She's my associate," Hectr said, casually passing a couple of coins when the corporal handed back the papers. "Also, my guard and general assistant. As you saw, our papers are in order."

"Yeah sure." He winked at his fellow guards who joined him. "Ya know, if yer that broke, perhaps we can come to a good price for her. We could use some 'assisting' ourselves." His colleagues chuckled.

Leonie's skin crawled. *How dare he consider me as property!* She had to concentrate on stopping her claws from sliding out.

"Perhaps under other circumstances, but she's far more valuable to me as a bodyguard," the old merchant replied curtly. "In my experience, the North Road can be unsafe."

"Too bad."

"Can you tell me what the road conditions are like ahead?"

Ignoring the question, the guard spat on the ground again and sauntered off with the others.

Leonie watched them return to the shade of the wall. Glancing up, she saw the crystal was still glowing. "Time to go I reckon," she muttered, pulling at her hood to cover her face more.

With a flick of the reins, the cart lurched through the gates.

A short distance past the city boundary, Feiron stopped at a traveller's shrine. He climbed off to toss in a few coins and mumble a brief prayer before he climbed back. "All part of the disguise," he said in response to Leonie's curious look. "Not doing this might be suspect. One never knows who's looking."

"I have a fair idea. Ever see those obelisks glowing?"

"Glowing? No. But now that you mention it, my mentor always suggested I avoid them when possible. She never said why, which I thought strange, but she's a strange woman."

"We'd best go now. If the guard tells them a rrell passed through, they might come after us."

Leaving the city behind, buildings became scarce, giving way to the encroaching jungle and swamp. True to its name, Delta was established on a delta. The road twisted and turned to avoid the worst of it, with dozens of bridges spanning the many waterways.

Leonie kept glancing over her shoulder for any sign of pursuit. Even though the road remained clear, she didn't relax for well over an hour.

Low-hanging, dark-leafed ferns hemmed the dank path. Argus stretched his neck in an attempt to eat a few fronds. Tree trunks, enveloped with a pallid fungus, loomed overhead. The air was heavy and damp and full of insects. Shortly after, Leonie climbed in the back in search of repellent.

"I knew that'd come in handy," Feiron said. "Luckily, I don't need it for myself."

"Maybe because your odour keeps them away?" She smiled to take the sting out of her words.

"Are we going to get onto that subject again?" Reverting to his original form, Feiron deposited the tome on the seat between them during the process. He didn't like to hold different shapes for more than a few hours.

"That's something I don't want to see again in a hurry." She grimaced.

At first, they followed the Urmaq River, but as the swamp became more prevalent, the road curved away to higher, firmer ground. Gradually moving inland, they lost the view of the river. Foetid air surrounded them. Little wind penetrated the dense foliage. Buzzing insects moved across the path in annoying clouds, making Leonie wish she was back in Delta already.

"What's the book about?" he asked. "It's heavy."

"Prophecy, spells, and other esoteric ranting." She shrugged. "Other than that, I couldn't say. I have to deliver it to a rollo—"

"A hroltahg? I've not seen one before. This will be exciting."

They had been on the road for a few hours before darkness descended, Leonie took over the reins since her night vision was better than the shapechanger's. Eating as they drove, they continued to put as much distance as possible between them, the city, and any potential followers.

Feiron plied her with questions since the sky was heavy with clouds and too dark for him to examine the book. She told him of the courier's death and Jade's information. Around midnight they stopped near the base of a hill; one of several through which the road meandered.

"I'm going to hide further in the foliage," Leonie said. "I don't expect anyone to be out at this time of night, but you never know."

A few minutes later, they found a suitable site obscured from the road by a small hillock and dense foliage, and they proceeded to set up the tent.

"If what you say is true, this *Seer's Codex* is no doubt full of prophetic events; perhaps it mentions the coming of the High Ones?" Feiron spoke as they worked. "If I recall, they predicted the city being built. It all seems coincidental."

"I don't believe in coincidences."

"Maybe fate... or destiny then. Those with the gift of foresight suggest what may occur." He paused. "A few hroltahgs have this gift."

"I see." She shrugged, but seeing how much interest Feiron had, she tried to sound enthusiastic. "How's the city involved?"

He followed her as she unhitched the cart and tethered Argus closer to the trees where he could graze on the leaves.

"When the High Ones arrived, they brought new ideas and techniques, including a different form of magic. They soon controlled the Brotherhood, or at least influenced them greatly. When word spread of this arrival, many people flocked here. As the city grew, the palace increased in size. Over the decades, it swallowed the old monastery tower. Many newcomers were powershapers and representatives of other religious orders. That's why Delta has several temples; they think it's special – blessed even."

"Ha," Leonie scoffed. "They can have it."

"Does anyone know who these High Ones are?"

"I thought it was obvious." Feiron shrugged. "The Lords Zander, and Brendon, and the Lady Dianah arrived under strange circumstances over a hundred and fifty years ago. Around the same time as this arrival."

"How many years?" A bolt of lightning creased the sky. Thunder rolled across the hills shortly after. It looked as if the dark clouds threatening rain all evening were finally about to fulfil their promise.

"That's what the scholars say." Feiron oozed into the tent. "Zander's the patron of Eternix and has been since his arrival. That's why the Eternix followers, known as the Temporal Brotherhood, or Watchers, are so invested with him."

"I think the scholars you've been talking to smoke too much lingorsa weed." Leonie ducked into the tent after him as the first drops fell around her. She yawned, closed the tent flap and settled down on her blanket. "It'll take a lot to convince me Zander is anything special. Didn't Lady Dianah and Lord Brendon die in that fire too?" She watched Feiron go to bed. It was fascinating to observe the illios get into a barrel. His blob shape flowed up around the sides and poured into the hollow.

"That is unclear. No one has been able to locate, or identify, their bodies. They strongly believe they have merely returned to their origins, not died."

"Crazy people," was all she said.

The drumming of the rain on the tent grew louder. Leonie checked her calf. The stab wound was healing well; she always healed quickly. Back under the covers and lulled by the rhythm of the rain, she finally dozed off.

5

THE RIVER INN

THE NEXT DAY PASSED SLOWLY. LEONIE COULD WAIT HOURS TO PICK a pocket or scale a wall into a merchant's warehouse, but she became quickly bored with this inaction. She measured the day in snoozes and irritating insect bites. The jolting of the cart did nothing to appease her mood. The trip soon lost any appeal and she itched everywhere.

Gradually, change occurred; hills petering out to undulating plains; the plains became a patchwork of assorted types of crops for the markets in the city. Her interest picked up when the road re-joined with the river and signs of civilisation appeared.

Leonie observed loaded barges making their way south. She was no expert, but it appeared they were having a hard time. Moving nimbly from one side to another, the bargemen were busy fending off flotsam or utilising long poles to steady their course. She'd heard the Urmaq was normally a placid river. Now it was a torrent of muddy water and debris.

She sat in the back of the cart, watching the river as they snacked. "I reckon the rain we've had is nothing like up north."

"Agreed," Feiron said beside her. "They say each year is getting warmer and more crops fail."

When it was time to go, Leonie took the reins. Feiron

remained in the rear to practise his shapechanging technique. As an apprentice, his final testing included his ability to assimilate into several objects or persons. First, he assumed the form of the vorien merchant, followed by a large serpent, a rock, and a wooden barrel. His final attempt was of a young girl wearing a faded yellow dress.

"I better stop before I lose concentration." Feiron came forward to join Leonie. "Bad practice makes for bad forms."

"Those shapes looked fine," she said. "The girl's hair needs a lot of attention. It's dull, too thick and lifeless. And the barrel, is it empty or full?"

"Hair causes me no end of trouble. It's too fine a detail to assimilate." He leaned closer to her and examined her hair. "I'm told no illios can do it, but it is a challenge I've set myself. As for the barrel, it's empty. Once I refine it, I can reduce the size and give it some content but what, I don't know. I can achieve sounds with further practice. But I don't think I'll be liquid. Someone might think I'm wine and attempt to taste me." He chuckled. "I find the concept of anyone consuming me abhorrent."

Leonie smiled at this scenario. "What more do you need to pass?"

"At this stage, the least requirement to pass my apprentice-ship is two of each shape; any race, plain objects and animals and hold them for several hours. I also have a crocodile in my repertoire. I'll practise more tonight."

"You can work on the hair problem too," Leonie suggested.

"I can but try." He didn't sound positive.

By late afternoon, another mass of clouds rolled in from the northwest. They reached the outskirts of Indras. Feiron took over the reins, changing back into the guise of Hectr when farm-houses became more numerous. "See that bridge over there?" He pointed to the stone structure spanning the Urmaq. "Any other time, we'd go that way. Although it's hillier, it's a much better road and passes through more villages. There's a turnoff to Qelay after a few days." He continued towards the congregation of cottages and warehouses. "However, our path is worse for wear, therefore less frequented, but more direct. It should save us several days."

"It'll do then. The fewer travellers on the road, the better." Leonie observed the town centre, checking if anyone seemed to take any undue interest in their arrival. There didn't appear to be many places to stay, but they found lodgings at the farthest end of town. Leonie went to check out the area, finding the tavern had a large stable at the rear, backing right up to the riverside, along with its own small pier.

"That's so Da can ship in goods and ales from the north," a young boy informed her. "He reckons it's silly to use roads when there's the river right under our feet."

"Thanks, son." Feiron tossed him a silver coin. "There be another of those if you take good care of Argus." He gave the animal a pat. "He's worked hard for the last couple of days."

The boy's eyes lit up at the coin. "Yes, mister. I sure will."

Leonie noted the number of horses in his care.

"A few of 'em are locals." He saw her look. "Here to celebrate the end to the drought. We 'av a group come from way up north. Nasty types, from the way they treated their mounts, though Da would cuff me for talkin' bad about customers. Mercenaries, I reckon."

"I see." Leonie grabbed her backpack from the rear of the cart. "And what makes you say that?"

"Cos' underneath their robes, some are wearin' mail."

"I see. Well-spotted." Leonie nodded in approval.

"We don't get many travellers 'ere, neither." The boy continued, filling Argus's food trough with an assortment of vegetable peelings. "Normally all we get are the locals and those that don't wanna be seen. Beggin' your pardon, I didn't mean you. Most travellers cross the river by the stone bridge; the road's better. Nothing much north, except small farms and more swamp."

"It's alright young fellow." Feiron tousled his hair. "We take no offence. You're very observant."

"Thanks, mister."

"It's time we sought lodgings before they take all the rooms." The old man waved as he followed Leonie out.

The inn was a two-storey building of smooth river-rock with large timber beams above the windows and doors, supporting the upper floor. Inside to the left of the rear entrance, past the cellar door, was a stairway. On the right was the bustling kitchen, evident by the banging of pots and the mix of aromas wafting through the door. The front portion of the building contained the dining room.

The chatter subsided when they entered. As the horses in the stable indicated, guests crowded the room. Many heads turned, and eyes marked their progress to a small table by the fireplace.

A serving girl came over to see to their needs. The hubbub resumed, though subdued.

"Welcome to the River Inn. I'm afraid there's not a great selection left tonight." She was polite but kept glancing at Leonie's eyes. "We've some salad, vegetable soup and roast mutton."

"Anything will be better than what I've been eating lately," Leonie said. "I'd like the roast thanks. As undercooked as you can."

"I'll have the salad, sweetie." Feiron smiled. "And a room for the night, if available."

"I'll check with my Da," she said, glancing at Leonie. "We might only have the one room left."

"I'm sure we'll cope," Feiron answered.

"So then. Let me guess," Leonie asked the young girl. "You don't get many of my kind here?"

"I'm sorry if I was staring." The girl blushed. "In truth, we don't. Your eyes are lovely."

"It's okay. I know what it's like to have a curious nature."

"Thank you. Dinner may be a bit longer than usual." She glanced at the crowd. "Would you like anything to drink?"

"Strong tea for me, and your best ale for my feline friend here," Feiron answered.

She moved off to get their dinner ready, weaving her way across the crowded floor with practised ease.

While they waited, Leonie became aware she was the only obvious non-human in the room.

"I wouldn't worry." The old merchant replied to her mutterings. "As the young lass said, they don't get many travellers here. I don't think they'd get many of any kind here. Humans are the majority in Athglenn, in fact, all of Shak'aran. It's in the cities you come across a greater variety of races, especially in the ports."

The young girl brought their drinks, then disappeared back into the kitchen.

Diners at the adjoining table, local farmers from their sturdy attire, stood to leave. One patron, having consumed too much ale, fell backwards, landing awkwardly by the fireplace.

Hectr and Leonie leapt to help, but Hectr was closer. He grabbed hold to help pull him to his feet. In the confusion that followed with the inebriated fellow, Hectr tripped, his hand ending up within the glowing coals scattering embers across the floor and sending sparks up the chimney. Even though it was only a few seconds, it was too late. Those who saw the incident murmured among themselves.

Helping the drunk farmer to his feet, she checked for injuries. Apart from any embarrassing stories soon to be recounted around the township, he was unscathed. His wife and a friend escorted him out the door to the sound of mixed laughter and sympathetic calls from the other patrons.

The portly owner of the inn appeared to soothe his guests and make sure all was well. The activity soon subsided and everyone resumed their seats. But now there were a few sidelong glances Feiron's way.

"How's your paw?" Leonie asked, concern in her voice.

Feiron looked at his hand. "Barely a mark," he said as they resumed their seats. "I should be fine." Then, in softer tones. "I'll be able to regenerate most of the damage, but I suspect some here may have seen too much. Having a high pain threshold can sometimes be a disadvantage. Too late to howl in pain, I suspect."

"Is that a problem? They don't appear to be a violent lot."

"Prejudice can affect people in different ways. I've seen it before," he continued. "It can make the most pleasant of crowds an ugly beast. You're only a bit different. You're warm-blooded and, forgive me for saying so... resemble an overgrown pet; you'll be fine. They may hate you, but they don't fear you. To most of them, illios are akin to monsters. 'Blobs', as you put it. Something alien, who can walk among them in disguise without their knowing. I've found people fear what they don't know or understand."

Further conversation stopped as the proprietor arrived with his daughter, helping to deliver the food. "Kind sir, you've my thanks for helping earlier. I hope you'll not come to harm by the incident."

They exchanged a 'that's an unusual way of putting it' glance.

"I'm Hectr and my companion is Leonie. Do I note a city accent?" Feiron asked.

"Indeed, from Reenat. I've met illios before and know them, in a fashion." He put out his hand. "If it's not too painful, may I shake your hand in thanks?" He added quietly, "I'm aware of the looks you're getting. Fine folk for the most part. I have, shall we say, a worldly reputation and they trust me. By this gesture, I hope we will avoid more harm."

Feiron stood up, grasping the man's hand. "Ladies and gents," he called out. "The next round is on me." This created much noise as most of the diners called for more ale and wine immediately.

The proprietor turned to his daughter. "Go fetch your brother from the stalls while I open another barrel." Soon the dining room again bustled with good cheer. Except for the table with the suspected mercenaries. They glanced over often, less jovial than other patrons, but drinking more.

As she ate, she continued watching them from the corner of

her eye. If there was trouble, Leonie was certain they'd be at its centre. At the behest of some diners, Hectr went to mingle, some wanted to thank him for the drinks and helping their friend.

Shattering glass silenced the room. One mercenary lurched to his feet; two of his companions held him back. He wasn't looking at the illios. His hate-filled eyes were on Leonie.

With a few terse words in his ear by a companion, the group dragged their hot-headed colleague up the stairs, words like *bitch* and *filth* carried across the tavern. The other mercs stood up and followed. Some were steadier on their feet than others.

Oh great, they're staying the night. "Let's hope they're too drunk to cause any more trouble," she muttered to Feiron.

Their leaving signalled an end to the revelry. Soon all the diners ambled out the door, and the inn became far quieter. Peals of thunder followed flashes of lightning.

They both followed the young girl upstairs. "Here's your room. Sorry for those men disturbing your evening. Thank Uthu they're leaving tomorrow." She hesitated, looking at Hectr. "We don't get many of your kind here either."

"You mean an illios; a shapechanger," Feiron supplied. "You may have seen us before, but been unaware." He shrugged. "Would you like a quick demonstration?"

"Yes, please. Very much." She nodded.

"I should warn you," he continued. "It can upset some people."

"I won't be scared." Her voice shook.

"But it might make you ill," Leonie muttered, stepping past.

"Don't listen to her." Feiron moulded his shape. First, he selected the vorien, then moved onto other forms from his repertoire, including the python and barrel.

"Show off," Leonie muttered, looking around the room.

The girl's eyes were wide. "Ooh. You can change into anything you want?"

"Up to a point." He tried to explain. "I can shrink or expand my body mass but the shape must be within a certain range of size—" Her father called for her.

"I must clean up, but thank you so much for showing me." Her face broke into a huge grin as she backed out of the room. "My brother will be so jealous when I tell him."

"My pleasure, lass. Could you get your brother or father to bring up a cauldron or an empty barrel for me to sleep in? I don't rest well on the floor or in a bed."

"I will," she replied over her shoulder as she skipped down the hall.

He closed the door behind her.

"Are you quite finished?" Leonie yawned, surprised by her tiredness.

"Yes, thank you. I love the look on their faces when I do that. It's fun and good experience." Feiron slid across the floor.

Shedding most of her travelling clothes to give her tail some freedom, Leonie stretched before climbing into the big, soft bed. Feeling mellow, she realised the ale affected her more than she would have liked. "I reckon I could sleep through a thunderstorm." She yawned again.

"That may be the case." He moved over to the small window. Water teemed out of the sky. It didn't look like it would stop soon. Lightning flashed to the northeast, with the faint sound of thunder heard over the rain.

Leonie dragged herself out of bed and walked over beside him to peer out, catching sight of the flashes of light. She rolled her eyes as she turned back to the bed muttering under her breath. "More rain. That's all I need." She yawned before dropping off to sleep.

Shortly after, there was a knock at the door. Feiron oozed over to open it. The innkeeper rolled a barrel expertly into the room and placed it in the corner by a small table.

"Ah. You're a wonder. Thank you so much."

"It's a pleasure. Goodnight to you both."

Feiron settled by a lamp with the book, amused by Leonie's snore, sounding much like a purr.

6
_____

RACE TO THE BRIDGE

LEONIE AWOKE TO HER TAIL BEING SHAKEN IN THE DIM ROOM.

"Rise and shine," said a cheerful voice from the foot of the bed.

Leonie rolled over slowly, squinting at Feiron sitting on the end of the bed. "Will you settle for one out of two?" Leonie sat up with care. "That brew last night was potent enough to curl the tails of Slistorf." She held her aching head in her paws. "What time is it?"

"Dawn."

"Uh-huh." *Why did he have to be so damn happy?* Her stomach churned like Delta's harbour at the tide-turn. Glancing at the barrel, she wondered if he'd mind too much if she threw up in it. "I gather you slept well?" It wasn't his fault she had no head for the local ale.

"Yes indeed. That lovely woman in the kitchen has brought up some fresh nut-loaf and fruit for breakfast," he said. "I've already eaten and paid for everything. Dig in and I'll get Argus harnessed." Feiron turned towards the door.

Biting into the oven-warm loaf, she hoped the food would quell her nausea. Leonie watched Feiron in fascination. Instead of opening the door, he oozed underneath it, shrinking like a deflated bladder.

When she finished her breakfast, she washed in the small basin before making her way down the stairs to the rear of the inn. The courtyard was a quagmire. The guilty clouds had now retreated to the southeast, but others were looming, ready to take their place. She tried to make her way to the stables without getting any mud on her but found that virtually impossible.

Feiron, again back in the guise of Hectr, led the di'anth and cart into the courtyard. The horses belonging to the mercenaries were absent; hoof-prints in the mud left a trail to the south.

The young lass stuck her head out the front door of the inn and waved as Leonie and Feiron rode off to the north. A few people braved the wet weather to carry out the necessary chores; otherwise, the streets of Indras were all but empty. The river, far more turbulent than yesterday, threatened to overrun the banks.

"Another downpour like last night will flood this place I reckon," she observed. Immersed in the book, Feiron managed a nod. Leonie shook her head, incredulous at the amount of interest he had taken in it. She rode on with the sound of Argus's feet sucking on the muddy road surface and the incessant buzzing of insects. The surrounding fields, newly tilled – now muddy, contrasted darkly with the green of the abundant crops in the adjacent fields. On the other side of the river was similar, all the way to the mountains to the distant west.

By mid-afternoon, they approached the banks of a tributary of the Urmaq. Water lapped at its banks; the bridge gone, washed away by the floodwaters. The road ended at the roiling water's edge where only a few remaining pylons could be seen.

On the opposite shore among a scattering of willows and poplars stood a handful of cottages. Several coracles leant against the walls of boat-sheds. Others had been dragged well away from the rising waterline. No villagers were visible. If not for the smoke whipping out of the chimneys with the fresh breeze from the west, it was easy to think it was deserted.

The pair contemplated their next move. Feiron suggested they try to entice someone from the village to ferry them across, but then they observed a lone rider approach from the hills to the east. They decided to wait as it became evident he was heading over to see them. Leonie prepared for the worst in case this was a trap.

"G'day folks," he called out as he rode up. "If ya not fancying a swim in this 'ere Deraz, there be an old bridge way up in yon hills." He hooked his thumb over his shoulder. The man looked to be well past middle age, though, because of his weather-beaten face, he may have been ten years younger. "No one in their right mind'll be takin' a boat to water. I had to use the other bridge me'self."

"How far is it?" Leonie asked, raising her voice as he stopped beside them. She hated water at the best of times and was not comfortable crossing, especially under these conditions.

"Why do you youngsters always think us oldsters are deaf? The bridge is about a half day's ride. Doubt you be getting there afore dark or the rain." He turned to ride off. "There be a lot of mud sliding there too, so ya better take care."

"Thank you," Feiron called out. The old man waved over his shoulder. They watched him ride south as they considered his words. "So, what to do?" he asked her.

"I'm not keen to retrace our path back to Indras and follow the main road if that's what you mean. The path less travelled is my preference."

"Well, that makes it easy then. I suppose we do as our friend suggests and go east into the hills." Feiron flicked the reins and Argus trundled off the road onto the muddy trail the old farmer had recently travelled.

No sooner had they started off again than the clouds let loose. Leonie scrambled to don her cloak. Feiron, changing back into natural form, seemed unperturbed; the drops running off his skin.

Travelling on the outskirts of the fields, they reached the start of the hills. Rough ground and woodlands forced them away from the waters' edge and, as the old farmer had said, mudslides were frequent. Trusting in the strength and stability of the di'anth, they took their time as the narrow, winding trail took them higher into the rough country.

Cresting a rise, they paused to survey the panorama of the countryside behind them – a checkerboard of fields split by the Urmaq, which continued to the base of the Central Ranges seen in the distance. Shafts of light from the setting sun streamed through gaps in the heavy clouds and danced across the fields, treetops and water. The undulating terrain and forest continued to the eastern horizon.

With the failing light, further travel in the dark would be folly in these slippery conditions. They camped within the shelter of a copse a short distance away.

Movement – a glint – to the west caught Leonie's eye as Argus started down the incline. Instead of getting Feiron to stop the cart, she hopped off, landing lightly.

"Keep going, I'll catch up," she called out as she loped back to the summit. Shading her eyes against the glare, Leonie scrutinised the muddy track below.

A group of horsemen were riding hard along the riverbank. In this waning light, the boggy soil and rough terrain made it easy for a horse to break a leg. At this distance, she couldn't make out details. Another glint. *Weapons? Armour. The mercenaries from the inn?* A sense of urgency struck her. *The numbers are about right!*

These riders must have good reason to risk their mounts with this foolishness, and only one came to her mind: *the Seer's Codex.*

Leonie considered her situation. Horses were faster and more manoeuvrable than a di'anth and cart, so they'd cut through the woods. At the rate they were travelling, assuming they didn't lame a horse in the effort, the riders would more than likely reach the bridge sooner and stop any chance of escape. *Coincidence? Not bloody likely!* She sprinted on all fours over the hill to catch up with Feiron who was about to set up camp.

"Riders coming fast," she shouted. "Mercenaries from the inn."

"I thought they went south." Feiron looked up in surprise as the feline ran up beside the cart, panting slightly.

"Me too," she said. "Stow that gear and I'll drive," Leonie called back, grabbing for the harness to hitch Argus to the cart. "You know, it would be really good if you could transform into something faster than a di'anth!"

"Afraid not, and I wouldn't be able haul–"

"Just kidding."

Trusting her instinct for danger, Feiron secured the load without hesitation.

The moment Leonie tightened the last strap she leapt to the seat and flicked the reins. Argus bellowed in protest as he tried to reach for another frond of the juicy leaves. A harder shake of the reins for extra encouragement and they were soon bouncing along the dim trail, mud splashing everywhere. Her night vision and the beast's stability allowed them to race headlong in the gloom. Branches and leaves whipped by as they sped along the path that wove through the woods. Leonie dodged as best she could. She avoided the worst, but now and then the sting of sharp-edged fronds left their mark, cutting into her despite the fur. Feiron, who had oozed into the seat beside her, absorbed the lashing with little regard.

The cart trundled over the rutted surface, jolting her to the bone; she had to clench her jaws tight to stop her teeth from rattling. The road was now more rock than mud. Feiron held onto the seat with a couple of tentacles. He sat amiably, wobbling now and then. It reminded Leonie of a dessert she'd seen once – except there were no fruit pieces. *There were some advantages to being a blob.* "What's stowed in back?" she asked aloud.

"Tools, mining and farming implements, food and camping gear. Enough to look legitimate but nothing to fend off half a dozen cut-throats."

Leonie considered this as she ducked under more low branches.

Argus's breath steamed in the cool air, as his sides heaved

like bellows. Di'anths were fine for the long haul, but sprinting was not their strong point.

Stars shone down through a patch of clear sky as the pair shot out of the forest; a small clearing unfolded. On the far side a narrow bridge, barely wider than the cart, spanned the ravine. The distant roar of the torrent below reached them. The clearing on other side was like the one they raced across now, surrounded by woods, with a path leading into hills beyond.

Halfway to the bridge, a shout erupted from the woods to their left and behind. Leonie didn't dare look back, as she aimed for the centre of the dilapidated wooden bridge. A paw's width, either way, would send them over.

Feiron glanced around, seeing nothing, but hearing a lot of thrashing within the trees. The riders trying a shortcut, but having difficulty making their way through the thick undergrowth.

"They're trying to cut us off!"

"I know. Let me think." She risked a glance to her left as the source of the noise grew louder. As soon as they cleared the trees, the riders would be upon them. "Have you anything flammable?" she blurted.

"Um yes, there's a small barrel—"

"Get it. If we break it open on the bridge, we can set it alight. That might delay them." She concentrated on keeping a straight line as she aimed for the bridge.

Feiron flowed to the rear before she finished, searching frantically. The cart rumbled onto the bridge. Hauling the barrel free from beneath the sacks, he rolled off the cart onto the bridge with a hatchet in his grip.

Argus wheezed, drawing in great shuddering breaths. Knowing the poor animal wouldn't be able to go on much longer, Leonie stopped as soon as they reached solid ground. Bounding from the cart, she raced to Feiron who had knocked a hole in the barrel's top and was pouring the contents onto the wooden planks. There was barely enough of the thick fluid to cover the narrow structure.

"Get out of here," she ordered.

"But you have no flint—"

"I don't need any. Go. I can do this."

As he backed away, a jubilant cry arose from across the ravine. Once the riders broke through the trees, they turned and sped across the open ground towards the bridge, sods of turf spraying in all directions.

Unsure what Leonie had in mind, Feiron flowed back onto the cart. If the contents were what he thought, the further the better. "Keep your distance from that stuff," he yelled.

Leonie heeded his advice and backed off the bridge. Anything else he said was lost as she slowed her breathing, cleared her mind and concentrated; ignoring the thunder of the approaching hooves. With only minimal guidance in the arts of spell-casting, she began to draw in the power. She had to be very careful; drawing too much power was a danger, even when using a magical item, like now.

The ring on her finger began to glow. A ball of heat, pitifully small, formed in her cupped paws. Why she did not feel any pain from the heat always surprised her. She focused on the oil slick at the centre of the bridge and sent the flame-ball across. Swiftly, it arced through the night.

Darkness suddenly blossomed with heat and radiance. The resulting explosion threw her back and to the ground. Fading with the distance, the sound echoed along the cliff. The di'anth bolted, taking Feiron along as it tore through the night bellowing in fear.

Across the ravine, the horses reared in fright, throwing all but two of the riders to the ground as they scattered around the clearing.

Leonie staggered to her feet; a stabbing pain in her side.

"Are you alright?" Feiron returned after regaining control of the animal.

"Oh yeah. Fine." Still shaken, she looked across the chasm. Struggling to control their terrified mounts, the riders were disorganised. The remains of the bridge supports jutted from the cliff face.

"What *was* that stuff?" she asked.

"That's what I was trying to remember. I think it was balbon, a concentrated oil derivative and volatile."

"It certainly did the job." She winced as she climbed into the cart.

"You're injured." He started to fuss over her.

"I'll deal with it later." She looked over her shoulder as they moved off. The cloaked riders watched, but the roar of the water obscured their shouts. "Let's put some distance between us and them."

7

ATTACK IN THE NIGHT

FEIRON SLOWED ARGUS AND STEERED HIM TOWARDS A CLEARING BY the side of the road. Even though they were only a short distance from the bridge, they remained out of sight from the riders behind a raised mound surrounded by trees.

"What is it?"

"Before we go any further, I better check your wound."

"I'll be fine."

Feiron ignored her and moved to the rear of the cart.

Leonie was tired and sore. Sighing, she examined the wound in more detail. In the fleshy area below her armpit, a piece of wood had embedded itself between her ribs. Any deeper could have been serious. *Feiron need not know that,* she decided. Extending a claw, she gingerly prised the splinter out, needing to cut a bit of skin to extract it. Hissing at the effort and nauseous with the pain, sweat matted her fur and trickled down her neck and back.

Feiron returned with a small ceramic flask stoppered with a waxed cork, a bowl of water and some cloth. He rinsed the matted blood from her fur then gently smeared the wound with an ugly, grey-coloured ointment. It was thick enough to slow the bleeding, but smelled hideous, reminding her of dead fish rotting in the sun.

"The Lyhosians call it *miwalli*," he said. "I'm told it does wonders for almost everything."

"I reckon I'll call it fish-rot. It certainly clears the lungs, though." She winced as he wrapped a length of the cloth around her ribs. "Why do you have it? I didn't think your type got cuts?"

"I try to prepare for every possibility."

Leonie carefully swung her arms around, turned and twisted to check her manoeuvrability, testing her limitations. "Those riders were in a hurry. Are you thinking what I'm thinking?"

"What and admit to my paranoia? That bridge is down for good. I think we're safe for now."

"Being paranoid has saved me before. I'd better check. I won't sleep if I don't. And you know how irritating I can be without sleep."

"Even with slee—"

Leonie cut him off. "Don't get too comfortable in case we need to leave in a hurry. Another run like that won't be good for Argus."

Slinking into the trees, she was nothing more than a whisper, using the foliage to keep out of sight. She reached the clearing in a matter of minutes, careful not to strain her wound. Across the ravine, Leonie saw the men between two fires. By their mannerisms, they were arguing, but the rumble of the water and distance proved sufficient to drown out any details. They had erected tents; the horses unsaddled and tethered to one side.

Maybe I am too paranoid. Leonie waited, pulling a face as the dampness seeped into her fur. The men were settling down. They wouldn't have bothered setting up a camp in the first place if they were intending to pursue tonight. Satisfied, she returned to Feiron with her news. Her injury had scabbed over while she watched, but the movement caused it to bleed again. *Feiron won't be happy.*

"You're sure they're the same ones from the River Inn?" Feiron asked when Leonie returned with her news.

"Positive. I recognised the one that spoke out last night. When I left, they were bickering around a fire. I think they'll wait for first light before they attempt to cross. Since they can't see in the dark, it'd be suicidal for them to try."

Setting up camp became routine. Fed and watered, Feiron gave Argus a good rub down while Leonie looked for firewood dry enough to set alight. By the time she returned with a meagre load of wood, Feiron had almost finished setting the tent. She dumped the wood in a pile, sorted out the kindling and larger pieces, then started a small fire with a minute dose of power. The damp wood hissed and steamed in protest as the flames licked around them.

"Let's keep this fire small and douse it as soon as we're finished. It doesn't feel right, knowing those mercenaries are so close – even if they are stranded."

They set a pot to boil; the fire put out straight after. Soon, with steaming cups of tea, nut-loaf and cheese from the inn, they had time to rest in relative comfort. Both relieved the rain hadn't spoiled their food.

The small amount of powershaping earlier had wearied her more than she expected. She decided she might not be thinking clearly. Leonie leant back against a wheel of the cart and tried to get comfortable, but couldn't settle down. Faint background noises kept intruding; Argus munching on leaves, his feet breaking twigs as he moved, his tail dragging along behind; Feiron's movements; the clink of cups, the swish of the tent flap opening and closing…

The clatter of tin pots woke her. She sat up, wincing at the twinge in her side, realising she had dropped off to sleep.

"Sorry to startle you," Feiron said. "More food, perhaps?"

She nodded, rubbing her eyes. While she nibbled, she recalled dreaming of the River Inn; images of patrons in farm attire eating. Robed figures, with a hint of metal armour underneath, burst in and set the place ablaze. Men and women ran screaming, but couldn't get out.

She described it to Feiron. "I can't shake this feeling. Am I tired or still being paranoid?"

"About those men? We can assume the search in Delta failed; they'd have to try somewhere else. They're looking for a half-rrell ... and here you are."

"But why didn't they grab us at the inn? Why wait until now? Why this mad dash across the country in the dark? And why," she finished, "are they wearing those cloaks with no insignia? What are they hiding?"

"Who knows? They might be mercenaries working with the Deltan guards. Maybe they received a message. There *are* spies in Delta, you know." He winked at her. "Those assassins certainly knew about the book. If we find who they were working for, we may find who our real enemy is. And not forgetting, south of Qelay, most guards answer to either Zander or one of the temples."

"Tell me," she said, gathering the tin plates, "you've been studying the book. What could it possibly say to get Zander, or anyone, so concerned? Assuming there's any truth about him being this High One. It's just a book."

"The future and the past." He put his cup down and picked up the book, flicking through it with a small tentacle. "One entry mentions the arrival of the eternal High Ones, as I mentioned earlier, strangers who arrive on a pillar of fire. It says they are eternal and will bring with them great secrets far beyond our understanding, bestowing blessings and good fortune on those who follow them and believe in them. The interpretation is ambiguous."

Feiron quoted from the tome. "... 'and a great light shall fall through the sky, bringing new wisdom and magic in a sky-vessel. Within lie those with great secrets that will enable the Chosen to return to their own origins.' Another entry, dated a century later, also mentions the arrival, but declares the strangers are not what they seem and will eventually bring ruin and damnation on those who follow. The more devout the worshipper, the further the fall."

"I bet that part isn't taught to them."

"There are several entries, all differ slightly."

"That's the way with all predictions," Leonie argued. "They say so many things – and none of it makes sense."

"Ah well, the essential details are similar. They do all agree with people coming from the sky. Perhaps the discrepancies are due to the amount of time between the different foretellings. The phrases are in differing styles and handwriting, an indication the book had been passed around a lot. We will have to ask Styx; to confirm the origins of the city and the rumours surrounding Zander, Dianah and Bren."

"Who actually wrote it? How old is it?"

"There is no mention of any specific author, but the earliest entry here is...," he paused, flicking through the pages, "... in 223. There's a century between some entries."

"That'd make the book over a thousand years old." She came over after cleaning up the dishes, wiping her paws on her loose shirt.

"Remarkable yes, and durable. I'm intrigued to know from what the pages are made."

Leonie considered this while she banked up the fire. "All this is about the past; does it mention anything about now or the future?"

"There's a reference to the races returning to their origins... and also a mention of the departing of the High Ones from this world."

"They die? You said they were eternal."

"Depends on your interpretation of *eternal*. It might mean *eternal life*, as some religions preach, which still involves death, but *'departing from this world'* does not have to mean dying. Remember, they were from another planet or world. I've heard sages speak of the theory of other worlds. They say the stars are like our own sun, though very distant."

"But—"

"It's only theory and far beyond my understanding. No need to lose any sleep over it I should think. It's not as if we will ever know the truth."

A few drops of rain began to fall, so they moved the conversation to the tent.

"Do you think other worlds would be like ours?" she persisted as they made themselves comfortable inside.

"Who knows what they are like? I'm no scholar, but I've been around, and a few things have occurred to me. All the races have their own unique mythology. We are all so very different; humans, rrell, voriens, seleth, glins'ool and hroltahgs, yet there is one thing common to all, hints that in the distant past we were not of this world. None of us."

"What do you mean?"

"For instance, in a lot of the legends from several races there is no mention of twin moons."

Leonie turned to him, waiting. "And?" she prompted.

"That's it. Only a mention of one moon; we have two. Where are the legends including both moons?"

"Myths and rumours," she muttered from the darkness. "Maybe bad translation ..." she yawned, "or just make-believe stories for the young."

"Ah yes, but all rumours and lies – at least the best ones – have an element of truth."

"So, you believe them?"

"Until I know for sure either way, I wouldn't discount them completely." Leonie's ears twitched. Her head came up sharply.

"Hear something?" Feiron asked.

She nodded. "Stay here," she whispered. "I'll take a look." Crawling under the rear tent flap, Leonie skirted the edge of the camp, avoiding the light from the fire. She made her way in the direction of the noise; her dark figure blending with the shadows of the underbrush. To her right, she heard Argus snorting and chomping on leaves, undisturbed.

Halfway to the tree line, her hackles rose. Deep within her

being, she sensed a familiar tug – *someone's drawing power*. Leonie gazed about anxiously. There – a faint glow off the trail where the trees were thickest – she saw a dark-robed figure raising an arm.

Running across the sodden earth and dodging trees, her injury prevented her from using all four paws. Maybe it was the images of the dream haunting her, but she had a sense of deja vu. As she closed the distance, she was both concerned and relieved to make out only the one figure. *Where are the others?*

Her best chance was to get him as he stood in concentration. Leonie recognised it before it happened; the releasing of the power. She was too late. There was a blinding flash followed by a thunderous explosion. Flames engulfed the tent.

She hurled herself at him, glimpsing the surprise on his face before they both went down in a ball of fur and robes. A cry of agony punctuated the brief struggle. At first, neither of them moved, and then slowly, the robed figure stood up and staggered off into the woods, back towards the chasm. The bellowing of the frightened di'anth drowned out the crackling of the burning tent.

Leonie lay unmoving in the long grass. A large snake slithered up to her through the underbrush, its tongue darting in and out. It blurred briefly as it transformed into the illios. He flattened his body and oozed underneath, lifted and carried her gently back to the cart. Placing her on the ground, he splashed a small amount of water on her face.

After a few moments, Leonie regained consciousness. With his help, she sat up slowly, ruefully rubbing her head. A large lump was already forming behind her left ear. "So much for landing on my feet. That's the second time tonight I've fallen flat on my face." She scanned the campsite noting the smoking ruins of their tent, then back up to the path. "Where's that bastard? I could've sworn I got him."

"You did, but it took a while. He collapsed a little beyond the tree line. Take it easy for a few minutes and catch your breath. Where do you hurt the most?"

"Everywhere." While waiting for her head to stop spinning, Leonie examined her bandaged wound. The brief tussle had reopened the gash, and it was bleeding again.

"I will get more bandage," Feiron offered, seeing her bloodied paws.

"Don't worry. This blood's not mine," she said.

"We better see to that at least." He pointed to her ribs.

"What happened? I left you back in the tent."

"Your hearing is superior. If you think you heard something to cause alarm, that's all I needed."

"The book?" Ignoring the throbbing in her head and side, she stumbled to where the tent had been, and searched the smouldering debris. She straightened up with the blackened tome in her grasp. The leather cover was charred. Thinking the book ruined, she thumbed through the pages. They were undamaged.

Feiron joined her. "An unusual material indeed."

Now that they had found the book, Feiron insisted she sit down to allow him to dress her wounds and examine her head properly. She complained, but kept still long enough for him to attend to the minor injuries.

When he finished, they went to examine the attacker's body. They found him face down in the underbrush.

"Thought so. One of the fellows from the inn." It was easy to see the manner of death; he had lost a lot of blood from a severed artery in his thigh.

"It would have been good to ask him some questions."

"He wasn't in a talkative mood." Leonie crouched to search him for some indication of whom he really worked for. "He's a soaker; he's removed his chain mail otherwise he wouldn't be able to cast. Metal interferes with drawing power," she explained. "Channelers cast using the power from within, so can wear armour."

"You seem to know a bit about powershaping," Feiron said. "I'm curious how you knew to cast the fire spell earlier."

"I didn't really cast anything." She brushed back some of her fur and showed him the ring on her finger. "I found this in my travels and managed to learn a bit about it. I thought you'd know more."

"We illios have no ability to cast; something to do with our body; the way we are formed."

"Yeah well, like I said, I'm no powershaper. I can see it, but only know the one trick, and that's purely because of the ring." She looked at the body again. "He was taking a risk to fireball us – unless he knew the book would be safe." She continued with her search, finding a belt-pouch containing several coins. Some were Deltan, but others were from Reenat, as indicated by the etching of a rampant gryphon and crown, the emblem of the Royal House of Athglenn.

"This chap's been on the road for a while. I wonder what he was doing all the way up there." Feiron pointed out the coin's origins.

"Spying perhaps." Leonie noticed a medallion under the robes with a motif of a flame. "This certainly explains a lot." She reached for it, but the moment she laid her paw upon it a flash of scorching heat assailed her. Dropping the disc with a hiss, she whipped her singed paw to her mouth. "You know what this means?" she asked, sucking her fingertips.

"More bandages?" Feiron recognised the Fire Temple motif on the round metal disc. "Indeed. The Brotherhood of the Flame. We have a group of Woorin zealots after us."

"This could be bad," she said.

"The Woorin Temple has been trying for decades to oust the Temporal Brotherhood – those worshipping Eternix – from being Zander's pets. Maybe this book can do it for them, or perhaps a force to be taken more seriously. But then again, perhaps Zander's still behind this. I hear he can be devious, pitting one group against the other."

"Let's hope other sects aren't in on it, otherwise we'll have a religious war on our paws." Leonie stood up and brushed the dirt off her knees. They turned to go back to camp. Halfway there, Leonie stopped abruptly.

"Idiot," she muttered. "How'd he get across?" She glanced at Feiron. "And where are the others?"

Both turned as one to the path and raced back to the cliff.

8

MISCHIEF IN DELTA

"There's a half-rrell involved master. I sense she knows something," Rodi said. Picking himself up from the temple floor, he wiped the trickle of blood from his ears onto his red Seeker robes. He had been focusing on the telepathic link made possible via the priest's amulet until the moment the troublesome feline touched it, causing a backlash. The female half-rrell was not a member of their temple. Discordant emanations relayed back through the link to stun him, resulting in his injuries.

"Pagh. One half-caste bitch?" Coundar ignored the Seeker's pain. "What could she possibly know or do?" The High Priest of the Woorin Temple paced the floor. "What in the blazing hells made that fool Karig go off by himself?"

"The others appeared to be... less committed, master. I understand they argued that the bridge being down was too much an obstacle."

"Are you still in contact or did you lose them when Karig died?" Coundar interrupted.

"I've lost it, master, but can attempt a transfer contact through another."

"Do so. Tell those other fools to get that book at any cost. They do not want to come back without it. Tell them to kill the interfering feline, and that illios." Coundar's eyes flashed a baleful red. "I want no one to know of this." He turned and stormed out.

Coundar strode down the wide corridor, his black robe billowing behind. The torches in the sconces flared as he passed. He entered another room at the far end of the passage. Three novice Seekers were in trances, each with a small burner on a low table in front of them.

"What news?" he demanded.

"The Watchers are still carrying out their futile searches in the city," one replied, unaware of his master's ire. "They lost the trail when the assassins struck, before the courier delivered the book into the hands of—"

One of the other acolytes went rigid, her mouth widening in a silent scream before she collapsed to the floor, a small amount of blood oozing from her eyes, ears, nose and mouth.

"That's Mina," the first Seeker said without emotion. "She was keeping surveillance on members of the Death Sect. They must've discovered her presence and now know we're also searching for the tome."

"Has she mentioned anything?" He stood over the female body twitching on the floor. He recognised her; she had been ambitious and, for a while, entertaining.

"Only that they sent agents out of the city in several directions."

"Lucky for her, then. Let them have her. She was careless." Coundar turned to the third acolyte who had several candles and personal items of the other temple High Priests in front of him. "And you?" Coundar barked.

"Master," he said in an irritating falsetto. "It's believed one of the sages was responsible for the Jart'lekk attack on the courier. The other sects still appear to know nothing. I'm scanning them all one at a time." Perspiration ran down his face, dripping onto the table as he placed one of the items down. He picked up another and began the intense concentration required. It was an awkward task, swapping mind-link from one recipient to another, especially over longer distances. The wet weather was an added hindrance. The mixing of the elements, in this case Air and Water, interfered with each other.

A hand lashed out and gripped Coundar's ankle with inhuman strength. He teetered, flailing his arms about as he lost balance. With an oath, he tumbled to the stone floor.

Mina crawled towards him, dead eyes glistening black orbs.

He kicked at her, trying to scramble away. "Guards!" he yelled, trying to get to his feet. "Guards!"

The Seekers, only vaguely aware of the events, fell out of their trances, stumbling over to help. Their initial efforts to pull her away were ineffective. Mina's strength was too great.

The door burst open as four guards ran in, believing they saw the three acolytes attacking the High Priest, but then they saw Mina's face. The guards stepped in and impaled her with their spears. This slowed her down, but her grip on the High Priest weakened.

With a vicious kick, Coundar freed himself and stumbled to his feet. He whirled around, enraged. Mina was now rising, reaching out for anyone, oblivious to the four spears embedded in her chest and abdomen. Blood ran freely, matting the robes to her body. A spear pulled free, severing a vein. Blood sprayed across the floor. The two remaining acolytes scattered in horror, their faces as pale as the dead woman.

"Beware my wrath." He raised his hand, palm facing forwards. The raging fire in the hearth died down as he drew in the power and focused. A thick shaft of scintillating red light struck out, hitting Mina's body squarely in the chest. The guards shielded their eyes from the intense magical heat, dropping their now smouldering weapons and moving back to safety.

As the fierce heat engulfed her, the undead body staggered around the room, arms windmilling. Her flaming robes threatened to ignite anything they touched. Acolytes and guards clambered over each other in fear, avoiding the conflagration.

One of the more courageous guards picked up a chair and used it to push her into a corner, away from the others. It immediately caught fire from the unnatural flames, but it was enough. Mina fell writhing to the floor. Within moments her body, blackened beyond recognition, was now a grotesque lump of bone, and charred, crackling flesh filled the room with an overpowering stench. One of the younger acolytes threw up in the far corner at the sight and smell.

"The Death Dealers want to play games, do they?" Coundar gathered his robes about him, breathing heavily and perspiring. "Maybe they delved into Mina's mind and found out more than we thought." He studied the corpse, noting the guards' reluctance to approach.

Contemptuously, he ordered them to dispose of the body with a wave. "Continue the surveillance," he commanded the telepaths as if nothing had occurred. "I want to hear of any new developments immediately." Coundar strode out.

The two remaining telepaths glanced at each other nervously. One of them opened a window to release the reek of death to the night air. The other acolyte, giving the guards and charred corpse a wide berth, went to rebuild the fire before resuming his seat.

It took them a long time to clear their heads enough to carry on with their tasks.

"So Alen," Lothas said. "You picked up Mina's last thoughts, did you? Good. You're progressing." He beamed at his capable apprentice sitting opposite. The High Priest of the Temple of Opsyss, aged in his forties, wore the customary blood-red robes of his station. Tattoos across his shaved head, ideograms of the Order, showed his rank and the events that influenced his rise. His pupil, a thin man of about nineteen summers, wore a black smock, his hair still intact, with beaded plaits.

The two men sat back in the cushioned chairs in the rear of the Temple of Opsyss and sipped wine. The incense burner on the marble table had expired.

"Did you note how sloppy her attempt was to penetrate my screen? Those telepaths from Woorin are pathetic. Very poorly trained."

"Yes, master, but that technique you used to control the body's movements." Alen moved to the edge of the seat in his eagerness. "I've not come across that before."

"Nor should you. You're still far from that level of training. One cannot rush these things. You were privy to it only because the occasion arose," Lothas pointed out. "Coundar needed a scare. It has been too long since I had a laugh. That is enough for this evening, young Alen. I doubt anyone they bring out tonight to replace her will be any better. Go and study on what you have witnessed, concentrate on the methods I used to thwart her probing."

"But—"

"I know you've tried it before." He lifted his wineglass in the general direction of the Woorin Temple across the plaza. "All students think they know enough; have practised enough, but like Mina, they won't know if they have perfected the skill until it's too late. Go now. I must consider the information I've gleaned from her dying mind. I feel tonight will show some promise." Lothas resumed his sipping, already deep in thought.

9

FIRE-FIGHT AT THE RAVINE

LEONIE AND FEIRON MOVED TO THE EDGE OF THE CLEARING NEXT TO where the bridge had once been.

"What are they up to?" Feiron deferred to Leonie's night vision.

"One of the brothers is nursing injuries and staying back with the horses. The others are heading for the ravine." She peered at the edge about thirty feet away. "There's a rope and a grapple spanning the gap. It looks like we've company coming."

"In your condition, I don't much like our odds."

"Let's see if we can even them out then." Leonie crawled forward.

"How did I know she'd say that?" Feiron's image blurred as he transformed into a serpent.

Leonie moved as close as she dared to the ravine without being seen, crouching behind one of the many small boulders scattered about. A large snake slithered through the grass towards the cliff as she waited. She watched as it progressed towards the hook embedded in the ground. "What's he up to now?"

One of the brothers started climbing along the rope while his companion watched. The climber hung upside-down with his legs over the rope, pulling himself along with his arms, then dragging his feet behind. The rope sagged with his bulk, making a wide *v*. His lack of fitness was telling, and it didn't take long for him to start wheezing.

The snake slithered onto the rope, coiling around as it moved out.

"A neat trick," Leonie acknowledged, glancing at the activities of the second group.

They were ten paces further up and attempting to cross near the ruined bridge. After a few swings, the grappling hook arched high into the night. It bounced off a rock and when the thrower pulled it taut, it came loose, ripping up tufts of grass. He hastily re-coiled the rope.

Meanwhile, the first climber was in difficulty. He slapped at the snake with little effect before he tried to reverse his direction and head back. His panicked movements caused the rope to bounce and sway. His companion called out, waving him on. The serpent continued its harassment.

When the man lost his grip he cried out, but his legs stopped him falling. Dangling upside-down, his tunic fell, obscuring his sight. Flailing his arms blindly, he only tangled his garment further. Seconds later, he slipped from sight, lost in the foaming waters below. His comrade on the other side baulked, but with a shouted order from a stocky brother, he prepared himself.

Feiron reversed his direction and slithered off the first rope to join Leonie.

"I'll take this one. I have a few questions." She began to crawl out to the rope.

After watching Leonie creep out, her belly low to the ground, Feiron slinked to an area opposite the second group and transformed into a shape similar to one of the many boulders. With the rope once again gathered, the second group threw again.

With a clang, the hook landed. Relying on the concealment of the night to protect him, the illios flicked it over the edge before it snagged. From their wild gesticulations, a furious argument was taking place between the two on the opposite bank. They re-coiled the rope and prepared for another throw.

The brother Leonie had been watching tapped into the power. A small ball of flame formed above his head, lighting the area around him for a few paces with a pale-yellow glow. He also drew a dagger from a sheath, gripping it between his teeth before lowering himself onto the rope. Climbing hand over hand, he seemed in better physical shape than his predecessor. The rope dipped rhythmically with his movement, placing him out of her sight intermittently. The small flame floating above his head bobbed in unison, causing distorted shadows to grow and shrink.

Leonie used these moments to edge closer to the grappling hook. Shortly after she arrived, a hand slapped the ground in front of her. They met face to face as he was about to haul himself up. His eyes grew wide in fear. Foetid breath washed over her as he swore between clenched teeth. The climber hung, one arm on the cliff edge and one still grasping the rope.

"Hello man." Leonie flashed him a smile. "So then," she flicked her violet eyes to the flame. "I see your sect likes fire, but tell me, how well do you like water?"

His answer was unintelligible. Spittle ran down his chin.

"Here, let me help." Leonie reached out with her left paw and took the dagger from his mouth. His reluctance to part with it caused him to receive a cut to his lip for his troubles. Blood and dribble mingled, flowing freely.

"Filthy wench," he raged, attempting to climb up. Leonie firmly placed her claws on his hand, with enough pressure to draw blood.

"Such language, and you a brother of the cloth too," she chided. "I want answers man, or else you can follow your friend and start swimming lessons."

He took the hint, being in no position to force the issue.

"Who're you working for? Why are you after us?"

He tried to retreat, but again she applied pressure with her claws, careful of her burnt fingers. "These are simple questions;

answer and you can go. Remember, you started this when your friend came over and tried to fry us."

He remained silent. Leonie noticed his arms trembling with fatigue, and doubted he'd be able to make it back, but she didn't dare let him up either.

The brother closed his eyes and began muttering under his breath. At first, she thought he was praying. Then sensed the familiar drawing of power. There was nowhere for her to run to in time. Frantically, she dragged the knife back and forth across the rope. The dagger was blunt. *I could chew through the rope faster than this!* Blocking the pain from her burn, she sawed madly using both paws.

The ball of light dimmed. A sneer creased the brother's bloodied lips. Then he began muttering a spell. The rope jerked as part of the cording twanged, but still, it held. Leonie didn't stop her frantic sawing.

The last strands unravelled with his weight. His eyes opened wide as he fell. The chanting faltered when he lost concentration. The built-up power had nowhere to go. His body could not contain it. The energy burst out of him as it sought a path back to freedom.

Leonie drew back from the edge. A bright flash lit up both sides of the clearing as rolls of thunder echoed up and down the ravine. The air reeked with the smell of bile and charred skin. Chunks of super-heated flesh rained down, hissing and steaming when they spattered on the damp ground. Crawling away in a daze, bright spots hampered her vision. She shook her head to clear it and the ringing in her ears.

Raised hackles gave a split-second warning as the ground to her right erupted in a fireball. Leonie instinctively rolled to the left and stumbled towards the trees on all four paws. Staggering behind a pile of rocks, she slumped in a heap, desperately trying to regain her senses. Sucking in a couple of long, deep breaths, she moved around, carefully glancing over the boulders.

Smoke rose from a charred area beside the grappling hook.

The three remaining brothers stood on the far edge, pointing and peering into the gloom.

"Are you alright?" Leonie jumped at Feiron's touch. "Didn't you hear me?"

"Slistorf!" She turned to see Feiron behind her. "I think I've gone deaf." She shook her head to clear it, but only made it worse.

"I doubt that. Maybe a bit shaken. Sit and catch your breath."

"I was doing that until you scared the crap out of me." She ran her fingers over herself. "No new injuries."

"You were lucky. If they could see in the dark, you'd be charred too."

Shrugging, she resumed her watch of the worshippers. "I was as weak as a kitten after I blew up the bridge. If we make them cast enough fireballs, they'll get tired, and we'll have a chance."

"Are you sure you're up to this?" Feiron asked, but then answered himself. "Forget it. You'd say you were, regardless. I have a counter-strategy. I'll distract them when the hook catches. You then fireball the rope. It will burn, or at least be too damaged for them to risk climbing over."

"Yeah. How many grappling hooks can they have? I like your plan better."

With a nod, he ambled off through the woods while Leonie slunk as close as she dared; the rocks keeping her approach obscured. They were preparing to throw the hook again. When it snagged, she saw Feiron rush out from the woods, angling his way across the clearing. He threw a rock to gain their attention.

Already one was casting while another brother lowered himself onto the rope. Leonie concentrated on her task; eyes steady on the rope. She needed only a small amount of power for her task. If she missed, she might conjure up one more attempt. Kneeling, she opened her palm and let fly. The fireball shot through the air, bursting on impact. The rope caught alight immediately.

It took the brother on the rope a moment to realise his

dilemma. He struggled to move back. When the rope burned through, he swung down and smashed into the opposite cliff face.

Their response had been swift as a flash of flame incinerated the area where Feiron had been. She hoped he avoided it as she crawled back to the edge of the wood. While waiting, she wondered what it would do to him – considering his fluid form.

Out of sight, they both watched from the tree line for any further attempts at crossing the ravine. The two remaining brothers stood on the opposite side. Whatever they discussed was unknown, but they eventually decided on a plan. Together, they removed their amulets and tossed them into the raging river far below and retreated to their campsite.

When satisfied they weren't up to any tricks, Leonie and Feiron wearily walked back to their camp site.

"I think we were lucky," Feiron said. "It's likely that group was inexperienced. Maybe we killed their leader? But either way, I suspect they relinquished their calling when they tossed the amulets into the ravine. They will not be returning to the temple. I hear Coundar is unforgiving of failure. However, I have no doubt others will come. And they will be far more experienced."

Back at their campsite, Leonie retrieved what she could from the remnants of the tent. Feiron went in search of Argus who had broken his tether when the first fireball struck. The cook-fire had been rekindled and a pot of tea simmered gently by the time he returned. Leonie leant against the cart, rubbing ointment into small cuts and her singed paw.

"How's Argus?" she asked, not looking up.

"Not as battered and bruised as you." Feiron placed a bag of meal around the di'anth's muzzle before slumping a short distance from the fire.

"I'll live." Leonie sat next to him with a groan. "Do you think there's a link through those amulets?"

"I think discarding them was more than symbolic." Feiron nodded. "We can assume Coundar, or whoever is behind this, is aware of tonight's activities. I suggest we get some rest and move off first thing in the morning." He reached for the pot. "But there's always time for another cup of tea before sleep."

Although the clouds had drifted away, the pair moved under the wagon in case the fickle weather turned. Sleep came quickly, any discomfort forgotten.

Dawn coated the horizon in an amber sheen and the clear sky promised a bright day ahead. A small sky island drifted off to the south. They watched it until it had dwindled into the distance. Feiron prepared breakfast while Leonie watered and fed Argus.

As the reptoid ate, she examined his legs and tail for any cuts or injuries from last night's run through the forest. "I'll check on our friends, see what they're up to," she said to Feiron afterwards. "I won't be long." Moving off, she bypassed the area where the body lay.

Crows hopped around on both sides of the deep ravine. There was no sign of the brothers other than the smouldering remains of the campfires. Wisps of smoke curled up into the still air.

Leonie ventured closer to the edge. Crows squawked and cawed at her approach, but didn't fly off, just hopped away until she passed. She didn't need to look to know what they were pecking at; the cloying smell of burnt flesh remained in her lungs.

Peering over the rim of the ravine, she guessed it was about three storeys down to the churning white froth. Further downstream, the chasm widened. Picking up one of the grappling hooks, she looked at it before tossing it over the cliff.

"Are you sure they left?" Feiron handed her a plate on her return from the ravine.

"As sure as one can be." Leonie squatted opposite him. "The place is deserted, and the fire is smouldering ash." Steam wafted off the strips of cured meat and mashed vegetables heaped in the centre. Her mouth salivated, and she wiped her lips in case she drooled.

"I thought after last night's activities you'd need a decent meal," he said. "We have enough, so dig in."

She nodded in reply, her mouth already full.

After breakfast, Feiron insisted on checking her injuries before they hooked up the cart. The gash near her ribs had bled, but otherwise, everything else looked clean enough. There was no harsh redness to show any infection. He reapplied more balm before wrapping the worst in a bandage.

"You must try to be more careful. This is the last of the bandage."

They moved along the little-used trail, giving Argus an easy time of it. The day proved to be warm and the roads dried quickly. The trail angled north-west, leading out of the foothills to another plain. After high-sun, they re-joined the trail about three leagues up the Urmaq River from where the Deraz fed into it. Even when she took her turn at the reins, Leonie spent much of the time looking over her shoulder. Argus kept to the road, regardless.

"I very much doubt anyone will be crossing yet," Feiron said.

"I know, but I get this feeling of being watched."

Feiron looked around. Some fields lay fallow, while some had ears of corn bent over from the recent weather. There were clumps of trees scattered about, but no dwellings were in sight. High above, a hawk pivoted and then hovered, searching for prey.

"Do you think they'll stop searching after we deliver the book?"

"Zander is an egomaniac – he won't stop; after last night, neither will the Woorin Brotherhood. Then there's the Jart'lekk to consider – they may not be after the book themselves, but they'll not forget the two dead colleagues you left back in Delta. No, I'm afraid to say things will not get any better soon."

"I didn't think so either," Leonie said.

"Besides, they probably think we know what's in it. If they don't get the book itself, then they'll continue in their efforts to get *us*, believing we'll be the only ones to tell them its contents."

"Doesn't sound promising."

By mid-afternoon, they arrived at a much more placid water-course with a small sturdy wharf. A simple system of ropes and pulleys indicated a ferry still operated. A gong hung from a low branch and from that, a mallet.

Feiron stopped in the tree's shade. Leonie ambled over to the gong and gave it a hard smack with the mallet. After the resonating sound faded, she saw movement on the other bank as a man emerged from the small hut. Shortly after, another figure joined him.

The pair of travellers snacked and watched as the ferry approached. There were two methods to move it; by gripping the thick rope and walking backwards from bow to stern, or standing and hauling on the rope. By the time the barge thumped into the wharf, Leonie, and Feiron in the guise of Hectr the merchant, were ready to board with the fee for their passage in hand.

Dusk found them entering Swangrove, another small village about four leagues to the north of the Deraz ferry.

The swelling of the Urmaq River left a distance of ten paces between the water and the road, the bent grass and debris evidence it had been higher recently. A cluster of about a dozen buildings lined the road. Cheery, yellow light from the larger one near the middle of the town cast long shadows across the road, beckoning weary travellers to enter.

They tethered the di'anth to a post and peered inside from the open door before they entered. A few patrons sat around the fire, mugs in hand. They looked up as the floorboards creaked to see an old man and a half-rrell entering.

Considering the troubles resulting from the last time they visited an inn, they ordered meals, booked a couple of rooms at the back and kept to themselves. After their meal, they took Argus to a stall around the back, leaving him in the capable care of the stable-hand.

10

GET OUT OF MY HEAD

AM I DREAMING? LEONIE WAS CONFUSED. A STRANGE BROWN GLOW began to throb in her head, and with it, a presence. *Who are you?*

Surprised at her awakening, Lothas controlled his response. *There, there,* the voice in her head soothed. *It doesn't matter who I am, other than a friend. My master requires me to use whatever means are necessary to obtain that tome by your feet. I'm inside your mind to direct you to bring it to me, and no, you are not dreaming. This is real.*

Where are you? What do you want? Leonie sensed a dim, brown light in the darkness.

Physically, I'm in Delta. Lothas, the High Priest of Death dared not let on she was at the extreme range of his abilities. *We require the Codex. Your body will feel no pain.* The brown pulse flickered black. *In fact, you'll not be aware of any part of the journey,* the voice assured her.

Who's your master? Leonie asked. Though the voice in her head spoke kind words, there seemed to be a darker presence.

The great Lord Opsyss.

I've heard a little bit about him.

He is most powerful. You will soon get to know him well for your service.

What service?

I sense your unease. Rest assured, ultimately, you will be well-rewarded. He knew now he should have tried harder to kill the wench in her sleep, but at this extreme range, it was difficult. Get her closer and her fate – and his success – would be sealed. Now she was aware, and there was that mysterious barrier in her mind, she might be troublesome. He had to try again later—

Get out, her mind screamed.

Darkness engulfed her. At first, she thought she would sleep, but then realised she was already asleep. Too late, she grasped the reality as cold darkness descended.

———

Hectr knocked on his companion's door. There was no reply. He checked to see he had the right room; certain it was the one diagonally opposite his own. As he knocked harder, the door slipped open.

"Leonie?" he called, pushing the door open further and stepping through.

The bed had been slept in, as evident by the twisted sheets, but was now empty. He felt the sheets. They were cold. Puzzled, he went downstairs to the front of the inn. The door stood ajar. He turned at a sound from the kitchen but found only the cook preparing the breakfast. The lass lifted a tray of fresh loaves from the oven. She shook her head when he asked if she'd seen Leonie. Picking up his pace up in concern, he went to the stables at the rear of the building.

Argus lay curled up in a divot in the dirt, but other than the cart and a donkey, the stable was empty. It was unusual for her to wander off. He ran around the inn to the road. There was no sign of her in either direction. At a loss, he spotted the stablehand collecting shellfish from traps by the river.

"Ho there, lad," he called.

Putting down the trap, the boy stood up quickly. "Will you be wanting your di'anth and cart readied?"

"I'm not sure. My young, hairy friend has wandered off. I was hoping you might have seen her."

"No, sir." The lad shook his head.

"Never mind, lad. I'm sure she'll turn up." Feiron hurried back to the inn, his mind racing. When he left her last night, she had retired with the book held in her paws. He searched her room. Her pack was still there by the bed, but there was no book.

Only now did he seriously consider her words the day before, about the feeling of being watched. Somehow, someone managed to get close enough to spirit her and the book away. He ran to the stable, wondering why they'd want her if they had the book. Another thought chilled him – what about the Jart'lekk? If they had been this close without discovery, Leonie would be a corpse; himself along with her. Her disappearance remained a mystery – it was not their way.

No matter which way he looked at it, none of this boded well. He dragged the saddle from the cart and strapped it onto Argus's broad back. When he grabbed the reins and swung up into the seat, the di'anth stomped several times at the awkward weight. It had been a while, Feiron recalled, since either of them had been near a saddle. As an afterthought, knowing Leonie's abilities in accumulating injuries, he extended an arm to reach over and grabbed his satchel from the back of the cart.

He gently backed the beast out of the enclosure and turned him into the lane. At the road, he turned to the south. It was a sheer guess. All he considered at that point was Delta; Jart'lekk, the Woorin Temple and anyone who had an interest in the *Seer's Codex* lay in this direction.

Argus stomped to the south, his webbed feet slapping the road as he picked up speed.

——

Leonie found herself in complete darkness and silence, making her feel claustrophobic. She didn't think she was dead.

The voice spoke the truth. She could feel nothing, hear nothing. Her senses registered nothing; only part of her mind seemed to be active. She could admit to herself her fear. Leonie heard that when you died, you could meet up with those who had passed away before. Death held no joy for her. The thought of the possibility of meeting those she had killed didn't make her feel good in the slightest. There was no one here, though. Nothing. That meant one of two things. Either what she'd heard had been lies, or she lived.

If she wasn't dead, then she was angry. *Someone* had entered her mind and taken over her body to do with as he pleased. Regardless of how sorry he said he was, it was her body. She wanted it back. She didn't enjoy being trapped in this dark place in her mind, *and* he was taking the book.

He worked for Lord Opsyss, not Woorin. *So, he isn't from the Brotherhood of the Flame. One is as bad as the other.* Leonie's thoughts raced. *Where am I? How do I get out of here?* She searched in vain. *How can I escape from my own mind?* This place reminded her of being stuck in a barrel.

Leonie panicked as forgotten childhood memories burst forth. Wandering the backstreets of Delta, a bunch of street kids had chased her. She had run off, hiding inside a barrel. They passed, but when she had lifted the lid to look one of the slower kids lagging behind his friends spotted her. Before she could get out of the awkward hiding place, they wedged the lid down tight, trapping her in the cramped dark. She remembered them laughing; kicking and banging the sides until her head rang like a drum. Leonie struggled to find a weak point. A final kick toppled the barrel, and it started to roll. Their laughter faded with the increasing rumbling and distance.

She became dizzy. The noise as it bounced over the cobbles was worse than anything she heard before.

The noise stopped abruptly. Her stomach heaved as the barrel fell. For a second, she thought everything was getting better, but then there was a big splash. Leonie had smacked her head hard. The next thing she knew, water surrounded her. Salt water. She had rolled into the harbour—

You will have to save yourself again. With her mind's eye, she perceived this thought as a pale, blue light pulsing faintly each time he spoke.

What?

Save yourself. Fight back. How is this any worse than your time in the barrel?

Who are you?

A friend.

The other voice said he was a friend too.

I am here to help you, not control you.

Her head throbbed again. Everyone wanted the book and to use her to get it. Confused and uncomfortable, the darkness swelled and rolled in her head. Was this another trick to get her to change her mind? All she wanted was peace and quiet. *Go away.*

That is it. Get angry. Do not let that priest use you like a puppet.

I said go AWAY. She didn't know what to do. Instinct took over. *I want you OUT OF MY HEAD.*

Make me go. Concentrate your Will. Fight as hard as you can.

She pushed, envisioning the blueness dwindling in size, becoming fainter. She was back in the barrel, using her legs and pushing her back against the sides—

You will have to push harder. Lothas will eventually kill you, you know. It is what he does. The blue light pulsed again. *You need to strengthen your mind as soon as possible.*

Lothas' brown pulse reappeared, dimmer. *What's happening here?*

You're leaving too!

You're supposed to be dead, girl. The brown pulse flared, remaining firm for a time before fading again. *Where have you been hiding?*

GO AWAY. Leonie pushed at the brown light.

It's not that easy. The brown light dimmed.

Leonie kept pushing. She could feel something give.

Is that the best you can do? The blue light flashed.

GET OUT. Leonie pushed as hard as she could.

Better. Much better. A nucleus of white glowed within the blue aura.

Who is in here with you? The brown light now had an orange fringe, then slowly faded.

Good girl. He is weakening.

Leonie's body stumbled, falling heavily to the stony ground, smacking her head against a rock. She lay in a muddy puddle at the edge of a path between two fields. Her body jerked the moment she touched the water. Her limbs moved woodenly, soft flesh scraped over the hard rocks, leaving small trails of blood swirling in the water until she was back on dry dirt. The book lay in the scraggy grass.

I sense pain. Her mind reeled.

Good, the blue aura said. *Lothas is losing control, but it is not over yet.*

Do you know how much reward my Lord Opsyss can give you? Lothas praised. Dim flashes of brown appeared with each word.

Leonie stumbled to her feet. *NOT ENOUGH TO PUT UP WITH YOU.* She staggered a few steps, and then stopped. Despite her resistance, she turned and went back in slow, jerky movements to retrieve the book as Lothas again regained control.

He's too strong. Leonie sighed. *I'm useless.*

Nonsense, you are untrained, Blue flashed.

How do I get better? Can you teach me?

Perhaps. First, you must survive long enough.

Where are you?

Close. Rest your mind, for now, you will need to battle him again.

Blissful silence. Her mind was still a roiling cloud of foulness, but from her little haven, she sensed the blue mind's withdrawal. Lothas still lurked inside her head. She now knew evil. Leonie heeded the advice and sank into the depths of her mind. It wasn't so bad now. She wondered if the bit of training helped or was it exhaustion? Perhaps she was now truly dying.

The sun rode high in the sky. On the top of the rise, Lothas, through his borrowed feline eyes, discerned the Urmaq as a silvery ribbon in the distance. The clarity of this creature's eyes amazed him. His mind registered the flies buzzing around the gashes in the knees, arms and head. It would be several hours before he'd have complete control. This half-rrell had apparently found a little hiding place for her mind. Once across the water boundary, he'd be stronger. He would pull her mind apart. She would have nowhere to hide.

As she stumbled over the rise, a small hut came into view. Lothas forced Leonie's damaged legs to move faster, heading directly for the ferry, arriving at the small tributary as the sun kissed the horizon. The girl remained passive, which was a relief. There was only a short way to go and once across the water, she would be his. Stepping onto the flat-bottomed barge, Lothas got her to untie the mooring line.

"Hey. What ya think ya doin'?" a gravelly voice called out.

Leonie / Lothas ignored it and continued with the task at hand. Footsteps approached and a firm, calloused hand grasped her shoulder, wrenching her around.

"I said wha—" The ferryman fell back with a stricken look when the half-rrell he had ferried only a day earlier turned to face him, now covered in mud and blood. A jagged cut to her head exposed bone. Many lacerations covered her knees and arms. The vacant stare from her eyes was as dark as midnight.

Unnerved by the sight, he fled screaming into the thatched cottage. The slammed door rattled the shutters on the windows.

Leonie / Lothas resumed moving the barge. Moving the vessel would take more strength than this body possessed. Lothas had no such trouble. The pain from tearing muscle and sinew was nothing to him as he forced her body to work far beyond its capacity.

11

NEW ALLIES

"WHAT WAS THAT SCREAM?" FEIRON ASKED AS HE TOPPED THE RISE. Below, he recognised the landing area of the barge and glimpsed a burly ferryman running into one of the cottages. Curious what would make the formidable man act in such a manner, Feiron approached with caution using the trees as cover. The barge came into view. It was about five paces from the bank and he saw Leonie working the ropes. Her movements were slow and jerky. She was alone.

Feiron hadn't expected this. Running to the bank, he called out, waving his arms to gain her attention. Any doubt about what made the man scream became clear when he saw Leonie turn.

"Fub. What's happened to her?" Feiron's initial confusion turned to shock and dismay when he saw her bloody face and legs. He poured out of the saddle and called again. "Leonie! Come back," he yelled desperately.

She didn't respond, carrying on as if he didn't exist.

The barge gradually moved further from the bank; the rope bowing as the flow of the water took hold. As the angle increased, the pulley knocked against its housing.

Feiron grabbed the rope to pull the barge back, but Leonie's strength surpassed his. A germ of an idea formed. He frantically searched the bank. Finding what he was looking for, seconds later he wedged the end of a small branch in the pulley. With luck, it would jam the rope and prevent the crossing.

The barge slowed to a stop and began rocking in the current.

Now Leonie, fight all you can, her blue glowing ally implored. *The water weakens him. Remember how I showed you.*

GET OUT OF MY MIND! Leonie directed her rage towards the dark brown malevolence.

Ah, little one, soon we will finish this. Lothas replied with a small but steady brown glow.

I WANT YOU OUT NOW! Not knowing where she found the strength to resist, she felt his control slip. Leonie slowly moved her arms by herself.

Good. The blue glowed brightly with encouragement.

No no, you cannot defeat me! Lothas cried out as his strength waned.

Do you require assistance, my master? A tan pulse intruded distantly.

Alen! Praise Opsyss you're here. Meld with me. Strengthen my hold on this creature's mind. The water elements drain me so. She will be ours once she crosses over.

It shall be as you command, master. Tendrils spread from the tan light towards the brown. Slowly, the intensity of the two flames increased.

Oh. He's got help. Leonie cried.

You must keep pushing, the blue aura implored.

… together they are … too powerful. Leonie struggled. Through tears of anguish she felt the combined strength of Lothas and Alen grow.

She saw Feiron standing on the far shore as an eddy gripped the barge, rocking it in the deeper water. Soon she would be under the total control of these evil minds and he'd be unable to enter the water to help her.

A thought struck her. She remembered what happened back on the road when she fell in the puddle. They hated the water. It caused them pain. Being close to the water was not enough to weaken both of them. She had to be in it. *I hate water too.* She looked at the river. It was deep and brown, churned up by the torrential rainfall over the last few days.

Leonie, do not do this! The blue entity grasped her train of thought.

It is our only chance, or we lose everything. Leonie picked up the heavy book from the deck and forced her legs to step towards the edge. She could feel the two evil minds gathering strength as they melded. *Can we do what they're doing?*

Another step.

Not at this time. The effort would destroy your mind. Hang on a moment longer, Blue flashed rapidly.

She looked up, feeling the evil presence building in her head. Soon they would have complete control. *I can't.* With an effort, she raised her arms. *I'm out of time.* Her head pounded with the effort; her muscles quivering in strain.

Now we have you! The brown lights joined, flaring brightly in her mind.

Her last step faltered. Teetering on the edge, her legs twitched as the joined minds of Lothas and Alen forced her to turn back.

The barge rocked ever so slightly in the rise and fall of the turbid water. In a last effort, she shifted her centre of gravity. The added weight of the book was sufficient for her to lose balance. Leonie toppled backwards, taking the book with her. The churning waters engulfed her instantly.

NO! Ahhh— The melded minds of Lothas and Alen blinked out; their hold snapped.

Gripping the tome tightly, Leonie sank to the murky depths. *Will you stay with me until the end?*

I am with you. The blue aura flashed in the emptiness. *But the end is a long way yet.*

From the riverbank, with his full attention on the barge, Feiron watched in dismay as his friend fell overboard. "It's times like this I'm glad I took swimming lessons," Feiron muttered, transforming into a vorien, and dived into the water.

Unperturbed about the drama on the water, the di'anth wandered over to the nearest leaves as the vorien slid into the water. Moments later, a huge shadow passed overhead before ploughing into the water. Jumping back in fear, the di'anth bolted towards the road and into the hills.

The water was murky but the shadow of the barge loomed overhead. Using the outline as a point of reference, Feiron swam with the flow, intent on searching as much of the riverbed he could between breaths.

He saw a dark form moving along the bottom. Flicking his tail, he surged forward only to find a dense mass of weed. It was time for air. Surfacing, he gulped in huge breaths, taking stock of his location before he dived again. He saw another shadow in the murk. He froze in sheer disbelief at the size. It was massive. The shape of the vorien merman dissolved as Feiron lost all concentration.

Unsure how much time had passed, Feiron found himself on the shoreline, his mind in turmoil. Confused. He glanced to the barge in the hope somehow Leonie made it back. It rocked in the middle of the turbulent river. Still unoccupied.

He tried to reform into the vorien, but it refused to take shape; his body had absorbed too much water. Moving like a bloated jellyfish, he ambled to the river's edge. He wondered how he had made it back to shore.

As hard as he tried, his body refused to shapeshift. "Leonie could be drowning. This is no time for timidity or incompetence," he cried, utterly frustrated. "I must find her." Feiron looked to the murky waters. He waddled into the water, determined to find her. His body rose and glided effortlessly above the ripples and back to the shore and there was nothing he could do to prevent it.

Back on dry land, he looked around, bewildered.

Further along the coarse sand and flotsam, he spied Leonie slumped on the grass. "How did she get there?" As fast as his ungainly body would allow, he squelched to her. Water seeped from the pores of his body as he examined her. Covered from head to foot in scrapes and lacerations, cleansed somewhat by the water, her recent wounds were bleeding.

Befuddled by recent events, it took several minutes before he noticed the massive head above the canopy of the trees.

Feiron froze while his bloated body oozed water continuously.

A stick rose from the ground and began scratching in the sand on its own volition. Surprised, Feiron glanced down at the sand quickly recognising words. The wyvern was writing.

'Greetings. It is clear your kind cannot mind-speak.'

Still too confused to respond, the silence stretched.

"You scared the shape out of me," Feiron blurted. "Was that you in the water? What's happened to Leonie?"

'My apologies for startling you. Yes. Your friend is in a coma.'

"What? Why?" He turned to look at her again. Her breathing was shallow but steady. He wondered what had made her do this; to run off alone with the *Codex*? How could she possibly move the barge by herself?

'An entity known as Lothas—'

"The High Priest of the Death Sect?"

'He took over Leonie's mind during the night, pushing her body far beyond its normal capabilities.' As he wrote, the *Seer's Codex* emerged from the murky waters, green lengths of weed hanging off it. Floating over the water's surface, the book settled by Leonie and Feiron. 'All to gain this tome.'

———

None of the inhabitants of the small village dared leave their homes with the wyvern present, leaving Leonie and Feiron the privacy of the barn to recover from their ordeal. Smelling musty after all the rain, the straw-littered floor showed spots of mildew. In one corner lay an overturned boat, its hull in need of repair. Oars, coils of rope, an old coracle that had seen better days, and other boating paraphernalia littered the area.

With Leonie's poor condition, it was better than being outside. Feiron administered what aid he could, applying his balm and wrapping her many wounds in any clean cloth he could find. Once her fur dried, he swathed her in blankets on a bed of the straw. He placed the tome next to her. Once she recovered consciousness, it would relieve her to know the wyvern found it.

Shadows flickered on the walls as flames licked up from the fire in a small hollow scraped in the dirt. The wyvern lay nearby, motionless, his tail protruding out the rear door.

High clouds, blotting out the stars, scudded across the sky. The twin moons, Luminor and Luxor, had already crested the horizon; the intermittent light shining through the doorway casting elongated shadows across the hay-covered floor.

Tossing another faggot onto the fire and sending sparks flying, he dragged out a small bundle from his pack. Since most of their gear was back in Swangrove, only a small amount of food was available. He glanced across to the wyvern.

A stick started scrawling in a cleared area of ground.

'If I perceive your intentions, I have no food requirements.'

Watching Leonie's chest rise and fall steadily, Feiron's mind had finally calmed. "I must thank you for saving her and finding the book. It will relieve Leonie to know of its return."

'It was no trouble.'

"I gather you can hear me?"

The large head nodded.

Feiron sat down by the fire and looked at him. He guessed the wyvern was eighty-feet long, mostly black and dark shades – a hint of blue when the moonlight reflected in a particular direction. Feiron started to chuckle – his distended body wobbling.

'Amused?'

"In a warped way. Leonie doesn't believe in coincidence. I was thinking of her reaction once she's recovered." Feiron rummaged through the bag for the rest of the nut-loaf broke off half and put the other half back.

'I do not understand your meaning.'

"My mentor has given me a task to fulfil for her research – to return with wyvern eggshells. We were travelling intending to find wyverns. And here you are. Too much coincidence."

'To be precise, I am an elemental.'

"Not a wyvern?"

'I was for a very long time. You might call it *transcending*. After my passing, I was granted access to dwell on a higher plane of existence as a reward for things I did – or did not do – during my time.'

It mystified Feiron, food halfway to his mouth.

'Perhaps a demonstration?'

While the illios watched, the elemental faded to nothingness. He reappeared moments later. The stick scribbled in the sand. 'I have no *body*, but can make myself corporeal – solid – if the need arises.'

"Amazing." Feiron began to nibble the stale bread idly. "Whether fate or coincidence – here I am, talking to one. I didn't really think it would happen."

'As for coincidence; I knew of your intentions.'

"And you just happened to be in the area, or was it foretold?"

'I am pursuing one of the many strands of prophecy. Some of us keep watch on the unusual events that transpire on the astral plane. I encountered the aura of a particularly nasty entity. I followed it and it led me to your friend. The aura had entered Leonie's mind. Possession is not something we condone.

'Leonie has hidden deep inside her mind. She should have died when he took over. Her mental endurance is extraordinary – enough to pique our interest.'

"*Our* interest?"

'There are others on the astral plane apart from hroltahgs.'

"Do you know one named Styx?"

'We have communicated.'

"Can you tell me, and forgive me if this sounds crazy... Is this part of prophecy?"

'Isn't everything to some extent?'

"I..." he started. "We..." Feiron stumbled with his thoughts. "Never mind. What about this Lothas, is he still about? What about the Brotherhood?" Feiron asked, moving on to a more tangible subject. He watched as the sand smoothed itself before more writing recommenced.

'I perceive no threat in the immediate area,' the elemental wrote.

Feiron took a few moments to digest this information. "If Lothas had control of her, why didn't you stop him, or Leonie jumping into the river?"

'Several reasons; intrusion in mind control can be very dangerous, especially untrained ones. Your friend knew the book was about to fall into the hands of someone evil and depraved. She discovered a weakness in Lothas's control. Water is a strong elemental disruptor. Leonie managed to gain control for a moment and fell off the boat on purpose.'

"But Leonie can't swim. She hates water."

'True, but her reasoning of the ramifications of Lothas gaining the book outweighed her fear. It worked. Lothas has gone.'

"Dead?"

'No. Incapacitated.'

Leonie groaned in her sleep. Feiron watched her for a moment.

"You couldn't lift her out of the water sooner? Before she drowned?"

'It is obscure and no doubt unsatisfactory to hear, but certain thresholds within prophecy must be crossed before the granting of any support. Also, we had to be certain Lothas had departed completely.'

Feiron considered this information.

'Her body heals remarkably well,' the wyvern continued, 'but my concern is with her mind.'

"I don't feel too good myself," Feiron muttered. His body seemed bloated and pale. "I might go for a walk. A bit of exercise might ease my discomfort." He stood up, leaving a muddy patch where he had been sitting and sloshed into the darkness.

On his return a short time later, he felt better but weary. He checked on Leonie, who twitched and softly moaned in her sleep.

'Her subconscious is working through a recent trauma.' The stick began scratching in the dirt again. 'It could take time. Get some rest. I will look out for you both this night.'

"Don't mind if I do." He squelched down away from the fire. Feiron made a depression in a pile of hay. He then laid a length of sailcloth over it and pooled himself within.

'As you are seeking wyverns, I know of a lair in the Ranges to the west. Tomorrow, I will take you there.'

When Feiron awoke, the old coracle sat outside with their few supplies inside. Leonie, still swathed in blankets, floated into it.

'This trip will take most of the day. I hope it is not too taxing for you.'

"Less than a day to the Ranges?"

'We will not be travelling by land. Now that your friend has gained the interest of a very dark entity, she will need help and protection. I have dallied overlong and must return to the astral plane. You will be well looked after. I am certain.'

"I see. Will we communicate like this too?"

'I do not believe their trainer has taught them to write.'

"Trainer?"

'There is a human. He will communicate. We should go.'

Feiron rose and carefully slipped over the edge of the small boat so as not to land on or disturb Leonie. Halfway over the side, he stopped. "What about Argus?"

'With regret, your di'anth has run off in a panic.'

"Can't we look for him?"

'We could, but to what aim? Transporting him would be awkward, not to mention a very unnerving experience. He would not do well in a wyvern lair.'

Inside the coracle now, Feiron slumped. "I was getting quite fond of him." Once seated within the small, round craft it lifted off the ground a few feet then drifted out the rear door of the barn. It was still dim outside, the small village still asleep, but he saw one wavering light through a curtained window.

As the craft rose higher and higher, Feiron checked Leonie was settled and covered from the cool breeze. The view below and around him – spectacular on any other occasion – was an alternate distraction to look at other than his bruised and battered companion. Without Leonie to converse with, it was a silent trip to the Central Ranges. On occasion she'd moan as if in a dream, but that – and the rush of the wind – were the only sounds. Even the wing-beats of the elemental were silent. With nothing to write on, communication with the wyvern was impossible. Now and then he'd work at deciphering a few pages of the *Seer's Codex* to pass the time.

The mountain range grew larger, and once-distant peaks became more detailed. Soon, one peak in particular stood out because of the wisps of smoke issuing from it. He thought he could see shapes flying in and around the smoke. Feiron realised the wyvern elemental had disappeared. Part of him knew he was safe, but it was very disconcerting to not see the wyvern. He hung on to the coracle sides, wondering why the secrecy. When they were about a league from the active volcano, they started a slow spiral down to a hilltop devoid of vegetation larger than small, thorny shrubs.

After the coracle gently nudged the ground, a stick started scrawling in the dirt. The elemental remained invisible.

'If you light a large fire, they will come to investigate. I must be away. I bid you and Leonie farewell.'

Feiron glanced around fruitlessly. "Oh. Umm... thank you for all your efforts." He awkwardly addressed the empty air. "Perhaps we'll meet again?"

No response came, and the stick lay motionless on the ground.

With a sigh, he checked on Leonie before exploring the hilltop. The southern and western sides ended with a sheer drop. Far below separating the base of the hill and the foothills of the volcano lay a steaming lake. When a gust of wind came up and over the precipice, it brought with it an appalling stench of sulphur. The buffeting wind also made loitering precarious. He moved to the east side, noting a rocky, unused trail leading down and turning to the north, towards Hallam, he suspected. He set about lighting two fires; a large one to summon the wyverns and a smaller one for cooking. He made enough dinner for two, but as there was no change in Leonie's state, he left her portion to cool.

In the shadow of the mountains, night descended early. He spent a short while trying to shapeshift, but his waterlogged consistency prevented any form from holding firm. Sullenly, he built up the bonfire, then also went to sleep.

The next day dawned clear and crisp.

Leonie's condition was unchanged. Feiron warmed some the food from the previous night for breakfast. A shadow passed overhead as he ate his solitary meal. He looked up, squinting in the glare of the early morning sun.

Tense moments passed. Forgetting the food, he watched in both awe and trepidation as the shadow banked and spiralled down, a rider visible on its back. The creature looked like a huge flying snake, but with legs. A pair of long wings sprouted about a third of the way down its back. Two taloned feet crunched into the gravel when it landed with a thud on the edge of the trail. The sun glinting off its scaly hide gave it a green glow. It wrapped its barbed tail around the base of the rock; a fearsome yet beautiful sight.

The huge green wyvern cocked its head to gaze down at them. When it opened its mouth slightly, it exposed fangs as long as Leonie's forearm. The serpentine neck lowered to ground level, and the creature emitted a loud hiss in his direction.

Feiron exuded more fluid at that moment than in all the previous days combined.

12

WYVERNS BEWARE

THE LANKY RIDER CLIMBED FROM THE STRANGE SADDLE. HE WAS heavily bearded, with long, fair hair pulled into a ponytail which draped down his back to his belt. His clothing comprised leather trousers, a tunic with sheepskin lining and gloves reaching to his elbows. In his knee-high boots, Feiron judged him to be a little taller than Leonie, and the mask covering his eyes gave him a bug-like look.

"Hello there." His mild Tesakian accent finished on a high note. He was about to jump down from the rock when the wyvern made a sound, more like a bark, or a cough. "Oops, nearly forgot." He turned and gave the beast a good scratch in the centre of its long snout between the amber eyes.

The air vibrated; the wyvern purred.

"She loves this," the rider said over his shoulder. After a few moments of scratching, he turned and lightly jumped to the ground, approaching with long, easy strides.

"Sorry if we alarmed you."

"Is it safe?" Feiron fought the urge to run and hide.

"Oh yes, as long as you mean no harm. Rare as these occasions are, there's a standing agreement not to eat my visitors. It gives them a bad name if they do."

"Well met. I gather you're the trainer of wyverns?" Feiron asked.

He flashed a smile. "I am Philbert." He bowed deeply then shook hands, only then realising he still wore his goggles. "Sorry. I forget I have them on sometimes." Removing them showed startling green eyes. "I'm so glad I finally get to speak to a traveller. They don't stay long—"

He was cut off by a soft hiss.

"All right, alright. May I also introduce Dorn, last daughter of Axorg, First Chosen of Noldor, and my wing commander." He turned, flamboyantly waving an arm in the wyvern's direction.

"You name it?"

Again, the wyvern inclined her head. She winked.

Unsure how to respond, Feiron gave a quick wave. "While meeting with you is very exciting, I'm afraid my companion here is in dire need of your help." Feiron indicated Leonie in the coracle.

"Your companion? She is injured?" The rider sounded sincere, noticing the cuts and gashes. "That is sad news. I'm limited in any aid, but will gladly help if I can. Dorn, what can you sense?"

The wyvern turned her gaze towards the prone figure in the coracle. *While she has severe physical injuries, I am more concerned with her mental state. Her mind is intact but unreachable. I cannot sense anything from the illios.*

Philbert looked around. "How did you come to be here, considering the state of your friend, and no mounts to be seen?"

"I can understand your confusion, but can easily explain – however implausible the tale may sound to you." Feiron had been wondering how much to reveal about their latest incident and was at a loss. "Umm... a wyvern moved us here."

"What's that you say?" Phil's head snapped up in surprise. "Dorn. Listen."

I hear. The wyvern responded at once. Her massive head swung around; amber eyes drilled into Feiron.

"Normally we can detect other wyverns in the area," Phil continued.

"I'm no expert, but I don't believe this was your typical wyvern. He was an elemental, to be precise," Feiron added.

"This is truly fascinating. Did this wyvern elemental have a name?"

"Not that he shared, no."

"Can you describe him?"

Feiron glanced at Dorn. "Massive, about three times Dorn's size. Black – when he wasn't invisible. He also had amber eyes. Does he sound familiar?"

Axorg, Dorn replied in surprise.

"Axorg? Can this be?" Phil shook his head in wonder.

It is rare, Dorn responded. *It is said that those of great age and with certain qualities can attain transcendence.*

That would be him. Phil nodded. *Axorg is now immortal?*

Feiron watched Philbert. "I gather you're using mind-speak?"

"What? Oh, yes. You cannot hear us? My apologies for the oversight."

Feiron sighed. "Axorg wrote in the sand with a stick."

"This is an extraordinary tale." Phil looked from Feiron to the prone figure in the coracle. "I didn't consider teaching the wyverns to write," he muttered.

Why would Axorg have any interest in our affairs? Dorn asked. *Transcendents are no longer of this plane.*

Phil repeated the question for Feiron's benefit.

"I cannot explain his motives," the illios replied. "He said he was keeping a watch on the happenings on the astral plane. It also appears prophecy may play a part. Have you heard of the Temple of Opsyss?"

"Vaguely. If I remember correctly, they tried to start a sect in Tesak. The Tesak'i would have none of it."

"So, you know what they do?"

"Not really. A cult that worships the dark arts, I guess? Did Axorg show the help he thought we could provide?"

"The head cleric possessed my colleague, Leonie, apparently using mind control."

She needs to be shielded from further violation? Dorn prompted.

Feiron nodded after Phil repeated the question aloud. "I believe so. Leonie has been like this for over a day now. Her body has been sorely abused. Perhaps her mind too."

A chilly gust of wind swirled around the clearing; the looming clouds indicated rain.

"I think we should move. We will take you both to the lair so we are out of the elements, and talk in comfort."

"Will you be able to transport us in the coracle? Axorg used telekinesis."

"I see. Dorn?"

Of course.

They doused the fires and Feiron once again slipped into the coracle. This trip was much shorter and it wasn't long before other inquisitive wyverns gathered to see the newcomers. The spectacle entranced Feiron; creatures so large, yet so agile. They ducked and weaved, swiftly circling around them until Dorn issued a loud growl. In seconds, they dispersed, back to the smoke cloud looming high above.

As the coracle with the strangers bobbed closer to the volcano, the shadowy area of a deep crevice became more defined. Soon, a cave entrance became visible, appearing too small for such large creatures as the wyverns. But, as they neared, the true size became clear. The edifice containing the volcano was massive; its real dimensions obscured by the mountainous terrain surrounding it.

"The locals call it Hell's Maw," Philbert called down over the wind. "We call it home."

Dorn landed on the ledge and Phil leapt off with practised grace. The coracle bobbed in through the entrance, glided silently past the rough walls and gently settled inside. The long and narrow path curved into a huge, irregular shaped cave. Dark sand and small rocks covered the floor. Multicoloured scales, piled to the side of the floor by the passing of wyverns over the years, contrasted with the dark rock.

Phil strode in behind him, followed by Dorn. "We don't normally get visitors here, but I'm sure it won't take long to organise a place to rest."

"I'm sure Leonie will be happy with whatever you can provide. I only require a barrel or container of some description to sleep."

"I find these are very handy – for beds and storage." Phil removed pots and jars from a cavity within the wall. "They were bubbles formed in the magma decades ago. They're all over the place and many sizes. Sleeping on the floor can be a hazard if a wyvern steps on you."

After locating a couple of fur blankets, Phil placed them within the niche. Together, Phil and Feiron lifted Leonie into place.

"Very handy." Feiron noted the smooth walls of the niche as he fussed over Leonie, bunching the blanket on the edge and ensuring she wouldn't roll out. At no stage did she moan or move – other than her breathing, she was as limp as jelly. He reached into his backpack, opened the jar of miwalli and generously applied it to all her cuts and abrasions. "She normally heals very well, but I'm sure this won't hurt."

Leaving Leonie to rest, Philbert showed Feiron around the lair. It was a brief tour. The trainer slept towards the rear of the cave, in a niche similar to that of Leonie. One area of the cave was a bit wider, with a fire pit, the cooking utensils stored nearby in the myriad of smooth, irregularly shaped alcoves.

As they settled by the fire, Feiron spoke. "First, I'd like to thank you for taking us in under such extraordinary circumstances." He had considered what to tell, or not tell, his host, finally deciding – as always – the truth was best.

Axorg saw reason to assist. To honour him, so shall we. Dorn answered before Philbert could.

He repeated her response aloud to the illios.

Feiron gazed upwards, considering what to say. Sloping

walls, with ridges and ledges on all sides, obscured the ceiling. Light filtered from above, indicating a hidden opening. The wyverns rested along these rocky outcrops. Through the rising smoke of the fire, dozens of large eyes returned his gaze. Dorn was the closest being one of the eldest and largest, while the younger, smaller wyverns rested higher up.

"We were heading to Qelay," Feiron started. "Leonie has a task, to deliver an important book to the hroltahgs there." He then went on into detail about recent events. "The *Seer's Codex* contains prophecies, or foretellings if you prefer, that may – or may not – come to pass." Feiron quickly retrieved the *Codex* from the coracle, placing it in Philbert's hands.

The rider almost dropped it. "It's heavy. If what you say is true, the knowledge contained within could gain a person some unique insights." Phil examined the book as he spoke. "Knowing the future would give power over others."

"Precisely. We know several people have already died in attempts to obtain it. Knowing of this book's existence could put you in great danger."

"My dear chap, I'm surrounded by a cloud of protective and inquisitive wyverns. No one and nothing could get close enough to cause us any harm."

"Except an elemental…"

"True, but transcendents are another matter entirely, and as you can imagine – an extremely rare event." Phil nodded, poring through the pages. "I'm unfamiliar with some languages and can only make out a few entries." After a few moments, he stopped. "We are being remiss. This is not assisting your friend. I'll request Dorn to see what she can do."

I am not a healer.

"No, but you trained your younglings."

This is not the same.

"Can't you try? Axorg thought we could do something."

I shall see what I can do.

"Thank you." He turned to Feiron, who was glancing

between Philbert and Dorn, on a ledge above them. "Dorn will gladly help."

"We are in both your debt."

"Nonsense. I'll hear nothing of it. It's the least we can do." Phil smiled.

For you, perhaps, Dorn quipped.

Leonie's physical condition improved, but with Dorn contacting her subconscious mind, the regular updates via Philbert also indicated progress. On the third day, she woke, looked around blearily, taking in her unusual surroundings before attempting to sit up.

Feiron, situated by the lair entrance, watched the wyverns flittering in and out of the misty lake below. He turned at a noise and flowed to Leonie's side.

Leonie coughed. She rolled over and leant on an elbow.

"Thank goodness you're awake." He wrapped himself around her.

"Not getting soft on me?" she croaked.

"I was born soft." Feiron was as himself, a grey translucent blob, though still distended.

"Never mind." She looked around blearily, staring at the smoky bonfire nearby.

"How are you feeling?"

She wrinkled her nose. "Terrible. I can hardly move and I ache all over. I'm as weak as a kitten, and my head's throbbing and I'm starving. To top it all off, my fur's a mess." She braced herself on the ledge, getting her bearings. "Other than a bit stiff, I'm sure I'll be fine soon enough." Leonie grimaced.

Feiron insisted on checking her injuries. Apart from her previous injuries, Leonie now sported a deep gash above the temple, several nasty lacerations to her arms and legs, and a singed paw. Miraculously, none of them appeared infected, and all were in the final stages of repair.

"It seems not a day can go past without you getting some injury."

Leonie shrugged. "May as well do what I'm good at." With

his assistance but against his advice, she carefully stood up. "I feel like I'm a hundred." Hissing and wincing with her every move, she limped around to get some movement back in her joints, cursing under her breath.

"Do you remember what happened?"

"Seems like a bad dream. Someone – Lothas – took over my body, then something looking like a blue light tried to help. Lothas also had help ... then I was drowning." She stumbled to the chair. "It's all a blur and my head aches at the thought of it."

He brought a cup of water and started to fill her in on all the details during her coma.

"No need." She sipped the water. "Dorn has filled me in on everything."

"She has?"

"Yep."

"So, you know where we are?"

"Hell's Maw." Leonie nodded. "It was a shock at first. I thought I was dreaming. Dorn showed me some images through her eyes."

"She can do that?"

"And I can't wait to learn to fly."

"Learn to— *What?*"

"Fly. You can too." Her grin reached pointy ear to pointy ear. "Maybe after you stop spinning."

A shadow in the entrance cut off his reply.

Welcome back to the land of the living, Dorn said.

"Ah. I am very glad to see you awake, Leonie."

"Hello, Philbert. Dorn has been telling me all about you—"

"Don't listen to gossip." He glanced to his wyvern.

"Thank you too, for your generous assistance," she said.

"It's a pleasure to help, and so good to meet you." Phil beamed at her, the corners of his eyes crinkling. "But it's Dorn and her wyverns who can take all the credit. I just do the cooking."

"Speaking of cooking. I'm famished."

"I'll get something started." Phil offered.

"In the meantime, how about some tea?" Feiron suggested.

"Lovely," Leonie called over her shoulder as she limped to the cave entrance. Dorn perched on the edge.

Leonie took a deep breath at the sight of her. She estimated Dorn to be an impressive twenty paces long from snout to barbed tail, covered in cobalt blue scales. The widest areas were the shoulders, twice as thick as a di'anth. With ridges over her deep-set eyes, the head was like a serpent's, but longer. There were many tendrils, resembling thick whiskers, hanging from the snout and lower jaw.

Two dots detached themselves from those circling the volcano mouth. They approached swiftly.

Feiron joined her with a steaming mug. "Who would've thought it would lead to this?"

"Not us. Back in Delta, we were more concerned with avoiding them for fear of becoming a snack."

Squinting in the afternoon sunshine, they watched the two silhouettes spiralling down to them, and averted their gaze to avoid the grit picked up by the wing-beats as the wyverns landed. When they looked back, two young wyverns stood each side of their mother. They were both mostly green, with a slightly lighter shade underneath.

"Dear friends, allow me to introduce Slana and Faldo, Dorn's twins." Phil spoke from the lair entrance.

The two new wyverns hissed softly in greeting.

"Truly, you are all a sight to behold," Leonie praised.

I like the furry one, Slana said.

Moving closer, Leonie reached out to touch the closest one. The green scales were warm, smooth, and hard, but not as hard as she would have first thought.

"Later, when fully recovered and prepared, we can try some real flying," Philbert offered.

"I can't wait."

Feiron looked dubious.

"In the meantime, enjoy the view. Dinner will still be a while.

A Tesakian staple diet. I hope you like mushrooms." Phil turned and stepped inside.

Dorn and her twins dropped off the ledge and soon joined the others.

Like Feiron had done over the last days, Leonie sat on the edge sipping her tea and watching the terrain below. The lair's entrance was about two-thirds of the way up the eastern face of Hell's Maw. The cliff was vertical down to the steaming lake. She wondered how Phil got up the first time. He didn't look like a mountain climber.

Noldor flew him. Slana answered her thought. *He was mother's mate.*

Leonie considered this as she watched the wyverns circle above.

"How are you really feeling?" Feiron asked.

"Seriously, I'm alright, just exhausted. Dorn tells me you were quite concerned."

"Of course. I'm sure you would have done the same for me."

"Speaking of which – you've put on weight."

"In a manner of speaking." The shading of his skin changed.

"Eating my share of the food?"

"Water retention."

"Are you blushing?" she watched curiously.

"It's nearly all gone now." Feiron's shading changed even more. "I spent far more time in the water – searching for you – than prudent."

Her smiling face turned serious. "I'm sorry for all I put you through—"

"Nonsense. It is Lothas who bears the blame for this."

"Don't worry. I will pay him a visit when we get back." She turned her gaze to the southern horizon. "He won't be doing that again."

"To you?"

"To anyone. I'm going to promote him from High Priest to his god's right hand."

13

RESTING IN THE WYVERN'S LAIR

Leonie spent the next days recovering and getting to know Philbert and the wyverns. It was one thing to have Dorn keep her abreast of everything, but the real thing was more satisfying.

"I have to say though," she said. "This communication through the mind is amazing, especially the time she allowed me to see through her eyes."

"Were you able to read her thoughts?" Feiron dished out the evening meal.

"No. She had to send everything to me. She taught me much about what I can and can't do, but I am no telepath. I reckon I'm far more sensitive to it now though. More aware."

"More susceptible?" Phil asked.

"On the contrary, as soon as I sense activity, I can home in on who it is. She showed me a few tricks and how to put up a wall. Apparently even she had difficulty in getting through once I learnt the basics. I can look after myself."

"I knew she'd be a great help to you," Phil praised them.

"Dorn is a marvel." Leonie agreed. "They all are."

You are too kind. The lair vibrated with the wyvern's purring.

Leonie studied the interior with a keen eye while she ate. She thought the lair tidy, but then she hadn't been sure what to expect.

"You were expecting bones strewn all over the floor, perhaps?" Phil laughed when she mentioned it. "A wyvern consumes everything. As they get older, their scales drop off as new ones grow to replace them." He picked up a handful from the floor and let the coarse grit sift through his fingers. "This sand is crushed volcanic rock and scales, which may give you a sign how long wyverns have been in the area."

When they looked up, they saw many serpentine heads gaze down, unblinking. Their eyes glowed in the gloom with a subtle radiance; the colour of the orbs matching the wyvern's scales; from the deep blue of the lake, to the orange of the lava bursting from Hell's Maw.

"All the luxuries of home." He pointed out the bathing area. "My very own mineral spa."

"How do you get water up here?" Leonie asked.

"The youngsters fetch it for me. I've made up a large leather bucket of sorts. They grip it by the long handle and drop it in the lake to fill up. There's a hole in the roof. Over the years, I've managed to cut a rough channel in the rock. They empty the water into it and by the time the water has flowed to the bath, it's cool enough not to scald."

"What made you consider this venture?" Feiron collected the empty plates and piled them to the side. He then retrieved a pot of boiling water for tea.

"Partly because I was young and foolish and wanted to make a name for myself." Phil reminisced about his earlier times in Tesak. "I got the idea in my head to train wyverns for the Tesak'i, the Lord of all Tesak. It has been done before, in Greol – a lost city I read about in our library. Reenat has its gryphons. I had visions of grandeur – thinking I could do something momentous."

"We all have those thoughts," Feiron agreed.

"I was one of the court's many Healers of Horses. Being part of the Tesak'i's retinue, even a lowly one such as myself, we all heard stories about other rulers from the staff of visiting nobles. Your accent reminds me of a couple who came from the Delta. A raven-haired woman and a large, hairy male—"

Leonie's whiskers twitched at this news. "How large?"

"One of the largest men I've seen. Not so much in height, though he was maybe a tad taller than me, he was very solid; broad-shouldered and thick limbs."

Feiron noticed Leonie's far-away look. "Are you alright?" He handed her a steaming mug.

"Hss? I was thinking of Brendon and Dianah; he was huge and hairy, and I recall she had jet-black hair."

"They died in the temple fire," Feiron reminded her.

"No bodies were recovered, you said." She shrugged. "I'll remain sceptical."

"It was over a decade ago," the illios pointed out, handing another mug to Phil.

"This encounter was also about a decade ago this summer," Phil continued, "but they named themselves Dana and Roland. They wore commoner's clothes but had the bearing of the noble-born. They claimed they were from Lyhosa, but their accents weren't right. In fact, I couldn't place their accents, but I realise now they sound similar to yours."

"Perhaps it's just coincidence." Feiron suggested to Leonie. "How long have you been training?" He turned to Phil.

"A couple of years now. It's taken longer than I anticipated."

"Why? Is training difficult?"

"No, it's actually very easy – once you get past the 'not being eaten' stage." Phil grinned. "It's more getting them to work together, not as individuals. They're very intelligent, you know, almost as intelligent as other races."

We can hear you. Dorn swayed her tail, the barbs leaving scratches in the rocks.

"Of course you can," he said. "I was teasing."

Humans. Sometimes I do not know why I bother.

"Yes, you do, silly lizard; because I'm great company and you love my singing."

Feiron looked at him quizzically until Leonie explained the conversation.

"You truly sing to them?" Feiron asked.

"Yes, every once in a while." Phil lowered his voice. "They have no voice for it themselves, sounding akin to a rock-fall."

We can hear you, Dorn responded.

"But it is true, yes?" He winked at Leonie.

We sing better than you can fly.

Phil burst out laughing.

"You indicated earlier you had another reason why you are here," Leonie said after sharing the conversation with Feiron.

Phil nodded. "It was an idea based on what this Roland said. He mentioned he was a scholar, travelling to inform whoever would listen of the impending doom we all faced."

"Impending doom?"

"He said Shak'aran was getting warmer each year, and – perhaps twenty years from now, an ancient race, the l'ithnamagri, would emerge from their hibernation."

"L'ithnamagri?"

The wyverns growled at the mention of the word.

"All I know is the l'ith are large and formidable creatures; here long before we were." He looked into his mug, swirling the tea. "Perhaps by then, we'll have enough wyverns to help protect the city and its people."

There are not enough wyverns in the whole world for that, Dorn said. *These creatures of which you speak are very numerous.*

Phil finished his tea and got up for a refill while Leonie stared into her mug.

Feiron broke the growing silence. "Well, this is nothing like what we expected. It has always been said wyverns were cruel," Feiron said.

"And the stories of how they destroy everything," Leonie added.

Dorn snorted in response. Other rumbles could be heard from the upper reaches.

"From narrow-minded individuals who couldn't communicate with them no doubt, present company excluded. We all tend to hate things we fear or don't understand," Philbert waxed philosophically.

"Yes, I agree. Remember what happened at Indras, Leonie? We illios are ridiculed because of our looks."

"It's the way of the world it seems." Phil nodded.

I like stories. Slana interrupted their thoughts.

"Hss, not these ones. These stories say your kind is evil, a threat to be removed."

Slana growled, her body vibrating. *But you and your friend are here.*

"We had a task... I didn't really believe you existed." She shrugged.

"You didn't?" Phil asked her in surprise.

"We were expecting some weird creature, but you can't go around believing everything you hear in taverns." Leonie continued.

"True enough," Phil agreed.

"Why haven't you returned to Tesak?" she asked.

"I'm waiting for the last of the eggs to hatch."

"How many are there?" Feiron asked eagerly. "How long does it take?"

"Three more eggs are due to hatch in a couple more weeks, and in a few more months, we should be good to head off. Finally. I can continue the training in Tesak."

"Do you know of a ready source of eggshells?"

"Eggshells? Ah, is this the quest you spoke of? This could prove tricky for you. The eggs hatch in caves way down inside the volcano. It isn't the heat alone they require, but certain gases as well. You came at the right time. The youngest wyverns you see around here are only a few months old, but they mature quickly. They are very long-lived and only breed every two decades or so.

"Noldor, the dominant male, was in a terrible state when I came across him, but the females were far more distraught. When the mating time comes upon them, the urge is so intense.

"He barely won the fights with the other suitors. But he was the victor, and the others left. If he died there wouldn't have been any mating, and if they don't mate at the right time, the ability to produce offspring can wane. I healed him as best I could, and for my troubles, they agreed to help me until the next mating. Though who's going to stop them if they decide to leave early is anyone's guess."

We gave our word.

"And very gracious of you too," Phil replied quite sincerely.

"Is Noldor still around?" Leonie asked.

"Not anymore. The male leaves a few months after the courtship, perhaps returning every few years. Noldor left several months back. No doubt he's off to find another brood."

"Typical," Leonie muttered.

Yes.

Leonie chuckled at Dorn's response.

"Did I miss something?" Feiron asked.

"A girl joke." Leonie grinned.

Sparks shot out as Feiron stoked the fire, grumbling about not hearing mind-speak.

"My friend, we also promise to let you know everything said in mind-speak from now on, won't we Leonie?" Philbert added.

"Only if he cheers up," she teased. "Phil, you said earlier Dorn was Noldor's First Chosen; why is that?"

"In the wyvern world, Dorn is very high up, almost royal—"

Pagh, Dorn butted in. *My father was renowned for his wisdom and fierceness in combat. He was also one of the oldest and wisest living wyverns. He had a certain nobility about him, but royalty – no. Even if he is an elemental, the world lost a great soul when he parted this life.*

"I'm sorry for your loss."

Thank you, but unnecessary. It was many years ago, even before you were born.

As the silence stretched, Feiron poured himself another cup of tea and moved the discussion to his own quest. "How hot does it get inside these caves?"

"Dorn?" Phil called out.

The big female wyvern's head appeared over the ledge, her bright eyes gleaming in the gloom. *The cave entrances start about a wingspan above the magma level. I do not know how you measure heat, but I would expect it to be far hotter than you could endure.*

Feiron turned to Phil. "Is there anywhere else I could find eggshells?"

"There are numerous areas where each wyvern chooses to lay the eggs, but only within the vent area where the gases can reach them. There may be dozens of fissures and crevices that could lead to a hatchery, but they would be tiny." He began ladling out the mushroom soup into bowls. "But they would be close enough for the weak telepathic signal of hatchlings to be picked up by the mothers."

Turning to study the back wall, Feiron sipped his tea silently considering his limited options.

———

As promised, the flying lessons started the following day.

I want the furry one. Slana thought, craning her sinuous neck around to watch.

All that hair? No, thank you, Faldo replied. *I bet you sneeze; she will fall and you will get into trouble.*

Behave, you two. Dorn chastened the pair before she directed her next thoughts to Leonie. *They are still young and have no manners when it comes to strangers.*

"It's alright," Leonie said. "I know a couple of impetuous youngsters back home." She remembered to keep Feiron abreast of the conversation.

"It will be a whole new experience for you both, but the principles are simple. Hang on tight and don't fall off." Phil chuckled at their looks. "Sorry, just joking, but it's still good advice." He pointed out the different aspects of the saddles. "I modified spare horse saddles. There's a pommel to hang onto and stirrups for your feet. These tethers are to stop you from falling. Each one wraps around your waist and hooks onto the back here." He pointed to where they attached to the saddles.

"What're these for?" Leonie asked. She had moved over to Dorn's flank and was examining Phil's saddle. On each side of the pommel was a curved flap of hardened leather.

"More modifications. I don't use the tethers any more. When I mount, my thighs fit snugly underneath each of those flares. It takes getting used to, but far more practicable. Also, in combat, it frees the hands for weapons." He moved on to describe flying techniques. "I've no need for reins. Any instructions are sent telepathically. All you'll have to do in this case is hang on. Dorn and I will help direct Slana and Faldo. Don't get me wrong, I know they are quite capable flyers, but sometimes they'll roll or flip to show off."

He saw the look on their faces.

"You're not serious?" There was a slight tremor in Leonie's voice.

"Please relax. Everything will be alright." He smiled to reassure them.

Neither looked convinced.

He is a great jester, but this time he is right, you will both be safe. We are far smarter than horses, and some people, I suspect.

When it was time to mount up, the creatures lowered their long necks so their jaws were almost touching the ground. Philbert guided the novice riders, Leonie on Slana, then Feiron on Faldo.

Placing a paw in the stirrups, Leonie grabbed the pommel and heaved herself up, throwing her leg over.

Feiron then oozed into position.

That looks interesting. I wish I could do that, Faldo said to him.

"He can't hear you, Faldo," Phil said out aloud.

You mean he is deaf? The young wyvern looked closely at his passenger.

Only to mind-speak, Phil replied. *So be nice.* After he'd checked they were both belted into their saddles, Philbert climbed onto Dorn.

"The take-off is probably the roughest part," he called out. "Lean forward, hang on very tightly and after a few wing-beats, it should smooth out."

Dorn launched herself. Slana readied herself for flight, as did Faldo.

Hang on, furry one. Slana crouched, bunched her leg muscles and raised her wings and, like a released spring, she threw herself into the air; her wings snapping down. The strength of the jump was unbelievable. Even with the warning, the jolt was so intense Leonie almost lost her grip. With a deep thrumming sound drowning out all other noise, Slana rose into the sky at an exhilarating rate. Peering below, Leonie could make out Feiron hanging on to Faldo, but couldn't tell if he was enjoying himself or not.

Her mind reeled at the height; her ears lowered slightly, turning sideways. She had never been so far above the ground before. Climbing around rooftops was one thing, but this was an entirely new experience, with no comparison. The wind beat at her fur, the fresh cold permeated her skin, the sound of wings beating drummed in her ears; the muscles rippled between her thighs. It was exciting beyond description. She felt so alive.

You like to fly, it seems.

"It's all very new to me. It's so wonderful."

It is pleasing to know this. Do you think your friend is enjoying himself?

Leonie looked across to Feiron and waved. He waved back, calling something, but the rushing air snatched away the sound of his voice.

"Yes," she replied. "I think he's enjoying himself."

The three wyverns levelled out and flew close to each other in a triangle formation. The younger wyverns were side by side, their wingtips almost touching with each languid beat. Dorn was behind and slightly higher, where she and Philbert could keep an eye on them and their novice passengers.

The group circled, using the thermals to gain altitude. One moment the cliffs raced by, close enough to see the details of the rough and craggy fascia, then suddenly as they flew out over the canyon, the ground dropped away revealing the shimmering surface of the lake. The landscape transformed into a mosaic of colours and textures, with the sparse forest spread out below like a carpet of dark green lace interspersed with the darker colour of the rocky ground.

The Central Ranges, sweeping to the north and south, faded with the distance. Beyond the lower peaks, a whole series of higher peaks came into view, and only now did Leonie comprehend their sheer immensity. It was no wonder they had described it as the Spine of the World. Another turn and the view changed again.

Leonie made out the spidery trail of a road below. She lifted her gaze. Out of sight beyond the southern horizon lay Delta. In a weird way, she actually missed the place; dark and dangerous, yes, but it was all she had known.

All too soon, the trio headed back to the lair.

As much as she hated to admit it, Leonie was tired and out of condition. After a quick bite to eat, she did a short series of stretches before resting. She slept through dinner, and both Feiron and Phil were reluctant to wake her. Her moans during her nightmares indicated she still had some recovering to do.

"Don't be overly concerned for your friend. The wyverns monitor her constantly," Phil reassured Feiron.

14

THE MELTING-POINT OF AN ILLIOS

Unlike Leonie, Feiron couldn't sleep, swirling all night in his barrel. Thinking collecting the eggshells would be a simple matter, he had been reluctant to leave Leonie alone in her comatose state and go exploring. His goal was so close and his friends wouldn't be able to help. He would have to go alone. Oozing out of his bed, he slid past the sleeping forms of Phil and Leonie. He hesitated when passing her. She'd be sorely put out being excluded, but if what Dorn said was true, then there was nothing Leonie could do. She might even try to stop him.

Soundlessly, and invisible to wyvern minds, he flowed over the many scales littering the floor to a cleft in the rear wall. Around and above, the wyverns slept; their snores filling the chamber with a low rumbling. Whenever he'd had the opportunity, Feiron had searched the cavern, confident in his ability to navigate the fissures that would lead to one of the alcoves. His body could deal with the noxious fumes the volcano emitted. His only concern would be the temperature. Creeping along the wall, he began to enter the narrow cleft. It took a while to get his entire body inside as he needed to spread himself extremely thinly and over a large area.

With his body spread out so much, his sensory organs could

pick up the differing temperatures and air currents more accurately. Since the alcove was supposed to be close to the magma, he made his way in the warmest direction. When that proved false, he backtracked and started again.

With the need to concentrate constantly, Feiron lost track of time. There were far more fractures than expected. Sometimes, he even met up with himself. To make matters worse, the air currents moved in many directions, confusing him. Finally, however, he spied one of the hatcheries directly below. Shell fragments littered the floor. He wasn't sure which cave it was, but that didn't matter now; he had made it. Eagerly he lowered himself.

It was a long stretch and his bulk, already touching the floor thirty feet below, broke his tenuous grip on the lip of the fracture. The sudden release almost caused him to splash. Hitting the bedrock stressed his endoplasm, and he barely maintained cohesion. He lost awareness. When his body recovered, he decided it was an experience never to be repeated. Still disoriented, it took a few moments to gather himself before he could start his shell collecting.

The fragments were of many hues and shades; greens, reds, blacks. Many wyverns must have traversed this cavern in the past, their great weight grinding the shells into a fine multi-coloured powder.

Collecting the eggshells was an easy task; a simple matter of moving around and scooping the fragments into his body mass, in the same fashion he had smuggled the *Seer's Codex* out of Delta. There were a couple of larger fragments nearer the entrance, but the heat became too intense, forcing him to remain to the rear of the cave. Quickly, he began to notice his consistency thinning from the heat; he decided he had enough to satisfy his master.

Feiron flowed towards the wall; only then aware of his predicament. The only fissure he could see was the one in the ceiling. He was annoyed with himself, blaming his eagerness for being so foolish as to drop into the cave without checking for other exits first.

He oozed up the wall but as the wall curved to become the ceiling, his grip on the rocky surface loosened. Feiron hung like a steaming, wet curtain. If he stretched out too thinly, the heat would make his body bubble and blister, yet if he retained his mass in a thick layer, he'd lose his grip. Either way, it doomed him to fail. Dejectedly, the illios dripped to the floor. He flowed around the cave, even risking a foray towards the entrance in the hope he'd be lucky enough to find something missed, but the intense heat drove him back.

Reaching up to the crack proved futile; even if he could stretch that far, he doubted he'd be able to haul his mass all the way, especially now he was so fluid. He moved as far back as he could to think, but he'd need to make another attempt before percolating away. While motionless, he noticed the droplets beading on his skin. He was evaporating!

——

Leonie awoke from another dark dream; the lair was empty.

Grabbing a chunk of bread, she went out to the ledge fully expecting to see the blob-form of the illios. She looked in all directions, but his grey mass was nowhere to be seen. She turned back at a noise. Phil was emerging from a storage alcove.

"Have you seen Feiron?" Leonie asked him.

"No. I thought he might have gone outside." Phil looked up from his breakfast preparations. "I know he loves the view."

"No. I've already checked."

Anyone seen the illios? Phil sent out a general query.

No, I haven't seen him since last night, Dorn responded. Many others had the same thoughts. None of the wyverns had seen the shapechanger all day.

Do not forget, telepathically, he is invisible to us. We can only see him physically, Dorn said.

Phil suggested they go for a fly, in case the eccentric illios tried his luck at mountain climbing. "Do you think he may have tried for the eggshells by himself?" Phil asked Leonie as they mounted the wyverns. "He was very keen on the idea."

"It would be like him to go off alone so as not to be a nuisance."

"Then that's where we should be looking." *Dorn?*

Very well, she answered the unasked question. *The youngsters will help search for him.*

Dorn and Slana landed so Phil and Leonie could mount then the pair spiralled up to the lip of the crater, moving upwind, away from the nauseous fumes. At the rim, others joined them. Faldo was first to volunteer flying down to look around the alcoves. A few of the more adventurous wyverns assisted.

As the minutes passed, Dorn and Slana idly glided in the shifting wind.

Glancing down through the rising smoke, Phil and Leonie observed the wyverns darting in between the crevices, disappearing completely when they entered the many alcoves.

I think I have found him, a blue wyvern said.

Faldo's form shot out from a grotto. He raced over to where the blue hovered, disappearing into the indicated cave.

Leonie leant over the saddle, craning her neck to see.

The heat has melted him. Faldo emerged from the cave and moved away from the heat.

"Why didn't you bring him?" she yelled when he reappeared alone.

He is too drippy, like water.

"How can we cool him down?" she asked desperately. "Any cold water or ice nearby?"

"Snow or the river," Phil said. "Best to get him out first."

"We'll need something to carry him." Leonie thought quickly. "That bucket you mentioned, can we use it?"

"Yes of course. It would be ideal, as long as the heat isn't too much for it."

As the suggestion formed in Leonie's mind, Slana, who wanted to do her bit to help, darted back towards the top entrance of the sleeping cavern.

Hang on, furry one. Slana dropped through the roof. There was little room for flying. She tucked her wings, using levitation alone. *This is a shortcut.*

Leaning over and looking down into the gloom was a bad idea, Leonie decided, especially with rock ledges rushing towards her. She had to trust in the young wyvern's skills. Sure enough, within moments of darting into the cave, Slana's claws latched around the handles of the large leather sack. She pivoted to return to the light.

Leonie's stomach lurched with the sudden change in direction, but she remained silent and hung on tightly. "Go as fast as you can Slana," she said aloud, forgetting to think it.

Faldo isn't half as fast as I am.

All Leonie could see was a blur of rocks whizzing past. Suddenly they were awash with sunlight. Slana pivoted and flew like an arrow to the others on the rim.

Leonie gritted her teeth hoping they were still in time.

Faldo, catch. Slana released the handle. The heavy bag fell towards the bubbling lava.

Leonie's body tensed and her breath caught in her throat.

Faldo fell like a stone after it. *Got it.* Within seconds of it becoming a smouldering piece of hide, he snatched the handles and continued the dive towards the cave where Feiron was situated.

Tricked you. Slana laughed over her sinuous neck.

Leonie hadn't realised she was holding her breath. She remained quiet, exhaling in relief. The wait for Faldo's reappearance was interminable. "Have you heard anything?" she asked impatiently.

Faldo?

On my way. His thought reached them as they saw him step out from the alcove. He slowly lifted off the ground for a few feet before flapping his wings.

"Get down lower," Leonie told Slana.

What about the heat? she asked as she descended.

"I'll manage. I need to see how he is." Leonie urged her

down. "Feiron. Are you alright?" she yelled when they met Faldo halfway. Waves of heat washed over them, threatening to singe her fur.

There was no immediate response. She was about to call again, but her hearing picked up the faintest reply.

"Tea... good."

"You idiot. What did you think you were doing?"

This time there was no response at all and Leonie hoped whatever gods that were out there would look after him. The group of wyverns swarmed back to the lair, waiting outside as Faldo lowered Feiron through the roof.

Leonie and Phil arrived through the main entrance as Faldo came to hover above the cave floor. They laid the illios inside his barrel. There was no other way than to tip the bucket over and watch the grey, fluid mass flow over the rim.

He had difficulty moving. I had to lay the bag flat on the floor and hold it open so he could pour in, Faldo explained. He joined Slana to watch the activity from the alcoves above. Dorn sat on the floor, her long body extending to the entrance.

"Have you any idea of how to treat him, since you're a healer of sorts?" Leonie's ears were flat.

"I was hoping you'd have some idea. All I can suggest is cool water. He evidently lost a lot of fluid with the heat; see how the barrel isn't as full as usual." He went off to fetch the water-skin. "Looks like breakfast will have to be done again," he called back as he passed the smoking remains of the forgotten strips of meat that had been laid out in the skillet earlier.

It will not go to waste, Faldo snickered.

How can you think of food now? Slana said.

I am always hungry, he protested mildly to his sister.

Hush, children.

"How much do we add?" Leonie asked Phil on his return, hating not knowing how to help. "Do we pour it on? They absorb stuff, don't they?"

"I guess so. There's only one way to find out. Let's see how a little bit goes first." Phil opened one of the skins and poured a few drops onto the grey mass. "We wouldn't want to drown him."

Leonie had never seen Feiron so still before; even when asleep, his form would ripple slightly. She noticed areas of discolouration. "See those dark areas?" She pointed them out to Phil.

"Hmm, burns? We'll not know until he tells us himself."

As they watched, the water slowly disappeared, absorbing into the skin.

"I hope that means he's still alive." Her voice cracked.

Taking turns, they poured small amounts, but it wasn't long before both water-skins were depleted.

"I'll go get some more fresh water."

Leonie nodded, handing him her water-skin.

"I won't be long." Phil climbed onto Dorn's back as she reversed out of the lair.

Leonie watched Feiron intently. She remembered the time back at the chasm when the Brothers of the Flame had attacked. Feiron had produced some balm to help heal her burns. She leapt up and went to search through the packs, to see if there was any left. Hastily dumping the pack's contents onto the sleeping pallet, the flask of miwalli fell out, luckily landing on a blanket and not the stone floor. She took the ceramic jar to him and examined its contents, unsure of how to apply it.

When Phil returned with the water, she scooped out a cup and mixed in some miwalli. It had a foul smell, like decayed vegetation. Holding her breath, Leonie poured the concoction over the grey mass. "How could anyone think this would be good for anything?"

"Ah yes, miwalli," Phil recounted. "I recall that particular medicine from my horse-healing days in Tesak. It's very expensive for all its putridness, but quite good for many ailments."

"We'll see soon enough."

"I don't know about you but I'm famished. I'll fix us another breakfast." He went to the fire, noting the pan was now empty.

"You'll be too fat to fly soon." He spied Faldo's smug face peered down at him. "I reckon you'll be staying behind."

Ha. Fatty Faldo! Slana chortled.

All day and night Leonie waited for some sign of his recovery. She realised she had forgotten to thank Faldo for his efforts. In fact, nearly everyone helped out one way or another, especially the blue wyvern who initially found her friend.

We are happy to do these things. Your customs are strange, but Singer has taught us well.

Leonie recognised Dorn's thoughts. "Thanks all the same. I only hope once Feiron gets better and starts to write about you all, everyone will know what you're really like, not vile and evil beasts."

"Not everyone will believe it, regardless of who tells them." Phil returned with firewood. "They'll believe whatever they want."

"I guess," she answered. "We can only try."

It was almost midday the next day before Feiron recovered enough to speak with them.

Leonie raced over the moment she saw a tendril appear over the rim of the bath. "We were so worried."

"Where am I?"

"Back in the lair."

"Lair? Did we meet any wyverns?"

"You could say that." Leonie swapped a concerned glance with Phil before turning back. "How are you feeling?"

"My body's worked hard regenerating, though I fear some areas are too injured for repair. Thank you for your concern, but we're tougher than we look though I admit I was worried."

"I bet. What happened?" She couldn't tell much from his looks, but his voice had become softer, almost raspy as he described his search for the eggshells.

"The damaged area is absorbed, and I believe I've lost some of my memory," he said.

"How?"

"Because of our make-up, the organs are spread throughout the body. They can all be remade, but if it is a portion where information stored then it will be lost."

"How will you know?"

"I'll let you know when I can't think of something," he joked. "Is there any tea left? I do recall a liking for it." He slowly oozed over the lip of the barrel, remaining a good distance from the small cook-fire.

"I think, to celebrate your survival, it's time I introduced you to some Tesakian Redleaf, very rare, but full of everything you could want... in a non-alcoholic beverage."

As the day progressed, Feiron's recovery improved, but slowly. He sat on the ledge in front of the lair entrance watching the rain and scudding clouds, marvelling at the way they moved along the range, swirling up and over the peaks.

"I reckon it's a dangerous way to lose weight." Leonie came to join him. "You're a lot smaller than normal."

"It's true, most of my mass is liquid. Even with the extra fluid I gained from the river, I've dehydrated too much," Feiron said. "Water will only replace a small part of my loss. The rest, the damaged portion that's been absorbed, will have to be regrown. Only time will heal all, but tea makes it seem better." He paused. "I do feel... different somehow."

"Why didn't you go for the eggshells earlier? Although it is hindsight, the extra fluid retention may have made it safer."

"Leaving you to recover alone didn't feel right."

"For what it's worth, I'm amazed at your patience." She patted him on the back. "You are too kind."

They saw the wyverns return from their flying as dusk turned to night. Feiron waddled inside to thank them for saving him. The twins acknowledged his thanks, inclining their heads and winking; physical indication the only way they could communicate with him.

I am very disappointed. Tell your illios friend he is not to attempt such a foolish thing again. In a flurry of wind and dust, Dorn unfurled her great wings and leapt off the ground, soaring into the dark sky.

Leonie relayed the message. Feiron's colour changed in embarrassment. "She has my word on that, and my sincere apologies. I vow to do what I can to rectify my ignorance of their ways. Now, if you'll excuse me, I'll go and rest."

The next day dawned overcast and misty. Leonie worried Feiron had still not recovered his usual joviality. Philbert brought in some large eggs; mixing them with his mountain herbs made for a tasty breakfast.

Feiron wasn't in his barrel and did not appear for breakfast. Leonie sought him out finding him eventually in a rear alcove. "What are you doing in here?"

"I've found out what I lost." Feiron greeted her.

"Your innocence?" She smiled, hoping a joke would lighten his mood.

"That went ages ago. I can barely shapechange into anything."

"What's a shapechanger who can't shapechange? How does that happen?"

"We learn by experience and practice. Muscle memory can be quite good with enough training. Unfortunately, it appears I didn't retain sufficient muscle memory."

"Do you recall what you could do? The serpent, or Hectr the merchant, or Drial the vorien—"

"I know what I could do – I can picture it – just not the how."

"Does that mean longer training with your mentor?"

"I hope not." He shrugged. "I will endeavour to put every waking moment into shaping in an effort to regain my abilities."

Leonie watched him forming into different shapes for a while, giving encouragement where she could. "I'll leave you to it, but don't overexert yourself. Resting is just as important. So is eating."

"I'll be out soon," he said, then to reassure Leonie, he added, "and I'll make up for the missed breakfast. No leftovers for Faldo this time."

A strong breeze came in from the east, whistling along the rock face near the entrance. As promised, Feiron joined them for lunch and didn't argue with the double-serving put before him.

"After all that trouble, did you manage to get any eggshells?" Leonie asked her sullen companion over the noise, watching him eat everything on his plate.

"I can't seem to find any evidence."

"Would your body absorb them?" Phil asked.

Feiron paused in thought. "I'm not sure, it's possible, I guess. Maybe I was too weak to retain them, or too fluid."

"Well, we've seen none of it out here."

"I don't know what to do now. I promised not to go back without them, and I'll keep my word." He nodded to Philbert. "But I'm sure my mentor will be surely vexed if I turn up with nothing."

"Better her wrath than dying."

"I'm not so sure."

"It wasn't as if you didn't try."

"Nonetheless, I wonder if there's anything else I can procure to mollify her temper somewhat before we leave."

"What about these wyvern scales?" she suggested. "It's the only thing left. There're hundreds of them, and it isn't as if one comes across them every day."

Feiron picked up one of the many scales from the floor and examined it closely, noting the colouring and texture. "It will have to suffice." He sounded slightly mollified.

15

A NEW PLAN

FULLY RECOVERED, LEONIE STILL HAD HER TASK TO COMPLETE, BUT Feiron's condition was an extra delay. A pang of guilt settled over her; Feiron had waited patiently enough for her to recover. Now it was her turn, and she would just have to wait.

She only had a rudimentary idea who Styx was, but surely, he was waiting for someone to deliver this book. It had been unavoidable, but their detour, intriguing as it was, had to come to an end. She hoped they weren't too much of a burden and getting in the way of their training. Any annoyance or ill-feeling about Feiron's rescue was short-lived, the wyverns continued with their perpetual antics in and around the volcano smoke.

Phil was rubbing oil into the saddles. Leonie lent him a paw and voiced her concerns.

"Nonsense," he replied. "Yes, Dorn took umbrage to what Feiron did, but trust me, she is forgiving. We are all impetuous, sometimes for very good reasons which seem ludicrous when you look back on it. Look at me. Here, hundreds of leagues from my home and family, on a dream to return with a swirl of wyverns for our city's defence. I'm sure, right now, those that I left behind think I'm a complete dill. And most probably dead."

"You've been so understanding—"

"Pagh. We'll hear nothing of it. But you are lucky we have taught you to fly, though."

"It was truly wonderful, but why lucky?"

"There are many leagues of extremely rugged terrain surrounding us before you get to the nearest road, and twice that before you get to the closest town. What better way to get to Qelay, other than flying? Surely you didn't want to sit in that coracle or travel on foot?"

"Oh." Leonie paused. "I didn't think of that."

"As pleasant as it's been for company, we all knew you would have to leave sooner or later. This is my dream, not yours. You have your quest to fulfil too. That *Codex* is fascinating. I'm certain this rollo is keen to get it."

"Like many others, it seems. Won't your appearance in Qelay cause alarm?"

"I dare say three wyverns descending on the fair city would bring on much involuntary bowel movement," Phil said, chuckling. "No. I propose we land on the outskirts; probably early morning is best. That way, by the time you get into town, it will be daylight. My understanding is many towns are suspicious of strange folk entering town after dark."

Feiron, when he wasn't practising, sat outside watching the wyverns go through their manoeuvres. When the wind picked up, he came inside and rummaged through his pack, studying the scales he had collected; sometimes swapping one for another he had found. His physical recovery was complete, though his shapechanging still required work, but he was ever-mindful of Leonie's mood when she needed a change of scenery. On the seventh day after their arrival, when they were together for lunch, he announced his fitness to travel.

"Are you sure?" Leonie asked, turning to Philbert. "We can wait longer if need be."

"Of course," Phil added. "I was not lying when I offered you to stay as long as you needed."

"I'm healthy enough to travel and deliver this tome. By my reckoning, we left Delta about twelve days ago. Our bosses would be expecting us to return any day now, and we haven't completed the main task. My lack of shapechanging is not reason enough to delay longer than necessary. I might add I am also keen to meet this rollo."

While excited at the prospect of the move, Leonie also had a pang of guilt, hoping Feiron hadn't overheard her earlier conversation with Phil. "If you say so…"

"I do. What needs to be done?"

"I suggest a brief flight this afternoon. That way we'll know for certain as to your readiness to travel."

Take-off was far less of a physical jolt, but a far greater jolt on the nerves. Once mounted, each wyvern simply dropped off the outer ledge and spread its wings to capture the air. The acceleration was enough to make the novice passengers gasp for air. In turn, Slana, Faldo and Dorn turned the dive into a huge swoop. They utilised warm air currents to assist in gaining altitude. The updrafts along the cliff face were ideal for this.

Leonie watched the wings move up and down, marvelling at the way they seemed to pivot at the shoulder. They really didn't look big enough to support the weight of the creatures. Once again, other wyverns gathered to observe the strangers. If there was any mind-talk, it was directed solely to other wyverns.

Blinking back tears caused by the rush of frigid air, Leonie was mesmerised by the sight of the landscape, but now it was from a much greater height. The forest spread towards the east like a map. The deep green of conifers blended into the brighter, more vibrant emerald of broad-leafed plants along riverbeds and in the lowlands.

Soon her nose picked up a foul, familiar odour. The wyverns were almost directly over the volcano, staying out of the fumes, as it would make the passengers sick. Blasts of dry heat washed over them. Looking down deep within the crater, Leonie saw a dull orange glow. The lava looked like a living thing, surging and bubbling, constantly moving. It was incredible to believe it was molten rock. Hell's Maw was an apt name. She watched other wyverns dart through the fumes, and some even flew into the crater itself.

Further west, and as far as the eye could see north and south, it looked as if the land was broken, the remains swept up in huge piles. There were other volcanoes further inland. Observing the deep ravines and sheer cliffs they'd have to traverse, Leonie was glad Hell's Maw wasn't one of them.

They climbed higher, wheeling away from the crater and the heat. The air grew intensely cold; Leonie tightened her grip on the pommel as her fingers numbed and she shivered, scared of losing her grip.

You are vibrating, Slana noted.

"C-cold," Leonie stammered.

I thought your fur coat would keep you warm. I will not go any higher.

"Thanks, but the fur isn't as thick as you might think, and I'm used to warmer weather," she stammered.

Slana began to descend in a broad spiral, sending her intentions to Faldo, Dorn and Philbert. As this happened, Leonie spotted a large sky island far off.

Dorn said to her. *Skylands seem to follow the line of the mountains, though why, I know not.*

Fascinating as it was, thoughts of the skyland quickly vanished as the wyverns increased their rate of descent. Leonie showed more confidence in her riding, with gradual increases in boldness. She glanced across to see how Feiron was doing. He also appeared confident, but Leonie noticed his body changing shape, billowing slightly like a sail.

They both laughed when the young twins flew in and out of the huge ravines that cut great swathes through the mountains, swooping and diving, banking sharply at the last minute. It became a merry chase, involving most of the wyverns. The sight of so many wyverns wheeling in the air above, with such spectacular scenery, would stay in Leonie's mind until the end of her days.

After dropping their passengers at the *front door* as Philbert called it, the twins joined the other young wyverns. Leonie and Feiron helped Phil stow the saddles on plinths to the side of the entrance.

"Was that okay?" she asked Feiron as they walked back into the lair.

"Most enjoyable, though I'm more sensitive to the cold now. Why do you ask?"

"You looked funny. When we were diving, you looked like a sail on one of the ships back in Delta harbour."

"Oh. Yes, I suspect I did look a bit strange. The force of the wind against my skin was far greater than I anticipated. I found by making myself narrower, I had less resistance, much like a ship's bow cutting through water."

With the impending departure, Phil tried to make dinner as enjoyable as possible by using his culinary skills and spices to make traditional Tesakian dishes. Afterwards, Leonie recounted their travels and adventures from the earlier portion of their trip; about their troubles with the Brotherhood and how it all started with the assassination of the courier. She told Philbert of Delta and all its goings-on, asking him what he knew about it. Since he was more educated and had been in the company of nobles in Tesak, she thought he may have some knowledge to impart.

The Tesakian confessed to knowing very little about Delta, other than the rumours he'd already shared with them of Zander's ruthlessness. He then described the forest city of Tesak, built high up in the giant Ironwood Forests.

"It would seem in some instances there are similarities between your Delta and my Tesak," he said. "Whereas you have many islands connected by bridges, we too have many small communities. Nestled within the boughs of each of the giant trees, they are connected at many levels by walkways suspended hundreds of feet above the forest floor." His hands and arms were animated as he described the bridges. "It also boasts one of the largest broods of glins'ool on all of Shak'aran."

"Friends shouldn't tell each other such tales. Trees large enough to house a community?" Leonie couldn't bring herself to believe in trees being so large.

"Ah. It is too grand for my inadequate words. You will simply have to visit one day. Then you can trust your own eyes." He winked at Feiron. "When you pick your jaw off the ground, I'll accept your apology."

To arrive at Qelay before sunrise they would need to leave at midnight. No one was in the mood to sleep.

It was a quiet, almost relaxing evening. Philbert then spoke at length of his time with the wyverns, naming them all, describing each of their mannerisms and traits in detail – with interjections from a few wyverns – and more of his plans to bring them to his home city. As the conversation died down, like the waning fire, he pulled out his lyre and while his voice may not have been as clear as a bard's, he made up for it with his antics, jumping around as he sang, threatening to fall and crush his lyre any moment. Wyvern hisses and barks echoed around the lair.

Leonie spoke loudly to Feiron over the din. "I hope his horse-healing is better than his singing."

The sky was crystal clear, the eastern horizon glowed with the rising of the twin moons halfway through their cycle, and a southerly breeze ensured a swift trip. Dorn, Slana and Faldo were quickly saddled. Apart from the sack of wyvern scales, there was little else to pack since the remainder of their belongings had been left at Swangrove.

"Will you be staying to see Qelay for yourself?" Feiron asked.

Phil was strapping a wooden chest to the back of his saddle. "No. Not at this time. There are still a couple of the youngest wyverns to finish training. I wouldn't want to jeopardise anything by cutting corners."

"A shame. Would I be able to come back here? I'd still very much like to write about the wyverns – I feel I owe them that much – and later, any of the other creatures we happen to come across; perhaps hippogryphs or the odd cockatrice."

"My friend, you are welcome to stay for as long as you can stand my singing. Who knows where this new venture will lead? You might even want to join me in visiting my homeland of Tesak. I don't know about the cockatrice, but hippogryphs dwell in the Northern Reaches and there are always the l'ith, those fell creatures lurking beneath the Vale of Dromas." He winked to Leonie.

They were about to launch when Philbert snapped his fingers and slid off Dorn's back. He raced back into the lair, returning moments later with a couple of old jackets.

"I hope you'll forgive my being a bit absent-minded. I set these aside earlier and only remembered. They may not be the best fit, but, warm is warm." He passed them around. "We'll follow the mountains north for a few hours. I reckon when the moons are overhead, it will be time to turn east. This way we can avoid most settlements."

Leonie donned the fur-lined coat as Phil spoke. The coat was slightly large for her, but using her belt, she wrapped it around snugly, sufficient to keep out the wind.

Feiron had little trouble, slipping inside and conforming to whatever size best suited his coat.

The take-off was still a stomach-churner. Instead of leaping into the sky, the wyverns dropped off the edge one by one, skimming down the sheer cliff before snapping their wings out and turning the plummet into a graceful arc to the north.

Leonie thought the night sky was as intriguing to look at as was the darkened landscape. There seemed to be as many stars as there were leaves in the forests below. The jagged peaks of the Ranges swiftly drifted by, but there were many more to the north. Lost in their own thoughts, the riders were silent for the majority of the northern leg of the journey. Whether the wyverns sensed the mood, or they too had wyvern-thoughts of their own, the usual jibes between the twins was absent.

I propose we rest for a quick meal and to stretch our legs.

Phil's message jolted Leonie out of her reverie. She acknowledged this message with a thumbs-up signal. As they banked to a gradual spiral, Feiron realised their intent, and he waved to Leonie.

In a small clearing between massive trees, Phil heaved the wooden chest off Dorn's back and carried it to a fallen tree, which made a good enough place to sit.

The three wyverns took off, quickly disappearing in the dark.

"Don't be alarmed." Phil saw the looks on his companion's faces. "They'll return soon enough. All this flying has made them hungry. Speaking of which, I have a pleasant surprise for you." Lifting the lid of the chest he pulled out ceramic jugs with cork stoppers, handing one each to the travellers.

Intrigued by this, Leonie and Feiron reached for the jars with curiosity. To their delight, the jugs were still very warm. Removing the lids revealed hot soup. Inside the chest, rocks radiated heat onto their inquisitive faces.

"I thought you'd approve." Phil smiled back at them as he handed them each a spoon. "I recall long night-flights can be so cold and monotonous. Also, some interesting news. Dorn has been in contact with the rollos. Qelay is on the north shore of Lake Urmaq. Styx will meet us near a bridge to the west of the lake.

"That means there'll be no need to go into Qelay. Once Styx has the *Codex*, we can head straight to Delta."

"Of course, but we'll need to collect more provisions with a quick detour back to the lair."

"How far can a wyvern send messages?"

"Several leagues, I believe. However, in this case, the rollos sensed the wyvern's minds. They initiated contact."

As Phil promised, their rides returned in good time. The banter between the twins was back, evidence of their change in mood too now that their hunger was assuaged.

"I suspect they found something nice to eat," Leonie said to Feiron.

We ate—

"Slana! I don't need to hear the gory details." Leonie rubbed her neck.

With spirits lifted, the remainder of the trip seemed far quicker and less depressing.

———

In the pre-dawn light, the lake was bordered by the darker forests on the south and west and the lighter shade of the fields to the north and east. As the sun appeared on the horizon, they glimpsed a bridge below, between large trees, and a strip of rocky ground nearby.

Dorn commenced a wide spiralling descent, the twins following. Just above the treetops, she straightened up and gracefully landed by a small scattering of boulders.

Faldo and Slana landed behind.

"Is this the place? Are we early?" Leonie looked around.

Dorn snorted. *We are at the correct place, at the correct time.*

"Then where—" She stopped as a boulder rolled forward. She noticed the furrow it left in its trail. It uncurled itself, forming a triangular shape with stubby legs and arms, each ending in short, sharp talons. It was a dark grey, like slate. She could see no face – no eyes, mouth, or nose.

Greetings. I am Styx, at your service, the squat figure said. *And no, Faldo, I do not expect I would taste good.*

Faldo! Dorn thumped her tail. *How rude.*

"Is that who I think it is?" Feiron looked down quizzically.

"I believe it is. Philbert, ever met a hroltahg before?"

"I have not." He stepped down from his saddle, joining Leonie. "Very pleased to meet you, Styx." He took in a deep breath. "I am—"

No need for introductions. I have been expecting you. I am glad Axorg managed to find you in time.

"You sent Axorg?"

I requested. One cannot leave these matters to chance... or coincidence.

Leonie quickly shared the conversation with Feiron who dripped down to join them.

Forgive me if I am blunt. I am getting used to those who cannot mind-speak, Styx admitted.

"How far is it to Qelay?" Feiron added his voice. "I couldn't see it anywhere."

We have several hours of walking as it is on the northern bank of the lake. There are quite a few farms between here and there. This location is a precaution to ensure no cattle are startled, which may hinder the produce of the dairies. Qelay relies heavily on this trade. There is also a swamp.

"A swamp. How lovely." Leonie's tail lashed in annoyance. "Luckily though, I have the *Codex* right here." She pulled the heavy book from her pack and held it out to him. "Now that you have this, my part is over." She was curious to see how the little fellow would carry it.

That you have brought it this far is a marvel. Styx made no move to collect the book. *On behalf of the hroltahgs, please allow me to show our gratitude by inviting you and your illios companion to relax in White Cliffs. Dorn has informed me of your recent travails. I understand you have had some difficulty, and I am at your disposal to render whatever assistance I can.*

"By taking the book, our troubles will be over. No one will need to harass us again." She smiled, relieved at not having to enter a stagnant festering swamp.

I am aware those seeking this Codex *are relentless. They will continue to seek whatever information they can. If not from the book itself, then from those with the knowledge of its contents. I would feel neglectful by not assisting you in protecting yourself from future assaults.*

"Seems I've heard similar words before." Leonie's smile waned. Obviously, Styx was not going to take the *Codex*. She shoved it back into the satchel, dropped her arms and turned to

Phil. "Looks like we're heading into Qelay after all." Leonie took off her flying jacket and strapped it behind her saddle. Feiron did the same on Faldo.

"I'm sure it's for the best," Phil said in an effort to ease the situation. "Always remember though, you are both welcome to visit any time." He hugged her briefly and shook the tentacle Feiron extended.

Leonie moved to each of the wyverns and rubbed their snouts. "I don't know how to thank you for all that you've done for us."

There is no need. Dorn inclined her head. *Your company has been most pleasant and intriguing, even Feiron's little escapade.*

Phil mounted, and with a last wave, the three wyverns lifted off and turned to the south.

Before they were out of sight, Dorn sent a last message. *For whatever reason he had, Axorg chose well.*

16

MARSH OF THE UNDEAD

CAUTIOUSLY CROSSING A DILAPIDATED BRIDGE, THE TRIO MADE THEIR way east. In his rolling mode, Styx trundled alongside Leonie and Feiron without difficulty. The forest quickly thinned out and within the hour they entered the swamp.

"You don't talk much." Leonie broke the silence.

I do not talk at all, but I am quite adept at communicating.

She rolled her eyes at Feiron. "Have you had much contact with... non-hroltahgs?"

A little. I find you all... curious.

"Well, you are the first rollo we've met."

I know this. Dorn communicated all with me.

"How does telepathy work?" she asked. "If I'm not tele-pathic, how can I... hear you?"

When you speak, I hear you, but my reply is done mentally. For mundanes – non-telepaths – I need to put the thought into your mind. When you think of something, I, as a telepath, can read those surface thoughts. If you were telepathic, you would be able to read mine freely as well and send your thoughts to me. The illios it seems, cannot receive our thoughts, as we cannot detect their thought patterns.

"Can anyone become a telepath?"

If not a natural trait, gaining the ability is extremely unlikely, but do not despair. I am sure you and your friend have very good talents in other areas.

"I'm a thief. I make my living by taking from others," she said matter-of-factly.

You utilise the skills you have: good balance, nocturnal vision, keen smell, taste, hearing, as well as the eyesight, lightning reflexes, and a limited ability to utilise power. Your mixed origins have caused you hardship, but this has also given some great advantages; you have everything you require to do what you do. I would not complain about any of that. You would be quite formidable if you had psionics too. I might add, for a thief, you appear to have good awareness of morality.

"You sure know what to say to please a girl. What can you tell us about yourself and your kind?"

My race is totally psionic and able to detect features of the local terrain by the reverberation of sound waves. Some of us have ability to register when the power is being used, but we all have the ability to utilise the physical senses of those creatures around us. It is very difficult to sneak up on us, any creature with a mind can be detected.

"You mean you can see through my eyes?"

Yours, or that eagle overhead; the lizard under those shrubs; or the fish in the water. Styx transferred these animal sensations to Leonie.

One moment she was soaring high above the ground, viewing the land below with a clarity putting her eyesight to shame; a cool, tingling sensation crossed her body when the wind ruffled feathers. The vision changed; she was now staring intently between grass shoots and pebbles – it was very disconcerting as each eye had a different view; then sudden murkiness enveloped her, and she felt the different water pressure as she swam through the river. It was almost too much. She gasped in wonder at it all, almost losing her balance. Her head reeled at the swiftly changing perspectives.

Feiron looked to the rollo. "Is everything alright?" he asked Leonie.

Leonie, carried away with the conversation, had neglected to keep him in the picture. She remedied that quickly.

Styx continued. *My skin is tougher than iron yet as pliable as leather, movement is normally by rolling, but we can also jump.* He unfolded himself and leapt into the air, landing with a thump about ten paces down the road, leaving a sizeable dent where he landed. *I forgot about that.*

Styx waited until they caught up. *We are extremely heavy for our size too. I weigh about six hundred pounds. I have talons on my hands and feet that are more resilient and sharper than any dagger.*

"I see modesty doesn't become you."

Modesty does not come into it when communicating mind to mind. We cannot lie. That is probably our biggest weakness.

"Is that all?"

We live about a thousand years. I am a mere fifty years old.

"I suppose you can do magic?"

No, though we can persuade others to utilise the power on our behalf.

"No offence, but I think I know why Zander banned your kind from Delta. I doubt he'd be in such control otherwise. Where's your mouth and nose?"

Non-existent. We have no need.

"So how do you eat or smell?"

Osmosis.

"I reckon he's being rude," she said to Feiron.

Styx explained. *We absorb any required nutrition, whether it is food, fluid or gas, through our skin, like your friend does.*

"We illios eat the same way?" Feiron responded after Leonie's update. "Something in common at last."

She grinned. "I'd think nothing could stop hroltahgs if you wanted to do something. Why are you pacifists?"

We believe violence is a result of anger. Anger clouds judgement. A clear mind, one that can see all aspects of a situation, is more likely to come to a more logical, peaceful resolution. There have been stories of rogues, but they are extremely rare in our society and considered abominations. We can sense aggressive thoughts. We shut them out in fear the madness might spread. One of us rogue is a bad thing. Several would be beyond terrible.

"So, you'd not raise a finger to save your own life?"

We only infiltrate minds to garner information. Self-defence is slightly different, but even then, our intent would not be to kill. It is hard for me to describe it to one who is not a telepath. We have a belief in a higher consciousness. Our bodies, whether covered in fur, scales or feathers, whether they be bone and sinew or translucent ectoplasm, are merely transitory shells. When our bodies die our soul, or spirit if you prefer, is released to join those already released. Some call it a universal consciousness; an all-pervading force. You have already encountered such an entity.

"We have?"

"Axorg, the elemental wyvern," Feiron said after Leonie's update.

Precisely, Styx continued, *we evolved to utilise our abilities not so much for offence, but for protection. For survival.*

"What's the difference? You said no one could touch you."

True, but I do not refer to danger from people – I have not been in a dire situation in my entire life – I meant protection from our natural environment.

Leonie looked about. "Okay, I know we had a lot of rain and storms lately, but nothing that bad."

Not this environment.

"Is Reenat so much worse?"

Not Reenat either.

"I thought you said you were from Reenat." Her tail lashed in exasperation.

Do you think you are ready to hear this?

She sighed. "You'd know."

There was a pause before Styx replied. *We are not from this world.*

She frowned as her mind went back to an earlier discussion with Feiron. "What world are you talking about?" she asked, eventually.

My race's home world. I have not been there myself, so lack the imagery to show you. There really is no one word to name it in your languages. I can only describe it in words from your own mind; hot, steaming land of acrid air, volcanoes, vertical rock strata and very strong winds, with two suns and four moons. The vegetation can kill. That is the kind of world where my kind originated.

"Sounds ghastly. I can understand why you left. Where is it and how did you get here?"

We do not know its whereabouts. We came into this world via a portal — like every other race. None of the constellations here are familiar to us.

Feiron listened as Leonie continued to relay the conversation. "You see. Other worlds, like I said. Four moons and two suns though would be fascinating."

"Can you go back through this *portal*, whatever that is?" Leonie asked.

It is a doorway, harnessing powerful forces to connect different places, and no, we do not know yet how to return.

"Why not? Where is this portal? When will you be able to return?"

It is believed the portal — or portals, since we have many races here and therefore as many home worlds — were destroyed in the area now known as the Vale of Dromas during the Powershaper Wars. As to returning, that remains to be seen. We wait. Some think the book may contain an answer for us.

"Last week life was far less complicated." She sighed.

Some say ignorance is bliss.

"Hmmph." She reached into her pack for food. "What do you say?"

The more you know, the more you realise how little you know.

Her face screwed up in a frown. "That's not helpful." She bit savagely into a slice of smoked meat she'd pulled out of the backpack. "I get the impression life's going to get more difficult?"

There is that possibility. Would you have chosen to stay in Delta, knowing what is happening now?

"Nope," she finally answered. "I suppose I'm too curious. I like to have my claw on the pulse." Too many new concepts had entered her previously simple life and it would take a while for it all to sink in.

The slimy, dirty slum of Delta was her world. After listening to stories of travellers and bards, she knew the continent was far larger, and that there were lands, each with dozens of cities far larger than Delta, across the sea. This talk of other worlds was not something occurring to her in her daily activities. Now Styx calmly told her he was from one of them. Did that mean she was from another world? And Feiron?

Your ancestors would have been. But you are very different. Your unusual origins make you unique.

"How do you mean?" The tip of her tail twitched in anticipation. "There are plenty half-castes in Delta."

Not quite like you. There was another pause before Styx answered. *I promise to explain all in due course, but now is not the best time.*

Leonie updated Feiron, noting the air had steadily become stale. The trail they were on meandered to the east, hemmed in both sides by stunted trees and masses of reeds.

"I have a question," Feiron said. "The *Codex* we carry is very heavy. Do you know what it is made of?"

Essentially, the tome is made of... us, Styx replied.

"Made of hroltahgs?" Leonie blurted, translating for her friend.

"What? Like leather – from skin?" Feiron asked, puzzled.

Our bodies are very efficient at utilising energy, so it does not happen often, but now and then, we shed waste. Even for us it is considered a normal bodily function. I believe illios aren't so different? Your kind, however, does it far more often, depending on what and how much you consume and your body's ability to digest. Quite by chance one of your academics discovered its unusual properties and found ways to utilise— Styx stopped as Leonie burst out laughing. Her tail flicked back and forth; her whiskers twitched wildly as an image formed in her mind.

"What's wrong?" Feiron asked, confused when Leonie fell against him in a fit of uncontrollable laughter.

Did I say something humorous? The discovery was quite providential.

"I'm sure it was." She tried to control her chuckles.

"It's made of *what*?" Feiron exclaimed when Leonie was finally able to explain the origins of the book. "And to think, I had it inside me. I am not feeling well."

"You do look greener than grey." She slapped him on the back.

"How much longer before we get to White Cliffs?" she asked. It was mid-morning, and the day was showing signs of warming up. "What can you tell us about the road ahead?" Leonie could hear the buzz of insects, but not one bothered her, which was fortunate as the repellent had been left in Swangrove.

Lots, but it is as you see it; encroaching flora and foetid waters. We are almost through, about a league to go... and the insects are deterred by the output of my psionics. It upsets them.

She sighed with relief and relayed this information to Feiron, who was attempting to form a human hand. They continued for a short distance. Her nose wrinkled in revulsion. "Something reeks around here!"

"It wasn't me this time." Feiron tried to look innocent.

I sense decay.

"Perhaps there's a carcass nearby?" Feiron suggested.

"The breeze is coming from over there." She pointed to her left.

I have just monitored the immediate vicinity. We have company.

"Now you tell us! The Brotherhood or the Jart'lekk?"

Neither. A bear and a small pack of wolves.

"Why couldn't you detect them before?"

I only sense the minds of living entities.

"This's no time for riddles," Leonie gasped. Styx sent her clear images of several animals bounding through the wild underbrush. The wolves were skeletal, the fur tattered or missing, exposing bone and decayed flesh beneath. Bringing up the rear was a huge bear – a shambling mound of muscle, teeth and claws.

"I don't understand. You said they were dead?"

Yes, that is correct. I understand your confusion. The animals have been re-animated.

"Are they being controlled?"

Without a doubt, but not mentally, otherwise I would have detected them long before this.

"Then how?"

Power use, I suspect, from our friends of Opsyss.

"Necromancy?" she growled.

In a fashion.

"How do we stop them?"

Severing the head should immobilise them; incinerating the bodies is the surest way, or wait until the spell fades, though I suspect they will catch us long before that occurrence.

"You're full of laughs." She started jogging. Her companions kept pace.

They soon left the sparse covering of moss-covered trees. Leonie took the opportunity to look at the terrain ahead. The path rose slightly. Murky water, bordered by masses of reeds could be seen. In the far distance, she spotted tree-covered hills.

The creatures are getting closer.

"How're you holding out?" she gasped to Feiron.

"I'm fine." Feiron snatched a look behind. "But we should do something about those beasts."

"You think?" The sound of the wolves bounding through the undergrowth could be heard clearly. "Styx. How's the mind of undead work?"

It does not, but the Death Sect obviously has a way around that little problem. They will obey certain spells.

"Then they'll not be thinking as wild animals?"

I would imagine not.

"Would it be like possession?"

Uncertain.

"Hss." Leonie considered quickly. "Are there any other animals around?"

I detect nothing close other than insects, fish and eels in the water. There are firedrakes off to our right.

Feiron noticed a small island a short distance away with an old swamp-oak at its centre, with leafless branches clawing skyward. "Can we make it to that?"

The water is not too deep. Styx said after a pause.

"But the path goes that way." Leonie pointed, reluctant to enter the putrid waters.

"Yes, but if we stay on the road," the illios argued, "they'll catch up to us in no time. When we reach the island, we should at least have an advantage on the higher ground."

"Then what?" she called as Feiron turned towards the water.

"With luck we'll be able to beat them off while they flounder in the mud."

"How deep is this?" she asked, studying the swamp in front of her with distaste.

No higher than your waist.

Leonie growled. "Would the water weaken control?"

We shall find out presently.

Feiron pushed his way through the reeds, appearing far less stressed as he splashed into the water.

Leonie hesitated on the muddy bank. "I really don't like water."

It will be alright. Styx soothed, realising her surface thoughts were in turmoil about the water.

Reluctantly she stepped into the stagnant water and pushed through the reeds, testing each step carefully. "I'll stink for a week," she hissed to no one in particular as the rank water soaked into her fur. A scowl crossed her face when her paws sank in the thick mud. She followed in Feiron's wake where the scum had been broken up, though bits of it clung to her tail.

The steep, muddy shoreline of the islet proved difficult to drag themselves out of the slippery mire.

"Here they come." Feiron pointed past her shoulder.

The undead wolves burst through the reeds by the edge of the road and hit the water in a frenzy.

"Grab a branch or something," Leonie called out as she struggled out of the marsh, grabbing the nearest length of wood. "Aim for the heads and neck."

To add to the confusion, a horde of firedrakes burst from a hollow in the nearby swamp-oak. Irate at the invasion of their territory, the leathery flying lizards attacked the animals in the water. Small bursts of fire issued from their tiny mouths.

Two wolves were almost to the shoreline, unhindered by smouldering fur. Leonie hastily stepped closer as the first wolf approached the bank, yellow teeth bared. She lifted her branch high and swung, grunting with the effort. The club hit its snout, crushing the jaw. Unperturbed, it continued to clamber up the muddy slope as she staggered backwards.

Feiron had more success. The blow caved in the creature's skull. It squirmed for a moment before laying still. He yanked it free ready for the next one.

With a sound like a splitting melon, one of Leonie's wild swings struck her wolf in the side of the head. "Got you," she exclaimed in jubilation. The head lolled to one side, hanging on by sinew and rotten skin for a moment before it dropped. The jaws still gnashed at her. She kicked the head into the bog, avoiding the yellowed fangs while the body flopped around aimlessly.

As Leonie prowled back and forth waiting for the next wolf to appear, she chanced a look up at the colourful firedrakes, hoping they wouldn't attack them. Something peculiar caught her attention. "Styx. That bird is hovering." She jumped back when snapping jaws appeared through the reeds. She raised her branch for another swipe.

Styx concentrated, lightly probing the falcon. With part of his mind now on the ethereal plane, the bird's aura appeared as a small, grey luminescence. The landscape materialised in hazy ethereal shades. A spider-web of threads, controlling the undead, emanated from the bird. A thicker brown filament connected the bird to a distant mind in the south. He recognised it as Lothas's assistant, Alen.

The rollo willed a mental barrier into existence; a translucent pearl-coloured sphere enveloped the bird's aura severing the connection with Alen. The spider-web filaments faded. The brown filament writhed like a whip, retreating south with haste.

Across the ethereal plane, a scream of pain and frustration echoed through the stillness. Sensing the threat had been neutralised, Styx followed the receding tendril to the south, allowing the mental barrier to disintegrate, and sent his mind to follow the thread.

Distance on the ethereal plane was insignificant. In a matter of moments, he was looking upon the scene in the Temple of Opsyss. Below him, sprawled unconscious on the floor in a dark, round chamber lay a young robed man with a tattooed face and long dark hair. Blood dripped from his nose and ears. Several members of the order rushed into the room and began to give aid.

Styx withdrew his mind, returning to the swamp.

The falcon cartwheeled into the mire, but the other animals remained animated.

It would appear we still need to wait until the influence of the spell fully dissipates.

"Your powers of observation are amazing."

Indeed.

Two wolves struggled onto the island, slower and not as focused as the previous pair. Leonie jumped to the nearest, the swing of her branch knocking it into the path of the approaching bear. It caught the wolf in its massive paws and ripped it apart. The other wolf caught her eye. She dodged the creature's jaws, but at the expense of losing her footing. Sprawled in the mud under its foaming jaws, she reacted quickly, shoving the branch into its face. It gripped the wood, the teeth biting deeply.

Leonie used the branch to keep the jaws out of reach. It shook its head aggressively. Her arms jarred to the shoulder. With a final shake, the branch pulled free from her grasp and flew to the side.

Leonie scrambled backwards, whipping her tail from the snapping jaws. Her eyes widened in shock at what she saw next. The brown bear reared up. It stood half again as tall as her. The beast drove its claws into the back of the wolf. There was an audible crunch as the spine and ribcage of the wolf broke under the great weight. Huge claws tore the animal in two.

Rotten entrails spilled out onto Leonie's legs.

"Slistorf's balls!" For the merest second Leonie hesitated before scuttling back in fear, dodging the bear's claws. The air whistled with each swipe as it approached.

Stay back. Styx jumped in front of Leonie, splattering her with mud.

"Stay back he says?" she mumbled in a daze. "No problem."

The bear battered the rollo, but the claws made no impression on him. Styx barely moved under the barrage. The bear tried to lift him off the ground, but failed. The assault slowed, then faltered as the beast slumped forward. The massive body collapsed on top of the rollo.

The marsh became silent, except for the firedrakes. They gathered in a small buzzing cloud, and then promptly arrowed back to their nest within the ancient bole.

"What happened?" Feiron slid out from under the rotting carcass of the last wolf which had managed to leap onto him before the spell faded. "Where's Styx?"

Dazed, Leonie dragged herself to her feet and pointed to the bear's body. "Under that."

As they approached warily, the bear moved again. Leonie scrambled back over the dismembered wolves, heart racing. The fur on the back of the bear parted.

Styx emerged from the body, coagulated blood clinging to his body. *That was uncomfortable.* He was dripping in gore, but otherwise seemingly untouched. *To answer Feiron's earlier question, your Opsyss friends have reappeared.*

Leonie turned away, gagging at the stench.

All were keen to leave the area, not only because of the attack, but because swarms of insects appeared around the foetid carcasses and there was no dry ground on which to camp. After a few moments the marsh gradually came back to life. Other animals would soon be drawn in by the reek of death.

Leonie was about to step into the brackish water, the distaste evident in her scowl, when she started floating over the surface.

"What the—" She looked around in alarm.

Perhaps I can be of assistance.

She needed a few deep breaths to calm herself. "You didn't think to do this earlier?" Leonie growled.

When they located a safe, dry place to rest, Leonie vigorously brushed the scum out of her fur, fuming at Styx for letting her get this filthy, and initially decided not to talk to him.

"How did Lothas do it?" Feiron asked, oblivious to her frustration.

As Styx replied she reluctantly relayed the information, scowling as she found more muck on the back of her legs and tail.

It was his apprentice, Alen. I am unaware of the full capabilities of the Death Sect. Other than rudimentary telepathic abilities, he was able to gain control over these creatures through the worship of his god. Being closer would have provided a strong link.

"Will they be back?" he asked.

I doubt it, at least not before we get to Qelay. After that, who knows? At the moment his mind will need time to recover from the shock of the premature severing of his link.

"But I didn't think you could be aggressive." Feiron considered the bear.

It may be a technicality, but I merely blocked his mental projection. The animals were already dead, they could not be harmed further. I merely distracted the bear until the spell's effects faded.

"You call that a mere distraction? I thought he was going to rip you apart."

Remember, I am not of this world. My natural environment is potentially far more damaging than a bear.

"Well, thanks all the same." Feiron performed a slight bow.

At your service.

They soon stopped in a small copse where a small stream fed into the swamp. Keen to get clean, Leonie stepped into it and scrubbed vigorously. "I'll need to soak in a hot tub for a week to be rid of these smells," she muttered, noting how the slime had simply slid off her companions.

We are almost there. Shall we continue? Styx said after a few minutes.

The trail became a paved road hugging the banks of Lake Urmaq. Tilled fields became more prominent and by late afternoon they came to the outskirts of Qelay, entering the city shortly after. Any town folk downwind screwed up their faces at the foul odour and moved away quickly.

This was the first city she had seen other than Delta. Leonie surveyed it with curiosity. Where the streets in her town were closed in, here the streets were broad, with trees lining the sides. Spread out evenly on each side, the flat-roofed, mud-brick buildings were daubed in earthy colours. Only a few had more than two levels, the rest were low and wide. Every one of them had flowering plants hanging from boxes underneath the windows. Their fragrance wafted all along the streets, but not quite enough to mask her odour.

"The only green things growing around the houses in Delta were weeds," she muttered at the looks she was getting.

17

WHITE CLIFFS

For the last few hours Evlin sensed her prey getting closer and quivered with anticipation of the kill. In company with a couple of her guild members, she had scoured the North Road between Delta and Qelay to no avail. She was furious at her leader for not listening to her when she realised the Enemy had taken an alternative path.

Looking down at the main street from the tower of a Death Temple, Evlin couldn't keep the smugness from her voice. "Finally, the Enemy has arrived. As I've been saying." She studied the half-rrell below to formulate the best method of attack.

Her companion nodded. "I'll go and inform Gorrud. Stay here and keep watch. Inform us of any movements they make." He stood up, stretching briefly before striding to the door. "And don't remove the helmet, or all Gorrud's plans will be lost."

"You don't give me orders. Unlike you and Gorrud, I'm not an imbecile." Her breath misted the window slightly as she spoke. "Don't presume to treat me as such. Gorrud's plan is too complicated. If he'd listened to me, we'd be back in Delta by now, revelling in the master's pleasure."

"You forget to whom you speak!" Tunif spluttered.

"Your rank means as much to me as the lives of those down there. I don't forget whom I address; I simply do not care. Go and lick the boots of Gorrud, it's what you excel at."

Tunif stopped at the threshold when she spoke. At her last words, he silently pulled his dagger from its sheath and turned to her, his face contorted with anger.

Evlin continued to watch the travellers as they headed towards the large building built into the nearby hill. "And put that pig-sticker away, cretin. You never managed to hold your temper. How did you ever make it this far in the guild? Do not forget, it was *I* who discovered the Enemy. It is *I* who has our master's backing in this." She had not taken her gaze from the window, and the street beyond.

The enraged man stopped mid-stride, his mouth hanging open.

"Do you honestly think you're a match for me?" Evlin continued snidely. "Even from behind?"

"There's a fault in your helmet. You can read my thoughts."

"You truly are a cretin." Her chuckle was ominous. "Remember, we trained together; I know you for the snivelling coward you are. Run away now before I get annoyed."

"There'll be a time when I'll make you pay for those words." The only reply he received was her soft whistling. Tunif whirled, slamming the door behind him.

Even with her recent success, Evlin was still a junior member. It didn't take a genius to realise Gorrud's plans were far too elaborate. Simple plans are best. She didn't trust powershapers or illios. Unless they were dead. *I only trust the dead.*

Promotion wouldn't be far off. Her first priority was the book, then the Enemy and, Evlin allowed herself a brief smile, she would take care of Tunif once and for all. Out here, so far away from Delta, anything was possible in this line of work. No one would be the wiser, and promotion would be all the swifter.

———

Styx guided the pair through the wide streets of Qelay to White Cliffs. He explained to them the area was riddled with underground caverns.

"But why's it so popular with rollos?" Leonie asked.

Consider it as a resort for us. There are powerful forces at work here. There are areas inside the cavern system, which to some degree, have been modified to resemble our own world environment. I would advise you not to enter those areas; you will more than likely be squashed flat. The gravity on our world is much stronger. There are also some sulphur springs, which give off a gas similar to home. This may also prove harmful.

"What a charming place."

Styx led them to a strongroom on a lower level. *This is where the Seer's* Codex *will be safest. As you can see, the security is ample.*

"I've not seen a place that couldn't be broken into yet, given enough time or motive." Leonie looked critically at the safe.

"You've done all you needed to do, Leonie," Feiron said. "It's time to let go of this burden."

Reluctantly, Leonie left the book behind, but not before she witnessed it locked in the safe. They were soon taken to their adjoining suites in the west wing. The rooms were spacious and far better furnished than anything Leonie had seen before. Remarkably detailed tapestries adorned the walls. It was then that she noticed the lack of windows, realising they were completely within the hill. The maid, doing her best not to gag at the rank aroma, kept her distance and hastily ushered Leonie through her suite into the bathroom. The rooms were full of scented candles. It became clear they had anticipated this urgent requirement. She looked accusingly at Styx, who chose that moment to roll out to the hallway. *Did he scamper behind the door?*

Hroltahgs do not scamper. His parting thought made her chuckle.

"I still reckon they should set guards or something," Leonie said to Feiron when he visited later. She was squirming in a new outfit of clothes after pampering herself for an hour, luxuriating in the steaming, scented water. Three times, she called the maids to replenish the hot water.

The illios chuckled. "You? Wanting guards? Unbelievable. Need I point out we are surrounded by over a dozen hroltahgs. Do you honestly think anyone with criminal intent on their mind would be able to get close enough to be a threat?"

"If you put it like that, I suppose not. I must be tired."

"I confess all this has depleted my reserves also," Feiron sighed. "I cannot hold a shape, feeble as they may be, for more than a few minutes before losing consistency. We should both have a good, long rest. The book is now safe and in the care of those who can deal with it. Oh, and on the subject of a dozen or so telepaths around the place, I'd keep those paws in your own pockets if I were you."

She feigned shock. "I'm surprised you'd think I'd do such a thing."

"I'm merely suggesting you curb your excessive curiosity." He turned to the door, but stopped halfway. "Something I've been meaning to ask though. What's it like, Styx talking I mean?"

"It's weird; a sound right inside my head." She grasped for words. "I see images, as if I was there. It's amazing, though I suppose it's normal for those with psionic abilities."

"As much as being able to see in the dark is for you, or shapechanging for me I'd imagine." He still sounded disappointed in not being able to communicate directly. "We all have our own talents and use them to do whatever needs doing."

"Look at it this way," Leonie offered. "He detects your voice, but not your thoughts. All your secrets will be safe from prying minds. If a rollo can't read it, then who? A benefit, to my way of thinking."

"I hadn't thought of it like that." Feiron cheered up. "I'm pleased you have such a suspicious way of thinking."

"Thanks... I think."

———

After a healer checked her for physical wounds, Leonie and Feiron were ushered to an expansive dining room for breakfast. Several human guests were chatting amiably at another table on the other side of the room. They didn't bat an eye at either of them.

"What happens with the *Codex* now?" Leonie asked.

I have gone through the tome in its entirety. A number of the elders are also interested in its contents. They will no doubt have a forum on the matter in Reenat.

"Can you tell us any more about it?" Once again, Leonie kept Feiron updated on the conversation.

I would prefer to seek confirmation before I reveal anything. There appears to be information that may correlate with other tomes in our possession. I do not want you to be misinformed, besides, I am sure you can work some things out for yourself, if you think about it deeply enough.

"We understand." Leonie tried to hide her disappointment. "Don't forget, though."

We do not forget, but you have my word. I will let you know any new developments. He assured her before he left.

———

Feiron decided to attend the city library, having heard it contained a very good selection of contemporary works. The library in Delta was subjected to rigorous censorship; he was keen to find any information on wyverns.

Leonie considered how to occupy herself, when another rollo appeared at her door.

I am here at the request of Styx. I understand you have had some trauma. The brain, or mind, is very much like a muscle in its peculiar way. If not exercised, it can become weak, vulnerable and liable to attrition.

"And what will this training do for me?"

Make you more aware of telepathic contact. Enable you to protect yourself to some extent, but it will take some time.

The next few days became routine; after breakfast, Feiron headed off to the library and Leonie underwent her mind-training. It took a toll, requiring her to take regular afternoon naps. Afterwards, in the few remaining hours before dinner, Leonie explored much of the fascinating building. And, being Styx's guest, she refrained from picking up anything in her travels. Apart from the cave system, she had soon investigated every corner of White Cliffs.

———

Something was wrong.

Leonie looked around the dark room from her bed, moving as little as possible. Experience taught her to rely on instinct, and with the powerful enemies she managed to accumulate, she wasn't about to ignore it now.

Certain nothing was amiss here, she eased out from under the covers and crossed the floor. Padding silently along the deserted passage, she checked on Feiron sleeping in a large, ornate bowl in the room next to hers. Vague patterns of pastel blue and green shades swirled beneath his translucent grey skin.

The feeling of unease remained. Leonie's next thought was the *Codex*. Trying to console herself with Feiron's words about how safe everything would be with the hroltahgs' presence, she still succumbed to her nagging doubts. She had to act on her instincts before she'd be able to consider going back to sleep.

She tapped his bowl to wake him. "Feiron." The bowl gave off a musical ringing sound.

"Leonie?" he responded sluggishly. "What's up?"

"Something doesn't feel right. I'm going to check on the book. Want to come along?"

"Why are we still talking?" He flowed out of the bowl and coalesced beside her on the floor.

Within moments, they were in the corridor and moving swiftly to the lower level. Access to the manager's office was easy enough. She always had her belt-pouch with her containing the everyday items no decent thief would be caught without.

Or preferably not caught at all.

"Damn it."

"What is it?" Feiron asked from behind her.

"Styx's talking to me." Selecting the appropriate implement, she set to work.

I sensed your unease, but perceive no threat or intruder. I am curious as to what distresses you so.

"Just a bad feeling," she muttered, continuing her work. "A gut feeling. Nothing to do with the mind." The lock mechanism made a faint click. Satisfied, Leonie moved silently through the now unlocked office door, Feiron on her heels. They went straight across the sparsely furnished room. A tapestry behind the large solitary desk covered an entrance to a vault.

She pulled the tapestry aside to study the vault closely. "The door isn't guarded magically."

"Would there be any point, with all these telepaths about?"

"You keep saying that, yet I'm here. And I'm still uneasy." The main feature of the vault was an elaborate key and dial lock. She'd encountered one a few months ago and, though difficult, it hadn't stopped her then. This one should prove no hindrance either.

"At last," she whispered, cracking her knuckles. "I can finally do something."

There is no need. I have summoned the manager. It is protocol.

Leonie clamped her mouth shut, cutting off a snarl. She turned quickly at the sound of sandals scuffing on carpet coming from the passageway.

"All right, miss. I'll open it, if you don't mind." The manager's gruff voice came from the doorway. The manager, holding a flickering candle in his chubby hand and clad only in his night-robe, entered. He didn't seem surprised at their presence; more annoyed.

Leonie put on a smile to hide her disappointment and moved aside; but not too far.

The manager stomped to the vault. He manipulated the dial, blocking their view with his bulk. With a swift turn of the key and a jerk, the heavy door swung open. A search among the pile of papers, scrolls and other registration books proved fruitless.

"Damn." Leonie spat.

The book is gone.

He looked at her accusingly, then checked to see if anything else was missing.

"How did this happen without you rollos knowing?" Leonie asked Styx, ignoring the manager's look.

That truly is a puzzle. We are discussing it presently.

"We?"

Yes, I summoned others the moment things were amiss. The city authorities have also been alerted, but they are busy. There appears to be a fire in town.

Coincidence? Leonie stalked out of the office, looking for anything out of place. The feeling of unease remained, telling her whoever was responsible was still about. She updated Feiron with the conversation.

We have surveyed the minds of some horses and people in the area. Nothing has— Wait. There is movement. Two humans are crossing an alley a block away, moving swiftly. Interesting. Their thoughts are... shielded!

Leonie raced towards the lobby, Feiron at her heels. The front door was closed and locked. "Which side's this alley?" she asked.

On the south side. He sent her images.

On the first floor landing she spied an open window. She bounded up the stairs two at a time. "This will be faster."

The protectors are closing in on the culprits as we speak.

Leonie glanced outside the window. Several uniformed men ran down a lane below. There was a smoky glow above the rooftops in the distance to the west. Fire raged a few blocks away, billowing grey clouds masking the starlight. The wind blew the smoke towards them.

She slumped against the sill as unbidden memories surfaced, of smoke and embers...

"Are you okay, Leonie?" Concern tinged Feiron's voice.

She looked at him briefly before her eyes focused. "Yeah. I'm fine." Before he said anything else, she turned, dropped to the road and ran off.

The two men are fighting the protectors, Styx informed her.

Feiron stretched out of the window until he touched the ground, then slid down the wall. He changed form into Hectr immediately and followed Leonie.

They heard the ringing of metal on metal. Leonie dropped to all four paws to increase her pace. Soon she came upon three protectors surrounding the two thieves. As she approached, a protector watched her warily. Hectr joined them a moment later.

"Who would you two be?" a protector asked.

"Friends of the rollos." Leonie's manner was abrupt. She wasn't comfortable with guards, good or bad.

"Ah," he nodded. "It said you'd be here."

"That *It* has a name." She pointed to the two prisoners. "Have you searched them yet?"

"Just about to, miss," the protector replied. He turned back to the thieves. "Okay, you two. The fun's over."

More protectors appeared at the other end of the alley and made their way towards the group. With a curse, two swords clattered to the flagstones. Three protectors moved in quickly, restraining the thieves while another kicked the swords away.

"Where's the book?" Leonie asked harshly. They ignored her.

"If it's alright with you, we'll manage this," one of the protectors said brusquely.

Leonie stepped back with a growl, clenching and unclenching her claws. She had dragged the damn book all this way; she wasn't going to lose it now.

At sword point, the pair of thieves removed their cowls, revealing their faces and shaved heads. The protectors made a quick but efficient search of the thieves. "They got nothin'," one called out.

"You're sure they took something?" The first protector questioned Leonie and Hectr?

"The rollos seem to think so. You reckon they're lying?" she snapped.

The protector's head tilted slightly to the side, as if trying to hear a distant sound. The faint smile forming on his lips faded. "I guess not, miss. Maybe these two dropped it along the way." He looked back down the lane.

Leonie knew she'd have seen it. Compared to Delta, these streets were clean. A reminiscent odour tweaked her nostrils as Hectr stepped closer to her.

"Do your people normally shave their eyebrows?" he asked softly. "If you recall, I too have difficulty with hair."

"Illios? That'd explain why the rollos couldn't read their thoughts." She raised her voice. "These two are shapeshifters."

A number of protectors moved back, wary. "What d'you mean?" one asked.

"How do you know?" the first protector asked.

"They have no body hair," Feiron answered.

Suddenly the two thieves shrank. A protector stepped in and wrapped his arms tightly around one of them, to no avail. Both thieves liquefied. Too late they realised they were standing near a grille leading to the city drains. Three swords pierced their bodies with little effect. Within moments the two illios had gone.

"We've been tricked," Leonie stated.

"How so?" the lead protector asked.

"If they took the book, it'd be lying on top of that grille."

"I'll follow them," Feiron said.

"You'll do no such thing." She looked at Hectr. "They were only decoys. Let's get back. Something isn't right here."

18

THE HEAVY CAVERNS

"So, where's that leave us?" Leonie and Hectr jogged back to White Cliffs, and the vault. Half the household seemed to be awake; humans and rollos were searching everywhere.

The caverns.

"I thought you said only rollos can go in there," Leonie said.

Not completely true. We have grav-harnesses, suitable for use by others, Styx told her. *They assist in negating the heavy gravity effects within the caverns.*

"Okay then. Where are these harnesses?" An image bloomed in her mind showing several passages and stairs she remembered passing by earlier during her explorations. "Great, thanks."

They swiftly made their way down the passageway to the stairs. The temperature dropped slightly while they descended. About forty feet down, there was another passage; this one proved to be largely naturally formed, with a few areas hewn out of the rock to make it wider. At the base of the stairs was a junction of three tunnels. The door leading to the storeroom was set into an alcove opposite the stairs. It showed evidence of being tampered with.

Leonie examined the floor at the intersection. Although most

of it was bare rock, there were areas of dust and loose dirt, difficult to see among the ruts and grooves the rollos left over the
years. Eventually she spotted scuff marks and what she thought
might be partial boot-prints. "I can see three, maybe four sets of
tracks here."

Engravings and sigils on the wall warned of the beginning of
spell effects. This part of the passage was the edge of normal
gravity; past the sigils, gravity increased to over three times the
norm. Ducking into the storeroom, she found three harnesses
scattered on the floor.

There are normally eight.

Leonie grabbed one, examining it curiously. From the rear of
the belt, pliable metal bands formed a criss-cross, designed to go
over the shoulders to connect at the front where there was a
small dial alongside a slot for a shard of crystal, glowing with
the aura. She adjusted and secured it around her waist. Feiron
conformed his shape to fit and donned a harness as well.

They then moved back into the tunnel, following the tracks.
"I'm hoping they'll not be expecting discovery, and may be over-
confident. Can you trust everyone working here?"

Of course. You suspect inside help?

"Maybe, or you've been spied on for a while without
knowing."

We find both postulations doubtful.

"As doubtful as thieves getting in here and stealing the book
from under your noses?"

We do not have nos—

"A figure of speech. How long before you get here?"

Presently.

Leonie felt rumbling as half a dozen rollos, each an almost
perfect sphere, came around the corner. Her ears picked up a
ringing sound. She stopped outside the boundaries of the spell
area to watch.

Three rollos moved ahead, taking another route into the
caverns. Those remaining unfolded in precise timing, and now
resembled slightly flattened cones with short arms and legs.

Leonie smiled, seeing Feiron watching their movements with interest.

Allow me to introduce Riff and Dwer.

"Pleased to meet you," she said, though she had no idea who was who.

I am Riff.

I am Dwer.

She looked blankly at the three of them and threw her paws up.

Riff is on your right, Dwer on your left. It is curious there are no mental emanations in the vicinity other than your own. We can only sense Feiron's physical presence.

"So that means either more illios are about, they've escaped, or the rock is in your way?"

Crystals affect our sending somewhat, but rock is only a minor hindrance. There is nowhere for them to run. We find this behaviour most peculiar.

Stepping away, she moved down one of the tunnels, keeping an eye on the tracks. As soon as she passed the threshold, she staggered under the increased weight.

You must turn the dial.

Leonie turned the dial on the front where the two bands crossed. The effect was immediate as the weight lifted off. After a brief play with the control, Leonie discovered she could also be totally weightless.

It should be noted there is a finite amount of power in each crystal. The higher the workload, the quicker the power is drained.

"I'm in difficulty," Feiron gasped, forcing the words out.

Leonie turned. The rollos stopped with her. Just inside the boundary, Feiron lay looking like a pool of grey syrup.

"There are benefits with a skeletal system it seems," he wheezed. "My harness is not working for me. I can't... go on."

It would appear illios are not suitable for its use. Interesting. It may have something to do with the physical aspects of their body.

"Can you make it back?" She jumped from the boulder to be closer to him to help.

Feiron managed to ooze back to the safe section of the passage. "Keep going. I'll be fine."

"You sure?"

"Yes. Go on, but be careful," he said, slowly dribbling along the passage.

Leonie watched him for a moment before turning back to the task. "I guess that rules out more illios."

True, but the question still remains.

Riff and Dwer moved along the passage at a faster rate while Styx remained close to Leonie. She felt the trembling in the ground fade as well as the strange ringing in her ears. It was not really a sound, more of a subsonic vibration.

The ringing you are sensing is our way of seeing. You are very perceptive to hear it, but it is also likely a combination of several hroltahgs in close proximity in a confined space.

Leonie nodded. The tunnel descended a short way. A smooth rut exactly the size of a rollo had been worn down the centre. Past the base of the slope the tunnel branched. Down here, the floor was covered in sand and rock dust. Human footprints led off in the same direction.

Without a mental signature, the only way we can perceive them is with our soundings.

Following the markings, she jogged along the tunnel to the left, the dark interior being no problem for her night vision. Again, the tunnel branched. "Where do these lead?" The sand gradually dwindled, leaving bare rock.

Ahead is the Rainbow Cavern. The one to the right is the Hall of Spears.

"Do any of the caverns lead anywhere in particular? Is there a path to the outside?" Leonie bent down to examine the floor for any signs of the thieves, noting a few scuff marks heading to the left.

There are no exits to the outside at all, but one can access other, deeper systems. It is not logical they go this way if there is no escape but, we find a lot of what your kind does illogical.

"So, it's all a big dead-end, and the only way out is behind us?"

Correct.

"Maybe they are circling behind us. They seem to like sending us on wild goose chases."

It would accomplish little. The household is awake and aware. They cannot escape that way either.

The tunnel they followed gradually ascended. As they neared the crest, a dim glow appeared ahead. Riff and Dwer awaited them. Leonie's gaze was drawn to the ceiling as she stepped through a large archway. Among the stalactites were faint light sources. It was so enchanting—

Stop!

A hidden force stopped Leonie mid-stride, snapping her head down. In front of her was a sharp drop of about fifty-foot to a rock-strewn shelf in a cliff. She stepped back quickly. "Thanks." Her eyes returned to the stunning sight overhead.

The Rainbow Cavern. Styx informed her. *What you can see is moonlight filtering down the length of the crystal structures. The moons' movement causes the light to refract, forming the many colours, hence the name.*

"It's lovely. I bet it looks even more spectacular by day." Dragging her gaze away, even with squinting, she barely made out the far end of the enormous space. Far below, the floor was hidden in a swirl of yellowish clouds.

This is the longest cave. It has a large fissure across its centre that drops about three hundred feet in some places.

Leonie looked at the cliff face beneath her, trying to find the best way down. Partially illuminated by the glow from above, sections of the level below seemed to be boiling in a yellow mist. It was an eerie, yet beautiful sight. "I'm going to have to get down there to look for footprints or something." She turned as she heard the now familiar rumble of a fast approaching rollo.

Since we are entering this part of the system, you will require a face-mask for the toxic gases. I have taken the liberty of sending for one. It should mould around your face sufficiently, despite the hair.

A rollo soon arrived and handed her a leathery contraption roughly in the shape of a face; it had a bulbous front and a long, thin crystalline plate for the eyes. It felt horrible and awkward to wear, but once she managed to tuck in her whiskers, she was ready to go.

One more thing, you must learn to purge the mask. If you detect any gas, you must tighten the straps, and then clear the mask with your remaining breath. He sent mental imagery of how to purge; covering the filter – the bulbous front – with her palm and blowing hard. *Excess air is forced out the sides, taking any contaminants with it. If you have difficulty, I will remove you from harm immediately.*

"I guess there's only one way to test it." She moved over to the edge after a practise purge. "I'll climb down to that ledge. The ledge is too narrow to risk jumping." Leonie lowered herself over the edge and made her way down to the ledge. "So far so good," she muttered. Struggling to see through the mask, she concentrated on her footing, not wanting to risk a hundred-foot fall. She continued her descent to the next level.

The two young rollos had already disappeared below.

19

MELEE IN YELLOW MIST

TAKING TENTATIVE STEPS, LEONIE ENTERED THE YELLOW MIST. THERE was a moment when she detected a foul odour. She held her breath and climbed back up a few feet to clearer air. She then tightened the straps of the mask and purged before taking a tentative breath.

"You can *see* through this?" She peered into the yellowish cloud below.

In a fashion.

"Can Riff and Dwer check out the nooks and crannies, even the ceiling."

Riff is making his way to the end of the cavern. Dwer will climb to the roof on the left. To get a better picture of the overall terrain, they will compare soundings as they go.

Leonie nodded, concentrating on her movement.

Why not float down?

With a bit of experimentation, Leonie was able to adjust the harness's setting to slow her descent. All around her yellow clouds slowly billowed. At the bottom, she changed the settings to normal.

Riff and Dwer have detected movement. In her mind, she saw strange images in multiple shades of grey and black, initially finding it perplexing. With guidance from Styx, and concentration, it soon made sense. Closing her eyes made it easier, but now and then, more out of reflex than a real need, she opened them.

A pattern soon emerged as she continued, the lighter the shade, the closer the obstacle. Conversely, the darker it was, the further away. With that in mind, the terrain about her came into perspective. As she turned her head, Styx fine-tuned the image to match.

"This is incredible. Is this what it looks like to you?" she whispered.

Similar. What you are visualising is your brain's interpretation of the signal. I can only work with what is already inside your head.

"Good luck with that." Leonie moved on as his thoughts entered her mind.

Styx rolled along beside her. *A faint aura follows the left wall. Can you sense it?*

"Nope. It must be very weak." Leonie squinted, but saw nothing through the cloudy gas. "That's all I need. A power-shaper." She moved to the left, slowly. "That'd explain how they can see in the dark; he must've cast a spell."

In front of Leonie was a small depression. It took her a few moments to realise it was full of water and was roughly circular. Choosing to go to the left, she carefully moved around the columns and stalagmites. A faint noise reached her. A boot scraping on ground?

There. A different image formed in her mind; the path ahead descended in a series of natural steps. Five figures moved halfway along the floor on the other side of the pool.

Leonie continued confidently. Shortly, a wall loomed in front of her. It was cold and damp; rippled but smooth to touch.

From centuries of limestone deposits, Styx explained.

There was a small path between the pool and the wall. "Can you tell if they have the book?" Leonie whispered, placing her hand lightly on the wall and proceeding with caution.

There is not enough detail to be sure. One of them appears to be injured.

"That'll slow them down a bit." Leonie kept on moving, concentrating on the shifting shades in front of her. She soon came to the area where the floor angled downwards. Mindful of the slope, she moved slowly.

She jumped in fright when an ear-piercing scream split the silence, rapidly fading to nothing.

There are now four of them. The injured individual has fallen into the chasm.

"What are the others doing?"

They seem to be unconcerned and are making their way across the fissure one at a time.

"If they're not panicking, he hasn't got the book. I wonder why he fell. Wouldn't his harness support him?"

Unknown.

The mist diminished slightly, leaving a patch of clear air around her. They were now at the top of the steps. The area below was devoid of obstacles, so she took advantage of the situation and rapidly jumped down each level. Turning the dial to the lightest setting, she barely heard herself land. Within moments she reached the bottom, but waited for Styx. The mist gathered around her again.

They are moving across the edge of the chasm by way of a narrow ledge.

To stop her heart racing, Leonie concentrated. With four of them, any lapse would be costly. As she approached, she heard a muffled grunt. "I can hear them," she whispered, moving silently across the floor. So far, she'd had to contend with the Woorin Brotherhood and, indirectly, those sick fanatics from the Death Sect. She idly wondered who this bunch was.

One has successfully crossed over, one is in transit, two are still on this side. Riff confirms there is a new exit at the end of the recess, created by the powershaper. There is small tunnel showing a residual aura of power.

"Hmm." The news confirmed Leonie's suspicion a power-shaper was present. "Is it possible to send a message to Feiron?"

Yes. I am relaying information to other staff.

"Good. See if he can locate the exit outside and keep an eye on it."

Your illios friend has no eyes, but I understand your meaning. Riff will block this side.

"Give him my thanks."

You just did. He can detect your thoughts as well as I.

Leonie heard soft muttering from one of the two still waiting to cross. With eyes open now since she was so close, she made out dim figures as the mist thinned and swirled.

They kept no watch, apparently confident of not being discovered or pursued. They were also wearing masks and strange looking helmets, but it was the dark grey leather armour that alarmed her.

"What are Jart'lekk doing here?" Leonie muttered to herself, considering her next move as she crept closer. "Can you see those helmets they're wearing?"

Not clearly. I will get closer.

Leonie briefly saw Styx roll towards the intruders, almost underneath their feet.

Intriguing. I can only suggest it somehow blocks our psionics. There are certain rudimentary exercises that can accomplish this, but never before has a device been able to do it. This is a serious matter.

"You want one?"

We will retrieve the one from their fallen companion to examine. Our preference is to get them all, but the book has priority, even over this.

Leonie was almost upon them. Three paces separated them when a clear patch suddenly developed, exposing them all. She froze. The two leather-clad assassins watched as their comrade climbed across the chasm and up to the other side.

The figure on the far side turned. He called out and pointed. His voice was muffled, but his comrades understood the warning. With startling swiftness, they both spun with short swords released from their scabbards.

Crap! Leonie barely managed to dodge the first swing as she dived to the side, back into the clouds. She landed, turning her momentum into a roll. The metallic clang of the blade rang out as it struck the ground inches away.

She leapt up and darted to her right, away from the chasm.

Stop. There is a stalagmite in front of you. Move left a pace.

In the sudden melee, she had forgotten about the input from Styx. It was completely against her nature, but the only way she'd be able to navigate in this mist was to close her eyes and concentrate. She slid behind the stalagmite and composed herself. Images of the two intruders came; they were behind her, closer to the chasm. They were both stationary.

Leonie reached down, picked up a pebble and tossed it to her left. When they shifted to face the threat, she stepped with utmost care to the right, making her way towards the closer one.

The two on the other side are making their way to the exit. They must not escape.

Leonie couldn't afford a prolonged fight with these two. She had to assume the book was with the others and these two would now try to stop her pursuit. If she got close enough, she might be able to remove their masks. That would certainly distract them and allow her to move on. She'd deal with them if the need arose on her return; right now she had more important things to do.

Time seemed to stand still as she carefully closed the distance. She was now within arm's reach of one of them. She wouldn't be able to undo the mask straps, but a hard-enough swipe should dislodge it enough to put them out of the immediate picture. Raising her paw above her head, claws out, she swung, striking as the target turned, landing a glancing blow to the head.

The reaction was almost instantaneous. His sword came up in an arc, grazing Leonie's forearm as she whipped her arm back, but the sword-wielder's racking cough brought him to his knees.

Hearing the attack, the other intruder rapidly closed the distance. Leonie knew there was nothing behind her for about ten feet. She twisted the harness dial and leapt backwards with a somersault, landing next to a ribbed column of limestone.

The remaining leather-clad thief protected his companion while he adjusted his mask. However enough gas had entered to do damage; he remained on his knees coughing almost continuously.

Leonie realised their weakness. "Are they arrogant or stupid?" she said to herself. The assassins hadn't considered all the options the harness allowed, only considering attacks from ground level.

Gauging the distance as accurately as possible, and assuring herself she wasn't going to crash into any of the spikes above, she jumped at them, turning her harness to the maximum setting briefly. With claws extended, she sailed through the air in a graceful curve, emerging above the mist momentarily before descending upon the unwitting pair.

"Sometimes, I amaze myself." With the advantage of surprise, she kicked at each one, again slashing at the masks. The impact sent both reeling backwards as a sword whistled past her face.

Both assassins went down coughing and gagging, crawling further away from the chasm.

Leonie had to admire their dedication, for they continued to swing the swords about until the effects of the fumes took their toll. They dropped the swords, unable to re-adjust the masks one-handed. While they were doing this, Leonie tiptoed in, grabbed their weapons and tossed them into the fissure. "Let's see them use blowpipes now." She chuckled to herself.

You joke?

"I always try." Remembering they might have throwing daggers, she considered twisting their dials off. Her thoughts were interrupted.

Riff has been discovered.

"Can he be hurt?" she asked as she quickly moved away from the pair of incapacitated intruders. "That's two I won't have to worry about," she muttered.

Not easily, but if there is a powershaper, who knows what will transpire.

"Guide me." With his help, she pictured the chasm clearly in front of her. Again, gauging the distance, she ran towards it. She leapt off the edge and landed in a run on the other side.

Dwer confirms the book is not with the body below. There was a loud thump as Styx landed beside her. *Other than a series of columns in the centre, there are about forty paces of clear ground in front of us.*

"I see them. Now that stealth isn't an issue we can move quicker." Leonie adjusted her dial back to normal. After a few strides, she realised its charge was waning. "I'm starting to feel heavier." There was a brief pause.

I agree. Your harness's aura has lessened. Perhaps your acrobatics were not part of the designer's intent.

"You don't say." She didn't have to think too hard on the ramifications of this. If too much power were lost, she'd be useless in defending herself, leaving little doubt regarding the outcome of another encounter with any disgruntled assassins.

Leonie and Styx quickly covered the distance to the far side. In front of them lay the steep slope leading to the new tunnel. Ascending in relative silence, they left the cloud cover. The way ahead was completely visible. From out of the shadows of the rift to her left she spied sudden movement.

20

WRATH REDISCOVERED

THERE IS AN AMBUSH AHEAD.

"Watching the sorcerer's back, no doubt." Leonie noticed the crossbow in the intruder's hands. "How tough did you say your skin is?" She was totally exposed in this position.

Very.

"Do you think—"

Certainly. Styx anticipated her question, manoeuvring himself between the archer and Leonie.

"Thanks."

At your service.

They continued climbing, keeping an eye on the archer. Moments later there was a dull twang. Styx swiftly adjusted his position, deflecting the bolt. The archer cursed as he reloaded.

"I bet he wasn't expecting that," she purred.

You make light of the strangest situations.

"Survival instinct, otherwise I'd go mad." Leonie tried to push the archer from her thoughts, concentrating on the climb and retrieving the book.

Riff is in trouble!

The shock and power in his thoughts startled Leonie, causing her to slip momentarily. "What? How?" Now she had a headache.

This powershaper has a device. It does not require a mental signal to activate it. He jumped again as another bolt came their way.

"What's it doing."

Freezing him.

"That's bad, isn't it?"

Yes, very. It is about the only way we can be injured.

They were almost at the beginning of the fissure now. The slope levelled out slightly, allowing Leonie a direct view. About twenty paces away she saw a stooped figure pointing something at the small, round shape in front of him. A bright aura emanated from the device.

And there was no time for her to get there.

"Two can play at that game." Confident Styx had her back, she braced herself on the narrow ledge and concentrated, attempting to draw in power. Slowing her breathing, Leonie shut out all interference to focus on the ring. She released the power. A ball of energy, larger than any she had previously drawn, covered the distance quickly.

The powershaper was engrossed in his own affairs; unaware of anything else. The fireball burst on impact with the square of his back. In the confined space, the released energy propelled the man into the wall before he crumpled to the ground. Stone and crystal fragments rained down. He lay there unmoving while flames spread across his robes.

The aura dissipated as the rod fell to the ground. Riff lay unmoving.

Beware; the archer approaches.

"How's Riff now?" Leonie gasped as she felt her weight increase dramatically, realising the spell all but depleted the harness. The extra power to create the larger fireball had come from her surrounds, including the energised crystal. She turned her head to watch the last intruder make his way across the slope towards her, undeterred by the rollo's presence. It took great effort to reach for the dial, hoping there was some residual energy. If there was, it wouldn't last long.

Riff cannot signal, though I sense he is still alive. Relief flooded from him.

The archer closed the distance drawing his short sword.

Leonie turned her dial to maximum. Nothing happened. She strained to dodge the swinging blade. Styx deflected the blade by jumping into its path.

Drawing a dagger, the assassin lunged again, thrusting both weapons at his target simultaneously, but from different directions. Again, Styx jumped. The dagger blade was easily blocked, but the sword passed Styx's small form. The sword struck the wall above Leonie's face. Chips of limestone glanced off her mask.

The man prepared for another attack.

"Styx?" she gasped, barely able to move.

His helmet prevents me from reading his thoughts or controlling his actions, and I am forbidden to injure.

Both were in awkward positions; hanging onto the rocky slope to stop from sliding into the deadly mist below, but the assassin still had a functioning harness.

Styx unfolded himself and continued to move between them as a shield, managing to deflect the jabs and thrusts with his claws.

The fighter grunted something inarticulate. He sheathed his weapons, moved to the edge and climbed the last few feet of the cliff. Moments later, he reappeared above them, this time holding the wand. He aimed it at Leonie.

Immediately, coldness hit her in the shoulder, spreading rapidly to her neck, head and chest. Breathing became difficult. She tried to move, but her limbs responded like dead wood. Numbness overcame her rapidly. *So cold.* She gasped for air; her mask now becoming a hindrance. Raising her paw to remove it was too hard.

The wand attack stopped. With a determined effort that left her panting, Leonie managed to turn her head slightly.

Styx had leapt up to intervene and now took the brunt of the attack. The wand now aimed towards him; a bright aura lanced out, surrounding him as he strove to push forward. In self-preservation, Styx coiled back into his ball shape.

Leonie was horrified as the assassin continued to freeze the rollo. Inwardly she raged; her mind seethed at this cowardly act. She tried to yell, but only a pathetic growl escaped her lips, muffled by the face-mask. *Fight back,* she fumed. Her fingers clenched. Mobility was gradually returning. She was almost overcome with relief when she noticed the aura stop. Battling numbness and the heavier gravity, she tried desperately to flex her arms to circulate some blood.

The assassin bent down and pushed Styx towards the cliff. It was a tremendous effort considering the sheer weight, only the hroltahg's spherical shape making it possible. As if in slow motion, Styx rolled over the edge, landed on the ledge she was on before rolling off. Moments later, the cavern resounded to a loud thud.

"No!" she grunted. In disbelief, Leonie stared down at the murky, yellowish clouds.

A few pebbles clattered as the assassin slid down to the ledge Leonie was on. They turned to face each other. Through his mask, the crinkling around his eyes indicated he was smiling. He slowly removed his mask and tossed it into the yellow clouds below. He then unsheathed his dagger and stepped up to Leonie, running the flat of it up and down her back.

"Ain't losing a bitch? Did you like the part where I killed your *invincible* friend? I could cut your head off and you'd be unable to do anything about it," he whispered in her ear. The point pricked her skin as he traced a line down her arm from her shoulder. "Or even better, I could slice you open and watch you bleed to death," he continued. "That'd be fun, don't you think? But, I ain't got time to play much."

She stiffened with a groan, feeling the blade penetrate below her ribs. Pain raced up her side. Darkness beckoned.

"I bet that hurt. Lucky I didn't do much damage. You're

gonna die good and slow." He slowly twisted the blade before pulling the blade free. "A shame you ain't got no movement. I heard what you did back in Delta, I reckoned you'd fight better. Coulda been fun." He turned her around, wiping the blade on her fur. "You must think you're pretty special to take on all of us. But no one defeats the Jart'lekk"

Leonie glared at him. "There's one... thing you're forgetting." Her wheeze was barely audible.

"And what's that, kitten?" He moved right up to her confidently to listen, grabbed her ear and snapped her head back, exposing her neck.

If she was about to die, she wasn't going alone. "If the Jart'lekk... are so good," she gasped. She concentrated on her pain, and her loss. *He killed Styx and Riff!* "Why am I the one... always walking away?"

Putting all her pent-up wrath into one last-ditch effort, her sharp claws dug deeply into soft flesh as she clutched his groin. She squeezed and ripped.

He howled, doubling over, slashing at her in the process.

Leonie was too slow. The dagger cut deep, slicing her neck and shoulder. Her legs collapsed. As she crumpled, her paw came free; ripped flesh hanging from her claws. She toppled down the cliff like a stone, disappearing into the yellow mist like Styx did moments earlier.

Dropping his dagger, the assassin clenched the ruins of his groin. Blood freely seeped through his shredded trousers. He slumped against the cliff, agony etched on his face. By slow, painful increments, he clambered up the slope, crawling to where his fallen comrade lay smouldering. He grabbed the book as he contemplated the escape route. The frozen hroltahg remained tightly wedged in the exit.

Placing the book on the ground, the assassin spent several desperate moments working his sword through a small gap to lever the creature out of the way. With urgent desperation, he cleared enough room to get his hands around it. Soon, the obstruction rolled back enough for him to crawl past.

The assassin grabbed the book and squirmed into the narrow exit, lying down and pushing the book in front of him. With his body inside the fissure, he barely had enough room to move. His boots found purchase against the frozen rollo and he forced himself further into the crevice. He felt the rollo shift with his kick, but there was little he could do about that. Slowly and with much grunting, he painfully wormed his way up the smooth tunnel to freedom, leaving a trail of blood in his wake.

———

Leonie landed on her paws more by instinct than planning, immediately collapsing in a furry ball of agony a short distance from the base of the cliff; the three-gravities pulled incessantly at her body. Blood seeped out of the deep cuts as well as all those she received on the way down. Intense pain radiated from her ribs.

Her face-mask had dislodged and try as she might, there seemed to be nothing to stop the fumes from seeping in. She struggled to move her paw pinned beneath her before clutching her wound to staunch the blood flow. Now and then spasms of uncontrollable coughing wracked her body as the fumes did their work.

Fading in and out of consciousness, Leonie decided being numb was a good thing. There was no input from Styx. Even in this condition, she missed his banter.

"Well, well. Look what we have here – the Enemy," a female voice rasped. "I told you I heard coughing." Evlin broke out into a coughing fit herself. "She really isn't much to look at, is she?"

"Finish her off so we can get out of here." Tunif looked around warily. "The rollos will be swarming around here soon."

"And what're they going to do?" Evlin kicked the injured half-rrell in the already bloodied ribs. "Nothing. They won't help her." She lashed out with her boot again. "And they won't be hurting us. I think I'll get myself a souvenir first." She dropped to her knees and drew her long, thin dagger. With a deft cut, she had a good length of tail in her hands.

Leonie shrieked in agony.

"Yep, this'll do fine." The assassin watched the blood pool on the sandy floor with mild interest. "Who woulda thought so much blood would come from a tail."

"Can you hear that?" Tunif peered into the yellowish mist.

"I told you before, you're nothing but a coward." Evlin admired Leonie's tail in her hands, running her fingers along the fine fur. "Go then. I'll have my fun and complete this mission once and for all. If you ask nicely, I might even share the gory details."

"No." Tunif licked his lips, eyes searching the mist. "I'll wait."

Evlin cackled. "You can watch and learn then." She looped the tail through her belt and then rolled the body over onto its back. "Damn. I think she's died on me." She moved closer to check Leonie's breathing. "Not as tough as I thought. And I was anticipating all the fun." She reached to remove the Enemy's mask "What do you really look like?"

Suddenly Evlin fell forward heavily. A furry arm slowly snaked around her neck, pulling her closer.

"Time... to die," Leonie croaked faintly. The crystal she'd just removed from the assassin's harness fell from her paw. Claws sank into Evlin's windpipe, gripping tightly. She gargled blood; choking as it filled her mask. Struggling feebly, darkness descended swiftly.

Watching through the swirling gas for the approaching rollo, it took a few moments before Tunif noticed Evlin's fall. He swore at her clumsiness, then saw the pooling blood. He whipped out his dagger and stepped around Evlin's body to cut the half-rrell's throat.

Wary of any more tricks, he stepped on both the arms of the rrell thief.

"You failed, Evlin, but her head will give me much pleasure, and all the reward," he gloated. "Now it is I who will succeed in avenging our slain brothers in Delta."

Tunif looked up as a rollo appeared through the mist. He had never seen one with spikes before. The spikes, the same colour as the rollo, were about a hand-width long. They looked... lethal. "Stop there, little monster," he called nervously. "Come any closer and I'll show you the true wrath of the Jart'lekk." Tunif brandished his dagger, watching warily for movement.

Surprisingly, the rollo stopped.

Tunif risked glancing down at the thief. It would only take a second to cut her throat. Determined to fulfil his duty, he bent down to complete his task. Poised with dagger against the thief's well-muscled neck, his hand froze. He looked around anxiously hearing more faint rumbling.

With regards to wrath, let me show you mine.

An invisible force flung the assassin backwards like a rag doll, striking the cliff face.

Dazed, Tunif picked himself off the ground and adjusted his mask. "Is that the best you can do?" he panted nervously, searching for his blade.

It will suffice.

"For what?" The clatter of pebbles made him look up.

The impact of Riff's falling body crushed him, shattering his bones and turning the rest of his body to pulp.

For that.

21

MEMORIES UNDONE

WHEN FEIRON RECEIVED THE MESSAGE ABOUT THE RECENTLY discovered exit, one of the human staff volunteered to lead him to the area. Given the cavern layout, they quickly found the new tunnel opening on the north bank of a grassy knoll behind a few dense, thorny bushes.

Feiron and his guide sat down to wait. He looked at the view with interest, not having seen this part of Qelay before. The hill overlooked a small but picturesque lake, a mill with a water-wheel nestling among a copse of trees below.

His guide suddenly shook him.

"Sir, I regret to say, your friend has fallen... Styx and Riff were also attacked."

Feiron completely missed the shock on the young man's face when the last words were uttered. The moment he heard Leonie was in trouble he oozed into the dark hole to render any possible assistance.

"The protectors have been summoned," the guide called.

Encountering the assassin in the tunnel was a complete surprise, but Feiron was in a better position to react. With the news of the slaying of his best friend, he didn't hesitate. His method of attack was simply to smother. There was no room to do anything else. Feiron oozed around him, his viscous body filling all the air pockets, then he began constricting. He felt the assassin thrashing within the confined space.

Feiron shuddered the moment he felt the freezing energy. It was a matter of who lasted the longest; his endurance to the effects of the cold, against the lack of oxygen for the attacker. Feiron hoped the assassin's frenzied struggles would tire before too much of his endoplasm froze. Regardless of the outcome, at least the assassin's suffocation would in a small way pay for Leonie's death.

———

Riff rolled to a stop a few feet away from the bloody mess.

Styx concentrated, plying all his sensors to study Riff's form until assured his companion would recover. The tough skin was frozen solid, but deep within he sensed the life-aura strongly. He then waddled to Leonie's crumpled form partially covered by Evlin's body. With his telekinesis, he lifted the female assassin and tossed it aside.

Leonie...... Leonie.

Styx?

She swiftly rose, floating clear of the noxious fumes. Styx then gently propelled her forwards. *Stay with me. I will get you to safety.* He summoned a healer to meet them in her room and tend Leonie's wounds.

Are you dead? Am I dead?

Foolish woman. You know I cannot converse with the dead.

Somehow, she understood something was wrong. His mental contact had always seemed bright. She always thought it a shade of blue – like a cloudless, spring sky – but now it was darker, as if an autumn storm was pending.

What's... happened to you? What've you done? Leonie's thoughts drifted.

Too little, too late it would seem. I... caused a death.

Oh. An accident?

There was a pause. *No.*

Styx erected a mental barrier to ward off any outbursts from his peers, not wholly prepared to answer the questions and accusations that would surely be directed at him.

Leonie's body sluggishly floated towards the cavern's main entrance. Recovering from his recent freezing, Styx didn't push his telekinetic ability too hard. He moved along underneath her; staying close. There was an anxious moment when he leapt the chasm stretching across his path. He didn't make the entire distance, crashing into the opposite cliff face. He dug his claws into the rock, barely managing to regain control before Leonie fell back into the poisonous vapour. As he climbed out, her body flopped like the rag dolls the young human females played with in Reenat.

With only the steps to go, they were both soon above the cloud layer. Styx deftly moved her body along the labyrinthine passages, then up to her room. Two rollos followed him the moment he returned to the main living area. He could understand their disquiet; hroltahgs had never been directly involved with a death. They were fearful he had gone rogue.

The chambermaid squealed when the injured half-rrell floated into the room. Styx sent her to gather hot water and cloths to clean Leonie's wounds while they waited for the healer.

Are you still with me? Styx nudged Leonie's mind gently.

Uh-huh.

Your death was imminent. The only thing left for me to do was to intervene… physically.

If you saved my life, what's wrong with me?

You are in a coma. Your body has gone into shock due to the immense pain and the loss of blood. I find this the most unfortunate aspect about non-telepaths; you think because the body does not respond, everything else will not. It is the other way around; under certain circumstances your mind can survive without your body, but your body cannot survive without your mind.

If you say so. How are you, though?

I will recover.

I mean after what you did? I thought you said it was against your cultural beliefs.

Correct.

Then why? Not that I'm complaining. Why was saving me so important?

The elders recently furnished me with information from several other sources of prophecy. Singly, this information would mean little, but taken in unison, led them to conclude you may play an important part in our future.

Me?

Yes.

And you believe it?

I considered it worthy of my attention. If we are wrong, then I am the only one who may suffer, but, if we are right, you will potentially be the one to save us all.

Sure.

You find it difficult to understand.

Of course. I think your elders are nuts. And what's this stuff about saving you all? In case you didn't notice, I got my arse kicked. She cut off my tail!

The method of how you will save us, like most events in prophecy, is unclear.

Let me ask the question in a different way. From what will you need to be saved?

Extinction. Our race has not been able to reproduce offspring for the last couple of centuries – I am one of the last. We need to be returned to our own environment to do this. If this does not happen, we will eventually die out. The longer we are away from our true home, the harder it will become. White Cliffs was an attempt to simulate our world; to see if it would revive our ability to reproduce. It has failed. Styx paused.

I'm not sure I like the sound of me helping your race reproduce.

There was a knock at the door.

Here is the healer. We will converse more on this another time.

————

True to his word, the guide had summoned help, but with the illios wedged in the tunnel, there was little anyone could do. As soon as possible they extricated his unconscious and ice-cold form, frozen in the shape of the tunnel section they found him, and moved him to his heated room where a large bathtub had been installed.

Hoping a warm and humid environment would be beneficial, the healer monitored his condition. It was the best that he could do since he had little experience with illios. With the insistence of the rollos, he even poured a fresh brew of warm tea twice a day into the tub. "What a waste of good Redleaf!" he muttered.

Feiron thawed out slowly, revealing the body of one of the assassins. Once examined, the assassin was cremated like the others had been several days earlier. Styx regularly visited in the shapechanger's rooms to see how he fared.

Two days later, Feiron had recovered sufficiently to communicate. He was shocked by the lethal looking spikes, and his new colouring.

By using chalk and slate, Styx updated him on Leonie's condition. In turn, Feiron slowly recounted his encounter with the assassin. Though the use of the wand had caused inconvenience to the shapechanger, it turned out his pain threshold was much higher than the assassin's.

"I have to admit while I can admire the skeletal form of the other races, we illios also have advantages. Withstanding extreme cold temperatures is one of them. It was certainly better than melting."

The chalk danced across the dark slate. 'The assassin suffocated.'

"Good. That was my intent." Feiron nodded in satisfaction.

'I confess to venting anger myself recently. It has left me... confused.'

"And you convinced us you were all pacifists."

'For the last ten thousand years, it was so. We thought we had eradicated violence from our race. We have always regarded it a base emotion, something for beasts and less-developed races. Too bad we had not erased arrogance as well.'

"I didn't think you could eradicate either of them."

The previous writing disappeared from the board before being replaced. 'Then it seems you are far wiser than all of us.'

"If that's what you really think, perhaps I am."

'I sense frustration?'

"Stop blaming yourself. If you are a moral, sentient race, then the most appropriate thing to do, the right thing to do, is protect those that are—"

'Weaker?'

"I was going to say *unable* to defend themselves," Feiron finished.

'I see.'

"Do you? No matter what the cost?"

'This is acceptable to me, now. This is logical, otherwise given enough time, only the most violent race would dominate, and all other would be subjugated by that violence; controlled by it.'

"And self-defence is *not* violence or aggression."

'I find solace with your reasoning.'

"Will your peers see it that way? What do they think?"

'That is their decision to make. Suspecting I am rogue, they have erected barriers to block me from their thoughts, so I am unaware of their views; and they mine...' Reaching the bottom of the slate, he erased his previous words and continued.

'I recall, when dealing with the assassins, I was overwhelmed by the injuries to Riff and Leonie, and at their total lack of compassion. This sort of mentality should never be allowed to become the norm. I will go and contemplate before I contact the elders again. I will return afterwards, once my fate has been determined.'

"Styx," Feiron asked gently. "Do they hurt?" Referring to the spikes.

'Only on the inside.' With recent experience of what rolling spikes did to carpet and wooden flooring, Styx waddled out of the room, leaving the slate and chalk behind. The two rollo guards positioned themselves behind him and followed.

Feiron ordered a pot of strong tea and some balm before pouring himself back into his tub to recuperate. He wanted desperately to see Leonie for himself, but his cell structure was severely damaged and would take a lot of energy to repair. The effects of the regeneration process were swift, but tiring.

Propped up on pillows, Leonie drifted in and out of sleep. Her eyelids fluttered open when she became aware of a familiar aroma, but it was a rollo in the doorway.

"Are you awake, Leonie?"

She smiled. "Hi Feiron." Leonie's voice rasped.

"Damn!"

"What are you up to?"

"I am attempting to be a rollo as it's such an easy shape to mimic. Did my smell give me away again?" Feiron rolled to the bedside.

"Perhaps." She smiled feebly. "But how many rollos can *speak*?"

"Oh." He slumped.

"It's good you are trying new shapes," Leonie murmured, her voice still weak.

"With only staff to converse with, I needed to do something to stop from being bored. Talking to you is much better."

"Um, thanks. I don't think your new shape will work out though. You move too lightly. Remember, they're very heavy."

"But how do I *look*?"

She cast a critical eye over him. He certainly had the right skin tone. Even the texture was accurate. "Can you stand up like they do?"

Feiron unfolded. She had to admit his resemblance was excellent. He was now a rotund triangle with stubby legs and arms. His full height measured to the top of the mattress.

"If I can imitate the sound of their roll, perhaps that will suffice."

"And the ground shaking."

He slumped again. "Well, it's a start."

"And it's a great one too." She tried to cheer him up. "I'm sure your mentor will be impressed. How long have I been out?"

"Almost four days." Feiron changed into his native form. "I can't let you out alone can I? How are you feeling?"

"Other than that assassin bitch taking my tail?" Leonie shrugged. "Not too bad I guess."

"So, you're better than you look?" he asked casually, reverting to his natural form. She was covered in bandages and her arm was in a sling. "You look pretty bad."

Leonie look at him steadily for a moment. "Is there anyone else out there to cheer me up?" Now that he was in himself, she noticed his discoloured complexion. Within his translucent grey darker blotches could be seen. "You don't look so great either."

"Yes, well. I had a bit of excitement too." Feiron related his view of the events. "The bodies of the assassins, what was left of them, were cremated. I understand none of the rollos have communicated more than a couple of words since Styx went rogue."

"Speaking of whom, where is he?"

"He's around. I should warn you though… he has changed."

"How so?"

"He's now multicoloured and covered in spikes. Apparently, it's a regressive trait, reminiscent of their violent origins. One they thought they had eradicated."

"Looks like no one got out of this ruckus unscathed, not even the untouchable hroltahgs."

———

The door opened soundlessly as Styx ambled in. A pair of rollo sentinels waited beyond the door.

"Ooh, this looks serious." Leonie sat up, noting the spikes

Feiron mentioned. Whereas before he was a dark grey, now his tone hinted a deep red patterning, swirling randomly. "That colour suits you."

I have communicated with the elders in Reenat. They have left some decisions for me.

"About what in particular?"

You. There is a recess in your mind you should know about. It concerns your origins; how you came to be.

"You mean my childhood? Who my parents are?"

If you prefer... yes, but origins would be more accurate. You wonder why you are so different from all others, and uncomfortable about your unique abilities. He waddled to the side of the bed. *Your immunity to poisons, high pain threshold, the capacity to heal quickly, far superior reflexes than your counterparts and your ability to use power, and telepathy.*

Leonie considered. "Can't anyone else do these things?"

Some are able to do one or two. I know of no other rrell – pureblood or half-caste – with the capability to do as you do. I would be hard-pressed to come up with any other entity that can do all. Potentially, you can do much more. Anyone with all these abilities could be virtually unstoppable. You are far more than human and far more than rrell.

In silence, Leonie sat unmoving, staring out the window. The stub of her tail twitched in agitation. She fought the urge to scratch it.

I now know how it all came to be. I have also worked out a few of the answers from the Codex.

"And you're here to tell me this?" she murmured.

Correct, if you are strong enough.

"I recall we've had a similar discussion."

I cannot determine how this news will affect you.

She took a deep breath. "Bring it on, then we'll soon both know."

The door swung closed with a resounding thud, shutting out the sentinel rollos.

Then let us begin.

. . .

Leonie woke to silence. She eased herself up and reached for the glass of water by the bed, draining it in one gulp. There was a bell there too. She rang it to see who would appear. She felt extremely depleted after Styx's last visit and her head throbbed incessantly.

In a few moments her chambermaid arrived.

"Yes ma'am?"

"Any chance of getting food?" she croaked. "I'm starving."

"Certainly ma'am. Have you any preference?"

"Anything as long as it's meat, preferably raw."

"I'll see what I can do." The maid curtsied as she left, almost bumping into Feiron as he flowed through the open doorway.

"Is Styx with you?" Leonie croaked in greeting, holding her head between her paws.

"Hello to you too, and yes, I'm fine thanks. No doubt he'll turn up. Have you heard the good news?"

"I doubt it, considering I've been stuck in this bed all week."

"We're heroes, but dead ones."

"That's good, is it?"

"Well… not the dead part."

"I'm bored, and for me that's almost dead…" Leonie tried to get up but slumped back with a groan.

"But we are *heroes*!" he repeated joyfully.

"You get excited over the strangest things." She smiled wanly. "What's happening with the book?"

"The *Codex* is well-protected and soon to be on its way to Reenat with fifty soldiers from the Royal Athglenese Guards and two rollos. Hopefully that'll be the last of it. If I see another book on prophecy in the next decade it will be ten years too soon. I need a long holiday."

"Are you sure you're alright? This doesn't sound like the Feiron I once knew."

"The Feiron you knew wasn't about to become a block of ice," he continued. "The rollos have five of those helmets to study and will conduct extensive searches to try to locate their origins. And, although you don't believe in coincidences – it seems the illios we chased were sent by the local Woorin Temple, not decoys after all. The rollos have ordered all priests from the Brotherhood to leave, and refused any replacements for the time being."

"I'm surprised Delta listened."

"At first there was reluctance, but they are nervous – it's rare for a group of Jart'lekk to be wiped out along with their powershaper."

"Second time for me; don't forget why I left Delta in the first place."

22

REALM OF THE DEAD

"MASTER LOTHAS, THERE'S NO INFORMATION OF A HALF-RRELL OR illios entering the Realm of the Dead. Do you think the rumours of their demise are false?"

"Hroltahgs are renowned for their inability to lie." The High Priest of Opsyss looked up from the scroll he was studying. "Are you certain we haven't missed them, Alen? Many entities die every moment."

"No, master. I can assure you. We've located and questioned the assassins who recently entered the Realm. One assures me the feline died, stabbed with his poisoned sword before she fell into a pit of poisonous gas, and the illios froze to death by his hand. But, the lack of either entity suggests the assassin is mistaken. Could they have gone straight to their Realm?"

"Unheard of except for the most devout followers. These minions were most definitely not devout whatsoever. Everyone travels via Purgatory when they die. It has been this way since the first death. If they died, we have somehow missed them; if they are not dead, then their location is a mystery and we have deceitful hroltahgs. This poses several potential conundrums."

"Perhaps they've moved on to Reenat, hidden by the hroltahgs accompanying the guards?"

"Possibly. They may still be within White Cliffs. Send word to all our followers to continue searching. Whatever happens, keep this information from the Woorin Brotherhood; the idea of them thinking all was in vain appeals to me. In the meantime, I have things to consider." Lothas absently waved him away, lighting incense to commence meditation.

"We have word from our people in Qelay, my master." The young messenger licked his lips nervously.

Coundar continued his admiration of the view of the harbour and the Plaza below. "And what would those words be?" the Woorin High Priest asked from where he stood on the temple's roof garden. He looked briefly at the youngster. "Come now lad, I'll not bite your head off."

"There was an attempt to steal the *Codex*, master."

"Yes, yes. Those miscreant illios will be dealt with for their failure."

"Not *our* attempt, my lord. Another one."

"Truly? Qelay *was* a busy little town wasn't it?" He smiled, lifting a hand to his eyes as a gust of wind brushed his black, unbound hair across his face. "So, who was it, boy?" he asked.

"The Jart'lekk, my lord. And a powershaper. It was why our attempt failed."

"I'm curious as to whom they are working for," he murmured before speaking up. "I presume the rollos put a stop to that; slapped the Jart'lekk on the wrists and sent them on their way."

"N-no my lord. All the Jart'lekk are dead."

"Truly!" He looked surprised. "So, the hroltahgs called in the local garrison to help? I'm surprised they had the skill to kill a handful of assassins; they couldn't even contain my two shapechangers."

"Begging my master's pardon, they didn't. The information

is a female half-rrell, an illios and one hroltahg were responsible."

"Rollos are non-violent, and the Jart'lekk aren't push-overs." Coundar turned slowly. "Do not toy with me, boy," he said ominously.

"I'm not." The boy's voice squeaked as he dropped to his knees, head bowed. "These are the findings of our Seekers. I'm relaying their message only, master. May the Great Lord Woorin flame me now if I speak false!"

Coundar waited a moment, looking for a sign from above. "Oh well," he chuckled. "I guess there's truth in what you say. Get up, boy. Continue. What news of this half-caste bitch and her blob sidekick? Do we know any details about them yet, their names for instance?"

The young messenger nervously stood, and related the details of the failed attack to the High Priest. "No, master. Word is they also died from the effects of the assassin's poison. The book is believed to be headed for Reenat, escorted by the hroltahgs and a company of Athglenn guards."

Coundar considered the ramifications of this news. If the *Codex* was on its way to Reenat, they would never get their hands on it. Not without starting a war. A war his church could not hope to win. Yet. All in all, it was a shame the Jart'lekk failed. At least with them, there would have been a chance to negotiate. He turned to the messenger.

"Send a message. Get our priests out of Qelay before they slip up and reveal something they shouldn't. I'll organise replacements. One or two here are getting a bit underfoot as it is – a few years up there will put them in their place."

"Master," he squeaked. "The hroltahgs have expelled our order from Qelay."

Coundar gripped the railing firmly to control his ire. He dismissed the boy with a frustrated wave. The view suddenly held little interest for him. He strode into his rooms to locate his snuffbox.

Opening the small box on his desk, he pulled out a sachet

and carefully opened it so as not to spill any of the delectable powder. Placing the yellowish dust on the desk, he picked up a reed straw. Bending down, he quickly sniffed through the straw.

"At least those Watchers didn't get their grubby little hands on it," he said to his reflection in the mirror, noticing his hair could do with further brushing. "And if that meddling pair of miscreants hadn't died, you could have wrung information from them. They got their just rewards for their interference. They've caused the deaths of at least half a dozen of his men, worthless dogs as they were." He chuckled, looking at his reflection with a hint of suspicion in his eyes. "You're going mad you know, talking to yourself like this?" His voiced changed slightly as responded. "I could have you flogged for saying that! Do you know to whom you speak?" he said to his reflection sternly.

He held his own gaze for a moment before looking away, resuming his preening. "Yes." The High Priest continued his monologue. "If only she had survived and come back here to Delta. I'd have something special for her. For both of them, I would, yes indeed. But if I can't get *her*, at least I can take it out on others like her. Sacrifices, to make amends for all my efforts! All her half-breed friends will pay for her interference. And I know the person to do the job." Coundar put his brush down and giggled as he struck the small gong by the bed then lay back on his lounge, waiting. Giorgi, his personal assistant entered shortly.

"Send for that young powershaper... what's her name? The overly-ambitious rrell at the palace."

"Mage Grigorid, master?"

"Yes. Niaarin, that's the one. I have a proposition for her, if she's interested."

———

The silence was absolute as the priest in red robes walked into the gloomy depths. Though he'd never physically set foot on this path before, he felt mild pain inside his head whenever he took a wrong turn. He was being guided to his destination, feeling no sensation as he walked. It was as if his feet weren't touching the ground, yet with each step, the scenery changed around him. On the edge of his vision, beyond the shadows, he discerned vague shapes ambling about as if in slow motion.

The man cast his gaze about, surveying his surroundings, trying to memorise everything. He thought it would be cavernous, but he was wrong. This place was open landscape with low, angry looking clouds sweeping rapidly by, yet there was no wind here. Random flashes on the horizon, or deep within the clouds, cast a bluish radiance across the landscape, but there was no thunder complementing the lightning. Boulders and scraggly bushes flanked the path. Leafless trees stood stark against the horizon. When the sky lit up, their branches reached like skeletal fingers for redemption. The gelid air was thick with the subtle, yet pungent, odour of rot.

"Hmm, not too dissimilar to my dungeons," he mused.

The Realm of the Dead – Limbo, Purgatory – was a holding yard for the recently deceased and as such, was a bleak and barren place. It was supposed to be. It was neutral territory, where gods contemplated the future of their deceased followers. Were they faithful enough to be raised to the plane of their religion – their *heaven*, or to remain here for eternity as a lesson for their lack of piety? One day he too would be here, but with the blessings of his god, not as a victim. When his time came, he would welcome death with open arms. It was simply another path to travel. He knew it. He believed it.

Ahead, he saw the figure he sought, dressed in the dark grey attire of her profession. She looked the worse for wear and would continue to do so as long as she remained in this Realm. The manner of her death was also evident; her neck and cheek were deeply lacerated, flaps of skin hung from the cuts – teeth and jawbone visible. Her left arm hung uselessly by her side. There was a stupor about her; her reactions to his arrival were slow, and her movements ponderous. Unless, or until she was called to her own heaven, she would continue to decay slowly.

Nothing ever happened quickly here. The dead didn't mind. The dead didn't know any different.

"You are Evlin," he said, more of a statement than a question.

She slowly looked up with her rheumy eyes at the tall stranger with the tattooed scalp standing in front of her. It took a moment for her to comprehend, and longer still to answer.

"Yes," she croaked.

"I understand the Jart'lekk have an interest in a particular half-rrell." Lothas noted Evlin's slurred and raspy voice. Evidently her vocal cords had also been damaged. "I too have an interest in this creature. Perhaps we can come to an arrangement, accommodating both our needs? I'm sure you'd want revenge."

A look of confusion crossed her face. Her head lolled from side to side. The neck wound opened and closed, creating a faint sucking sound. "I am dead ... aren't I?"

"Yes, very much so, but all is not lost. I've a task for you to perform, and the ways and means to enable you to do it." He paused to let Evlin digest his proposal.

"You mean, I can live again?"

"In a manner of speaking, yes."

"I can hardly move. It's as if I'm walking in mud. What use am I to you?"

"You will have all the abilities you had before, maybe even better. The rewards for success would be high but the price of failure would be even higher. In here, death is no escape."

"I will not fail. I know what you want me to do."

"Do you?"

"You too want the Enemy dead."

"What I'm after is her knowledge of a particular book. I understand you were a Jart'lekk Seeker and have the talent to find this creature?"

"Yes. All my life, if I wanted something bad enough, I was able to locate it."

"Splendid. That's what I want you to do. Find her and kill her. Once her soul enters this Realm, she will be unable to avoid answering my questions. In here, the dead *do* talk."

"I will do anything to get the Enemy." Her hand absently reached for the tail around her neck and stroked it. "I need to complete my mission."

"Never forget you will be working for *me*. You are no longer a member of the Jart'lekk, or of the living, for that matter."

"My vows—"

"Ceased the moment the blood stopped flowing through your black heart. You are no longer beholden to the Jart'lekk."

"Then, to whom?"

"I am Lothas, High Priest of Opsyss. He is the Overlord of this Realm, but you will call *me* master now."

23

WYVERNS REVISITED

Leonie was chafing to leave. Sometimes patience was not one of her best qualities. As soon as she felt able to be up and about, she pestered Styx for a plan to get them out of there before she started making her own.

At your service, was all he said in his brief visit.

She had become withdrawn after he exposed her origins to her. It wasn't his fault, being the bearer of the news, and she berated herself for the frustration she couldn't quell. Styx had enough to worry about, and didn't need her being a burden.

"You still need to recover, child." The healer protested when he heard of the pending departure. "Some of the internal injuries could recur if you are not careful."

"I've had worse," she growled. *And I'll give you some internal injuries if you call me child again!* she fumed silently.

"If we stay here much longer, someone's bound to notice," Feiron pointed out. He had heard the growing noise from his adjoining room and came to assist. "We'll have the temples and assassins after us again. We don't want to be responsible for causing the rollos more trouble. I think fresh air will be what she needs for a speedy recovery, and a small – gentle – road trip would do her health wonders," he argued.

"And yours." Leonie bared her fangs at the healer. "If you get my meaning."

"I'll vouch for her care," Feiron assured him.

The healer threw his arms up and pronounced her fit to go and do whatever she pleased. He packed his medicines and was out of the room within moments, muttering under his breath all the while.

"Thanks for that," Leonie said.

"You're welcome. I'll be glad to leave too, but are you sure you've recovered sufficiently?"

"Believe me, I'll live." She began tentative stretching. "Styx assured me of that."

"Is he prophetic?"

"Nope, but there are things I need to do and I can't do much about it cooped up in this place. The sooner we're out of here, the sooner we'll get back to Delta."

"And then?"

"I suggest you find another city to live in, because when I'm finished, there won't be much of it left."

"I see."

"No, Feiron," Leonie said, her voice icy. "No, you don't see at all."

Feiron went to pack his bags. He hadn't seen her like this before and he wondered what Styx told her to make her so angry. No. Angry wasn't the word. She was furious, but a controlled rage he had never seen in her before. He felt a short burst of sympathy for the poor individuals who would face her wrath.

True to his word, Styx began making arrangements to get Leonie and Feiron out of Qelay. While his fellow hroltahgs continued to ignore or block communication, other staff members were ready to do his bidding. Styx sensed now they responded more out of fear than anything else.

We will need to keep you both hidden, he explained. *Reports have already been generated to indicate you both died in the attempted robbery. There is the hope interested parties will cease looking for you.*

"I thought your kind couldn't lie?"

We cannot. We have other people to do that for us.

"How do you plan on us getting out of here?"

You will both be smuggled across the lake on a barge after dark. Those assisting are totally trustworthy. Also, I have an apology to make. I am unable to accompany you to Delta, having been summoned by my elders.

"Can't you ignore them, or at least postpone your return?"

"What's that?" Feiron looked to Leonie, who then related the disappointing news.

I will escort you across the lake. However, you may be pleased to hear I have already arranged for more entertaining company – and they can protect you better than I.

"Wyverns?" she guessed, a smile on her face.

Correct. I hope you do not mind.

"I mind you not coming, but understand you have to do this. Seeing Philbert and the wyverns again will be nice though."

The barge slowed, edging closer to the wharf. Dockhands hauled on the thrown ropes and secured them to the bollards once the vessel pulled alongside. They set the gangplank and the unloading began.

"You lot, stow those crates and barrel in the back of the store-room, and be careful. The rollos were explicit in their instructions, and you know they detect lies. If any damage happens, they'll know who to come and see." The overseer, arms as thick as thighs, spoke to them levelly. "And you know what I'll do to you afterwards. Everything else goes on the wagons. See to it."

Long after the sound of the workers subsided, Styx pried off the top of the crate with his talons.

I am satisfied we are safe and unobserved.

"It's about time. My legs have gone numb," a muffled voice responded. Leonie pushed against the wooden slats that had been her prison since the morning. She stood and tentatively climbed out, her joints aching. "I hope it was worth it," she groaned. After a bit of walking around to get the blood flowing, she started a slow series of stretches to ease the tension out her joints.

Your survival is worth much more than you can imagine.

"Not to me." The normally clean rollo had slime and dirt all over him. "Why are you covered in mud?"

I could not be seen. The colouring can be managed, but these spikes leave no question as to who I am, therefore I went under.

"You can travel underwater? For how long?"

More or less indefinitely. I am able to absorb what I need from the water.

Feiron unfolded out of his barrel when Styx lifted the lid. "I'm certain all our woes will be rectified after a pot of tea." He looked around the back of the warehouse, finding several dusty pots by the fireplace. "You did think of food?" he directed the question to Styx.

Of course. Another crate, a smaller one floated across the room. Styx used his talons to pry the lid off, revealing the assorted contents and two backpacks. *Ample supplies for your return trip. I trust we catered for your tastes?*

Feiron noted the box of Tesakian Redleaf. "Excellent, and more than enough," he stated after examining the contents. "Can I assume we have time before the next leg of our journey?"

We have several hours before we head off. The wyverns will meet us on the outskirts of the village.

"There better not be any more excursions through swamps," she growled.

There is not.

Humming to himself, Feiron selected a few choice items and began preparations for dinner. "Leonie, would you do the honours?" He pointed to the fireplace.

"Sure." A minute ball of flame instantly materialised and shot across the room.

"Is it me, or was that done differently?" Feiron noted.

"More controlled, I think you mean. With all the mental training, I'm able to use the power almost effortlessly."

"Outstanding," he said while she continued with her stretching. "Dinner won't be too long."

The sound of the southerly breeze through the treetops seemed like a constant sigh, and occasionally, Leonie spotted movement in the depths; the scurrying of a squirrel up a tree, or a bird searching for food. Breathing deeply, she thought how refreshing the scent of the forest was, though crispy cold.

"Smells much better than a swamp. And, no annoying insects. I could get to like this place."

"What would Jade do without you?"

"Stress less I reckon." Leonie grinned back at him.

Greetings, Leonie and Feiron.

The wyverns were still hidden by darkness, but it was obvious they knew of their presence.

"Here they come." To Leonie's acute hearing, their massive bodies moving swiftly through the air had a distinctive thrum. This was what she could hear now, getting louder and louder. Even with full knowledge of what it was, it was fearsome.

"How do you know? I thought it was the wind through the trees." Feiron followed Leonie and Styx as they moved out from under the canopy of the trees, onto the ploughed field as three dark shadowy figures materialised in the gloom. Phil alighted nimbly off Dorn the moment her talons clutched the dirt.

"I was so hoping we'd meet up again," he said, giving Leonie a quick hug, and slapping Feiron on the back.

"We feel the same." Leonie looked pleased, though surprised at Phil's exuberance. "Have you all been well?"

"Wyverns are rarely unwell." Phil turned to her little companion. Useless as it was to hide feelings from the hroltahg,

Phil tried not to look distressed at the spikes protruding from the rollo. "Brave Styx, I hear you have been through hell and back in looking after our friends."

You could say that to a degree. I believe I am still in hell, and awaiting to return eventually.

"You must tell me everything that has happened to you all in Qelay," Phil said, still smiling.

I will leave that to Leonie and Feiron. I have a long way to travel. Styx turned to Leonie. He reached out a stubby, clawed hand.

As this was the first time she would physically contact him, she was unsure what to do. The others shrugged in their ignorance when she looked to them.

She reached out and clasped his paw. The smooth, hard *skin* was like holding a pebble; pleasingly solid and smooth. The warmth surprised her.

This communication is solely between you and I, he thought to her. *We owe you a great debt for the perils you have undergone to fulfil this task – and for what lies ahead – and for that, the elders are extremely grateful and full of anticipation. You have come a long way, both physically and mentally. I am soon to depart to Reenat, but will endeavour to keep in contact with you somehow.*

Leonie thought her response. *'I'm just glad it's over, but it was interesting meeting you and your kind. Also, thank you for telling me about my... past.'*

I just showed you how; the information was inside your mind. My last advice to you is to trust in yourself completely. I do not mean to constantly remind you, as I know it brings you discomfort on many levels, but I cannot assure you enough!

Leonie, you are a truly unique individual with huge untapped potential; the legacy of being created from the genetic structure of several species. It is hoped the training you have undertaken is sufficient for you to tap the resource brimming within.

'Sufficient for what?'

For what is to come. Prophecy... your destiny.... No need to roll your eyes. You must learn to trust yourself implicitly – there is abso-

lutely nothing – NOTHING – you cannot accomplish if you have the right attitude. You have to put your mind to it. It is that simple.

Leonie considered a reply. *'My job is done. Once back in Delta, I'll probably keep doing what I do. Other than a few answers, life will be the same.'*

Like it or not, events have already come into play. It will be easier for you if you accept these things.

'Did it occur to you that the elders are also using you as a pawn in all these prophecies, like me?'

Of course. We do what we do. He released his clasp of her paw. *Farewell all.* With his final broadcast, he folded and rolled off into the night at speed, his spikes churning up sods.

Leonie remained silent for a long time after his departure.

"-you okay?" Feiron was saying.

"Yeah. Sorry. Styx gave me another headache." She looked at them, taking in the three wyvern heads towering above. "It's is good to see you all again. Shall we go?"

"Most certainly. We can catch up on all the details back at the lair." Phil brought out their flying jackets and once on, made sure they mounted correctly, even though it wasn't too long ago since they'd ridden. "Let's fly."

The wyverns launched into the night and angled to the south and west. It was an uneventful journey. The wyverns glided most of the time, only occasionally flapping their wings to adjust height or course, making the flight almost leisurely.

Upon arrival at Hell's Maw, they removed their packs and unsaddled the wyverns before heading inside to relax.

Late the next morning, the aroma of breakfast wafted through the lair. Leonie sauntered to the fire where Feiron was adding tea leaves to a pot of hot water, and Phil was scrambling eggs.

"Hello there," he greeted her with a grin. "Look what friend Styx has provided." Phil, almost as exuberant as a small boy with a new toy, showed the box of Tesakian Redleaf. "I haven't seen this much Redleaf since I was in the employ of the Tesak'i.

Very expensive, I might add. Only the most affluent in Tesak could afford such a luxury."

"Oh, we drank it all the time in White Cliffs. We had so much, half-pots were tipped out unfinished." She burst out laughing at the crestfallen look on Phil's face. "Sorry." She patted him on the shoulder. "I'm joking. I reckon I was unconscious most of the time, and I hardly touched a drop."

"Obviously you are in fine spirits. Your headache is gone now?" Feiron asked, handing her a cup. "What brought that on?"

She sipped the hot beverage before replying, blowing at the steam. "Styx. When he takes on a mission, he's like a... a wyvern on a thermal; there's nothing you can do to stop them.

It would be unwise to try, Dorn warned.

"He was quite insistent that I have an important role to play. When we parted, he drummed it into my head."

"He has changed..."

"After what he's been through, who could blame him."

"Certainly not I, but I think his change is for the better. It makes me wonder though, and something you said earlier about none of us getting through this unscathed. If he changed so profoundly... what has happened to us?"

"Well—" Leonie accepted her breakfast from Phil. "I can use the power more easily. I'm also supposed to be better at warding off any uninvited guests in my head."

"No more possession?" Phil asked, handing Feiron his breakfast.

Leonie shuddered. "I hope so! What about you, Feiron. How have you changed?"

He shrugged. "That is yet to be determined. I have almost regained my shapechanging memory, so can hold most of my repertoire of shapes. Maybe something will show up eventually." He put his plate down. "Leonie, I have something for you."

"Oh?"

"You better close your eyes."

"What're you up to?"

"I'm about to do something I recall you saying you'd rather not see again." He sounded jovial, almost quivering with anticipation. "I have only your best interests in mind."

"Hss. Okay then." She closed her eyes as requested. Hearing a wet, slurping sound – much like a boot being pulled out of thick mud – she realised what he was up to.

"Agh. That's gross." Phil gagged. "Better warn me next time, too."

"My apologies. Leonie, you can look now."

She turned. Her inquisitive look turned into a huge grin as soon as she felt the weight and shape of the wrapped package. "Feiron, you're a wonder." Her violet eyes lit up, whiskers quivering.

"I have my moments."

Leonie unwrapped the package to reveal one of the gravharnesses. "Surely they didn't give you this?"

"Umm, no. Not really. What better place to hide it than within my body, which the rollo mind cannot penetrate."

"*I'm* supposed to be the thief." Leonie examined it closely. The harness looked in good repair, but she could see by the dull aura the crystal's charge was negligible.

"I'm sure we can find another source of those crystals," Phil offered.

"This is fantastic." Her whiskers twitched. "I don't know how to thank you."

"Your happiness will suffice. I see now there's convenience in *not* being able to have one's mind read. I think I may yet get over my lack of psionic ability."

"I didn't think you were so sneaky," she commented.

"Maybe that's what's changed – you're bringing out the worst in me?"

"There's hope for you yet."

"Others might disagree." He recounted how he'd smuggled the harness around the last few days, not daring to leave it in his room in case the chambermaid saw it. "I couldn't say anything in case your thoughts gave the knowledge to the rollos."

"I think it's high time you filled me in on what happened back there," Phil suggested.

Feiron resumed his eating and started recounting the events at White Cliffs between mouthfuls. Leonie reluctantly put the harness down and finished her meal, adding her account of the details when required.

Phil sat back afterwards. "I think it's amazing you are still with us. Have you been praying for divine intervention?"

"Not likely." Leonie sipped her tea, rolling her eyes at the thought.

"Me neither," Feiron said. "It must be as Styx stated; Leonie has a destiny to fulfil."

"No one better mention *destiny* or *prophecy* again," Leonie growled.

"And you?" Phil to Feiron. "What is your role in this?"

"Me?" he sputtered. "No idea. Jovial sidekick, I suppose."

"I wouldn't be too sure. These hroltahg foretellings are not trifling matters."

"Add *foretellings* to the list!" Leonie drained her cup.

"Then you too have a role to play," Feiron continued.

"Of course." Phil bowed his head. "I'm your mode of transport." A deep-throated rumble could be heard from above. "All of us, I mean."

"Which leads to the next question—"

"When do we depart for Delta?" Phil chuckled. "Tomorrow morning should suffice. Depending on wind and weather, it should only take a couple of days. So, we'll take food for three days just to be sure."

After the breakfast dishes were cleared away, they set about organising the supplies for the long trip, which kept them busy until lunch. While idly sipping her mushroom stew, Leonie examined the crystal from the grav-harness.

"Any ideas how to charge it?" Feiron asked her.

Leonie looked at him suspiciously. "You developing a telepathic ability?"

He concentrated. "I don't believe so," he answered after a pause. "Unless you sensed something?"

She shook her head. "Crystals can recharge themselves as they absorb power around it, but it takes a while." Leonie put her bowl down and gazed intently at the crystal. A short while later she slumped with fatigue.

"No good?" Feiron asked. Phil paused from eating to watch.

She winked and reached for the harness by her feet. "Let's find out." Sliding the crystal into the slot, she strapped the harness on and stood up. With a small twist, she turned the dial and her body rose off the sandy floor.

Philbert clapped in joy. "Excellent," he said. "That solves that, but how did you do it?"

"It's hard to describe." She spoke as she floated to the ledges above. "It's a bit like using the ring. I've got to relax and concentrate; to feel the energy around me, then pull it in carefully. It can't be held for long." She waved at a couple of inquisitive wyverns. "I wanted to store it inside the crystal. Recharging is a slow process so I drew it in slowly, releasing it slowly."

Feiron sighed. "It's a shame we illios do not possess these skills."

"I reckon shapechanging is a great ability." Leonie reduced the power to descend. She removed the harness and stowed it in a sack once on the ground. "But powershaping is different to what I can do. All I do is pull a bit in and put it in something; whether it be a ring or a crystal. To the power, it's all the same."

"Hmm. Oh well, we do what we do." He shrugged.

Leonie swore under her breath. "Now you're quoting Styx!"

As the sun set, all three of them were sitting on the outside ledge, watching the antics of their winged friends above the mouth of the volcano.

"Tell me something," Feiron said as he passed around a wineskin. "When we were camping by the chasm and that fellow from the Woorin Brotherhood tried to fry us, you spoke a bit about powershaping. It seems there are two areas of lore of which I am ignorant; telepathy and use of the power. Phil, do you know any powershapers"

"I know *of* powershapers, but not personally, no. Not until now."

"And you still don't. I am *not* a powershaper."

"You shape power, yes?"

"In a manner—"

"It was fireballs, wasn't it, Feiron?" Phil turned to the illios.

"Several times. Quite powerful too."

"And now she charges crystals."

"I believe so." Feiron nodded.

"Powershaper," they said in unison with a chuckle.

Leonie sighed, scratching in the dirt. "Quite a while back, I came to the assistance of a young thief who was also a novice powershaper at the time. He'd *obtained* something from an associate. Unfortunately for him, he got caught and was about to experience a different aspect of the art – as a target. I happened to be in the area, so lent a helping paw. As thanks, and since I seemed to show an interest, he tried to teach me the rudiments of it. It takes concentration to focus the energy correctly."

"Like we illios have to concentrate on keeping a particular form."

"I guess so. They say there's power all around us; stronger in some areas than others – leylines I think they call them – but only a few have the ability to tap into it directly. I can *feel* it, and see magical auras… and I've been able to for as long as I can remember. It helps in my work, but I can't work spells, only this ring. All I can do is release it and recharge it. Without it, I can't cast a thing. I wouldn't want to anyway."

"Why not?" Phil asked. "It all sounds fascinating."

"Back when the Woorin Brotherhood attacked us, one of them made a fatal error when he was about to cast a spell."

Feiron grimaced. "He blew up."

"When you draw power, it gets a life of its own – a purpose, if you will. It's got to go somewhere; do something. If you lose concentration, that's what happens. I'd need a lot of convincing to want to even think about pulling that much power."

"I think Styx has other plans for you."

Axorg also saw something in you, and I can sense a change in you too. Dorn glided past them. *Something that was not there previously. Your aura on the astral plane has strengthened considerably.*

"I'm not sure what that means, but I'll take your word for it."

It means you have the ability to do many things, given the correct incentive and state of mind.

"That's what Styx said," she hissed in annoyance.

24

TROUBLE IN THE NORTH

FAR TO THE NORTH OF QELAY, THE GUARD CONTINGENT ESCORTING the three hroltahgs and the *Seer's Codex* to Reenat were in the midst of setting up camp. As the shadows of the setting sun stretched across the broad plains of southern Athglenn a lone Gryphon Ryder returned.

Styx sensed the alarm of both rider and beast as they approached. After scanning their surface thoughts, he too was surprised at what had been witnessed. He waited for them to arrive so they could make their report to their young commander.

Massive wings beating down and forward to slow the rapid descent, the beast landed heavily to the side of the camp. The billowing cloud of dust, aided by a steady easterly breeze, rolled along the ground to disperse in an uncultivated field. The Ryder's lone and premature return had spurred interest throughout the guards who gathered around, murmuring among themselves.

"Darga. What have you to report? Where are the others?" the young officer in charge called out as he made his way through the crowd.

Be calm. Styx sent advice and calming thoughts to the nervous Ryder.

The scout nodded as he slid off his mount and saluted his superior. "Forgive the hesitation, Captain, but I fear you will not believe my words." He bowed his head.

"I've no doubt you're more than capable of carrying out your tasks. You wouldn't be here now otherwise. What I need from you though, is a clear and concise report."

Darga licked his parched lips before continuing. "The Ryders patrolled to the north as ordered. When we turned to the west we encountered ... something ... unheard of previously. We spotted many carrion-eaters. The ground was black with them. As we approached, they dispersed. On the ground ... was a whole *clutch* of gnashers. At least fifty of them – wiped out!"

Stunned silence met the report .

"I left immediately to report as the rest of the wing spread out to comb the foothills." The scout held the reins tightly in his gloved fist. "That's it, Captain."

Styx sensed the young commander's disbelief, but, true to his word, he showed no doubts.

"This surely is astounding news." He looked around, taking in the camp, the tired guardsmen and the fact it would be dark in a short time. "At first light, we will make haste to this site and see if we can determine what transpired. Lord Styx, by your leave, we must investigate this. It will delay our arrival in the city though."

Stress not, Captain Doran. I will journey to the scene forthwith. My senses are not hampered by a lack of light. I am not weary, and no, he added as the thought arose in the captain's mind, *for this, I will need no guards. Let Darga and his mount eat and rest for the evening. I have scanned his surface thoughts and am aware of the location. I suggest you continue directly to Reenat as planned.* Without any further delay Styx rolled off into the twilight, ignoring his two sentinels who remained like silent statues.

A few less experienced guards looked nervously between his departing shadow and the two other hroltahg escorts.

. . .

Styx disappeared into the gloom almost instantly, given his small stature. He could understand their concern; even when his mind had been linked to others of his kind, it was unheard of for a large number of gnashers to be attacked, let alone defeated completely.

Many things had changed since the incident at Qelay, but it was not a physical change, though it took time to recover from the freezing. Styx sensed his mind changing – not a common thing for hroltahgs. It was only logical he accept the truth. He had felt an emotion. Anger.

As he travelled through the night, he reflected long and hard on his actions. One of the prophecies indicated Leonie had a role to play that may influence the future of all races here on Yarnik. Fates be damned! Her premature death had the potential to be catastrophic for his race, and he had done what was necessary to prevent that from happening.

Prophecies were a myriad of twists and turns; as certain events occur destinies take other paths. Some foretellings fall by the wayside as other possibilities become more dominant. Did the elders foresee his actions? Did they determine the same outcome as himself... or did they have other plans – like now? Were they following other prophecies unknown to him?

Was he escorting the *Codex* to remove him from the greater community, or were they working to some other prophecy? Maybe they simply knew him better than himself, and anticipated what actions he would take.

Only time would tell.

By mid-morning, with the sun blazing down, he arrived at a scene of carnage a few leagues from the foothills of the eastern edge of the Central Ranges. Among the pools of congealed blood, bones and feathers, the remains of the huge, fearsome birds, with the bulk of their bodies missing, lay scattered across the dry ground; . It was unlikely any survived.

A flock of carrion-eaters took to the air shrieking their objection at the intrusion to their gruesome feast. Deliberately manipulating the mind of one of them – something he would not have considered a week ago – Styx influenced its flight so he could survey the area through its eyes.

He investigated the many identical depressions found on the ground. Individually, they indicated nothing significant, but as the vulture crisscrossed the area, a pattern emerged. Towards the centre of the bloodbath, the disturbed ground revealed little; on its extremities however, things became clearer.

Several lines of these depressions led from the scene.

With a minor mental nudge, the vulture banked around to follow the trail. Behind a low hill, the number of depressions increased. Originally one large group, the attackers had split up to come in from different directions to decimate the gnashers. After which, they regrouped and moved on.

There was no doubt in his mind what this indicated. As foreseen in the oldest prophecies, the l'ithnamagri were returning. If they were out in great numbers, there would be many more deaths and only a large, powerful army would have any hope of stopping them. As far as he was aware, there was no such army. He now suspected this was why the elders summoned him here.

Following the trail, Styx began the long journey west, into and beyond the mountains. Releasing control of the carrioneater, it let out a raucous squawk and flapped its way back to rejoin the flock returning to their frenzied feeding.

―――

"You've been quiet." Feiron looked up from the notes he had been making all afternoon.

For a change, Leonie decided to prepare the dinner. Her inner turmoil, building up over the last few days since her memories were laid bare, got the better of her. She thought about how to answer Feiron's question.

"Years ago, Lady Dianah formed a group where certain

women became the Favoured of the Temple of Eternix. My mother was one of those women.

"All the Favoured were taken into the sanctum, deep within the lower levels of the palace, where they were to live. A few weeks later, they were all with child. If anyone knew the truth of how that came to be, there'd be a riot. This was considered a miracle – a blessing from Eternix herself – and only happened to the worthiest."

"I've heard of this. It sounds like a great honour, but wasn't the temple destroyed in a fire? I understood many people died that night."

"They rebuilt the temple, but the sanctum below was destroyed. My mother perished, along with the other Favoured."

"A tragedy, to be sure," Phil offered.

"I'm obviously a mix of rrell and human stock. Styx says I am unique, but surely there were others. How long have the Favoured been around?

"No one knows for sure how, but there were miracle births. I have no knowledge of a father. Dianah somehow changed things so instead of a human child, they got something else, a unique crossbreed." She looked to Feiron. "That's why I can heal so quickly, why I have heightened perception and reflexes."

They listened silently as tears trickled down her face. Droplets weighed down the end of her whiskers briefly before dropping to hiss on the stones surrounding the fire.

"Now I know why I heal faster and can survive poisons. I understand why I get treated the way I do. I'm not natural. I'm an abomination to most people; similar to what you said about how people respond to the illios, I guess. The real tragedy is fire destroyed the temple and everyone I knew died; thugs caught anyone escaping."

"How do you know this?" Feiron came over to put an arm around her.

"Styx said part of my memory had a wall around it; something in my childhood so horrifying, my instinct for survival buried it deep." She shrugged him off gently, moving away. "A few nights ago, to complete my mental training, he removed it."

Silently Phil took over the cooking, but the meal was ready. Quietly, he dished it out.

"This is indeed a tragic tale," Feiron said softly. "You should have told me and not been burdened alone."

The closest wyvern's heads craned over the ledges, looking down, including Slana's and Faldo's.

Oblivious to the silent audience, Leonie started pacing. "It is a burden for no one else to carry."

"You have my admiration and respect for surviving without the need to seek revenge."

"Revenge?" Leonie sat down and accepted the meal Phil presented with a wan smile. "Oh, I will be seeking revenge. If there's a price, someone's going to pay it in full." She ate her food, but didn't really taste it. "If I had known this earlier, I wouldn't be here now – neither would Dianah. I don't deserve any respect or admiration. I was simply ignorant."

"How is it you survived the fire?"

"You know me. As usual, I snuck out at night and explored the city. When I saw the flames and smoke, I headed back. By then it was too late and I was caught."

"But yet you live," Phil said.

"Someone rescued me. A friend."

"Jade?" Feiron guessed.

Mutely, Leonie nodded, looking at her empty plate. There was more to the tale, much more, but she couldn't bring herself to talk about it. Not now, maybe not ever. She wished Styx hadn't delved *that* deep. "If you don't mind, I think it's time to get some sleep." With a slight nod, she walked to her alcove.

Feiron banked up the remainder of the fire then helped Phil quietly clean up.

. . .

Styx removed the barrier her mind had erected a decade ago; tossing and turning in the alcove, her dark memories returned, over and over...

... it was ten years ago. She'd been out exploring the big, exciting city when she saw the smoke and flames coming from the temple; her home for eight years. Soon, the bells of several other temples were ringing to alert the city.

She tried to reach her mother, but the inferno beat her back. Wandering around in a smoky haze, she found herself in a side street by a wharf. Suddenly, a rope was flung around her neck and pulled tight. She was hauled her off her feet as she struggled for breath.

"Ere's another," a man with rough hands said. "Ain't she a beauty?"

A small man on a large horse looked down at the young half-rrell with disdain. "I care not for your thoughts. Our Lord wanted any strays taken care of."

"I'll take care of her." He started rubbing his hands over her body tearing at her shirt.

"You vile, despicable wretch." The man on the horse looked down. "That is disgusting. Stop it at once!"

Swearing under his breath, the brute with the rough hands punched her on the side of her head, dazing her. He then tied the rope around her wrists and feet and dragged her to the edge of the wharf and left her. He then walked to a cart to the side of a warehouse.

She could see the dark water glinting through the gaps in the planking. When her head cleared, she looked around. Half hidden between some nearby crates were two other half-rrells, tied up just like her.

"Is that you, Pasha?" she asked one hunched deeply within a sodden cloak, in too much shock to respond. If it was Pasha – Leonie's gaze went to the still form beside him – then that was her brother Casp. She thought she recognised his tunic.

"What's wrong with him?" Leonie asked.

Still there was no response from the other. Leonie watched Casp for a moment, fearing the worst, but soon saw what she was hoping for – a slight movement of the chest. "At least he's alive." She sighed with relief.

The sound of hooves on the cobblestones made her look up. The small man turned his horse. "Get rid of them," he called out. "I believe I've spotted another stray."

The cart rocked when the ruffian jumped off and hawked into the street. He walked over to a wall and faced it for a few moments. The sound of the man pissing in the gutter reached her ears, soon followed by the smell. Leonie turned her attention back to talking softly to Pasha, trying to coax her back to reality.

The footsteps got louder. Rough Hands grabbed the noose.

Instinctively she reached up to stop it from choking her when he pulled on it.

He tied the other end of the rope to a weighted sack. Rough Hands then repeated the process with Pasha and Casp, dragging them closer and tying each one to the same bulky sack.

"Pasha," Leonie whispered fiercely. "Wake up!"

"Shut it!" Rough Hands stepped over and kicked her in the side. "She'll wake up soon enough." He laughed.

With a grunt, he picked up the sack and heaved it over the side.

The line arced out, but pulled taught once the slack was taken. If Leonie hadn't been grasping the noose, she would have choked, but the weight dragged her closer to the water with a jolt. Splinters dug into her skin. Through bleary eyes, she noticed the sack had landed on a small pontoon below. Rough Hands had miscalculated how far he could throw.

Swearing, he picked her up like a rag doll and swung her into the dark water. She splashed to the surface coughing and spitting.

"That's it, kitten." She heard him chuckle. "Make noise and attract the crocs. We'll see if ya get eaten or drowned first." He then pulled out a knife and knelt by her friends, but she couldn't see what he was doing. When he stood up, he had a tail in each hand, tossing them into the water beside her. She saw the blood staining the water around her as she went under again. A huge splash nearby caught her attention. The man had thrown Pasha in and was now flinging Casp.

Leonie struggled to stay afloat, but dipped underwater several times. Try as she might to avoid it, she always sucked in water, *wracking her body with coughing fits, depriving her of more air before she went under again.*

Futile as it was, she tried to kick closer to her friends.

"Keep churning that bloody water," he crowed as he climbed down a ladder to the pontoon.

Struggling in earnest, to survive one gasp at a time, she witnessed Rough Hands' progress intermittently.

He stomped over to the sack and picked it up. Rocks tumbled out the top. One fell on his foot, causing him to curse again. He started collecting rocks.

Leonie nudged Casp, trying to get him onto her back, then she heard Pasha coughing. Leonie went under several times, and each time she took in seawater and could barely manage a breath between the rasping coughs.

Her vision started to blur. Through her struggles she somehow managed to glimpse a dark figure silently climb down the ladder. She went under again.

He knelt to retie the sack. The figure bent down behind the chuckling man. His laugh became a gurgle. As he fell forward his mouth made a silent cry, shirt already dark with a growing circle of blood. Rough Hands toppled into the water, taking the sack with him. Moments later she felt herself pulled down into the depths by the weight.

Half an eternity later, her lungs bursting and her wrists and ankles raw from her struggles, she felt a hand grab her by the collar and pull her up. Through sheer force of will, her lungs screaming, Leonie desperately clung to the last iota of air as she felt herself rising. Her head began to throb; muscles were cramping —

With intense relief, she felt the cool air hit her face. Her breath came in ragged, heaving gasps. She still managed to inhale water, but more air than water this time. As she coughed and spluttered, Leonie became aware the pontoon was right behind her. As she twisted around, the dark figure she saw earlier took hold of her paws.

The woman then drew her blade and deftly cut the bindings and noose. "Get your breath back and get out before the crocs get you." It was a woman's voice. Then she disappeared in the water.

It was enough incentive to give Leonie the energy to drag herself onto the pontoon. It seemed like ages before the woman reappeared with a body.

Leonie grabbed a paw. "There's one more — "

Suddenly the water nearby thrashed, becoming a different hue.

With an adrenalin-fuelled heave the woman surged onto the pontoon. "Don't look!"

Too late, the red churning water was etched into her vision. Dumbly, she looked at the body beside her. Pasha?

Pasha coughed, heaving in a gasp of air.

"She's alive!" Leonie cried as the woman cut all the bonds.

"You ok? Can you walk?" she asked.

Leonie nodded. "Yes."

The woman stood, then gently lifted Pasha. "After you." She nodded for Leonie to move. "We need to go."

It was gloomy in the Realm of the Dead. Evlin knelt in the muck by a foetid pond, brushing the scum away from the surface. She saw her healed face, barely recognising it. Her eyes, now two black orbs, returned her gaze. Evlin shuddered at the memory of her meeting with Lothas; partly in horror at what had become of her, and partly with glee for the chance of vengeance.

"The powers of Opsyss are unlimited within His plane, but not out there," Lothas had told her. "In time, your abilities will diminish and your body will revert quickly to your appearance in death. I dare say most of the living would blanch at the sight and smell of you, not to mention your mount. Keep away from crowds. Keep away from sunlight; any strong light for that matter." He withdrew a gleaming dagger secreted within a fold of his robes. "This dagger will provide for your sustenance. When you kill someone with it, it will drain their life-force."

"But how does that help me?"

"You must stab yourself in the heart. The life-force will then be transferred into your body. The pain of each sacrifice must be shared, for without it, without the understanding, there is no gain."

Evlin looked uncertainly at the weapon, at the crystal blades. The handle itself was plain and simple but the two long, thin blades made it look like a two-tined fork. Spidery runes ran along each edge.

Lothas's lips rose in a quirky smile as he continued. "But, don't overdo it. Your body can only handle so much." Her expression clearly showed that she didn't relish the idea of sliding a knife between her own ribs. "You will get used to it." He smiled thinly. "Or you'll be too weak to fulfil our goal, and therefore useless to me. Your time in Purgatory can be short... or very long."

"I've had my fill of this dump already."

Lothas ignored her. "Getting here was the easy part, you simply had to die. And anyone can do that. Leaving is a different matter altogether. The nearest exit is well hidden deep within the Central Ranges. Walking out would be nigh impossible. The only way out is by using the power or flight. As it so happens, I came upon this creature recently; its body lay broken at the base of a gorge deep within the Central Ranges." A winged monster dropped from the sky behind him as he spoke. "He's young and boisterous, but should be adequate for our purpose."

Evlin stepped back. The creature had too many legs and was almost see-through, so bodily fluids could be discerned coursing through veins. "What is it? It looks hideous."

The monster turned and hissed, making the dead assassin take a further step back.

"It's a l'ithnamagri. The l'ith were here long before any of us. He can't understand our language, but senses thoughts and moods, like an empath. I've managed to instil some discipline; as long as he isn't provoked too much he can be controlled. He has needs too, which I've promised to be fulfilled if there is complete cooperation.

"Now then," Lothas explained. "If your body weakens too much, you will be returned here. He will return also. To a minimal extent, I've bonded him with you; if you fail, he fails. At the end of this plain, you'll see a dark chasm in which lies a portal." He pointed. "Only through there will you arrive back in Athglenn, deep within the Central Ranges. Find this half-rrell. Use the crystal dagger as instructed and you can name your reward."

When he said this, she fingered the tail looped in her belt, the souvenir she removed from her nemesis. "My dagger will—"

"You forget she's already survived your poisons. The dagger I've given you will do the job. I guarantee it. Even the slightest scratch will bring her into the arms of our Lord."

"How will I contact you to inform you of my success?" Evlin studied the weapon before sliding it into her sheath, tossing her old dagger to the ground without a second thought.

"Never fear, when you use this dagger, I will know of it."

Emerging from that dark, dreadful place Evlin felt relieved to be out in the open air again. She wasn't sure how long she'd been in the Realm of the Dead, but from the phases of the moons hanging low on the horizon, she guessed it had been less than two weeks. Stroking the furry tail about her neck, she sped through the clear night.

The prayers of Lothas had repaired her body, but he warned her about exposure to the sunlight. When dawn approached, she searched the ground below for shelter. Evlin nudged her ride to fly lower. The horizon was glowing by the time she located a cave in the foothills of the Ranges, on the edge of a heavily wooded area. They didn't sleep as such, but their bodies seemed to shut down while the sun was prominent. At an unknown signal, both undead awoke after dusk to continue the journey.

The Enemy was here! It was faint, but Evlin could *feel* her goal far to the south. Her mood picked up; her body quivered in anticipation. She urged the l'ith with her heels to increase speed.

You will soon be mine. A vicious grin creased the assassin's face.

25

REVELATIONS

THE FLAP TO THE TENT ENTRANCE MOVED TO THE SIDE AS BRENDON entered to escape the dry wind. Raising her head from her bunk, Dianah looked up momentarily before dropping back onto her pillow.

Stepping around the desk, Brendon slouched onto a pile of cushions opposite her with a sigh. Chairs that could take his huge weight were scarce. "How are you feeling?" he asked with concern, a rolled strip of paper in his hands.

"I'll be ok. I need a bit of rest," Dianah said.

"You've been needing more rest far more frequently," Brendon pointed out.

"We *are* both over a hundred and eighty you know. One does get tired, especially with all this hiding and fake persona."

"We agreed it has to be this way. For now. You've not been this tired in ages. We'll seriously need to consider returning to Delta and the *Skydancer*." He examined his arms. His body hair was coming back in force. "Time for Rejuve."

Dianah sat up and reached for a cup of water, the skin of her arms had a dark, metallic look, as did her face. "What's that?" she asked about the note in his hands.

"A message from Magda. You know, it's remarkable her pigeons can find us in this mess."

"I did what I could to imprint this location on their minds." She slumped back into the pillows.

"She says Leonie has reappeared," he read from the miniature scroll.

"Leonie? That's amazing!" Dianah jolted upright, spilling her cup.

"There's more. Zander is off for a trade delegation in Lyhosa. He'll be gone for about ten days."

"What an opportunity! If Alexander is visiting Lyhosa, this is the ideal time to get back to the *Skydancer* and the medicomp." Bringing the cup with her, she climbed out of bed and walked over to the chair by the desk to refill it.

"This is too convenient if you ask me."

"Perhaps. I'm certain Magda wouldn't send us into a trap, but we will remain wary. The opportunity though to get more research material from my last and greatest project; I thought it had all been lost." She sighed, lost in her thoughts while Brendon went through some other notes. "So, how is it out there?" she asked, finally.

"Not great. If that sandstorm gets any closer, we won't see any l'ith until they're on top of us. So far though, the scouts report nothing unusual," he said.

"That's something, at least, but it would be good to know what we're facing before it happens." Dianah rubbed her tired eyes. "I've been going over these older reports and while they give great detail of the territory, we still don't even know where their lair is exactly, or its layout. We can't very well mount a counter-offensive if we don't know where to fight."

"Not sure if lair is the appropriate word, but I agree it's a concern. And it isn't like we haven't tried. There's rough ground out that way, and lots of it. We'd need to use half the men here just to cover the area, but even then, it would take a month. And that's a month of food we haven't got. A wing of glins'ool scouts would be ideal if they could see past this sand storm."

"I assume there's been no word from Reenat or Plenari?"

"I can't even guarantee the messengers made it through." Brendon shook his head. "We know there are a few l'ith raiding parties moving around the Vale's perimeters." He randomly selected a scroll from the table and looked over its contents. "It would be an awkward time to return to Delta."

There was a knock on the tent pole nearest the entrance. Dianah quickly covered her face and arms with her cloak.

"Enter," Brendon called out.

"Your pardon, Mistress Dana, Master Roland." The man bowed briefly. "We have word that a rollo is approaching from the east... at least, we think it is a rollo."

"Explain," Brendon said.

"Sir, this one has spikes. We've not heard of that before."

"Spikes?" Brendon looked to Dianah who had her eyes closed, concentrating. "Nothing registers," she said.

"I can't detect him either," Brendon said after a pause.

"Are you sure of this? And only the one?" Dianah directed the questions to the man-at-arms.

"It's what Egan told me. He was using the long-eye. And yes, only one was seen."

"Well then, I suspect we should prepare to meet our guest." Brendon stood up, tossing the scroll back onto the pile. "This could be interesting. Go and fetch Poul and Garth." The man-at-arms nodded and stepped out of the tent. "How is it we can't read him?" he asked Dianah as he lifted the tent flap for her to exit.

"He's hroltahg," she said simply as she ducked outside. "I know our abilities are greater now, but we still have limitations." She adjusted the cowl.

"You'd think, after all this time and all these experiments, something would've registered," Brendon said over the cutting wind.

"True, but we did leave in a hurry. I will have to look into it when we return, but for the moment, let's hear what our visitor has to say." They stood side by side in the sand-strewn area in front of their tent.

Poul and Garth, arriving at the same time as the rollo, looked at it quizzically as sand swirled around its squat form.

"Not seen one before?" Brendon asked them as he examined the spike adaptation and mottled colouring.

"No, sir," Garth mumbled. Poul shrugged his slight shoulders in response.

"Welcome, friend," Brendon said to their guest. "I must say, we're surprised to find you out this way."

Greetings. I am Styx. I have grave news for you. He directed his thoughts to everyone.

"Please enter. I don't suppose there's anything we can get you?"

Nothing is required, thank you. Styx followed them inside. Poul and Garth ducked in under the closing flap and sat on threadbare cushions by the entrance.

Several days ago, I came across a flock of gnashers. They were wiped out by a pack of l'ith. I tracked those l'ith in this direction, to your north. I reported my findings to Reenat, then I decided to seek you out as I heard you were attempting to gather an army.

"Ha. Farmers with no farms organised by a handful of retired soldiers with few weapons makes for a sad army to take on these l'ith. But the men are here and they choose to fight with us. We are grateful of that much."

"Friend Styx." Dianah nodded towards the rollo. "We thank you for this news, grave as it is. I'm curious though. We had no knowledge of your impending arrival. I thought it was normal protocol for rollos to send forth a message to the intended recipients?"

Indeed, and I apologise for my secretive behaviour. It was my fear that broadcasting my presence would reduce my chances of success in infiltrating the l'ith nest in an attempt to put a stop to them. One way or another.

Everyone's mouth hung open in shock at this statement.

"Um... The l'ith are not interested in negotiations. What

exactly did you have in mind?" Brendon asked the question on everyone's minds. "It's unheard of for hroltahgs to take an active role in this sort of endeavour."

As my spikes and colouring might indicate, I am no longer your average hroltahg. Recent events have led me to a... change of heart. Styx didn't need to use his telepathic powers to read the question in their eyes. *I was responsible for the death of a Jart'lekk assassin who was intent on killing someone of vital importance. It was no accident and, under similar circumstances, I would do it again. Since that day, my comrades have chosen to isolate me from our society for fear I am crazy. So instead, I have turned my efforts to assist in the current dilemma we face, the emergence of these l'ith.*

I believe they use a form of mental communication, but of a sort I am not familiar with. I am aware of it, but cannot fathom any of it, and it is overwhelming in strength; much like someone screaming directly into your ears. My suspicion is that it emanates from one source, the l'ith queen. It is my intention to attempt to open communications with her and come to a peaceful resolution before it goes too far.

"If you can't communicate—"

Physical contact may be necessary.

Before anyone could respond he added. *I will of course be going alone. I do not expect to return. Roland, you may still need every able-bodied person you can muster to fight, or at the least pass on what has occurred. I will attempt to send a message of the outcome, but one can assume that if they still attack, then I have not been successful. And you will not see me again.*

After a pause, Brendon spoke quietly. "You are right, of course. Our presence would merely hamper your progress. We have knowledge of the area if you require it."

I would appreciate that. Bring your best man here. I will, with permission, do a quick mind-scan to gather the information.

"Very well then. I'm the one you want, and you have my permission." Brendon sat on the carpet close to Styx.

Concentrate on the specific area in question, Styx instructed. He gently probed Brendon's surface thoughts and received all the needed details of the ground surrounding the entrance. *All done. Your information will be of great assistance.*

"I didn't sense a thing. You were quick." Brendon moved over to the cushions he had vacated earlier. "Did you get it all?"

I can only assume so. What I have seems complete enough. May I ask though, do you know what the l'ith are up to?

"I kept on hearing stories about them so I decided to research everything I could. I spent years at it, even travelling to the other continents to glean info."

And what did you find?

"Quite a lot, as it turns out. Do you have much time?"

If I understand your idiom, not much.

"Ah. Better take it out of my head then. It'll be quicker. Reenat should know of it too."

Again, Styx entered Brendon's mind, this time being more thorough with his reading. During his searching, a snippet of thought caught his attention. A week ago, he would have ignored it completely, perhaps not even noticed it, but now he had to take a peek. He moved back when he gleaned as much pertinent information.

That is disturbing work you have uncovered. And this device you used to determine the orbits and season... I have never seen its like before. The scholars in Reenat will no doubt endeavour to continue your work. I thank you. The time has come for me to depart. The sooner I begin, the lesser the chance of being detected. Without further preamble, the hroltahg trundled out of the tent into the dusty night.

"What a strange fellow." Brendon shook his head.

"Appealing colours, though," Dianah said.

26

A HIVE OF ACTIVITY

As HIS SMALL FORM NAVIGATED THE ROUGH GROUND, STYX contemplated the new information gathered from Brendon. The mind-scan revealed far more than mere details of the terrain and l'ith. There were fleeting images of a community of deformed humans living in caves. Other images of the interior of a vast alien building with many strangely garbed people. No other creatures were evident; no rrell, seleth or glins'ool. There was a scene of a flying vessel plummeting through the air before it crashed into a swamp.

It would appear the rumours of the origins of Zander, Dianah and Brendon were true. They came from a world called Earth, and their technology was very advanced compared to anywhere on Yarnik. There was much more; the early development of Delta, a nursery of some description with many juveniles – most of which seemed to be crossbreeds – or an adaptation of the major races on Shak'aran. This was where Leonie was born. He considered the most disturbing knowledge Brendon had uncovered.

Yarnik orbited a binary sun. There were minor and major seasons, each one hundreds of years in duration. Now at the tail end of a minor spring, Yarnik would move into a major summer as its orbit took it closer to the larger sun. Even though this would be several decades away, if the knowledge was correct, the temperatures would soar to levels beyond survivability of most of the races. Only the wyverns and l'ithnamagri would survive. Further deliberation would need to wait as he trundled to the edge of the broken lands.

The entrance to the l'ith hive was not far off. He proceeded cautiously, using Brendon's mind-map until he arrived at the worst of the ruined landscape. Deep fractures in the ground revealed sections of huge crystalline formations.

Styx risked sending the gentlest of probes into the depths. The angle of descent gradually increased to form a vertical shaft with ledges and jutting crystal at random distances. He also had vague impressions of several openings along the shaft.

With no other movement detected in the area, he trundled over the edge and began his descent. As the gradient steepened, he unfolded and began to climb, digging his claws into the rock face. All was good at first, but as the shaft became vertical the cliff face changed from rock to crystal. Styx's claws found little purchase. He slipped and fell into the darkness. He instinctively rolled into a ball and waited for the crash.

The impact onto a shelf far below splintered the structure, sending fragments of crystal and rock flying in all directions. The boom echoed up and down the shaft and into the various openings branching from it. Styx detected a change in the hive-mind, and soon after, large masses moving towards his location.

So much for stealth. If the cacophony of thoughts and outrage were any indication, half the hive must be looking for him.

As secrecy was no longer an issue, he probed the area to get an idea of where he could go. Below and opposite was another ledge, this time with an opening. The ledge was larger and a strange object caught his attention. He leapt off to investigate. His communal memory told him it was a portal – one of the many doorways between worlds – though which one he could not say. It was lying flat, and did not appear to be operating. There was no sign of the other portals, but were more than likely lying at the bottom of the shaft. History indicated these portals required massive amounts of power to operate. As the portals were only in Dromas, the city must have been directly above the hive.

With these thoughts running through his mind, he began to roll along the tunnel. With an innate ability to determine his bearings, Styx explored the tunnels of the hive for hours aided by the bare minimum of sensory input. While the tunnels diverged in seemingly random directions, his instincts and need to find the queen drove him to look for the lower levels. Pausing at a fork leading down, he heard a clatter of pebbles above him. Before he knew it, l'ith emerged from a tunnel overhead.

Each one hesitated as it came across the rollo in the middle of the path. Mandibles slightly apart, the lead l'ith traced Styx's skin with the tips of its antennae. Styx had the impression the l'ith were smelling him and kept perfectly still so as not to pose a threat. After a few moments and without any indication of aggression they stepped over and around him and continued along the path Styx was about to navigate.

Following at a discreet distance, he extended his awareness enough to discern the massive creatures. The path grew steeper. Styx dug his claws in, but managed to keep up. The tunnel was almost vertical when it widened abruptly. He moved forward slowly until he could no longer detect the walls. The group he had been following moved off in a northerly direction, crawling along the ceiling and using a column of crystal to descend to the floor.

Feeling confident by the lack of aggression shown by the l'ith he recently encountered, Styx gently extended his senses until he could detect something. As suspected, the walls of the tunnel he was in curved out in all directions, becoming an opening in the ceiling of a large cavern with huge columns of crystal, reminding him of the caverns in White Cliffs. Scattered across the floor were many unusual boulders and crystal shards from past rock-falls were everywhere. The boulders were regularly spaced.

Bracing himself for the drop to the floor, he released his grip.

The floor was uneven, causing him to roll into one of the boulders. Instead of stopping him, it broke and covered him with a thick fluid.

Almost instantly his senses overloaded with a powerful shockwave of emotion. The boulder was not what it seemed. Whatever he had done had sent the queen into a frenzy. The cavern starting rumbling with the sound of many feet and within moments l'ith were pouring in from every tunnel from every direction.

Styx rolled over quickly to the queen, attempting to communicate with her, but his message was bashed aside by wave after wave of her vitriolic emanations.

L'ith surrounded him, a protective barrier between him and their queen. Styx felt immense pressure as a pair of mandibles grabbed him. His stubby arms lashed out with the talons that could dig into rock, barely scratching the large pincers, which surprised him. He found himself picked up and hurled across the cavern by another l'ith with tremendous force.

After falling to the floor, he immediately jumped to the side as more l'ith attacked. Quite by accident, he landed on the thorax of one of the many creatures. His weight and impact cracked the shell and Styx found himself within the body of the giant creature. With immense sadness and guilt, he felt it writhe and stagger in its death throes.

For a few moments the cavern was quiet, but with another barrage of thought from the queen, the gathering of l'ith shredded their comrade to get to him. After his near-death from being frozen back in White Cliffs, Styx's confidence had lessened. Tough as hroltahgs were, they were not unbeatable. He realised it was inevitable they would get the better of him. There were far too many!

Once again, giant mandibles snatched him as he emerged from the dead l'ith, tossing him around like a toy. One l'ith threw him hard against the cavern wall in an attempt to break him.

Styx twisted, digging his claws in to the rock wall while he hung there to survey the cavern in its entirety. The floor was a seething mass of l'ith warriors, and the strength of their combined emanations dulled his own senses. Desperate as his situation was, he was still reluctant to kill any of them if he could help it. Some of creatures were now scuttling up the wall to reach him. He had to move.

Carefully choosing his path, he leapt to the nearest stalagmite, sailing over the heads and snapping pincers of the creatures below. Gripping the column, he gathered himself and leapt to another one, slowly getting closer to the source of their aggression. The constant telepathic blast affected him in a way he had never encountered before. He began to tire and lose concentration. Unless the queen stopped broadcasting with such intensity, he would soon make mistakes and once they got hold of him, it would mean his death.

At the last column, he climbed almost to the roof before once again jumping as far as he could. This time his impact cracked the stalagmite column. L'ith scuttled away as it collapsed, leaving a short but clear avenue across the cavern floor to the queen. Styx reacted immediately. L'ith moved in to block his path and grab him.

Styx fended them away and ducked underneath the swarming creatures, dodging through the forest of legs as he sped onwards. Now that he was closer, he realised the queen was immobile within a cradle. So lacking in concentration was he that it just dawned on him all those boulders littering the floor were in fact eggs. And he had crushed one!

L'ith were rushing up to him. He had only moments left. No hroltahg had died of an unnatural cause for several thousand years. Styx decided the new sensation he felt was desperation. With the near-death experience in White Cliffs, it was not something he relished to revisit.

Great queen, I implore you. Cease this violence. Everything that has occurred these last decades has been a mistake. An accident. We will endeavour to appease you and your kind, but you must call off your warriors so we can negotiate.

The queen, though limited for movement, lashed at him with

her claws. She was much bigger than other l'ith, with quicker reflexes. Styx found himself once again in the clutches of powerful mandibles, struggling to escape her grasp. He felt pain. And fear. Styx ceased his struggling, looking for any semblance of sanity within the queen's mind. He found nothing, the madness giving her strength.

The floor around and below him was a seething mass of l'ith warriors, their single-minded aggression towards him instigated by the insanity of their queen. There was no way any army could hope to repulse them; there were too many and too powerful. The only hope for the survival of Athglenn, and the only way to ensure the fulfilment of the prophecy, was to stop the queen at any cost.

Narrowing his mind to a pinpoint and aided by his close proximity, Styx rammed his thoughts into the l'ith-mother's mind. *STOP!* The moment her grip weakened, he thrashed out of her grasp and freed himself. With little time to spare, he leapt on top of her; driving his talons into her head, he ripped the shell apart and dove inside. Curling into a ball, he used the spikes to lethal effect, churning her brain into mush.

The queen careened around the floor, wildly shaking her head, crushing fellow l'ith and eggs in her path until her body collapsed in a heap of tangled legs.

Styx emerged from the skull of the fallen queen to utter silence. The cavern was eerily devoid of any emanations or sounds, though he sensed the masses of l'ith still gathered within the cavern. He began looking for an avenue of retreat, not that he expected to make it. But the l'ith were immobilised; every one of them. Whether stunned by the power of the queen's mind in her death, or some form of l'ith mourning ritual, was unclear. Not even their antennae twitched. They were statues.

Taking advantage of the respite, his departure would be the wisest course. In his weakened state Styx had to navigate his way out of the hive, and it was a long, arduous climb. Careful not to attract attention, he stealthily picked his way through the forest of legs to the nearest exit before gaining speed. In his mind, he tried to find solace in the fact that, while he had inadvertently killed one of the l'ith warriors, their own queen had killed many of her own kind. He also recalled a conversation he had with Feiron; that sometimes, to protect the weaker from violence, one must confront that violence.

27

MORE REVELATIONS

I RETURN.

Startled, Dianah and Brendon both looked up from their work.

"Bren— Roland, you hear that? Styx survived!"

"I can, yes. He feels... jubilant."

"Jubilant? I've not heard that characteristic given to rollos before."

"Perhaps not, but the fact he's broadcasting is a positive sign."

Styx rolled into camp shortly after his announcement. Many, if not all the camp's inhabitants, gathered to greet him and cheer him on.

"Welcome back, Styx. I gather you had success." Brendon stepped forward with Dianah right behind him in her heavy cloak.

It would depend on how you consider success – has the l'ith threat been averted? Yes, but only for a time. Unfortunately, the queen died in the process. As you said, the l'ith do not negotiate. It is a sad reality; one cannot converse reasonably with the insane.

"We can both vouch for that. For what it's worth, you have our gratitude. You saved hundreds, perhaps thousands of lives."

They might become a concern when they produce a new queen. I am convinced the previous queen was insane, possibly a combination of her nest being severely damaged during the Power Wars and coming out of hibernation several centuries prematurely.

However, I find the phrase 'for what it's worth' curious. Does it mean you believe your gratitude is of little regard, or that I might perhaps not value it?

"Not at all. We are extremely grateful for your efforts today. This was not something asked of you, and you have probably estranged yourself from your people."

The estrangement is manifest. Perhaps your gratitude could extend into sharing knowledge. I find humans on this world in general intriguing and difficult to fathom. I wonder if I would find those not of this world as difficult to comprehend?

Perhaps we could discuss this in private? Brendon answered. "Shall we retire to our tent?"

Of course.

Dianah lead, Styx followed. Brendon spoke briefly but eloquently to the gathering about the reprieve. An eruption of cheers and applause followed him as he stepped into the tent. The once-farmers now soldiers, celebrated.

Styx started immediately. *I mentioned in my initial visit, I am not your usual hroltahg. For instance, I know who you really are, Lady Dianah and Lord Brendon. These things cannot be hidden for us. With my previous communications with you, it did not serve any purpose to reveal your true identities to your colleagues. Humans are strange and mostly deceitful, and always have been.*

Dianah and Brendon looked to each other in alarm.

Fear not. Your pretence is not my concern. Now, with regards the situation we all face, I believe I now have a higher calling than before.

A higher calling? Brendon echoed. *You found religion?*

Inconceivable. Before, I was an ambassador. True, it is an important station, however, with recent prophecy coming to light, I am to take necessary actions to ensure certain events transpire. One of those events was for me to go rogue, but there are other events requiring attention.

Dinah looked at Brendon, then back to Styx. *Are we in a sharing mood?*

Styx shrugged his stubby shoulders, a human trait he picked up. *I am here, am I not? To continue. When I entered your mind earlier, Brendon, I detected many things, many memories. Some of those visions – those landscapes, the strange devices – are not of this world. One of our prophecies – and I believe your Zander, or should we call him* Alexander *– knows of this. You are depicted as 'High Ones', and not being from this world. Some choose to believe you are divine, however the indications are that, while you do possess certain powers and abilities far beyond our understanding, this does not make you divine. You are as mortal as I am. You are no doubt aware the Watchers knew of your arrival from similar prophecies. This is why there was a tower on the headland when you arrived. They were waiting for your arrival, and have been in Zander's service ever since.*

So, Styx continued. *To put a value on your gratitude for ending the l'ith problem, I require further knowledge.*

"Is there anything in particular you care to know?" Brendon offered. "About the studies I've done of this world, perhaps?"

Yes, Brendon, that is part of it. Styx turned his attention to Dianah. *While there is much I am curious about, not all of it concerns my current task. Tell me what you can of these experiments – particularly in relation to a half-rrell by the name of Leonie.*

———

"I have a headache," Dianah complained.

"Is it any wonder, with Styx in your head for so long? Does he know everything?" He held his head at his own discomfort.

"I can't be sure. I did what I could to compartmentalise the worst of it."

"That's a relief. You've one of the strongest minds I know. I'm sure if there was something you wanted hidden, it would stay that way," Brendon affirmed.

"I'd like to think I would notice his in-depth probing. I had absolutely no chance on penetrating his defences. I'm stunned at the news Leonie is still alive though."

"I thought you'd lost everything in the fire. You know what this means? You can use her to obtain more samples and continue your work."

"We'll definitely have to keep an eye out for her. Maybe Magda can be of use again?" she said.

"At least we can relax now that Styx has gone. We still have our minds intact, and our immediate problem has been nullified for now. I'm glad we don't have Alexander to deal with when we return to Delta. The last time we were together it didn't end well."

"We left because the only other option was for either him or us to die. I don't hate him that much, and prefer to live." Dianah shook her head. "Is it just me, or are these events, this *prophecy* Styx mentions, now involving us? A rogue hroltahg turns up and prevents a potential catastrophic swarming; brings news of Leonie's survival, and Zander's convenient trip allowing our return to Delta."

"We can't be certain, but either way, we need to take the chance. We both need the medicomp on the *Skydancer*, and you need Leonie to finish your life's work," Brendon said.

"Then we have no time to lose. We better get to Delta and grab the *Skydancer* before he gets back, otherwise we'll have no leverage over him whatsoever. I'll send a pigeon ahead to let Magda know of our arrival."

"And I'll send our troops back to their farms. They can take whatever supplies we can spare, and our thanks."

28

TROUBLE TO THE SOUTH

MOUNTING THE WYVERNS WAS MUCH EASIER NOW, BUT THE TAKE-OFF was still a stomach-churner. The landscape below changed from the charcoal grey of the rocky foothills, the deep green of the forests to a patchwork of varicoloured fields towards the east, where the land was flatter. It reminded Leonie of a map she'd once seen; she had always wondered how they could know the detail.

Following the line of the mountain ridges to the south to utilise the updraughts, the three wyverns hardly required flapping their wings, gliding when they could. The sky was cloudless, but an icy wind came in from the mountains to their right; the riders remained cosy and warm inside their jackets.

Phil spent the morning noting how Slana and Faldo coped with their passengers.

Singer. Look to the southwest.

"Is that smoke?" Leonie asked, looking westward.

"I believe so," Phil called down, "but I'm not aware of any settlements this far into the Ranges."

"If it is smoke, going straight up like that is weird."

"Especially considering the turbulence you'd expect among the mountains," Phil agreed.

All three wyverns banked gracefully, in order for them to investigate. When closer, they began a gentle spiralling descent, aiming for a deep ravine from where the smoke column emanated.

There is trouble below. Dorn pointed out.

"What kind?" Phil asked, but it was not long before all could see exactly the sort of trouble she meant.

L'ith kind.

Leonie screeched in shock at the sight of a huge ant climbing along the cliff face. As it turned towards them, Dorn dived in and ripped it from the face and hurled it to the ground. The creature landed with a cracking thud on its back, its many legs up in the air floundering about until it died.

There are others.

Can we mind blast them? Slana asked.

"No!" Phil answered. "Our two companions have no way to protect themselves from mind blast," he explained. "Whatever we do will have to be the old-fashioned way."

As it turned out, there was only one other l'ith in the area, which both Slana and Faldo dispatched. In a coordinated move, they dived in and grabbed it in their talons, ripped it apart and dropped the dead creature over the edge.

Deeper into the ravine, they found glins'ool bodies scattered around a number of ledges along the cliff-faces. Folding their wings because of the narrow confines, the wyverns levitated to the ground. By the time the three travellers dismounted and made their way to the source of the smoke, the column had begun to dissipate.

"I have limited knowledge of the glins'ool, but this would appear to be the body of the Nest's shaman." Phil knelt by a bird-man, his crumpled form lying against the stones surrounding the firepit in a pool of blood. His wings were broken and his legs bent at odd angles. "The torc around his neck indicates some familiarity with the power. Looks like he started the signal fire." Phil stood up.

They separated to explore the ravine and nearby cliffs for survivors.

"Slistorf's Hairy Balls!" Leonie exclaimed when she got closer to the l'ith Dorn had killed. "Feiron, get over here and look at the size of this. What Styx said is true."

It is one of the ancient races. Dorn said, looking down from her rocky perch above Slana. *From long before your time.*

There had been depressingly little to be accomplished at the destroyed glins'ool nest. "We should cremate the glins'ool bodies," Phil informed them quietly. "It is their way, to release their souls to the air elements."

The rough ground made it too dangerous to climb to all the bodies. With the wyverns' help, they used telekinesis to reach the inaccessible ones. No one wanted to stay there for the night. Once the gruesome task was complete, they left as quickly as possible before it became too dark to find a campsite. After putting some distance and another small mountain between themselves and the site of the massacre, the trio landed on a ledge to make an austere campsite. The wyverns departed to fend for themselves for the evening.

See you at dawn. Phil farewelled them. Too tired and disturbed by the day's events to chatter, the travellers made a cold dinner from their packs and settled down for a fitful sleep.

The wyverns returned as the sun crested the horizon and the solemn party gradually flew southeast, coming across layers of clouds stretching in ripples from north to south. Slana and Faldo darted through them, their long, lissom bodies zigzagging with much enthusiasm.

It would be nice if we all arrived in Delta. Phil reminded the two young wyverns of their responsibilities for their passengers' comfort and safety.

Bursting through a cloud-bank, drops of moisture streaking across her face, Leonie gasped at the cold. *Flying is all well and good, but freezing is not for me.* She snuggled into her thick coat, pulling it tighter around her.

When they saw a large lake far below, the wyverns glided downwards in slow, wide circles. Their long slender necks wove to and fro as they searched for lunch. They closed in on a school of fish.

"This will be quite safe. Hang on and don't make any sudden moves," Phil cautioned over the sound of the rushing air.

As befitting the eldest, Dorn struck first, gripping a fish in each taloned foot. Waiting for the fish to regroup, Slana skimmed the surface of the water, succeeding in snaring one fish. Judging his approach too soon and not letting the fish recover, Faldo clawed empty water. Wheeling around for another attempt, this time he waited for the fish to bunch up.

Dorn and Slana climbed higher where they turned big circles, munching on their meal as they waited patiently. As Slana began to eat, the saddle tilted forwards and down as she reached for the fish in her claws. Leonie instinctively threw her weight backwards, jerking on the reins. Slana's head reared up with a hiss of protest.

Be still, child. Dorn scolded.

"It's alright, Leonie," Phil called.

"Sorry," Leonie gasped. Breathing deeply, she braced herself for the next lurch. Looking down, she saw the *v* rippling the surface in Faldo's wake. A spray of water showed he had success this time and was climbing to join them with his meal.

Brother, try not to lose your passenger, Slana cautioned.

Surrounding the lake, cultivated fields crisscrossed with irrigation channels and dirt roads spread out like a tapestry. Farmhouses dotted the land. Not wanting to cause attention, the riders ate their meal in the saddle, gaining more altitude to use the clouds as cover. The lunch of nut-loaf, dried meat and fruit was washed down with wine from leather bladders hanging on the side of the saddles. Leonie found it a challenge to drink and juggle food with the wind's constant buffeting. She looked across to see how Feiron fared. He simply created limbs as required.

Later in the afternoon the group spied a skyland to the east. After paralleling its course for a short time, they judged it to be drifting slowly south. It wasn't until they got closer before Leonie guessed it to be over a hundred paces across the widest section, much larger than she'd imagined. Towards the centre was a rocky hillock surrounded by boulders and scree.

Something glinted in the sunlight. Leonie looked around but no one seemed to have noticed. Maybe she'd get a chance later to get a closer look though the rough edges made it appear inhospitable terrain.

Phil and Dorn banked, sliding across the sky to view the other side of the skyland. He pointed to a small area to camp. "May I suggest spending the evening here?"

"But there's still plenty of light left," Feiron pointed out.

"Way up here there is, but look below."

They both followed his gaze; fingers of shadow, formed by every contour, spread across the landscape, creating a surrealistic image.

"This will be an opportunity for us all to experience something vastly different," Phil continued.

"Assuming we don't fall off," Leonie added.

"You have to admit though, *that* would be vastly different experience," Feiron quipped.

Leonie looked at her companion, slowly shaking her head. "You know, I don't think you've fully recovered."

29

SKYLAND ENCOUNTER

LANDING THIS TIME WAS EASIER, BUT THE MOMENT LEONIE dismounted, her joints and muscles screamed in protest. She'd been astride for such a long time, even walking caused pain. Dumping her backpack, she gingerly began a series of stretches in an effort to ease the discomfort and get her circulation going.

Once the passengers safely dismounted, the wyvern trio dropped off the skyland to look for dinner. Feiron and Phil bustled about, setting up camp among the large boulders out of the cool breeze.

"Someone has been here before." Phil knelt by an old fire pit, stirring the remnants. "And only a few months, is my guess."

"Glins'ool?"

Phil shrugged. "More than likely, but anyone who can fly. If these things travel as far as I've heard, then it could have been someone in the far north, or even a flyer from Reenat. The Royal Guards fly gryphons."

"I've heard of them. Something else I'd like to see," Feiron stated.

"You and me both," Phil agreed.

After digging through the packs, two pots were brought out

and filled from a water-skin, then set to boil: one for tea, the other as it turned out, for a thick stew of Phil's concocting.

"I should bring you two with me more often." Leonie sat back to relax by the fire, aches and pains niggling at her. "It's good to have someone doing the menial tasks."

"That's fine with us, isn't it Feiron?" Philbert answered. "And I think since we did dinner, she can handle breakfast."

"I'm not so certain. I've noticed when rrells are about, we don't see rodents to plague us," Feiron added. "Are you *sure* you want her to cook?"

"Maybe I'll go join the wyverns instead," Leonie said in mock indignation, pleased to see his sense of humour returning. His recovery was improving since his ordeal in the volcano. "At least they don't answer back."

Rodents are far too small to worry about and it takes so long to get a sufficient sized meal, Faldo grumbled.

"Hss. I can't win with you lot."

"So, don't argue." Phil smiled. "Here's your dinner." He passed over a steaming wooden bowl.

They all looked up to the sound of rushing air as the wyverns returned.

Leonie wasn't sure if it was her imagination, but it seemed the skyland tilted slightly when the wyverns landed. She wondered if the whole thing would topple, like a boat capsizing in a turbulent river. Shuddering, she pushed the image from her mind by watching the antics of the twins. Dorn had nestled in among the boulders still radiating heat from the sun, but Slana and Faldo shifted around until they were comfortable, their barbed tails leaving grooves in the ground. Finally, they curled up, wrapping tails around their green, scaled bodies.

With Phil's permission, Feiron had packed the leather bucket used to save him from the volcano cave. He now hooked a handle over the stub of a branch on a dead tree and poured inside.

Leonie briefly contemplated exploring the strange sky island, but when she stood up the ache in her muscles changed her mind. Spreading her bedroll near the fire opposite Phil, she lay down, pulled the blanket up and slept soundly to the rumbling of the wyvern's snores.

Leonie awoke with a rough nudge. She looked up bleary-eyed, scrambling back briefly in shock. The sight of an emerald-coloured serpent head the size of a barrel a few feet from her was still a new experience.

Here's breakfast. We'll show those men who can come up with the best meal.

Lying on the ground a few feet away was the biggest fish she had ever seen. Quickly she got up to make a breakfast the men wouldn't forget. Leonie stoked the fire with the remainder of the wood, setting the pot for the tea before turning her attention to the fish. She had no idea of its type but it was so big, the fillets were going to be the size of steaks.

When the tea brewed, she spread out the fire slightly and tossed the slabs of white meat into a pan. She frowned when the pieces draped over both sides of the pan. *Can't be helped.* The morning breeze quickly whisked away the mouth-watering aroma. The remainder of the fish was shared with the three wyverns.

"Thanks for getting this."

Our pleasure. Dorn gulped down the remains of the entrails.

Leonie didn't need to wake the others; the wyverns did that in the same manner they woke her. Enthused by the sounds and smells of frying fish, the men were soon digging into the hot breakfast with gusto.

Afterwards, leaving her travelling companions to their tea and talk, Leonie went for a stroll around the skyland, partly to exercise but mainly to take a moment to investigate the shiny object she saw on her arrival. She was at the base of the knoll and from this angle it looked a much easier climb than she previously thought.

Sweating slightly and climbing steadily, she reached the

summit. It wasn't a large area, and the mysteriously glinting object was in plain view; a huge crystal jutting out of the ground, surrounded by a collapsed stone wall. As Leonie approached, the crystal's facets glinted with the changing angle of the sun's rays. Unsure what to expect, her whiskers drooped. The thief in her had yearned for ancient treasure.

She was amazed at the crystal's size; her outstretched arms barely reached across the face. It had a bluish tint and when she peered closer, it was like viewing a five-sided glass tunnel. It was cold to touch, and her breath misted fleetingly. Leonie could only guess how deep it went. Her refracted shadow caused many strange shapes to flicker within, and she amused herself for a few minutes by waving her arms to see the effect. When she changed her position, a kaleidoscope of warped reflections faded into bluish obscurity.

Curiosity assuaged Leonie's mind turned to other things; the entire skyland awaited her. She walked to the edge and looked down. Thousands of feet below, past the wheeling wyverns, the approaching southern coastline spread out east and west. The dense jungle stretched along the coastline from the base of the Ranges and far to the east, as well as transitioning from jungle to sweeping plains as the eye travelled north.

The ocean is so vast! Leonie sat down and stared for a long time watching the tiny ripples out to sea form into waves, eventually dashing themselves onto the rocks along the shore. The colour of the water changed closer to the shoreline; from a dark blue to aquamarine. It was truly beautiful. Leonie was awestruck, she hadn't realised there were so many shades of blue.

We have found something you might like. Slana flew up. Faldo continued to wheel nearby.

"What do you mean?"

We will show you. Slana gingerly landed on the lip of the skyland, her huge talons gripping the rock. After Leonie mounted, the wyvern dropped off and positioned herself underneath the floating land mass.

Being so close, Leonie could clearly see the roughness where the rock sheared after it broke away from the ground. Crystals of different shapes and sizes were embedded everywhere, all angled in the same direction.

With Slana hovering ever closer towards the centre of the structure. Leonie discerned a darker area; she became so preoccupied, it didn't occur to her the slightest change in wind could squash her between the hard rock and the young wyvern.

The dark area resolved into an entrance. Leonie saw a tunnel; rough stairs led into the depths of the floating land. They were almost directly beneath the knoll.

I have stuck my head in there, but its length is beyond my reach.

Without hesitation, Leonie undid her tether and stood in the saddle, disregarding the fact she was several thousand feet above oblivion. She reached up, grabbed hold of the rough walls and climbed into the cracked stairway.

"I won't be long." She quickly climbed the stairs, her mind full of curiosity.

The walls and ceiling were formed out of finely cracked crystal. The stairs were littered with crystalline shards, presumably loosened by the forces that created the skyland. After about twenty paces, the passage became wider, forming a small chamber. It had a bluish light source in the ceiling, and glancing up Leonie realised it was the large crystal from the hill. There were carvings and inscriptions along the wall: strange runes, geometric symbols and several diagrams resembling maps. She was certain a sage would want to spend many hours or even days in here, studying the maps and deciphering the runes.

What was once a wooden table near the centre had succumbed to rot and collapsed under its own weight. Dust and gritty residue covered the cracked floor. On the far wall she could see another set of stairs going up but now blocked by fallen crystals and rocks.

The floor shifted under her paws. Leonie braced herself, but other than a slight vibration, nothing else happened. Dust and crystal shards filtered down from the domed ceiling. Not knowing how stable skylands were, Leonie reckoned it prudent to hasten her departure. Turning away, a niche to one side of the tunnel opening caught her eye. She peered in but found it full of grit and debris. When she scraped at the dirt, something fell to the floor. Leonie only became aware of it because of the faint clunk it made bouncing down the stairs. It had a dull glow.

Leonie leapt after it, hooking it easily with a claw, realising it was too fine to be a ring. An earring, she decided. Further study would have to wait until she was back in the air. She quickly loped down the stairs, putting the earring in a belt-pouch.

Slana wasn't at the exit. The tunnel vibrated again and the drop into emptiness made Leonie's stomach lurch.

"Hey, Slana. I can't fly by myself," she yelled into the emptiness, high above the Sea of Tears. The coastline spread out to the east, but to the west it was cut by the southern end of the Ranges.

The next jolt, far more severe than the last, caused her to stumble sideways. Her arms flailed as she tried to regain her balance, but the lower step cracked and fell away. Leonie fell with it. Spinning around, she grabbed hold of the next step up. The bottom step she had fallen on tumbled over and over as it plummeted to the water far below. Her legs kicked wildly in empty space as she hung over the edge. Slana was still nowhere in sight. Struggling back up, the step she was clutching tilted with her weight. Try as she might, any other paw-holds were out of reach. The step tore free from the crumbling mortar.

"SLANA!"

No sooner had she begun to fall when the young green wyvern appeared underneath her. *You can't fly, silly,* Slana said as the step bounced off her scaled neck.

Leonie winded herself when she landed across the saddle. The pommel hit her in the ribs. All the aches and pains of yesterday returned anew. Gasping, she quickly seated herself, sank her claws into the leather of the saddle and wedged her feet firmly into the stirrups, her heart in her throat.

Slana dropped away from the underside of the skyland as more debris rained down upon them. *An anomaly within the skyland prevents contact.* She explained her delay as they re-joined the others already in the air. *I went to inform Singer of your whereabouts.*

Leonie didn't reply, still getting over the close call.

Faldo glided closer.

"You always have to go off exploring, don't you?" Feiron called out, sounding both annoyed and relieved on her return.

"Yes." Leonie hoped her voice didn't betray her fear. "It's in my blood. Who went off exploring volcanoes alone I wonder?" Her paws were steady enough now to do up the belt.

Feiron shrugged, smiling. "That was different."

"Ah." Leonie rolled her eyes with a nervous chuckle.

"You weren't wearing your harness then?"

"It digs into my back when in the saddle." She shook her head. "Maybe I will from now on."

"Are you alright?" Phil moved Dorn closer to the other side. "Dorn senses your distress."

"A bit bruised and shaken, but fine now." Taking a few breaths to steady her voice, she told them of the chamber and the fall from the stairs. "Any idea what happened?" They circled back over the skyland. From here it looked as if nothing had changed.

"I don't know. If I had to guess, I'd say the shift from land to water affects them," Philbert said, looking down to the skyland, now well beyond the coastline. It turned ponderously towards the west where storm clouds loomed on the distant horizon. "If we stayed long enough, we'd probably find ourselves in Lyhosa within a week or two."

"Assuming it didn't drop out of the sky in our sleep. What makes them move the way they do? Where'd they come from?" Leonie asked.

"I've heard it's all to do with the power."

Well over a century ago, as you measure time, there was a war in the centre of this land, further to the north and west. Dorn informed them. *The breaking of the land caused the end of the war and the formation of these sky islands.*

"Yes. Who won?" Leonie asked, recalling the conversation with Styx.

I am not certain. Your history is not our concern. However, they do make good resting places on journeys such as this. I have not encountered one going over the ocean before; otherwise I would have warned you.

"So, I could've been in someone's home?"

"It could have been anything. Maybe even part of an old castle. Who knows?" Phil shrugged. "Maybe one day someone will study them."

"Maybe Feiron, once he's finished with the wyverns."

"Somehow I don't think so," Feiron said. "It would require a lot of flying. I'd want to find a way of communicating with the wyverns first."

30

AN UNEXPECTED ARRIVAL

LEONIE'S THROAT WAS GETTING RAW WITH THE CONSTANT SHOUTING. It became too much of a chore to be heard over the rushing wind and beating wings, so the conversation waned. She still shuddered from time to time, thinking of what could have happened if she fell. The thrill of flying, for now at least, abandoned her.

Continuing east, they admired the ever-changing terrain below. The coastline became a vast stretch of rocky shoreline interspersed with white sandy beaches. Unanimously, the group decided to land for a rest and lunch. The first thing Leonie did after landing was don her harness.

As they baked fresh fish over a large fire fuelled by driftwood, the twins revelled in the sand, lying on it and dragging themselves through it. Afterwards, they spent time harassing the numerous gulls, sending them squawking with indignation into the air. When they tired of that, the two young wyverns dived into the water, moving to and fro in a snake-like manner.

"I didn't know they could swim," Feiron said.

"It isn't something I've seen before either." Phil sat up, taking mental notes.

After lunch and a quick walk along the beach to stretch their legs, the trio mounted and continued their easterly course, passing yet another small skyland drifting further inland. After their recent experience, no one suggested a visit, especially so close to the coast.

By late evening they could see the city twinkling far below. Drawing closer, they began to look for a safe place to land. The area along the coast turned out to be too treacherous with cliffs and rocks. All they could find inland was dense jungle. Leonie knew of no area large or safe enough for the three wyverns to land near the city.

"What about the roads leading out of the city. Couldn't we land there?" Phil called out.

"They'll be patrolling them, and I'd rather not be seen." They returned to circle high above the city centre after flying around the boundaries for one final look.

"We could try the pier by the tannery." She pointed down to the south-eastern arm of the harbour. "It's set away from every-thing because of the smell, and at this time of night should be deserted. I don't think it'll support the weight of a wyvern though."

That is of no consequence. You forget we can hover. We need not touch the pier.

From out of the darkness a shadow rushed into view. There was a sickening crunch as a hideous creature slammed into Slana's back. The creature's shriek drowned Slana's screech of pain.

The jolt snapped the tethers, throwing Leonie from the saddle. Time slowed. With arms flailing the air, she slipped side-ways. Her fall was arrested when her paw caught in the stirrup, jarring her leg and leaving her hanging upside-down below Slana's chest. Her recovery was hampered by the green wyvern's efforts to dislodge a giant, grey bug.

Slana snaked her head around, barely able to latch onto the monster's body. Her teeth snagged a leg. Slana clenched her jaws and ripped them away. The limb cracked at a joint, pulling free from the body. Screeching in pain, the attacking l'ith sank its claws deeper into Slana's back.

Desperate for a paw-hold, Leonie spied the broken leather strap flapping in the wind above her. Beyond was the bulk of the attacking creature. She froze at the sight of its rider, recognising her as the Jart'lekk assassin from the caverns. *But, she's dead? I killed her.*

Evlin's face broke into a manic grin. "You'll not escape me so easily this time," the assassin declared. Without hesitation she climbed off her ride and dropped onto the green wyvern's thick neck. From there she reached down to fulfil her goal, but her prey was still out of reach.

Evlin slid off the wyvern's neck to grapple bodily with her long sought-after nemesis. Her added weight strained the damaged leather, ripping the stirrup from the saddle. The pair tumbled towards the dark waters of Delta's harbour.

Totally unprepared for the attack, the others were stunned by Slana's cry of pain.

Dorn's head snapped down in alarm. Her daughter was spiralling out of control, losing height rapidly. Recognising the l'ith, she instinctively sent a bolt of rage at the attacking monster only to find nothing there. The mind was empty! Recovering from her initial shock, a mental probe confirmed Dorn's suspicions. The l'ith had no aura about it at all. It was undead.

Ye Gods! Quick Dorn. Leonie's fallen. Phil mentally cried.

Faldo, go after Leonie. Dorn put a lot of force into her thought, knowing he'd want to prove himself and try to assist his sister. *I will deal with this creature.* Her son was no match for this undead l'ith. *Brace yourself,* she warned Philbert as she hurled herself after her daughter.

Philbert wedged himself into the saddle flares, using his years of working with horses and wyverns to cope with the sudden manoeuvres. He focused his mind to keep an eye both on Faldo and Slana's progress, looking for any advantage to exploit.

In horror, he saw Leonie fall. At first, he thought she'd disappeared in the darkness, but then glimpsed her dangling upside-down, being jostled by Slana's movements. With disbelief he witnessed another woman leap from the l'ith's back to Slana's then, inconceivably, slide down to grapple with the half-rrell. Then the leather strap snapped. He lost sight of them when Dorn's bulk blocked the view as she pivoted, intent on saving her daughter. All he could do now was watch and advise.

Feiron heard the loud screech a moment after the impact of the wyvern and the monster. He'd been looking down like everyone else, thinking of the nice, comfortable barrel awaiting him, and it took a couple of moments for him to grasp what was happening.

First, he saw one of those l'ith creatures clinging behind Slana's shoulders. Then he realised the saddle was empty. He couldn't believe his eyes when he saw a black-clad woman reaching for Leonie with a large dagger. They both suddenly dropped into the darkness.

"Leonie!" A wind gust ripped the cry into the night. Faldo dipped sharply and Feiron hung on grimly, wrapping his arms around any conceivable support. It was moments like these Feiron regretted not being able to communicate with wyverns.

"Finally, I have you." Evlin jabbed swiftly at her nemesis's heart.

Relying on instinct, Leonie barely managed to deflect Evlin's wrist. The blade glowed malevolently. The thick jacket, proving little protection against it, tore open at the shoulder.

Everything happened so quickly, yet time seemed indeterminate. It was hard to think with the sea rushing up and the air screaming in her ears. Instinctively Leonie grabbed the assassin's

CITY OF BRIDGES | 255

wrist, preventing another thrust. Even when her claws cut the assassin's flesh, Leonie's struggles proved futile. The assassin had amazing strength, far more than in the caves, and far more than any human should.

The twin-bladed dagger moved relentlessly closer to her heart.

Leonie twisted and lunged; latching her teeth onto the woman's shoulder in the hope the pain would weaken her. There was no reaction. Her sharp teeth pierced the skin and clothing, yet there was no blood. In fact, Leonie could've sworn the assassin was laughing!

"Your craving for life is futile, but death will be no escape either," Evlin yelled. "Once my master has finished with you, you'll be mine to play with forever."

Leonie saved her breath, redoubling her efforts, knowing the only reason she still breathed was because the both of them were spinning and tumbling through the air, struggling for any advantage.

Out of the corner of her eye she glimpsed Faldo swoop underneath. Instantly she realised he was manoeuvring below to attempt to catch them. *The dagger will kill him if it strikes.* She knew it in her bones. Leonie didn't want his death on her conscience. She twisted, in vain; the two women landed with a thump behind his beating wings.

It will not harm me. Faldo responded to her thoughts, regaining altitude.

Something jarred Leonie's spine on impact. She hissed in pain; then an idea blossomed.

With an evil glow behind her dark eyes, Evlin relentlessly pressed the dagger down. "When I've killed you, I'll take the life from your friend and his pet," she gloated. "My bug will be overjoyed with the taste of fresh meat. I believe wyvern is a delicacy to them." The assassin now had the advantage by being on top, but before she could react, a warm jelly substance oozed around her, starting to envelope the attacker.

"Feiron. No!" Leonie immediately realised he was trying to save her. She had to do something quickly, certain that if the dagger touched either Faldo or Feiron they'd die instantly. Leonie couldn't afford to release her two-pawed grip of the assassin's arm. Claws and teeth didn't seem to make any difference on this foul woman. She could see only one option to save her friends, but Feiron was hampering her. She turned her head and bit him. Hard.

He recoiled in surprise, letting go.

"Sorry, my friend." With a heave, she rolled off Faldo's back, dragging the assassin with her.

Dorn manoeuvred quickly above the attacking l'ith with the fury of a mother defending her young. Her vengeance was swift and sure. She sank her talons deeply into the central carapace and ripped the creature off her daughter's back. She then swung her massive head down and gripped the neck with her teeth, slowly crushing the shell between her jaws.

The night air filled with hissing, screeching and cracking. Dorn's claws raked the length of its body, shredding the wings and cracking the shell in several places. Though the foul creature didn't 'die', it could no longer fly. Damaged wings beat uselessly. Thick globs of dark ichor seeped from the gaping hole in its neck.

Dorn spat out the foul-tasting stuff, watching the creature spiral out of control to smash into one of the rocky outcrops in the harbour. She then pivoted towards Slana far below, flying limply to the nearest land.

Slana. How badly are you injured? Dorn waited for a reply, but none came.

Wind screamed in Leonie's ears. Borne out of desperation, she grasped at her idea. Her life depended on it. As they tumbled, she brought one leg up, then the other. Kicking and heaving with all her might, she timed her moment well.

In her initial struggles, Leonie had completely forgotten the harness from White Cliffs. It was only when she landed on Faldo's back she painfully remembered. After the episode on the skyland, she had donned the harness as a precaution.

The moment the assassin's grip loosened, Leonie put all her might into one final kick, then slipped a paw under her jacket and twisted the dial. A painful constriction around her ribs made her gasp as air squeezed out of her lungs. The harness did its work.

"Nooo!" Evlin cried as her nemesis slipped from her reach, moving farther away from her. She thrashed and swung her arms madly in an effort to strike. The blade slashed through thin air.

In a pique of rage, Leonie sent a fireball after her. It was fascinating to observe it trailing her, then flare brightly when it hit Evlin. Leonie watched, partly curious but relieved, as the assassin continued to plummet. A few seconds later, she saw the splash when the assassin's body hit. The water foamed up, but soon faded. Amazingly, the fire continued but dimmed as the body sank to the depths of the harbour as a shadow cut off her view.

Faldo's bulk loomed beneath her.

"You can have a seat as long as you don't bite," Feiron called out.

"With an invitation like that, how could I refuse? I can't make any promises though."

Are you going to stay on this time, furry one?

"That, I *can* promise. Stay right there, and I'll come down." She landed near the base of the tail and walked forwards, sitting awkwardly behind Feiron. "Sorry for biting you," she said to him.

"It's of no matter. Lucky I'm thick-skinned."

"More like all-skin." She chuckled, glancing down at the water, half expecting Evlin to appear.

Slana has landed. Come quick! Dorn's message was urgent.

We come. Faldo angled down sharply.

"We're going to land. Slana is down," Leonie explained to Feiron. "How is she, Faldo?"

She is in great pain. Faldo skimmed above the waves, wingtips touching the water with each beat.

"Where are we headed?" Leonie tried to pinpoint their location. A row of rocky pinnacles flashed towards them; the smashed body of the l'ith draped across one. She recognised it as Fang Rock. Faldo momentarily tucked in his wings before they clipped one of the massive edifices as he dashed between them. Her paw shaking, Leonie pointed beyond. "Slana's in the Plaza! Someone's bound to have seen her land even at this time of night."

Faldo flew directly to where his sister lay on the ground. Philbert had already dismounted to check the young wyvern's wounds, while Dorn hovered anxiously nearby.

"Can she crawl behind that?" Leonie called out when within earshot. She pointed to a three-tiered platform close to the canal. "It might block her from view of the garrison, assuming they don't already know she's here." Sadness wrenched her, watching the young female wyvern drag herself painfully along the paving; so agile in the air, now as mobile as a beached whale. "We may as well join her," she said to Feiron and Faldo. "It isn't exactly the way we'd planned it, but we're home now."

People are coming! Dorn's thoughts cut in.

Leonie cast her eyes around. The group, mostly guards, gathered on the edge of the plaza. Soon they'd gain enough courage to approach.

Faldo dropped quickly to the flagstones to allow his passengers to alight. As the wyvern landed, Leonie dropped to the ground, suppressing a groan from the pain of bruised ribs and over-strained muscles. Feiron dripped out of the saddle, reaching for his bag of scales as he dismounted. He joined Leonie by Slana's side.

Faldo launched immediately, lowering his head as he

streaked towards the mob. The roar he emitted scared them senseless. As one, they scattered white-faced for the protection of the nearest buildings.

"So much for a quiet arrival," Feiron muttered.

"How is she?" Leonie asked Phil.

"I think it's more shock than serious wounding." Phil straddled Slana's back, pouring a few drops of liquid onto each of the puncture marks. "There's muscle damage, painful but not lethal."

You do not know the half of it, Slana grumbled.

"Slana," Leonie called out. "There'll be many guards here soon."

Will they help?

"Only to your grave. You'll have to leave. Now!" Leonie added.

I cannot fly.

"Then swim, damn it, but if you stay, they'll slaughter you. These people don't understand."

You did.

"Remember I told you of the stories where you are evil creatures? These people believe those stories."

The men are returning. There are more this time, and they have a leader. Dorn was hovering in the sky, but she dipped her wings and dive-bombed the approaching group. Some men broke ranks and retreated, regardless of shouted commands, but the bulk of them remained steadfast.

Bows appeared and the night filled with shafts hurtling into the darkness. Most were fired in haste and fear, easily missing the wyverns, but others came too close. Dorn banked sharply to the right, but Faldo, following his mother's lead, hissed in pain as a shaft pierced his wing.

Singer. Prepare yourself. Dorn sent her intentions.

Phil spun to his companions to shout a warning. "You better hit the deck!"

Seconds later the squad of guards collapsed, dropping

weapons and clutching their heads, blood trickling from some ears.

Leonie looked around, wondering why they had to take cover.

Feiron shared her look of confusion. "What's happening?"

"Mind blast, but a restrained one," Phil answered. "One of the other tricks the wyverns have." He looked at them both quizzically. "Looks like you're both immune. Fascinating as that is, we should leave. Those men will be in a foul mood when they recover."

Phil turned to the young wyvern. "Slana, remember your training," he stressed. "Something like this could happen at any time. I know it hurts, but while you're feeling sorry for yourself, others are risking their lives trying to protect you. Get up. Now!"

I don't like you anymore.

"I can live with that."

Do not forget daughter, Dorn soothed. *There is a skyland nearby where you can recover. It is not too far.*

Very well, mother.

Phil slid off the young wyvern's back as she slowly rose from the hard surface.

Slana faltered slightly, and both Leonie and Philbert staggered as echoes of her pain rippled across their minds.

Dorn, Phil called.

I am here. Her massive form whipped around the tiered platform and dropped swiftly to the ground. The tiles cracked as she crunched down. She swung her tail away from where it almost swiped Feiron. *Apologies.*

Phil leapt into the saddle. "I hope to see you both again," he called as Dorn launched herself skyward.

After the two adventurers waved quickly, they moved to the shadows of the large dais used for public ceremonies.

Farewell from all of us. Dorn added as the three wyverns turned and winged their way back between the headlands. *We hope you will be able to fly with us again.*

"It'd be our pleasure, Dorn. Bye Faldo, Slana. Feiron sends

his regards too," Leonie said quietly, knowing the wyverns would hear her thoughts. The two adventurers ducked, bolting for the shadows of the dais.

"We aren't out of trouble yet," Feiron pointed out.

The guards helped each other to their feet; some still nursing their heads or wiping blood from their faces, others warily approached the area.

"I guess you'll be heading home?"

Feiron nodded. "I better report to my mentor first. She'll want to know about this straight away, and not second-hand in the morning."

"There will be dozens of guard patrols out now, all fired up and looking for something to vent their anger. Perhaps a quick dip up the Grand Canal to avoid them?"

"Sounds like a plan. What about you?"

"After what we've been through? I can manage these guys. Don't worry."

He didn't look convinced.

"How about we catch up in a few days?" she suggested.

"At the Heart?"

"Sunset." Leonie nodded. "Good luck." She climbed the stairs, looking back when she reached the top of the platform.

Feiron had shaped into the large serpent form he used at the chasm, the sack forming a bulge in his midsection. Keeping to the shadows, he slunk across the flagstones, disappearing the moment he entered the water. Leonie crouched and waited to see if the guards noticed either of them.

The men spread out below, their attention drawn to the south to where three dark shapes could be barely seen winging their way out to sea. One of the men, an officer as indicated by a sash across his right shoulder, looked down. He was standing in a splash of wyvern blood. The man jumped back with an oath and vigorously scraped his boots on the paving. Then he stopped, bending down to pick up something.

From the size and shape, Leonie guessed it was one of Slana's scales. The men gathered around to see. Leonie took that as her cue to depart.

———

Dragging herself out of the harbour, Evlin collapsed on the cobbled road in front of a row of warehouses. Gradually she was able to focus and get her bearings, discovering she was in Port-side. She must have lost her way, wandering through the forest of seaweed. Any other time the walk along the seabed may have been interesting, but not this night. This night the Enemy escaped.

Again, she had failed. Lothas would be displeased.

She scanned the harbour, but saw no wyverns, just drifting clouds and the silhouettes of ships.

'Where were they? Surely they didn't land in the city! And where was that damn flying lizard hiding?' her thoughts raged.

The horizon had the faintest touch of light from the pending sunrise. Half the night had passed while she made her way to dry land! She'd need shelter soon. The city was silent for now, only the sound of the waves from the harbour lapping against the stone wall reached her ears, but there were bound to be guards on patrol, and various merchants and fishermen would be up and about… if not already.

The assassin fingered the dagger, secured in its sheath while she pondered her next step. Going back to Lothas empty-handed wasn't an option she relished. She slowly stood up; the swaying of her weakened body reminded her of needed sustenance. Looking down, she was surprised her ruined legs could still support the weight; her clothes were in shreds and the ripped flesh beneath clearly visible. It was unnerving to witness so much damage. Tentatively, she touched her face, and could feel the previous wounds coming back. Once she renewed her life-force her body would recover quickly, all the damage would disappear and she'd be ready to deal with the Enemy and exact her revenge scratch for scratch. By the time she was finished with the half-rrell bitch, there'd be no skin left.

Her jet-black eyes surveyed the nearby buildings. There would be plenty of sleeping citizens for her to choose from here, and she had a lot of frustration to vent having been thwarted once again. Evlin skulked down the street to the closest dwelling. She would feel much better soon. And then, then she would find the Enemy once and for all.

31

THE RETURNING

STILL FEELING AS IF SHE HADN'T SLEPT A WINK, LEONIE WOKE WELL after sunrise. There was a momentary confusion while her foggy mind cleared. She winced at the bruising around her ribs; in fact, her whole body ached from the strain of last night's battle and days spent in the saddle. Leonie steadfastly carried out her stretching routine to loosen up before heading off discreetly to find food. Then she'd find Jade to report on the last month's activities.

Outside in the large square, people were busy shopping at the many stalls, going about their day-to-day tasks. The smells and sounds of the city were soothing in their familiarity, putting a spring into her step. Leonie looked around warily. On the far side of the square, she spied a couple of acolytes. Woorin noviciates, by their garb. She wondered if they were out for the fresh air and haggling, or something more devious. In case it was the latter she ensured her hood was up fully; she gave them a wide berth.

Curiosity burned inside Leonie when a flurry of activity near the garrison caught her attention. A squad of guardsmen, jogging in formation, headed towards Portside. Armoured guards in a hurry always raised her curiosity. As expected, any of a dozen taverns overflowed with information.

True to their kind, the rumourmongers were in full swing, spreading gossip quicker than a drunk could bring up his last meal. With a mug in paw, she milled through the crowd to listen.

"I seen it wit' me own eyes," one whispered hoarsely. "Four dragons fought furiously above the harbour, breathin' fire and lightnin' an' controlled by ethereal riders they was." He nodded vigorously. "They flew off south, back to Galhena, leavin' charred corpses to feed the crocs."

A few patrons turned away smirking, finding the contents of their mugs more to their liking.

"The 'arbour were foaming an' frothing like," he continued. "Red with the bloody frenzy I tell ya."

———

Reaching Jade's office, Rohan's bear-hug almost crushed her. When Leonie asked after Jade, his face darkened as he signed a reply with his big hands. His sharp hand signal reflected his mood. 'She can be found at the Heart. She's been there for two days.'

Leonie knew something was up immediately; Jade rarely left her office for long. She persuaded Rohan to come with her and they headed towards the Heart of Gold. When they entered the tavern, voices of the few patrons already present lowered to whispers.

"Another wine, Hilda. Now," a slurred voice called from Jade's private cubicle.

Leonie stalked over with the intention of removing whoever had the nerve to use Jade's table. She stopped in her tracks. She'd never seen her boss drunk like this; her hair was a mess, and she reeked worse than the clogged gutters in the back alley. Her leather clothing was loose, exposing more cleavage than the cheap harlots servicing the docks.

"Where's my drink?" Jade's bleary eyes slowly focused on

the shape by her table. "You're not Hilda." She struggled to her feet, falling against her friend in the attempt. "Leonie?"

Leonie held her, turning her head from Jade's foetid breath.

"Th-they said you'd been killed! I didn't want t-to believe it. Not you. Not like that, but you were away for so long," Jade slurred heavily.

"And you're drowning your sorrows? You shouldn't believe anything until you've seen a body, especially when it concerns mine. It'll take more than a few assassins to get me out of your fur. Let's get you cleaned up. I'll tell you all about it."

With much protest and cursing from Jade, Rohan picked her up like a doll and carried her up the stairs. Leonie ordered food and water before bounding upstairs. It took the two of them the best part of the morning to get Jade settled. She wanted a full report and promised to continue being recalcitrant until she heard everything.

Starting with the first attack of the worshippers of Woorin at the chasm, Leonie told of her possession by the High Priest of the Death Sect, the encounter with the undead creatures in the swamp, flying with wyverns, and about the incident at White Cliffs. When she began to talk about it, it all seemed so long ago.

Jade insisted she tell every detail of the fight with the assassins in the caverns. Even though she could hardly sit up in bed, she commiserated with her friend for losing her tail. "Lucky tha's all ya lost." She finished with a hiccup.

They stopped briefly when Netoha entered with the food. If the look on her face was any sign, Netoha showed great displeasure at Jade's recent behaviour. Rohan interceded, placing the tray on the table by the bed in case the tray somehow slipped from Netoha's grasp and landed on Jade.

Leonie smiled at the pair; sometimes his wife's temper got the better of her. She stood up and gave her a warm greeting. "How're you feeling, Nettie?"

"I'm well. Taking good care of myself. Unlike some." She glared at Jade, who was picking at the food oblivious to her vexation. "We're glad you decided to return from the dead." Netoha smiled at Leonie. "We all worried."

"I'm sorry for any distress. The rumours were meant to stop people trying to kill us, keep them off our backs. Then we could return without the need to look over our shoulders. Our paws were full as it was—"

"Never a dull moment." Jade stifled a yawn.

"Maybe for the first day or so. After that it got a bit lively," Leonie said. "Boss or not, you're going to rest. You can tell me everything that happened here later."

"But—"

"Can you finish your food, or do you need help? I'm sure I could find someone to assist."

"I can feed myself," Jade grumbled, sitting back. "Anyone would think you were talking to a kid."

Rohan turned towards the door so his boss couldn't see his grin.

"Well and good." Leonie didn't hide her mirth. "We'll see you and talk more tomorrow."

Back on the streets, Leonie made sure she kept a low profile as she wended her way home. Netoha had filled her in on the recent events in Delta. Strange things – vile things – had been occurring to other half-breeds and crossbreeds lately, some of them her friends. This problem had escalated beyond the simple harassment; people had gone missing. Bodies had been found in various parts of the city. Mutilated beyond belief, some could only be recognised by the remnants of clothing and personal belongings.

It horrified Leonie to the extent she vowed to resolve the problem once and for all. Leonie thought she knew the reason, feeling indirectly responsible. This situation had worsened since the *Codex* came to Delta. Whatever it took; whatever the risks, she'd deal with it. Those responsible would rue the day they drew their first breath.

She counted off who she'd be up against; The Flamers hadn't made an attack since the chasm. Perhaps the rumours of her demise at White Cliffs quelled them. The aerial fight over the harbour indicated that either the Deathers and possibly the Jart'lekk knew she was still alive, but who really controlled Evlin? What about Zander? What was his involvement? She couldn't go after them all.

"Not all at the same time," she muttered.

———

Jade looked recovered, apart from a bit of redness around the eyes.

"Your turn." Leonie started the conversation. "Did much happen while I was away?"

Her boss sat back taking a deep breath, thinking about what had occurred since she last saw her friend. "We discovered the Jart'lekk were hired by a sage, not Zander. If he believes the book concerns him, we have no confirmation."

"We did a lot of studying of the *Codex* on our way to Qelay. Feiron believes it has vague references to Zander, Dianah and Bren."

Jade picked at her dinner and continued with her side of the story. "Some of the temples were out and about more than usual, keeping an eye on the river and North Gate specifically."

"We returned last night on the backs of wyverns."

Jade's brows arched in surprise at this news. "Wyverns? I did hear rumours…"

"Rumours only, no mention of anyone actually seeing *us*." Leonie went on to describe Evlin's attack in what detail she could. "I'm certain she died in White Cliff's caverns; I felt her die with my claws in her throat. Her blood soaked my paw. I reckon the Death Sect got to her somehow, which would tie her and Lothas together. I'm not sure if the other sects know I'm alive yet."

"Then you better make sure you keep your head down so

they remain ignorant. The Jart'lekk alone are bad enough, let alone two of the more notorious temples. We don't need any more trouble. Anything else? Did Feiron get his eggshells?"

"Not exactly. He almost died in the attempt." She detailed Feiron's brush with death when he almost melted. "It's amazing what those illios can do. He ended up with a sack of wyvern scales instead. And I've collected an interesting toy; a harness that makes me as light as a feather. I'll show you one day.

"We also camped on one of those sky islands. I found this." She produced the earring from her pouch. "It has a very faint aura, so it's got some function, but what, I don't know yet." She tossed it to Jade, who dropped it on the bed.

Jade looked at it briefly. "Nice."

Leonie caught it when Jade tossed it back. "I'll work out what it does eventually, but earrings aren't my thing."

"Styx and the book should almost be in Reenat by now. I wonder what they'll do with it?"

"No doubt the Athglenn rulers are keen to see what it's all about. Unlike us, they've maintained close contacts with the rollos and therefore know a lot more about prophecy."

They fell silent for a while as they continued eating, the new information going through their minds.

"What are your plans, now you've returned from the dead?"

Leonie paused before she spoke again in a sombre tone. "Styx dredged out a few deep memories, especially about the night we met. It seems I owe you a great deal. Why didn't you mention anything about it?"

Jade sat down beside her when she realised what Leonie meant. "I wanted to, but you had such terrible nightmares. Then one day, it stopped. I was waiting for you to bring it up, but since you didn't, I felt you preferred to forget. So, I left it at that."

Leonie looked to her glass. "Any idea what happened to Pasha?"

"I arranged for her to be kept at a safehouse. A couple of days later, she disappeared."

"Did she run away? She was unconscious when you saved

her. Maybe she thought *you* were the kidnapper?"

Jade shrugged. "I looked everywhere I could, but she was nowhere to be found. I even sent messages via trusted people to the most frequented ports. Nothing. If she had simply run away, she wouldn't have been able to get far." Jade shrugged again. "Back then, the Takers Guild wasn't like it is now. I wasn't the boss and had little control."

"I can't believe I haven't thought about her all this time … either of them." Leonie put her head in her paws.

"It was a dreadful night. They would have lost their home and mother too." The talk went into greater depth, strengthening the bond between them as they reflected on years gone by. "You don't have to go through this alone you know."

"Yes, I do." Leonie took a deep breath, gripping the table edges. "This is my problem. And don't even think about sending someone out to look after me."

Jade didn't argue, knowing Leonie's tone, but silently promised to keep an eye out anyway. "Take this." She handed over the assassin's throwing dagger and scabbard from the night of the royal courier's death. "You'll need all the help you can get."

Leonie paused to wipe her eyes before taking it. "May as well add it to my collection." She hitched the scabbard on her belt. "Jade, thank you… for everything."

Leonie slipped out the room. She left with a great weight off her shoulders. Emotionally exhausted, all she wanted to do now was sleep. Wearily, she made her way back to her room.

———

Tossing and turning, dark thoughts flared up, Leonie decided there were better ways to spend the dead of night instead of wrestling with the sheets and her morbid childhood. Stretching wasn't enough and her random rooftop wanderings brought her to the Eternal Gardens. *Damn subconscious!* As she stared at the gardens, flashbacks of her youth quickly came and went; visions of fire and smoke, the sounds of women and children screaming resounded in her head, the yelling of guards assaulted her ears. These memories no longer caused the dizziness, but Leonie gouged her claws between the slate tiles to silently vent her anger. More memories of that night assailed her, this time with far more clarity than ever before. The night she lost her mother, her friends, her youth.

Using the lessons learnt in White Cliffs, Leonie calmed her mind and regained her composure, noting from the positions of the moons only a few minutes had elapsed. Thanks to the hroltahg training, she could now gaze upon the garden with greater hindsight, picturing where the original buildings had been situated; the gravel paths generally following the foundations of the old structures.

She recalled in her youthful expeditions the discovery of another exit from the dormitory area, a long dusty corridor and an entrance to an old storeroom. How and if they were connected was unclear.

As the recollections of another way in returned, she realised there might not be the need to dodge guards to enter the palace. She didn't want to get her hopes up as it may have collapsed or been blocked off over the years. Other people from the palace attended the numerous rituals, and they hadn't entered the same way as her mother, or the other Favoured.

She made herself comfortable against a chimney and waited, confirming the guard's movements. If the hidden entrance was blocked, the walls would be the next option. More or less on cue, the pair of guards returned along the path they repeatedly trod night after night, watch after watch.

Leonie lowered herself to the damp grass in the shadows at the rear of the warehouse and edged towards the open expanse. She'd have to cover a lot of distance before reaching the protection of the trees and shrubs, and time was running out. It was said Zander was due back soon. If she was going to have any chance of getting information, sooner was better than later. She had put it off for too long as it was.

32

SANCTUM

THE ENTRANCE, NOW COVERED BY OVERGROWN SHRUBS, WAS fortunately clear, except for cobwebs. Putting her shoulder to the weathered door and attempting to keep the squeak of the rusty hinges to a minimum, she entered the old storeroom. It took only a quick search to determine everything of value had been removed. All that remained were discarded boxes and a few crates. Underneath the refuse she found a couple of dusty barrels, with a reminiscent odour. It took a few moments for her to recognise it as balbon. She decided to keep well clear of that.

Outside the storeroom, wood panelling lined the walls of a long, dim passage. The whole place showed signs of ageing, as if it hadn't been maintained for a long time; the panelling had split with the dry air and the carpet was threadbare and faded. Small niches, each with an ornament, were spaced at regular intervals between dust-covered tables. After examining a few, Leonie decided the ornaments weren't particularly valuable, but must've come from all over the continent; they were so different in design and make. In the middle of each table was a large vase full of fresh-cut flowers, contrasting greatly with the dilapidated state of the passage. She was curious about the faint streaks in the dust near the edge of each table, like someone had run their fingers in it.

Leonie froze in surprise when she heard a sneeze behind her. She wasn't sure if it was by magic or a secret door, but whoever it was had silently entered the same passageway. There was little she could do to avoid detection without making her position even more obvious. All that remained was to stand perfectly still within the shadows.

Strangely, as the figure reached each table it paused, lingering over the flowers before moving off to the next table. A gloved hand traced the edge of the table, leaving a trail in the thick dust. Slippered feet trod the blue carpet stretching down the centre of the hall. The robed figure was a couple of steps past her before stopping, the hand poised in readiness to touch the next table.

With whiskers twitching, Leonie held her breath to see what would happen next, watching the figure closely. She could make little detail within the shadow of the hood, even with her night vision. The head moved around slightly from side to side, each shift punctuated by a faint snorting sound. Leonie realised the figure was blind.

"I smell a visitor?" The voice was a whisper, with a faint slurring. "Visitors don't normally come down here, or are you lost?" the female voice said a bit louder. "You know you shouldn't be here. Zander has strict instructions. He gets too angry for his own good – the last time he almost burnt down the place."

Before Leonie answered, the figure turned her head to the exact position to where Leonie was hiding. "I don't mean to offend, but you have an unusual odour. It *is* intriguing. These days there's little that intrigues me." The voice hesitated for a moment and the sound of sniffing could be heard. "A rrell? But the only rrell I know in the palace is Niaarin, the palace mage and *she* has no wish to visit me and uses redolent perfumes." The old crone shuffled a bit closer.

Leonie could see a small membrane on each nostril open and close as she sniffed. Her nose twitched and a forked tongue flickered out.

A seleth? Leonie thought in surprise.

"There's something else." The woman paused. "I smell sweat, but rrells don't sweat. So ...rrell *and*... human?" She turned full circle and sniffed the air behind her. "You are alone so you're a *true* half-breed?" The woman stepped back as if in shock.

"I won't hurt you," Leonie said quietly, fearing the woman would cry out.

The woman paused. "Can it be...?" she mumbled distantly.

Leonie was unsure what to say. She felt as though the question wasn't directed to her.

"Follow me," the woman said abruptly and continued in the direction Leonie had intended. As the woman scuttled down the hall, her hand came out to touch the tables as she passed, as if counting. She turned through a narrow archway.

Leonie warily followed her down a set of stairs.

"I'm Magda. I've spent well over a decade here, mostly alone," the crone said over her shoulder. "I don't get many visitors anymore – not since the fire."

Leonie knew this place the moment she entered the next passage; surprised and delighted at the accuracy of her information. "So, you know about the Favoured?" she asked, hurrying behind Magda.

The woman was silent for a moment, stopping before large ironbound double doors at the end of the passage. She leaned on one of the large doors at the end. It opened with a soft squeal of protest. Magda entered without answering. Leonie followed, pushing the door closed behind her.

Bookcases of indeterminate age lined the walls from floor to ceiling, with a row of them down the middle. To the left was a small hearth, a couple of worn chairs and a threadbare rug. Unerringly, the woman shuffled to a chair, indicating for Leonie to sit in the opposite one. "There are those that were born naturally, and those that were... a miracle," she said. "*They* were the Favoured—" The distant clang of an opening door and voices warned them of impending visitors.

"Quickly. This way." With the practised ease of familiarity, Magda shuffled down the side of the room, passing several rows of neat but dusty bookcases. In the far, dim corner she tugged open a small ironbound door. "You will be safe in here."

With the briefest glance at Magda, Leonie ducked low and stepped into a dark, narrow tunnel. The door shut behind her.

"If you are who I think you are," Magda's voice sounded faintly through a grille, "then you will recognise this place, and you'll be safe. If you aren't... then this will be goodbye. And don't eat the pigeons."

Leonie was sure she heard weeping as she tested the door. It was solid and seamless and wouldn't budge. No latch or locking mechanism to pick from this side. Cursing for her stupidity, she turned and moved down the passage. Descending a few steps, the sandstone bricks finished at what she assumed were the original tower foundations. Beyond, the passage continued into the bedrock of the headland. The astringent odour of salt filled the air, and very faintly, the occasional sounds of waves crashing into the cliffs. The tunnel opened into a low, wide cavern littered with fallen rocks. It took a moment for her to realise where she was. Home.

The sanctum stood to her left, dark and forbidding while the living area and dormitory took up the remainder of the large space. In her youth, the cavern had always been well-lit, with rugs and ornate decorations adorning the walls. Everything was gone now; in its place were burnt, charred remains. Though scorched, with a few remnants of the murals the children painted – the walls and floor were bare rock. Halfway along the east wall, the formal stairway that descended from the temple was full of fallen stonework and burnt beams of wood. To her immediate left was the nursery and to her right was where the older children played. Because of their differences – all being crossbreeds – none were allowed out into the city for fear of teasing and ridicule.

The area set aside for the dormitory and living area was a ruin. She walked through it, her childhood memories reminding her of the layout. Leonie stopped where she and her mother had slept. She wasn't expecting to see anything horrible, and she didn't. The bodies were long gone. It was merely her imagination of the sounds of conversation and laughter. Still, she stood motionless, silent tears running down her face, forlorn with her loss of the mother she hardly knew, at the loss of all the other mothers and children. *Why?* There was nothing more to gain here, yet she lingered for a few more minutes. *What her life would had been like...*

Wiping her face with the back of her paw, she turned abruptly and walked away.

How strange the sanctum looked through adult eyes. Her memories, returning in unconnected snippets, were of a completely different shape to what lay before her. Broken and charred wood littered the floor, and she realised these were the remains of an outer covering; a shell to disguise the alien shape. She had not seen it uncovered in its entirety until now. Like a cross between a bird and a fish, long and sleek; streamlined but huge. She wondered fleetingly if it was as large as those whales fishermen spoke about; they had seemed in awe of the creatures, always speaking in hushed tones. Touching the curved side, she nodded with a grim smile as the memories of the cold, hard metal returned.

Leonie walked around the entire sanctum; there was only the one door leading in about midway along the left side. One end of the sanctum formed a rounded wedge-shape held up by a strange structure sticking out from below. She decided this end was the head of the fish. What appeared to be windows were dark; not even her night vision could penetrate them. What amazed her was how they curved around the body. Just below the window read *Skydancer*. The metal here looked slightly dented and scorched. Bending down to look underneath she noted the scorch marks – as well as the long, deep scratches – trailed almost to the rear. In her memory, she recalled a multitude of flowers and plants all along the bottom, obscuring various parts of the sanctum.

At the tail end, two large cone-shaped tubes extended behind the body. Three fins splayed out here as well. One large fin sprouting up and out from the two tubes almost touched the cavern roof. Two shorter but wider fins stuck out each side and angled down, supporting the back end of the sanctum.

Walking back to the middle of the sanctum, sandstone steps lead to the threshold of a half-open door. She recalled it slid into a recess within the wall. As Leonie ascended, she spied a square indentation the size of her palm. It popped open at her touch revealing a dark blank rectangle, and ten small squares with rounded corners below it. They had symbols on each; they looked vaguely like numbers, but the order they were in meant nothing to her. Touching them revealed little other than the faintest of clicks when pressed.

With a shrug and the slightest bit of trepidation, she climbed inside. The interior wall was made of the same metal but a lighter colour. The floor had a firm, non-slip covering. She couldn't work out what it was. Not paint or carpet – she was barely able to scratch it with a claw. Opposite the entrance, but further in, a large column stretched from floor to ceiling. It was in the middle of the floor at the intersection of other passages. Leonie snatched her paw back in surprise when she touched it. It was warm. Cautiously, she placed her paw on it again. There was the faintest of vibrations. Further investigation disclosed little else; more of those little squares with numbers, a few dials and a lever, which did nothing when turned or pulled.

Following the passage to her right, she remembered the door her mother took her through as a child. All these doors were closed and try as she might, there was no way for her to open them. There was no aura of power and kicking it only bruised her toes. She stepped away in frustration.

Heading in the other direction, past the entrance and the warm, vibrating column, she walked towards the head. There were two closed doors on each wall. She didn't even attempt to open them. At the end of the passage, a partially open door led into a large room. Inside she saw the two large, darkened windows. Other strange objects and shapes occupied the centre of the room; weirdly designed chairs around a low table. Entering, she sat in one of the chairs, it moved, quickly moulding itself to her shape, even taking into account her stub of a tail. The material was smooth and tough yet flexible. Two of the front chairs had strange layouts of little squares in the armrest, but larger and with more squares of different colours as well as a few dials. Again, nothing changed when she pushed or turned them. *I wonder if Magda knows how to use these?*

She spent a few disappointing minutes exploring the room. The storage areas were empty; there was nothing here other than confusion. Everything here was beyond her comprehension and this palace visit was working out to be nothing like she had planned. *When had I really planned anything?*

Her conversations with Feiron echoed in her head. *These people really did come from another world!* Nothing here resembled anything familiar. She came here looking for answers, but now had more questions. Reluctantly, but at a loss at what else to do, she exited the sanctum and moved towards the sound of the surf.

As she approached, she heard a shuffling noise and the brief flapping of wings. She noticed a number of cages in a n alcove against the back end of the cavern. *'Don't eat my pigeons.'* Leonie recalled Magda's last words. She had a good mind to let them go, but decided against it. Knowing her luck, they'd crap on her as they flew about.

Turning her attention to this section of the wall, she noticed some of it was not natural stone. *Someone built it.* Stepping back again and comparing it with the sanctum – the *Skydancer* – she estimated the wall covered an entrance large enough so it could fit through.

There were several gaps where the rock-work had fallen. Leonie was about to look through when a pigeon came flapping through. When it landed, she noticed a band wrapped around its leg. *A message?* It flapped away when she tried to reach for it. *Who would be sending a message to Magda? Zander perhaps?*

With a shrug of disappointment, she returned to the gap. Craning her neck out in both directions, she could see no land. She was looking directly at the Southern Ocean glinting in the moonlight. Turning awkwardly, she looked up. The walls of the palace blended neatly into the cliff face.

Leonie climbed out and used her harness to ascend the wall. Buffeted by the wind, she gripped it to maintain direction. A dim light from a single window high in a tower intrigued her. The window was wide open, letting in the fresh sea air. The curtains, the worse for wear and stiff with salt residue, swayed stiffly in the breeze. Before her presence was noticed, she merged with the shadows near the ceiling. Her attention was immediately drawn to the far wall. The whole section glowed with aura.

It had a slight curve and a stone bench-top followed the contour. A cleric sat down in one of the many chairs along the bench. He sat, staring into the face of a large crystal before him.

Resembling mosaic tiles, row upon row of crystals were stacked on their sides to appear as a flat, hexagonal face. The many polished surfaces reminded her of honeycomb. Leonie was completely captivated. If it wasn't for the aura of magic surrounding it, she would have thought it an ornate mural, each facet depicting a different pattern. Her whiskers quivered in amazement.

Entranced, she risked exposure by moving closer to view the scene below. What she first thought as light playing along the crystal surface turned out to be moving pictures. Each facet showed an area of the city or harbour; some even showed glimpses of building interiors through windows.

Scanning the crystals on the wall, the cleric would adjust one of the silver knobs in front of him. It took a few moments for Leonie to comprehend what he saw on the large crystal was a more detailed image from one of the smaller ones. The dark of night made no difference to the view. *Bugger!*

Only now did it dawn on her! It was an ingenious method of spying. The pillars scattered around the city with the crystal decorations were strategically placed so Zander could keep an eye on his domain. No wonder he wanted the Temporal Brother-hood here.

Beside every large crystal display was an extremely detailed picture of a young man. Leonie had never seen a picture quite like it before. Dressed in strange, foreign garb, he had silver-white hair and startling blue eyes. No doubt someone of great interest to Zander, if the number of these pictures along the bench was any indication.

There were more crystals than she could count and after scru-tinising the closest ones, she recognised many locations. With enough clerics, the entire city could be observed. A few crystals remained blank, and she assumed they were faulty in some way. One particular location caught her eye, showing an area not too far from her abode. Her movements would need to be changed and Jade would need to be told.

Every so often the cleric would jot on a parchment beside him, looking at the large hourglass to note the time before moving onto a different scene. This one showed several furtive figures in the Merchants' Quarter. The cleric immediately tugged on a woven rope. She heard a bell ring faintly, no doubt summoning a messenger or guard. Either way, she'd have to come back and make a map.

Intent on his task, he failed to notice the dark shadow slip out the window. Within a few minutes Leonie was in the alleyways behind the large warehouses of Portside. Now more mindful of the obelisk's functions, it was preferable to the rooftops until she knew exactly which areas were safest. Heading back to the Web, her thoughts went back to the night of the slain courier. *Did these Watchers see her or the assassins? Did they witness the fight? Is that why the guards were riding down on horseback?*

"Slistorf's balls!" she hissed to herself. "How can I tell Jade if I'm supposed to be staying at home?"

33

DECISIONS MADE

Sleeping late was a luxury she was getting used to. Annoyed with herself, she quietly slipped back from the markets with her recently acquired breakfast. Leonie gathered her thoughts as she ate.

It had been almost forty days since the death of the courier; thirty-three days since the attack at the marsh and her possession – having that evil mind controlling her body still made her shudder. Her lessons in White Cliffs made the likelihood of that happening again extremely remote. The question vexing her constantly, who was the master that sent Evlin? Lothas was the obvious choice, but did the vows of the Jart'lekk extend into death? Did they know of Evlin's resurrection?

She had gained as much information about the *Codex* as Styx or Feiron could provide. Brief as it was, her words with Magda last night, and seeing the sanctum again, exposed hints of information still hidden deep in her memories. Leonie felt her next step was to visit another major player on her list. The recent undead assassin's attack made her consider the Deathers were aware of her return. *How long before others come knocking? How long before Evlin finds me again?* She had to put a stop to her somehow. If not for her own safety and peace of mind, then to prevent more unnecessary murders.

Determined to find answers, she decided to visit the Temple of Opsyss later that evening. If they were responsible, then she'd deal with them. And for his part in violating her, Lothas had a hefty price to pay.

———

"I'm so glad to see you." Feiron wrapped himself around her briefly. "I thought the guards had finally found you."

"Oh please. They've enough trouble finding tits in a brothel." She joined him in a chuckle as they moved to a corner booth at the back of the Heart of Gold. "Sorry I'm late."

"No rest for the wicked."

"How are you anyway? Did my bite hurt?" She tried to locate any signs of injury, but everything seemed in place. "You healed quick enough."

"Nothing I can't cope with, but yes, it was painful."

"Sorry. It's the only way I could stop you from being brave."

"That's the thanks I get for trying to save you?"

"I was saving *you*." She grinned. "That weapon was evil. I saw it glowing, and it wasn't normal magic. I could feel its *thirst*." She shrugged, having no other way to explain it. "Did you see the fireball? It stayed alight *underwater!*"

"Only for a moment, I was more concerned about you. Who was it you were wrestling with?"

She paused when their drinks arrived.

"The assassin I killed in Qelay. The one that cut my tail off," she said quietly.

"But—"

"I know. I know. She's dead. I hope she stays dead this time." She sipped her ale. "I reckon Lothas has a paw in this. His sect is the one dealing with corpses. Perhaps I should pay him a visit."

"When?"

"You know me. I don't plan. Things just *happen*." She took a swig.

The silence stretched.

"To think, we were standing here arguing about wyverns being a myth," Feiron finally spoke.

"Who would've thought we'd be riding them back."

"There was no hoard of treasure either, and there's still the promise of repayment for your assistance," Feiron said quietly. "Unless you want a couple of those scales as a memento?"

"Forget it. I've enough reward; new experiences, new friends, and of course the wonderful harness you borrowed from the rollos. It saved my life the other night. I have you to thank for that."

"You've changed. This isn't the thief I knew before."

"Maybe. I've learnt a lot more since then, but I'm still after answers."

"Can I help?"

"No, my friend. This is something I'll have to do by myself, for myself."

"When you talk about your memories, and what Styx uncovered... you change. To be honest, I think whoever has wronged you is in deep trouble. Delta may not be too safe."

"Perhaps. I doubt anything I do will make much of a difference, regardless of what Styx might think. What about you? What are you going to do?"

"I have a little bit more training to do—"

"I thought you could finish up when you returned?"

"It's my lost memory. Some of the shapes I was practising... need more practice. I have something really exciting to show you though." He almost bubbled with enthusiasm.

Leonie leant closer. "What is it?"

"Watch this." Ensuring no one in the tavern could see, he formed a tentacle. At first nothing special happened, but then it grew thin and long – much thinner than ever before. Soon, more extremely thin tendrils appeared. Then they changed hue.

"You can make hair?" Leonie watched wide-eyed.

284 | ANDRE JONES

"It needs work, but yes. I think perhaps melting may have done something to my structure."

"That's incredible. Can other illios do that?"

"None that I know. Remember the two shapeshifters in Qelay were hairless?"

Leonie nodded. "What's your mentor think?"

"She doesn't know yet, too busy with those wyvern scales. Even with all her bellyaching about not getting the eggshells, she's happy. I know her too well."

"So, in a way, we both got unexpected rewards. Your new ability, my harness and training – even your boss got more than she planned. Reckon you'll be chasing wyverns soon."

"If I can. I'd like to take Phil up on his offer, perhaps in a couple of weeks. Delta has been fine in its way, but it's time to move on. Maybe you'll come and visit?"

"Maybe I won't need to if I come too."

"Are you serious? Delta's your life."

"Ha. It's almost been my death a dozen times. But I don't know. It's a big decision. See how things pan out. I'll let you know, one way or the other in a few days."

They finished their drinks and exited the tavern at the rear. As they were about to depart, Leonie turned. "I almost forgot; remember I talked about the glow in the obelisks?" She continued at his nod. "They are used to spy on the city." She detailed what she'd seen in the palace.

"That is worthy news indeed. I'll pass it on to my mentor. Thank you." He waved farewell.

———

The candle was down to a stub by the time the High Priest of the Death Sect called out. "I require a sacrifice. See to it now."

The novice waiting by his door ran off towards the dungeons immediately.

Lothas donned ceremonial robes and made his way to the altar chamber to prepare for the ritual. He didn't have to wait long before one of the recent prisoners was dragged up from the cells far below by two female guards.

He raised his eyebrows in surprise when he noticed it was a dark female half-rrell. "I was unaware of this particular prisoner." He briefly contemplated on his luck changing, and it being Leonie. A brief glimpse into her mind ended that thought. This was a different half-caste altogether.

"*It* was brought in earlier this evening, m'Lord, caught down by the docks. If it's of no use, we have—"

"No, no, in fact it's most fortuitous. Coincidental even. Why is she unconscious?"

The guards finished securing the prisoner to the altar. "She's a hell-cat, m'Lord. It was easier this way."

"Hell-cat? An interesting term but perhaps premature. The ceremony will be more successful with her full awareness. We shall wait until she revives." He appraised the two guards as they efficiently stripped the half-rrell of her rags.

The victim on the altar moaned.

Lothas regarded her with flat, dark eyes. He'd not seen a half-rrell naked before and noted the fur, now matted with filth, covering the emaciated body. He was about to remark on the extra nipples when her eyes fluttered open. They were deep amber; the irises mere slits.

Her claws came out and her body tensed only to discover the bonds. Glancing around the curved room, her eyes took in her predicament, the two guards and finally came to rest on the old man by her side. She hissed, spitting at him.

Lothas ignored the phlegm dripping on his collar. He had plenty of other robes. Without preamble he raised the dagger and began chanting. His deep voice filled the chamber. The area around the altar darkened, and the air cooled dramatically as the High Priest's mantra grew louder, strengthened by the sacrifice's growing fear.

Panicking, the half-rrell began to struggle and mewl. Mist appeared in front of her face with each breath as the temperature plummeted. Her nerve wracking, high-pitched screech sent a shiver up the spines of the guards.

As the chanting reached a final crescendo, the dagger, now with a menacing glow, plunged towards her heart.

In desperation, she twisted to dodge the blade. The thongs held fast. The dagger missed her heart but sliced her left shoulder, opening it to the bone. Blood spurted as the blade severed an artery, spattering the priest and the altar with dark red fluid. Her face contorted, mouth wide in an agonised scream before slumping into unconsciousness.

"Damn it." He placed his palm over the wound. A glow appeared beneath his hand as he spoke a quick prayer. The blood flow stopped. Other than a livid scar, the area now showed damp, matted fur.

The chamber's temperature began to increase the moment the darkness waned.

"What shall we do with it?" One of the guards looked impassively at the pathetic creature.

"Leave her. I will return shortly. Restrain her more thoroughly, or I'll find another use for you both."

The two women hurried to obey.

34

HOT TIME IN DELTA

A CART TRUNDLED ALONG THE LANE, THE AXLES IN DIRE NEED OF OIL if the constant squeal was any indication. The driver, head down and concentrating on the darkened lane, failed to see the lithe figure sail overhead from one side of the lane to the other. Leonie bounded over the rooftops with ease, doing what she did best.

A gusty wind swept in from the east, bringing with it a nauseating stench from the bog. She wrinkled her nose, cursing under her breath. Clouds boiled overhead threatening rain, but giving good cover from the two crescent moons.

The lane below was clear. On the other side, the rear entrance of the temple beckoned. With a small twist of the harness dial, she leapt the ten paces to the top of the temple's outer wall, landing quietly behind one of the unadorned columns. Bits of the old render crumbled under the sudden weight. Dust filtered to the ground; the chips of mortar sounding like a hailstorm in the quiet of the night.

Muttering curses, she crouched in the shadow and surveyed the courtyard, waiting for someone to investigate the noise. Empty barrels and crates cluttered the area within the confines of the walls. Her nose picked up the unmistakeable odour of the stables to her left. She was about to drop to the ground when she heard a snuffling near the base of the crates. Her ears flattened automatically as two large dogs wandered around, broad snouts to the ground; one raised its leg for a moment before moving off after its companion.

Why is it always damn dogs?

She considered the distance to the main building. It would be a big leap, made difficult without a run-up. The scuff of a boot alerted her to the presence of others. Crouching even lower and glancing around, she spied five robed figures skulking in the shadows a few paces up the lane and heading towards her. Leonie was out of their line of sight for the moment, but that would soon change when they moved nearer; she was above the back gate. The figures continued their approach. In the court-yard, the dog's ears flicked. A low growl permeated the night as they trotted closer to the gate.

Preparing herself, she bunched her leg muscles and leapt forwards, twisting the dial to maximum the instant her paws left the wall. Brickwork cracked as she pushed off, reducing the effect of her leap. Behind her, she heard a muffled oath when loosened bricks hit the ground. The dogs below growled menac-ingly and trotted towards the sound.

Wind whistled through her ears as she sailed the distance. *I'm not going to make it.* All too quickly, she slowed, a body-length from the roof guttering. The dogs below started snarling in earnest. A glance down showed they were still interested in what was beyond the gate and not aware of her. *Good.*

Contemplating the temple's roofline, she became mindful of the wind buffeting her further away. She was directly above the courtyard; if she lowered to the ground those dogs would smell her out. *Not so good.*

Wracking her brain, she tried to come up with a plan. She knew she could keep the harness charged and stay in the air as long as she remained awake, but the stiff breeze seemed intent on blowing her out towards the harbour. She snatched her belt-pouch and rifled through the accumulated contents. Her lock-picks, a small blue wyvern scale, ball of twine, fluff, dirt and a pinecone. With the dawning of an idea, she separated the twine and pine cone, letting the wind take the fluff and dirt. Tying the twine to the stem, she looked at her work sceptically.

Deciding the roof was too smooth with its slate tiles, she lowered her height until level with a balcony and estimated the distance. All she had to do was use the cone's weight to loop over the railing. Keeping hold of the end of twine and leaning forward as much as possible, she tossed the cone towards the balcony, aiming above the balustrade.

It just reached, the cone barely hanging over the lip of the railing. With the utmost care, Leonie pulled on the twine and incrementally decreased the distance. When there was enough twine pulled in, she tugged on it to pull the cone to her. The next time she tossed it, the cone looped over the railing a couple of times, making the anchoring firmer. In short time, she was hovering over the balcony. She reduced the harness setting until she was on the floor then peered down to the courtyard for the other intruders. Leonie didn't want to be anywhere near them if they were caught.

Far below, the five shadows entered the courtyard via the gate. The two dogs lay unmoving by the gate, dark wisps of smoke rising from them.

Flamers? What are Woorin followers breaking into the Death Sect for? Shortly, the bulk of the building blocked her view of their progress.

Knowing little of the Temple's layout, Leonie considered her options. Other than the current surviving members, few citizens were privy to such knowledge. They weren't going to come forth with the information for fear of retribution. She dared not speak of it to Jade simply to avoid any argument.

"Maybe I should've asked Evlin," she muttered. A thought occurred. *If the Flamers are breaking in, they probably know their way around.* She had to go find them. Deftly turning, she darted to the glass doors leading to the interior. The doors were unlocked. Popping her head in and glancing each way, Leonie stepped into a gallery. A long, wide landing followed the curve of the building. The centre of the gallery, bordered with a stone-carved handrail, opened into empty space. Moving closer to the edge, she saw three more similar galleries below. The temple floor must be below ground level; it looked much lower than she expected.

The curved ceiling rose above, covered in artwork showing a dark, desolate place. She took a moment to take in the scene. Dark shapes were scattered across the barren landscape; some lying down, others crawling, standing or flying. All the major species were represented, some Leonie didn't recognise. From the forehead of each figure, white tendrils radiated towards the centre of the dome. As the eye followed the undulating path of each tendril, they grew darker, merging at the apex. The centre was so black, no light reflected from the area, even to her eyes. *Maybe light is being sucked in?* The scene made her uneasy. She shivered, her fur standing on end. Turning away, she tried to concentrate on the main task.

From this vantage point the floors below appeared empty. In her experiences, the fewer the people, the greater the chances of encountering magic of some description. *Then again, what imbecile breaks into the temple of Death?* Leonie proceeded cautiously, wary of traps and the tell-tale aura of power.

Pausing to check the charge on her harness, Leonie twisted the dial to a minimal setting and glided down the closest stairs, silent as a ghost. The descending stairway alternated sides at each level. The next lot were across the room.

Stopping by the balustrade, she considered the potential of getting caught if she floated down. The faint creaking of a door gave away the presence of others nearby. With the acoustics of the dome structure, it was difficult to gauge the precise direction. Her ears pricked up, twitching back and forth to gather as much information as possible. Her whiskers detected the faintest trace of air movement. A draft came from below and left, back towards the courtyard.

Leonie listened intently, ears twitching. *The Deathers? Have I*

or the others alerted someone, somehow? Was it the Woorin intruders?
Leonie wished she could blank her thoughts.

She padded silently across the floor to the stairs and warily descended.

On the level immediately above the main floor, Leonie estimated she was directly over the front entrance, which led out to the Grand Plaza. Crouching by the edge of the stone balustrade, she peered over. A door at the opposite end of the main floor stood ajar, but no figures could be seen. *The back door?* Leonie doubted they managed to cross the floor without her knowing. She considered the area on either side of the back doors, some of it obscured by the black stone pillars supporting the tiered floor system. She'd have to move quickly to catch up.

Leonie backed up, took a running jump over the balustrade and sailed across the void, using her harness to cover the entire distance, landing on the hard tiles a few paces from the doors.

No sooner had she landed when high-pitched screeching assaulted her ears. Instinctively she ducked and rolled behind the nearest pillar. No attack came, but the screams continued in ragged gasps. Leonie now realised what made the noise; only a rrell in sheer agony could make that blood-curdling sound.

The screaming came from her right. Ducking behind a thick tapestry, she came across an archway with stairs leading down. She felt power being drawn. She took the stairs two by two, all senses straining to ensure no surprises awaited her. The sound of steel on steel rang out shrilly, grew louder with her every stride.

The bottom opened into an alcove. Beyond lay a large rectangular chamber lit by torches, with two doors near each corner on the far side. A body in red lay smouldering inside the arched entrance. Further in, robed figures, six in red and four in black, were engaged in a vicious battle. Some of the Deathers looked scorched, their red robes trailing smoke as they moved to ring the centre of the room where an altar stood.

Unless her eyes deceived her, another half-rrell was chained to it!

"Pasha?" she hissed in disbelief almost forgetting to stay hidden.

Oblivious to the activity around him, a chanting priest stood over her, dagger held overhead. Leonie could barely hear his words, and his head was hooded. An ominous darkness loomed about him, and it didn't take much to deduce the half-rrell was about to be sacrificed. There was no way she could cover the distance in time. Whipping her throwing dagger out, she flung it towards him.

The praying abruptly halted. The darkness waned with a roll of thunder. Falling to his knees and dropping his own weapon, he clutched the hilt of the one in his chest. It took a few moments for the red-robed warriors to realise the priest's fate. But when they did, they doubled their efforts against the intruders. The priest lay on the floor, unmoving.

A distant door banged behind her. She heard voices and running footsteps, alerting her to the pending arrival of others. *But who?* Twisting her dial savagely, she quickly rose to the arched ceiling of the alcove, almost smashing her head in her haste. Flattening herself against the ceiling, she adjusted her harness to a lesser setting and tried her best to blend in with the wavering shadows.

She felt power being drawn. A fireball erupted, engulfing the chamber in a bright flare. The black-robed men were immune to the effects, but red-robed figures staggered or rolled blindly, attempting to fight and put out the flames at the same time. With the priest down, the Flamers quickly gained the upper hand. They closed in on the altar, stabbing any Death Dealers within reach, and began to undo the chains.

Leonie blinked away the flash-spots, disbelief at what she saw. *The Woorin Brotherhood were saving the half-rrell!*

Screaming, the scorched prisoner flinched, struggling as they tried to carry her away until one coshed her. With the body now limp, they moved hurriedly towards the stairs.

Opsyss reinforcements met them, flowing down the stairs like a river of blood in their red robes. They forced the Flamers back into the chamber. Before the Flamers could release another spell, another chanting priest, surrounded by gloom, appeared from one of the doors on the far side of the room. In his presence, the charred and smouldering bodies rose from the floor as tendrils of the darkness touched them, coiling around them like a serpent.

Flashing in the light of the flames, swords and daggers clashed. Caught off-guard, the four Flamers were overwhelmed by the living and the dead; the tiles were soon awash in their blood.

Smoke from the fires rose to the roof, billowing and roiling in the confined space. Leonie choked back a cough. Bile, caused by the reek of burnt flesh, threatened to give her away.

As one, the undead stumbled to the sides in a group. The surviving Opsyss warriors took up the smoking half-rrell body and laid her out on the altar. It was quickly determined their sacrifice had died. They began to bicker among themselves until a door behind them opened.

At a command from the hooded newcomer they dropped to their knees in silence, as did the undead. Leaning on a staff, he raised an open palm. He uttered a word. The undead dropped to the floor with a sigh the moment it left them, and the evil gloom dissipated as did the fires, casting the bulk of the chamber into shadow. Now only a few sconces shed a dim flickering light.

At the same moment, intrigued and appalled at the events below, Leonie felt heavier, her harness's power almost depleted by the spell-casting. She had overstayed her visit and didn't relish the idea of remaining in this place of carnage to recharge it. Trying to hold her breath and keep an eye below, Leonie kicked and crawled along the ceiling towards the stairs in an effort to get there before the harness's power dwindled completely. She wasn't going to make it in time.

With a quick glance she spied a dark corner. Silently, she dropped to the floor with a roll and blended with the shadows.

Striding to the body of the fallen priest, the new arrival rolled him over. After examining him, he pulled the dagger free, holding it close for a look. He then placed it on the altar, careful to not touch the blade's edge, then wiped his hands on his robes. He removed his hood, revealing an older face.

Immediately, the surviving red-robed men bowed.

"That is an assassin's weapon." The priest pointed. "It would appear the Jart'lekk are in league with these wretches." He looked with disdain at the four corpses from the Woorin Temple. He raised his voice. "Search everywhere; find the murderer. Bring him to me!"

"At once, Master Lothas," they replied as one.

Lothas? Leonie cursed silently. *Who had she killed?*

The group of surviving clerics moved. One stayed behind to assist the High Priest as the rest headed for her door.

"Leave it," Lothas commanded. "It won't be going anywhere. Join your brothers and bring Alen's killer to me."

The remaining acolyte bowed and ran after the others.

Lothas took a long last look at the feline corpse on the altar before turning to the rear door. He paused for a moment, then disappeared beyond the threshold.

When it became quiet Leonie crept out of the shadow and approached the altar. It was a gruesome sight, but Leonie felt she owed it to Pasha, for neglecting her all these years.

"I'm so sorry it came to this," she whispered. "If only I had known you were back I—" She spun at a noise.

"How touching." Lothas stood at the doorway. "We finally meet in the flesh, Leonie. I still have some questions for you."

"Good luck with that. You failed once before – you really think you have a chance face to face?"

"You were at extreme range and had some assistance. Now you are all alone and in my domain. I am feeling confident."

Leonie sensed his mind trying to enter hers; he failed.

"Get used to being disappointed," she chuckled at his surprised look. "I'm not the half-rrell you thought you knew. No longer will I succumb to being your puppet."

"Intriguing. Ah well. What I can't get in life, I will learn in your death." He raised his arms and started chanting. In moments the temperature dropped and the chamber darkened considerably. To make matters worse, Leonie heard familiar growling getting closer.

Stepping back, she sensed the altar behind her. Leonie spun around, grabbed the dagger and vaulted over the altar. A pair of glowing eyes came through the doorway leading from the stairs. *Undead hounds now?* She was about to toss the dagger at it, but realised the poison would probably have little effect on those already dead. She twisted, hurling it at Lothas instead.

Her aim was true. Inches before it struck Lothas, it stopped mid-air and dropped to the floor.

"Slistorf!" she hissed. The second hound had entered the chamber. They separated to cover both sides of the area. Leonie knew from her experience with Evlin that undead were strong and tenacious. There was only one obvious thing to do. Leonie leapt over the altar and raced to the third door in the other corner of the room.

The door opened easily. She jumped through, slammed it shut, and put her shoulder against it to brace it. Seconds later the hounds ran into it, jarring her to the bone. The door wouldn't last too long. Leonie hurriedly looked around the dark room.

A lounge along the wall to her right, with table and chairs in the centre. One door on the left and another set of stairs opposite. Leonie vaulted the table and hit the stairs three at a time. The door cracked and splintered behind her.

This night was not going as she had imagined. *You've still got Lothas to deal with!* There was an open door at the top of the stairs. She darted through the doorway and hid behind it. *This is a crazy idea.* Leonie held her breath as the two hounds bounded into the large room and kept going. She quietly stepped back into the stairway, softly closing the door behind her. It suddenly dawned on her she had not even contemplated Lothas might follow the hounds. Pivoting instantly, she was greeted by nothing but an empty stairway. *Stupid mistake!*

Leonie sighed with relief and considered her next options as she descended. She hoped Lothas didn't expect her to be returning so quickly – or at all. She had fleetingly considered that killing him in his own sanctuary might prove difficult, but Alen had died easily enough.

Carefully taking a moment to examine the room, she moved past the shattered door towards the smoky chamber. It was quiet, with only the dead scattered on the floor. *A smart girl would be leaving now.* As she entered Lothas's rooms she heard distant howling.

Lothas was nowhere to be found here. *He couldn't have gone too far.* She retraced her steps back to the sacrificial chamber. Fearing the hounds would burst through the door any moment, Leonie bounded through and jogged up the far stairs towards the main area.

Shouting and more clashing of weapons became louder as she neared the top. The fifth Woorin intruder was cornered. It looked like the Deathers were trying to take him prisoner, but he was not having any part of it. She recognised Lothas moving in from the edge of the group. He started a familiar chant. Once again, the immediate area grew dark and cold.

The Woorin brother dropped to his knees and shouted a phrase. He flared brightly. Leonie averted her eyes at the brilliant flash; a resounding boom shook the building. Even on the far side of the hall, the shockwave knocked her over. She sprawled across the tiles. When she managed to look back, the mob of red-robes were scattered across the floor, most unmoving. All were fire damaged and smoking. The nearest column cracked and the floor above tumbled, showering the area with plaster and rubble.

She knew there was very little time before the place would be crawling with every Opsyss follower, but she had to make sure Lothas was dead.

Jogging between the bodies, she checked each one, finally coming across the High Priest, crushed by a slab of the upper terrace. His face was mostly charred, but there was enough to recognise, and the bald head and tattoos confirmed it. He wasn't breathing.

Voices and the sound of many feet prompted Leonie to make

good her escape. The main doors, close to the fallen floor, were the nearest exit. She hoped there'd be enough confusion to slip through unnoticed.

There was a yell from above. Looking up she saw several acolytes looking over the second-level balcony and pointing at her. More acolytes appeared beside them to see, crowding around and leaning over the balustrade. There was another resounding crack and before any of them could move, the balcony on which they had gathered buckled, crashing to the one below. As the main support for that area was the column damaged by the heat blast, the whole section of balconies collapsed.

Leonie dived back from the huge cloud of falling debris as bodies, limbs and more rubble from the upper floors rained down around her. Stone chips and mortar glanced off her, but not sufficient to cause more than scratches and bruising. The main exit was now blocked. Screams and moaning assailed her ears as she turned and bolted to the stairs, coughing in the dust. Luckily, this side of the temple remained mostly intact. If no one barred her way, her best route would be the way she entered.

Without hesitation she bounded up the cracked structure. Racing around the next level, aiming for the next set of stairs, she heard a commotion below. She increased her pace and finally reached the exit. Cold wind buffeted her the moment she stepped onto the balcony. The weather had closed in and a light drizzle was falling. Thick rain clouds blotted the sky.

Leonie looked down, regaining her breath and clearing her lungs. She savoured the coolness of the rain as it helped soothe her burns. There were two options available – the stack of crates about thirty feet below and hard flagstones beyond that, or the roof of the adjacent stables. Perched on the railing, Leonie grabbed the eaves and flipped her body up as the hounds suddenly appeared on the balcony.

She had all but forgotten them in the confusion. It was sheer luck she jumped when she did as their approach had been uncannily silent. Their claws gained little purchase on the smooth tiles and they careened into the railing where she had just been standing. Snarling as they moved in confused circles, all too soon they picked up her scent. Two pairs of baleful orbs looked up.

Leonie slunk along the edge, and when directly across from the stables, she leapt the short distance. Distributing her weight evenly, Leonie landed on the shingles with barely a sound, performed a tight roll to absorb her momentum and stopped in a crouch. Glancing back to the balcony, the hounds were nowhere to be seen. She hoped they'd find something else to chase until whatever spell controlling them wore off.

The rain, which had been a light sprinkle soon increased to a downpour. Thunder and lightning to the north meant the night was going to become very wet.

Keeping low, she bounded along the ridge of the roof to the end. Gripping the eaves, she vaulted over the edge, dropped to the lane and raced back towards the Web. Always mindful of the glowing obelisks, she ducked and weaved in the shadows, avoiding the clerics of the various orders who were out and about in numbers investigating the ruckus.

What happened tonight was bizarre and needed much thought. While waiting for the lane to clear, she took shelter under the eaves and looked back. Seen through the rain, a portion of the Opsyss temple definitely looked lopsided and plumes of grey smoke swirled away in the wind. The explosion from the temple had awoken many people in the city. She could hear voices and the unmistakeable sound of boots stomping on the nearest bridges. *The city guard no doubt being mobilised.* Delta didn't need a religious war; no civilisation did. The Powershaper Wars flashed through her mind.

Tired, singed, sodden and blistered, all Leonie wanted to do was wash and rest. Knowing sleep wouldn't come until she thought things through, she made her way to Jade's apartments. *If she's not awake yet, she soon will be.* Leonie found it was always better to bounce her ideas off someone whose mind worked like hers.

. . .

Leonie paced the floor between the bed and window, leaving damp paw prints in her wake.

Jade sat bleary-eyed in her bed, pillows around her, exasperated by the news. "This is how you keep your head down, is it? You're drenched and wearing my carpet out."

"I thought you'd want to know straight away." Leonie continued pacing. "Besides, I've still got questions needing answers."

"You're right. I'd be annoyed if I heard about this in the morning; but more annoyed about you going there." Jade climbed out of bed and stomped to a cupboard. She grabbed a jar from a shelf and stood behind a chair. "Sit down and lean forward." Unstoppering the container, she gently applied some ointment to the worst of Leonie's blisters. "You don't deserve this."

"I know." Leonie paused. "Pasha's dead. They were going to sacrifice her. The Flamers arrived, and all hell broke loose. She didn't survive. Neither did Lothas or his sidekick, Alen."

"They killed Lothas?"

"No. I killed Alen with the assassin's dagger. Now they think the Jart'lekk did it. Lothas died when the building collapsed on him."

"What were the Woorin brothers doing there if not to kill Lothas? They've been feuding for decades."

"Can you believe they were trying to *rescue* Pasha."

"Rescue?" Jade paused rubbing the cream.

Leonie shrugged. "Looked like that."

"The Flamers went through a lot of trouble to rescue a half-rrell; no doubt thinking it was you." Jade continued working. "Now they think you're dead... again; let's keep it that way. Did anyone see you?"

"None living."

"Good. If we're lucky, both sects will be too busy to worry about you now."

"When have we ever been lucky?"

"If Lothas was killed," Jade continued, "then perhaps that undead assassin won't be making visits again either. As for what Styx may've done inside your head, I can't help you there. Right now, anything would be an improvement." She finished applying the cream. "Done. So... did you manage to garner any more information? Assuming that's what you went for?"

"Nothing." Leonie gingerly stood and stalked to the window, clenching and unclenching her claws in frustration. "Absolutely nothing, except their taste in tapestries is even worse than yours."

"Ah well, glad we found that piece of trivia." Jade grumbled through a yawn. "Watch the carpet, don't pull the weave. Do you know how hard it is to steal something that size?"

Leonie tried to relax. "If the sects are off my back, I can look for more answers."

"No, you can't. Go home and rest, and, although it pains me to repeat myself, keep your head down!" Jade tossed her the jar of cream. "Let them continue to think you're dead."

Leonie barely caught it in time and deposited it in her pouch. "Thanks, boss."

"You only say boss when it suits you. Don't thank me. I don't want my carpet ruined."

35

A FINAL MEETING

LEONIE WOKE FROM HER RESTLESS SLEEP AS THE CURTAINS PARTED.

Jade stepped in through the window. "Having no doors is a real pain."

"You're just getting old," Leonie quipped. "But you must admit, it does deter unwanted visitors." She cautiously rose from the bed, squinting at the glare through the parted curtains. "Checking up on me, are you?"

"The thought did cross my mind, however I did want to see how you were faring. The city is in an uproar – well, the religious sector anyway. All they're doing is blaming each other. The city guard is patrolling in earnest, keeping the two orders at arm's length from each other until things calm down."

"That could be a while."

"The good news is no one is talking about you. So, I'm reminding you of the need to stay out of sight. We don't want to stir any needless trouble. Understood?

"Perfectly." She began cautious stretching.

"Need any more cream?"

"No. I'm coming along fine. You know I heal well."

"A good thing for you; seems you can't go a day without getting injured in some way."

"Ha, that's what Feiron says."

"Great minds think alike. When did you speak with him?"

"A couple of days ago. He says he'll be heading off after his training."

"With the wyverns?"

Half bent over in mid-stretch Leonie nodded. "Maybe I'll join him. For a while at least."

"Will you?" Jade considered. "With what's happening, it would be the ideal time."

"What? No argument for losing your best thief?" Leonie tried to look hurt.

"We did manage without you quite well while you were away. No temples were destroyed for weeks!" Jade chuckled.

"I'm really hurt," Leonie said sarcastically.

"As you say, you heal well. But," Jade added, "you will be missed." Her tone turned more serious as she pulled a rolled note from her belt. "This was left on the bar at the Heart."

"For me? What's it say?"

Jade looked affronted. "As if I'd sneak a peek at a message to *you*."

"You're too funny."

"Keep resting, and keep off the streets." Jade turned to the door. "I'll catch up with you later."

"Don't you want to know what's in it?"

"I'm sure you'll let me know if it's important."

"Oh! Speaking of important – all those obelisks and monuments around the city are used for spying. The Watchers in the palace monitor them constantly."

"What? Damn!" Jade slapped the wall. "That means we'll need to change our routes to avoid them." She sat on the windowsill fuming.

Leonie quickly read the note, too impatient to wait.

'I have some exciting news. Come to the sanctum as soon as you can.'

The message was intriguing, if disappointingly short. *Why the sanctum and not in the library,* she wondered.

Leonie had an idea. She thought furiously. "You know, I could visit the palace and find out exactly what they see; map blind spots. It will keep me away from the temples; it's on the other side of the city and probably the next safest place other than being cooped up here."

"How did this news come about?" She looked up. "Did Feiron tell you?"

"It's amazing what information he gets." Leonie shrugged innocently, covering her relief for managing to tell Jade without actually lying to her face. "If I'm leaving Delta, now is surely the best opportunity," she enthused. "And although you won't admit it, you know I'm the best and only person to do it."

Jade swore under her breath. "And if I said no?"

Leonie idly studied her claws. "You could potentially lose half the guild profits, if not the Takers themselves. Nowhere would be safe."

"Tonight then. I'm coming too."

Crap! "Umm, you know. I don't think that's the best idea you've had. I mean, in your element you are fantastic, but in this situation I can move and climb faster, and can see in the dark. And of course, now more than anything, you need to be around for the others just in case…"

"Damn I hate it when you make sense."

"I agree, it is rare." Leonie nodded, trying to look serious.

"Fine. Come see me the moment you return. I know me being asleep doesn't stop you."

"Sure thing, boss! You'll be the first person I speak to."

"I better be." Shaking her head, Jade climbed out the window and down to the quiet lane.

Leonie paced the room. Before her trip to Qelay and meeting Styx, she would have been out the door in a heartbeat. Tempting as it was, she forced herself to relax and be more patient. Everything Jade said was true; she did have to keep a low profile, and running around with her current injuries in broad daylight with the extra patrols could prove disastrous. Taking a deep breath, she got busy. First thing was to get breakfast.

Once done, she searched through the drawer of her one cupboard to find something to draw on and a stick of charcoal. She found a roll of vorien leather in its case; very expensive because it was impervious to water damage – if one actually paid for it. From memory, and the occasional foray to the higher rooftops nearby for reference, she drew a map of the city. It was something she had always considered doing, so she concentrated in an effort to make it as accurate as possible.

Every now and then, when she got cramps, she alternately stretched and practised the various mind techniques until her stomach grumbled for more food. In a light, hooded cloak, a furtive visit to the nearest tavern provided her with a fulfilling meal, after which she forced herself to return to her room, determined to wait it out until nightfall.

Leonie donned her harness, tucked the scroll case inside her vest, and slipped out the window well after sunset. Her priority was to see Magda first and find out what was so exciting, then she could relax mapping the sections of the city under observation.

The streets had been chaotic earlier, but the fracas between the temples had now subsided in the evening. Even so, extra patrols were still out and about to discourage any over-curious citizens or vengeful clerics. Every second she waited for a clear route was an eternity and she chafed silently at each delay before continuing through the sprinkling rain.

Deciding it would be much quicker to enter via the cavern where the sanctum was located, she made her way along the shoreline below the palace headland, then ascended the cliff face with the aid of the harness. Avoiding bumping her blistered back, she spent a few awkward moments slinking through the orifice. Eventually, she emerged into the cavern. A few pigeons erupted from their roost. Her heart skipped a beat. *Slistorf's balls!* Leonie waited for them to settle.

As she approached the sanctum she heard voices coming from within. Quickly, she stepped behind the dilapidated structure that used to be part of the dormitory. Careful not to touch it and risk it collapsing, she used what she could as cover and edged closer. One sibilant voice was easily recognised as Magda, but the other one, she had no idea.

Deciding she'd have to roll under the sanctum if anyone approached, Leonie snuck up to the entrance, listening intently. The door was now wide open. The acoustics distorted the voices, making the conversation gibberish. *Slistorf! I've got to go in.* Still, she hesitated, not daring to think who was inside. *What was such exciting news?* Breathing slowly and deeply, she mounted the stairs and slipped into the central passage. The column in the centre of the floor now had blinking lights. There was a faint vibration through the floor and an unusual odour throughout.

Whoever was occupying the sanctum was ahead and to the right. Her ears twitched. *Another female was talking.* Leonie ducked around the corner, heading down the passage to the room her mother used to take her.

At first, Leonie saw one figure visible facing away from the door. It took a moment to realise Magda was laying on the strange bed her mother – and every other Favoured – had used. The stranger was taller and looked human, though the heavy cloak didn't help determine much more detail. The voice was vaguely familiar.

The cloaked woman stopped what she was doing. *Hello, Leonie,* she said.

Not trusting her legs, Leonie gripped the doorframe.

"Yes, it's me. Dianah." The figure turned.

"You're alive!" It *was* Dianah, though looking much older.

"We have returned, but only for a short time." *We mean you no harm.*

"Who's we?" Leonie's voice quivered. "You mean Magda?"

"Nope. She means me," said a deep, male voice behind her.

Leonie spun around, struggling to remain conscious. Her stunned mind was overwhelmed with feelings and emotion. *Remember what they did to you!* The massive man stood at the intersection of the passage, next to the vibrating column.

Brendon was much hairier than she remembered. He was aging as well.

"Looks like you're in worse shape than us. Lucky we came back. We can help you," he said.

"Yes child. You need healing," Dianah suggested.

Leonie studied her. Not quite hidden under the cowl, Dianah's facial features were wrong. Her skin was grey and harder. Any other time, Leonie would be hard-pressed to recognise her.

Magda looked up from the bed. "Leonie. I'm so glad you got my message. Lady Dianah and Lord Brendon can help you." She held her arms out to the side. There were weird tubes taped along her arms, then running into the base of the bed. "They helped me. I am no longer riddled with burns. The pain is but a memory and... I can see! You look wonderful. Everything looks so wonderful."

"Let's get you finished up." Dianah said to Magda, and started removing tubes.

"Why are you here now?" Leonie asked. "Why did you return?"

Brendon answered as Dianah was busy. "We needed the *Skydancer* – the sanctum. The last time, we left in such a rush... I thought Zander was going to kill Dianah. I've not seen him so mad. Until Magda sent us a message, we had no idea anyone survived the fires. We're glad to see someone."

"As Magda says, you are truly wonderful." Dianah finished and was helping the seleth to sit up. She turned. "It's so good to see you again." She stepped towards her.

"Stop right there," Leonie ordered, surprised at the tone in her voice. "I've been wanting to kill you ever since the fire. And get answers. The answers first, would be better though."

"I understand—"

"You *understand*?" Leonie hissed. "You *make* me, then leave me and the others to die? My mother died!"

"I can explain—"

"Yes, you will." Leonie stepped forward, claws unsheathed.

STOP! Brendon ordered from the door.

Leonie froze mid-step as an invisible force clamped her body as if in iron. A switch in her mind clicked the moment she recognised what was happening. She placed her paw firmly on the floor and looked at Brendon. The shocked look on his face told her the story. "I don't reckon you'll be doing that to me anymore," she said to cover her sigh of relief.

"How?" he almost whispered, eyes wide.

Leonie started to appreciate Styx's constant training. "A little friend's been working in my head."

"Styx?" Dianah frowned. "We spoke with him. He was... curious about you."

Leonie's turn to her, curious. "Is this another trick? Another lie? Last I heard, he was heading to Reenat."

"So he said." Imploringly, Dianah put her arms out. "Leonie, whatever you think of us, of me... I'm not your enemy. True, you have the right to think unkindly of what was done to you, and the way it was done, but that wasn't how it was meant to be."

"My mother was murdered, along with many others," she repeated. Dianah almost sounded sincere. Leonie focused on her anger. "You were responsible for us. You deserted us!"

"Because of Zander." Brendon found his voice. "You can blame us for many things if need be, but not that."

"You ran and left us. Surely you could have done something. Aren't you the 'High Ones'?"

"Please, Leonie," Magda pleaded from the bed. "Lady Dianah and Lord Brendon only meant the best. What happened was not their doing. Please believe me, if not them. They can heal almost anything. Am I not proof?"

"Now I'm not so sure. Perhaps this was a trap." The rage burning inside her diminished slowly, but not completely. "You could have told me they were here instead of some cryptic note." Embers still glowed hot, fanned by despair and her yearning for answers.

"Anyone could have read it. I had to be careful."

"Okay. Talk then." She locked eyes on Dianah.

"Shall we get more comfortable?" she smiled. "We have refreshments, or we can heal—"

"No healing. Not yet. I want to hear answers before I even consider you *helping* me ever again."

"Fair enough." Brendon stepped away from the door, leading towards the head of the sanctum. "We can all sit comfortably in the lounge."

Leonie guessed right; the lounge was the large curved room towards the front. She sat upright, not resting on her blistered back. "Where's Magda?" she asked suspiciously.

"I sent Magda back to her rooms for more rest," Dianah said. "In our world, I was a scientist," Dianah explained. "While I have the knowledge in helping the sick to heal, I can do so much more. In my efforts to develop a body that could repair itself, I used many techniques and samples from a variety of sources." Her voice took on a clinical tone; forthright and cold. "In so doing, I created your line using a rrell embryo." Whilst she talked, Brendon collected the drinks, placing a tray of glasses on the low table.

"What am I? What sources did you use to—?"

"To create you? I conducted so many trials... many failed until you came along. You are a perfect combination of human, illios and hroltahg genes in a human host."

Leonie sat silent, letting this horror sink in.

"You were impressive while growing up," Dianah added. "From what Magda has told us, you were one of the best and last results that escaped the fires. If you know of others, it would be a great benefit to further the studies." She paused. "Leonie?"

"There is no one else," she replied, dragged back from her thoughts. "But if you think I'd hand over anyone for your experiments, you are sorely mistaken."

"I understand." Dianah's eyes dropped. "I'm only human, and as guilty with ego and ambition as the next person – perhaps more so. In my efforts to increase my own meagre telepathic abilities, I started using genetic samples from the hroltahgs – they are truly incredible specimens. Perhaps I've been punished – in my eagerness for results, I modified myself." She fully lowered her cowl. The extent of the skin change covered her body. "My aim was only partially successful, while my abilities increased slightly, my skin has taken on the hue and texture of a rollo. This was one of the reasons Zander went crazy, he couldn't handle the change in me or my resolve to continue. I'm guilty of many things, but there's no excuse. We argued, we fought and there was an accident. We cannot find it within ourselves to punish him for what he has done – either to you and those that perished, or to us."

"What about my father?"

Dianah smiled wryly. "He's not from this world I can assure you."

Not of this world. Breathing steadily while this all sank in, Leonie sipped at the unusually flavoured drink Brendon had offered her earlier. Studying the glass, she was amazed at its thinness. "If Zander disapproved of all this, where does he fit in?"

"Back home, on my world, Zander – or Alexander – was my lover and confidante. He was as ruthless, if not as crazy, then too. Weak-minded, untrusting, almost paranoid, but extremely wealthy. Some things don't change between worlds. Wealth always means power."

"What, or where, is your world?" Leonie asked. "You have power there too?"

Dianah paused for a moment, thinking.

"Not power, like in magic," Brendon filled in the silence. "She means control. Our world is called Earth. Can't say for sure where it is from here."

"Ah." Leonie took a moment to digest this. "So, you wanted control?"

"Not I," Diana replied. "It's what drove Zander. To control everything. On Earth, power also means wealth. I needed his resources to continue my experiments."

"So that's what's driving you. What about you, Brendon?"

"Initially, I was part of her experiments," he replied. "I helped her; she helped me."

"But it all came crashing down," Brendon added. "It's complicated, but for various reasons we had to flee home; all three of us. We used this craft to escape, but crashed here instead."

"And that vexed Zander so much." Dianah shrugged. "More than anyone guessed. Being marooned here eventually took its toll. On him. On all of us."

"Don't look to me for any sympathy." Leonie drained the glass and put it down. There was a moment of dizziness as she struggled trying to fathom all this information. She needed to hear something more familiar. "When did you meet up with Styx?"

Brendon sat up leaning forward. The chair adjusted to the new position. "In short, I was trying to amass an army to fight the l'ith – you know about them?"

"Only a little. I saw some a few weeks ago. In the mountains west of here. They had killed a nest of the glins'ool."

"Big buggers, aren't they. Anyway, we were up near the pass to the Vale and along comes this rollo. Stops for a visit, then goes off and kills the l'ith queen."

"That's not the Styx I know." Leonie felt odd. *Maybe I'm tired?*

"Well. He had changed – gone rogue – and covered in spikes. But you're right, it wasn't as straightforward as that. He said he was going to try negotiating with her first."

"Yep. That's more like him." She started feeling dizzy and lethargic.

"But he failed, and killed her instead. He survived, told us the good news, and left for Reenat." Brendon and Dianah paused, watching her.

"You look weary. You should relax, and I'll get you another drink?" Brendon rose to collect her glass.

Her mind tingled briefly. In a flash of insight, she twisted and tried to leap to the side. *Too slow!*

Brendon grabbed her in a vice-like grip, and kept his face

away from her jaws. Struggle as she might, Leonie could barely breathe. With her arms pinned and his massive weight holding her legs down, her claws were useless.

Dianah was by her side in an instant.

Leonie felt a sharp sting in her neck and the fight fell out of her. She dropped into unconsciousness.

———

The voices she could hear were faint, but distinguishable.

"… look at this … the previous sequence did have its merits, but these new vectors show far more potential. I think we should pursue that now," she heard Dianah say.

"What about Leonie?"

"We'll gather more DNA samples, but she's of no further use. She could even pose a threat, especially now Styx has meddled with her mind."

"And then?"

Dianah shrugged. "We trade her for the ship, and Zander can get the information he wants."

"After all she has been through?"

"You're getting emotional. If she finds out this was our fault and framed Zander, you think she'll be forgiving?"

"I forgot how cold-hearted you could be."

"Cold-hearted? No. I'm still a scientist, and desperate for a remedy."

The voices got louder. They entered the room seconds later.

Leonie looked around, faking confusion as if she'd just revived. "What happened?"

Dianah turned to Brendon, surprised. "I gave her so much sedative even you would've struggled to stay awake. Her abilities are uncanny. Far more successful than I had thought possible, even with Styx's modifications."

"What… have you done?" Leonie looked at the bandage on her arm and the various tubes.

"I require more material to continue my research. We ran a

few tests for further analysis; we'll probably need a bit more: hair, skin, blood—"

"All those words before were lies! I should have known."

"Not all of them. But I am ambitious." She shrugged. "I couldn't help myself."

"Seems you just did."

"You wouldn't be here without me—"

"*Here* where I'd rather not be." Slowly, feeling came back to her limbs. She did feel better, but she continued to act listless. "What are your... plans now? I gather... letting me go isn't... part of it?"

"Zander has a desire for any knowledge of this *Codex*, and we need this ship," she replied with indifference. We think it a fair trade."

"And what? You think Zander will have a chat and then release me?"

"Probably not. Bren, better get more sedative. She's too lucid for my liking." There was no pretence of empathy or compassion now.

Damn. Time to relax. Breathe in slowly. "You say you aren't responsible for any deaths? What about mine, or Zander's?" *I'm dead if they sedate me again.* "Either way – him or me – only one is going to be walking away."

Brendon returned with a vial and needle and handed them to Dianah. She filled the syringe with a pale green liquid from the vial.

Leonie tested the bindings; two straps across her legs, another for her torso and one each forearm. "Against my better judgement, I'll give you both one last chance," Leonie said as they turned and approached the bed.

"You are persistent." Brendon held her steady. "And hardly in a position to argue."

Dianah brought the needle up. "We probably won't see each other after this."

Gritting her teeth, Leonie released the power she had been slowly absorbing. The powerful fireball exploded among them.

In the confined space, the blast was effective. Dianah flew back, smacking into the wall; Brendon flew across the bench behind the bed. Both collapsed in unmoving heaps.

Secured on the bed with nowhere to go, the intense heat washed over her, singeing her fur. Already weak, she blacked out.

36

RESOLUTIONS

A MISTY SPRAY CAME OUT OF THE CEILING.

Leonie had no idea how long she'd been unconscious, but her fur was soaking. She blinked water from her eyes. Craning her head to the side, Dianah and Brendon lay on the floor with water pooling around them. The bed throbbed beneath her, and there was a faint humming.

Dazed, she tested her straps again. With effort, the scorched one finally snapped; she had no idea what it was made from, something *other-worldly* not cloth or leather. Reaching across, she realised she still had tubes attached to her arms and legs, like Magda had. Carefully removing the melted remnants, she was surprised at how little blood escaped before clotting. Clumsily she released the rest of her bindings and swung her legs around to the side. Sliding gingerly off the bed, she remained there until the room stopped spinning, breathing deeply, looking at the two sprawled, unmoving bodies.

Checking for her own wounds, she couldn't find any. She had healed completely, even her fur had been repaired. Her tail had regrown! Leonie couldn't believe it. When she got off the bed, the humming stopped, as did the vibrating.

She walked around in a tight circle, watching her reformed

tail flow behind like a streamer on a kite. She stopped when she got dizzy, but rejoiced in swishing her tail back and forth numerous times before getting back to her current situation.

Dianah's clothes were charred rags and Brendon's hair was severely singed. Both were badly burnt, except for the portions of Dianah with hroltahg skin, blisters already visible. The walls closest to the fireball were darkened by the intense heat and some of the furniture had melted. She had a brief pang of regret, but squashed that when she thought of the trickery and lies, dosing her and reverting to their original plans. No. No remorse for them. *They don't deserve it.*

She found her grav-harness on the floor and clipped it on, then her pouches and the scroll case. She took a brief moment to swish her tail back and forth, never believing that she would ever feel that sensation again!

Determined to make sure nothing like this was ever repeated, Leonie decided to permanently block access to the sanctum. In her earlier exploration of the palace she had found a storeroom along the passage before the library doors. With any luck she'd find what she was looking for. Leonie carefully jogged through the library, wondering where Magda had gone. The storeroom was located where she remembered along the wood-panelled corridor. In earnest, she searched through the pile of discarded boxes. A familiar odour assailed her nostrils. The barrels of balbon she'd found earlier. There was a large barrel, half-full, and two smaller barrels. Leonie managed to get the two in her arms. If she had time, perhaps she'd try rolling the bigger one, but she was not going to push her luck. It was awkward enough juggling these two casks to the cavern.

Leaving one barrel at the bottom of the stairs, she unstoppered the other and began pouring out the contents as she made her way towards the cliff exit, reaching about halfway before it ran out. She dropped the empty cask in the slick of oil and jogged to the exit. Knowing full well the volatility of the oil, and not wanting to get roasted again tonight, Leonie put as much distance as she could between herself and the ensuing blast. She spent a few minutes releasing the pigeons by opening their cages to the hole in the wall before crawling through it herself. Turning and hanging onto the edge, she wedged herself in the entrance. She needed a clear line of sight. Once in place, she slowly drew in power, wondering at the extent of her new capabilities. The fireball she cast in the sanctum was far bigger than anything she had created before and she doubted she had enough to do that again. *Was this the result of Styx's training plan?*

In a shallow arc, another ball of fire just as powerful as the previous one, sailed into the cavern, igniting the fumes before it reached the oil. The shockwave deafened her, the force of the air shooting through the hole caught her off-guard, blowing her back end over end. In a reflex action that saved her from plummeting into the cold water, she twisted the harness dial and her fall slowed to a stop as rock fragments flew past and splashed in the water below.

Since the harness only provided up and down motion, Leonie adjusted the dial slightly. Descending until her paws were in the water, she started paddling to get closer to the cliff and the rocks; she still had some mapping to do. A chance look up caused her to keep still; a couple of heads were peering out. "Do you reckon they heard that explosion?" she muttered to herself. *Think, next time, stupid.* Leonie castigated herself for arousing the palace when what she really needed was everyone to be relaxed and sleeping.

The heads disappeared after a couple of minutes. No alarm was raised that she was aware, so she continued to paddle, glad the Watchers couldn't see well in the dark. *And damn lucky they haven't got an obelisk looking out to sea.*

Upon reaching the rocks, she clawed her way closer to the cliff face and started rising. Pausing at the now slightly larger opening, she took a moment to look inside. The cavern was full of smoke, leaving little opportunity to see her work other than a few flames here and there. She continued to rise.

Eventually the ringing in her ears abated, but a slight headache remained as the window loomed above her. Leonie stopped to listen, but heard nothing. Peering over the sill, two Watchers sat and stared intently at the crystal displays. Checking for any other presence in the chamber, she slunk inside and rose to the same spot as before.

Carefully she pulled out the map and charcoal stick and began adding the details of what areas of the city were visible. She deduced each monument or obelisk had several points of view; all had at least two, but the ones nearer the centre of the city had three or four angles of sight. The charcoal stick was down to a stub before she was satisfied.

Fearing the harness would soon drain, she rolled up her map and made her exit, relieved everything had gone smoothly.

Perhaps it was just her paranoia coming through, but during her trip home, she was extra cautious. "I've never been this lucky," she muttered as she navigated her way along the shore-line to the waterfront docks.

Pausing in the shadows as a couple of late-night walkers ambled down the street, she recognised the lane where the royal courier was assassinated. Looking back, there was little sign of anything amiss in the darkness. Perhaps the combination of distance, thunder, the roiling waves and the cave exit facing away from the city was sufficient to suppress the noise, which might account for the lack of alarm being raised.

Deciding there was no need to wake Jade on her return, she left the unrolled map on her desk instead and headed home to sleep.

Sitting astride the apex of the roof of her room, Leonie surveyed the cityscape as she munched on her breakfast. It was going to be a warm, sunny day. Every now and then, she flicked her tail just because she could.

Across the uneven rooftops of the Web, the larger buildings near the Plaza and merchant quarters obscured the bulk of the ships in the harbour. While she had been mapping, a brief opportunity had availed itself for her to get closer to the crystal displays. It took a few moments, but finally she spotted the area nearest where she lived. It lay on the edge of a blind spot; the two closest obelisks did not directly view her section of the rooftops. To be safe though, she determined to keep to the south and west side from now on.

The short time after her return from Qelay had been busy. Brendon and Dianah were now history and Zander had no knowledge of her specifically. Lothas and Alen, including many of the Death sect were no longer a threat. And, thankfully, that meant no further encounters with Evlin.

The Woorin Brotherhood could still be a menace if Coundar thought she was alive and kicking. Best to keep him unaware then, she decided. Without a doubt, the death of another High Priest would get other temples nervous, not to mention the possibility of raising the ire of their gods. "Irate temples is one thing, angry gods could be a worry," she said, sighing.

Although she didn't like the answers, her burning questions were resolved. More could be done, but vengeance wasn't what she sought anymore. She felt no exultation. While she might be good at it, killing left her feeling hollow. It was simply one way to survive. Leaving and putting all this behind her was another way. She had to believe it was a better way.

She would tell Jade of her decision to definitely leave with Feiron. It was the only sure way to keep everyone out of trouble, and she suspected her presence was putting a strain on the Takers Guild as well. She was looking forward to flying with Slana, Dorn and Faldo, sometimes missing their banter.

———

"Here you are. Where have you been?" Feiron oozed up from the alley and formed into the old merchant to sit beside her.

"Regrowing my tail." She swished her tail in his face.

"What? How did you do that?"

"It's all this training Styx had me go through." She found it a struggle to keep a straight face. "You know how you need to concentrate to form a shape?" She continued after his dubious nod. "Me too. I just spent all night concentrating, and here it is. All fluffy and shiny; better than new."

Feiron looked stunned. He almost dripped off the roof.

Leonie burst out laughing.

He pulled himself together and reformed. "I see. Hilarious." He grabbed her tail and pulled.

"Ow!" She winced.

"It's real?"

"Yes."

"I mean really real!"

"Really real." She laughed, then filled him in on the recent palace visit. "I left the map with Jade on my return. Once she's studied it, I'll make copies and let you have one for your mentor as well. We all need to be wary."

"That would be a good thing to have. Thank you again. Very handy indeed."

"Hey. Maybe if there's time when you get back, I'll take you up there and let you see it for yourself."

Feiron looked to the palace in the distance. "We've handled undead, assassins and wyverns; what dangers can the palace possibly hold to thwart us?"

"That's what I reckon." She nodded, her attention drawn to shouting.

They both looked down to the lane as some people started quarrelling. It looked like a drunk had wandered into the path of a merchant's cart. No one was injured, but a di'anth hopped from foot to foot in agitation. Then he bolted. The merchant gave chase and the drunk stumbled away in the other direction.

"City life," Feiron sighed. "I'll miss it."

"No, you won't." Leonie slapped him on the arm.

He grinned. "I have a question about the obelisks and the Watchers; if they can see where you live, why didn't they come to get you?"

"My place is just out of sight, but I reckon they're after someone else. There were pictures of this white-haired man everywhere around the room, and at every desk." She pulled out one of the pictures. "I grabbed this last night. Zander may not be a murderer as I first thought, but he is definitely paranoid."

"Any idea why?" Feiron looked at the picture with, flipping it over and studying it in detail. "This is incredible."

Leonie shrugged. "He's wearing some strange clothing though. He looks very pale, but not sickly pale; just needing more sun."

"A foreigner perhaps, from the north?"

Leonie shrugged. "And what brings you to visit?"

"A message from Phil. They will collect us at the end of next week."

"How did you get a message from them?" she asked.

"My mentor won't reveal her sources."

"I don't suppose it was carrier pigeon?"

"Carrier pigeon? I doubt it." He shrugged. "I've not seen one around there. Why?"

She shook her head. "I saw one recently. Just coincidence. So, we have just over a week? I reckon I can stay out of mischief for that long."

"You'll have to do it alone," he said after a pause.

"Why is that?" Leonie looked at him quizzically. "Where are you off to?"

"I can't say where, but I'm being enrolled into the Guild of Sleuths."

"You? I've never heard of the *Guild of Sleuths*?"

"They're elite investigators, but they are not located in Delta, or Athglenn for that matter—"

"Where are they?" she asked.

"It doesn't matter, but I will be back in time for our exciting departure. This is a great honour. They normally only take illios with far more experience – several years at least."

"And – no offence – especially with your recent activities, shouldn't they wait for you to get all your faculties straight. How is your memory? Have you got all your shapes down now?"

"I have, but it's actually *because* of my recent activities this came about. The experiences I've undergone, especially with wyverns, hroltahgs and even melting, are apparently sufficient."

"Making mistakes has merit with your lot? Where do I get to enrol? I should be front of the line." Leonie smiled. "But I guess congratulations are in order."

"Thanks. Perhaps I'll put in a good word for you."

"Does this guild know about you going away?"

"My mentor has informed them. She assures me it is in fact ideal. The guild has very little contact with Plenari, or the Tesak'i."

Leonie considered her next question. "Do you reckon Phil would like the idea of you spying on his people."

"Spying? No indeed. Just keeping my people abreast of the goings-on, politics etc."

"Yes. Spying." She nodded.

"You make it sound so underhanded."

Leonie shrugged. "You're the spy. I'm just a thief."

"With very unique skills, but one with such poor eyesight. It's a shame really."

"Poor eyesight? How do you reckon?"

"I noticed your tail straight away, but I've sat here for quite a while, and yet you haven't noticed my hair. Very sad."

"Your– Hey, you've got eyebrows!"

"Your powers of observation never cease to amaze me."

THE END

continued in Book 2
Shadow of the Tower

END NOTES

Characters

Leonie: a hybrid (rrell/human) thief. Agile, black fur, violet eyes, heals fast, excellent senses, faster than average, stronger than average, 6', 160lbs

Jade: human. Taker Guild Master, Leonie's boss and friend/mentor. Agile

Feiron: illios (shapechanger). (aka Hectr Cerrin, aka Drial)

Styx: hroltahg from Reenat. Becomes Leonie's telepath trainer/mentor

Dwer: hroltahg from Qelay

Riff: hroltahg from Qelay

Lord Zander: human. Ruthless (generally absent) overlord of Delta city-state

Lord Brendon: human. (aka Roland) Partner to Dianah, co-ruler of Delta city-state

Lady Dianah: human. Partner to Brendon, co-ruler of Delta city-state

Evlin: human, Jart'lekk assassin

Tunif: human, Jart'lekk assassin

Philbert: human, Tesakian, wyvern trainer. Resides Hell's Maw

Dorn: female wyvern, green, and mate to Noldor. Leonie's telepath trainer/mentor. Resides Hell's Maw, Philbert's ride

Noldor: male wyvern, green, and mate to Dorn

Axorg: elemental wyvern

Slana: young wyvern, green, sibling to Faldo. Resides Hell's Maw, Feiron's ride

Faldo: young wyvern, green, sibling to Slana. Resides Hell's Maw, Leonie's ride

Daras: human, portly sage, corrupt

Ro: human Jade's 'bodyguard', bouncer. (plainsman from the Northern Reaches)

Netoha: human, Ro's partner, (plainswoman from the Northern Reaches)

Coundar: human, High Priest of the Woorin Temple in Delta

Karig: human, cleric/follower Brotherhood of the Flame

Lothas: human, High Priest of the Temple of Opsyss in Delta

Alen: human, Priest of the Temple of Opsyss in Delta

Magda: seleth aide to Lady Dianah

Rodi: human, acolyte/ seeker for the Woorin Temple in Delta

Mina: human, acolyte/ seeker for the Woorin Temple in Delta

Giorgi: Coundar's assistant

Garth: human, militiaman assisting Brendon and Dianah at Vale of Dromas

Poul: human, militiaman assisting Brendon and Dianah at Vale of Dromas

Argus: di'anth (reptile), Feiron's pack animal

Races of Yarnik

humans: fair skinned, bipedal, generally head and facial hair (males), average senses, strength and speed, 4'5"-6'5", 110-230lbs

rrell: (feline): generally bipedal, fur (can run faster on all four paws), any solid colour eg: white, brown, grey, ginger, black, but may have dual or tri-colours (rare), whiskers, claws, keen smell, acute hearing, highly agile and dexterous, acute hearing and vision/night vision. Between 5'-6', 80-150lbs, possibly telepathic

illios: (shapeshifter): greyish blobs (natural form), potentially can form many shapes (can't change mass), average senses, telepathic immunity, regenerative ability, 1'-7' (shape-dependant), average senses

hroltahg: (rollos): very heavy/dense individual, grey to black, 100% powerful telepathy (no eyes, nose, mouth, ears), very heavy: 250-500lbs, ball-shape approx. 1'-2' diameter

seleth: (reptoid): bipedal, scales/thick skin, variations of mottled green or brown (black or white rare), 150-350lbs, 4'-5', acute smell and taste, very strong, poor reflex and speed, possibly telepathic

vorien: (mermen/women): bipedal, fine scales, any colour/combination, fins*, acute smell and taste in water/poor on land, can survive on land for several hours*, slow on land, fast in water, 100-300lbs, 4'-6', possibly telepathic

glins'ool: (avian): bipedal & wings feathers, fast and agile (better in the air/flying), any colour combination*, 50-100lbs, 4'-6', possibly telepathic

wyverns: indigenous to Yarnik, bipedal & wings, long necks, spiked tail, various solid colours (offspring lighter shade than parents), all telepathic, keen senses, can fly/glide all day, 1000-3000lbs, 40'-80'

l'ithnamagri: indigenous to Yarnik, ten legs, mandibles, black, 500-800lbs, acute smell/hearing and vibration senses, poor eyesight, very fast, very strong, telepathic/ pheromones

Temples / Religious Orders

The religious orders on Shak'aran are based on the eight elements:
Air, Fire, Water, Earth, Spirit, Time, Life, and Death

Woorin Temple: Woorin - God of Fire,
Opsyss Temple: Opsyss - God of Death,

Temple of Eternix: **Eternix** - Goddess of Time
Temple of Life: **Mimmis** - Goddess of Life
Air Temple: **Oes'het** - God of Air
Water Temple: **Ler'eni** - Goddess of Water
Spirit Temple: **Emera** - Goddess of Spirit
Temple Of Earth: **Qevlir** - God of Earth

Locations / Places of Interest

Yarnik: the world

Shak'aran: major continent, includes countries: Athglenn, Lyhosa, Tesak, Fisbane, Ertuk, Gruarch, In'sha, Central Steppes, Northern Reaches, Shattered Isles

Delta: rogue 'city-state' trading port in southern Athglenn, at the mouth of the Urmaq River

Reenat: capital city of Athglenn, seat of the true rulers of Athglenn

Plenari: capital city of Tesak, built on and around the massive trees of the Tesakian

'The Web': poor quarter of Delta, generally for downtrodden, outcasts and misfits

Portside: western side of Delta harbour, for more prosperous traders, merchants and families

Dockside: eastern side of Delta harbour, for smaller, less prosperous traders and merchants

Indras: rural town on the North Road, half way to Qelay on the Urmaq River

Hell's Maw: volcano in the Central Ranges, lair to wyverns

Central Ranges: vast mountain range stretching from far north coast to south coast, also called 'Spine of the World'

Qelay: major rural city in Athglenn, halfway to Reenat. Head of the Urmaq River

White Cliffs: resort especially designed to cater for hroltahgs, located in Qelay

Swangrove: small rural town north of Indras on the Urmaq River

Urmaq River: Largest river in Athglenn, from springs in Lake Urmaq to south coast

Deraz River: small tributary feeds into the Urmaq River

Vale of Dromas: a region in the centre of the continent. Fabled to be home to the original and ancient city of Dromas. Historians believe it was destroyed during a Powershaper War, which had a devastating impact on the terrain

Skylands: hundreds of these sky islands of many and varied sizes, float around the Shak'aran continent. It is believed they are the remains of Dromas; the effects of the Powershaper War ripped the ground asunder. The unusual crystalline mantle – believed to be the source of 'power' (magic) – is repelled when drained of 'power'

Luminor & Luxor: twin moons orbiting Yarnik, believed to eclipse approx. every 100 years

ACKNOWLEDGMENTS

With a book that has taken over two decades from conception to get out (including 18 years in the Navy) … there are so many to thank – and I couldn't possibly name all of them. (not with my memory …)

First and foremost, to the many Purple Zoners (you know who you are) for the earliest beta-reads and critiques, Sharon Athanasos, Laura Comerford, and more recently Tracy Joyce, Pete Aldin, Stephen Kerwin and Aaron Cordy.

I'd also like to thank Belinda Crawford for her artwork for the series covers:

https://www.facebook.com/groups/designedbyboots/

and Barbara Holten for her editing prowess:

https://barbarajholten.com

And finally but most importantly, my wife Morag, for putting up with my absent-minded rantings, and our daughter, Meredith – for putting up with me, and also *her* mum for putting up with my absent-minded rantings.

ABOUT THE AUTHOR

Andre Jones made his debut appearance (unless you believe in reincarnation – in which case this is his third) in Wollongong, NSW Australia and has managed to stick around for 58 years... so far.

Okay, okay... enough of the third-person stuff...

My parents were Dutch immigrants, and since I had a gloomy and challenging childhood, (and I've forgotten most of it) I immersed myself with drawing, reading and sometimes writing. As a child, I devoured the works of Enid Blyton before progressing to Tolkien, McAffrey, Asimov, Heinlein and Bradbury. As a young adult, I got lost in many and varied roleplaying games, including: MERP, GURPS, Harn, Skyrealms of Jorune, good old D&D *(and its many variants)* and Traveller. (I never got into these new card games) .. and also spent far too much time on video games like Skyrealm (but nothing to regret).

This 'not so interesting' life led me to various occupations: Security Officer, Police Officer, Park Ranger and finally as a Petty Officer in the Royal Australian Navy for 18 years *(sadly, his roleplaying stopped there)*.

Currently residing in Melbourne with my lovely – and very understanding – Scottish wife and a British Shorthair cat, I'm now a retired Navy Veteran with the opportunity to write, roleplay, draw and potter to my heart's content.

Also by ...
Book 1
City of Bridges

coming soon
Book 2
Shadow of the Tower
Book 3
Ripples of Time

also coming soon
AND BY A A JONES
The Misadventures of Biff and Tiff
Book 1
Gnome Henge
Book 2
Lost Fairies

https://andrejonesauthor.site

www.ingramcontent.com/pod-product-compliance
Lightning Source LLC
Chambersburg PA
CBHW030245120726
47903CB00005B/1621